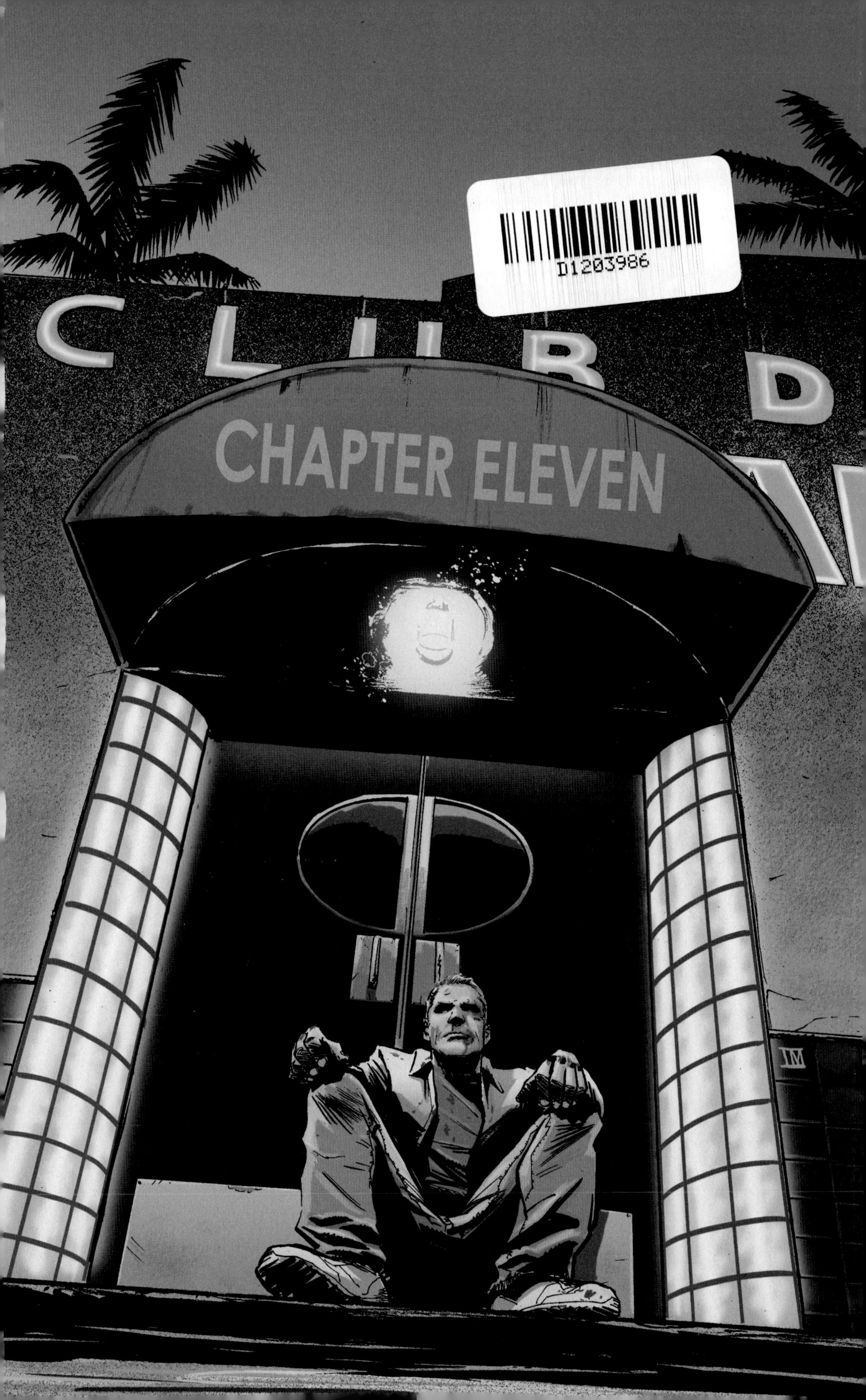
CHAPTER ELEVEN

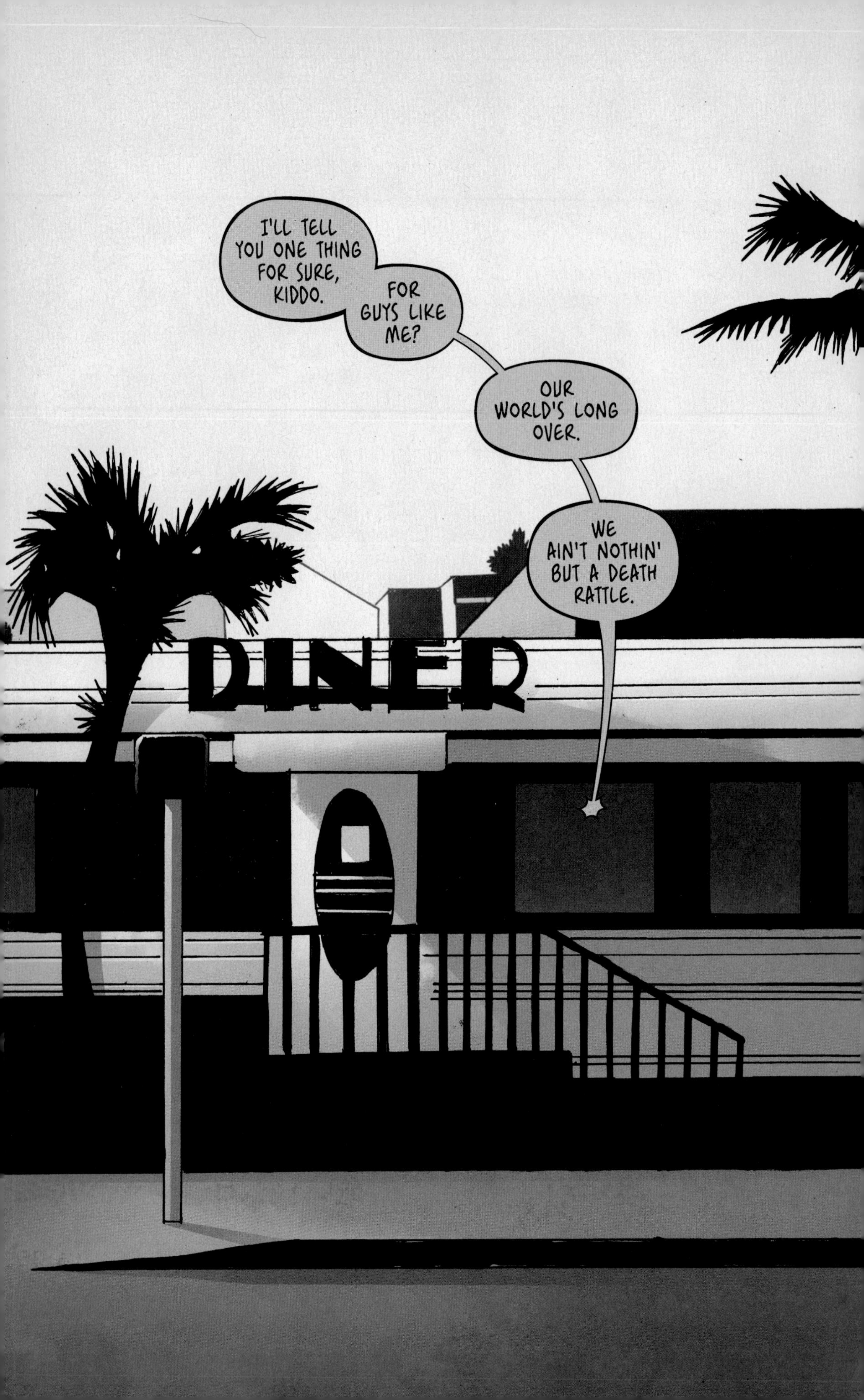
I'LL TELL YOU ONE THING FOR SURE, KIDDO.
FOR GUYS LIKE ME?
OUR WORLD'S LONG OVER.
WE AIN'T NOTHIN' BUT A DEATH RATTLE.
DINER

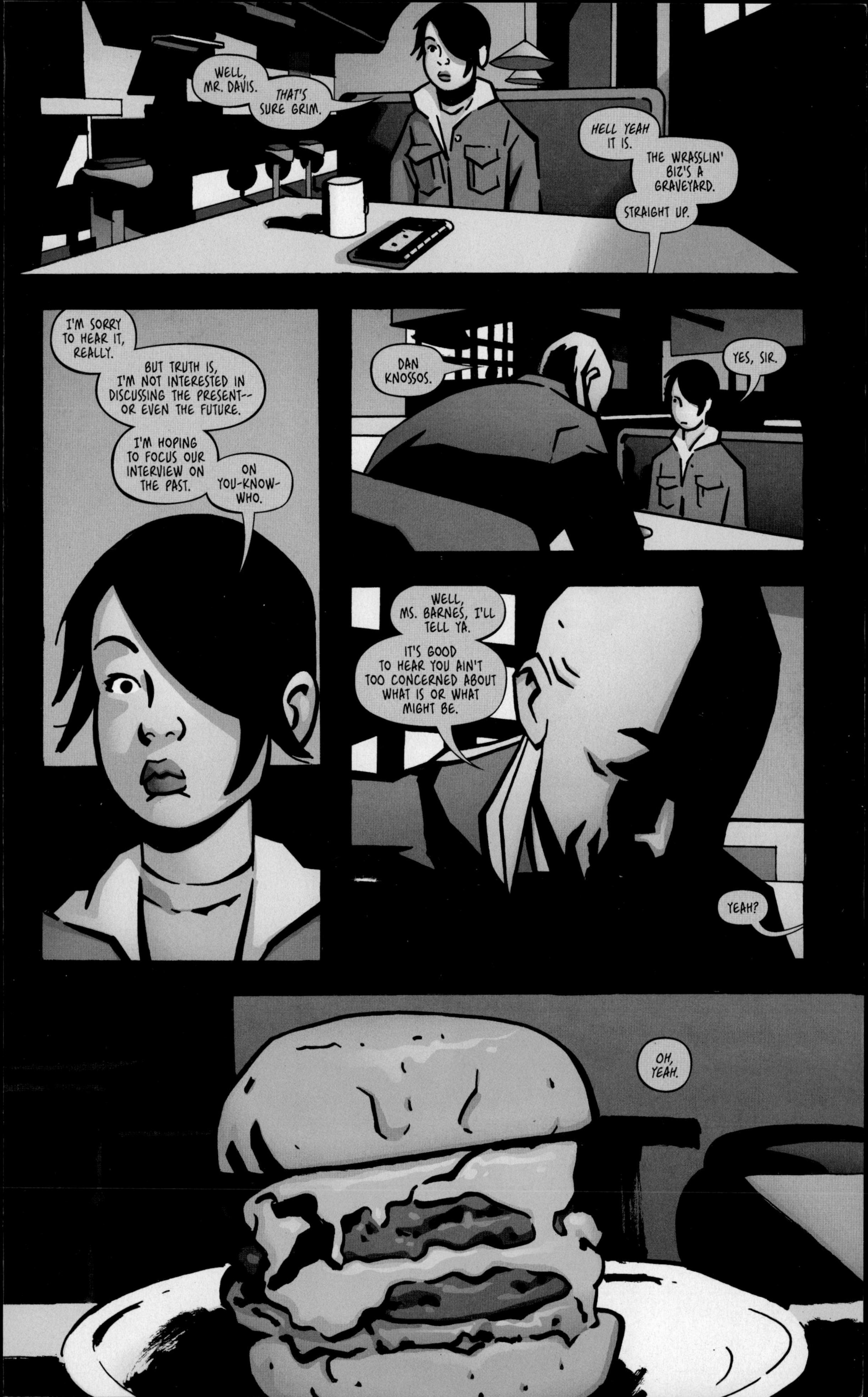
WELL, MR. DAVIS.
THAT'S SURE GRIM.
HELL YEAH IT IS.
THE WRASSLIN' BIZ'S A GRAVEYARD.
STRAIGHT UP.
I'M SORRY TO HEAR IT, REALLY.
BUT TRUTH IS, I'M NOT INTERESTED IN DISCUSSING THE PRESENT-- OR EVEN THE FUTURE.
I'M HOPING TO FOCUS OUR INTERVIEW ON THE PAST.
ON YOU-KNOW-WHO.
DAN KNOSSOS.
YES, SIR.
WELL, MS. BARNES, I'LL TELL YA.
IT'S GOOD TO HEAR YOU AIN'T TOO CONCERNED ABOUT WHAT IS OR WHAT MIGHT BE.
YEAH?
OH, YEAH.

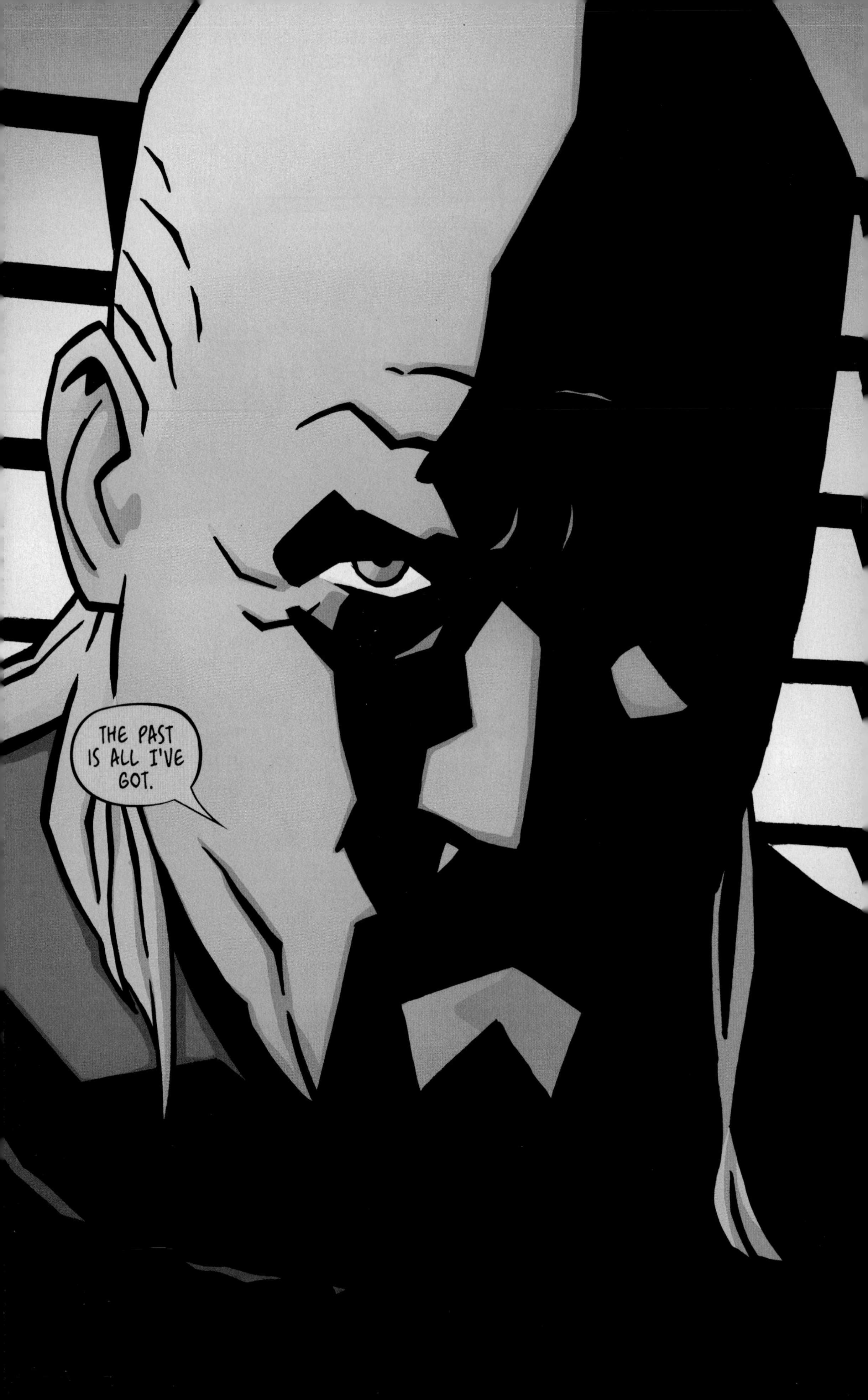
THE PAST IS ALL I'VE GOT.

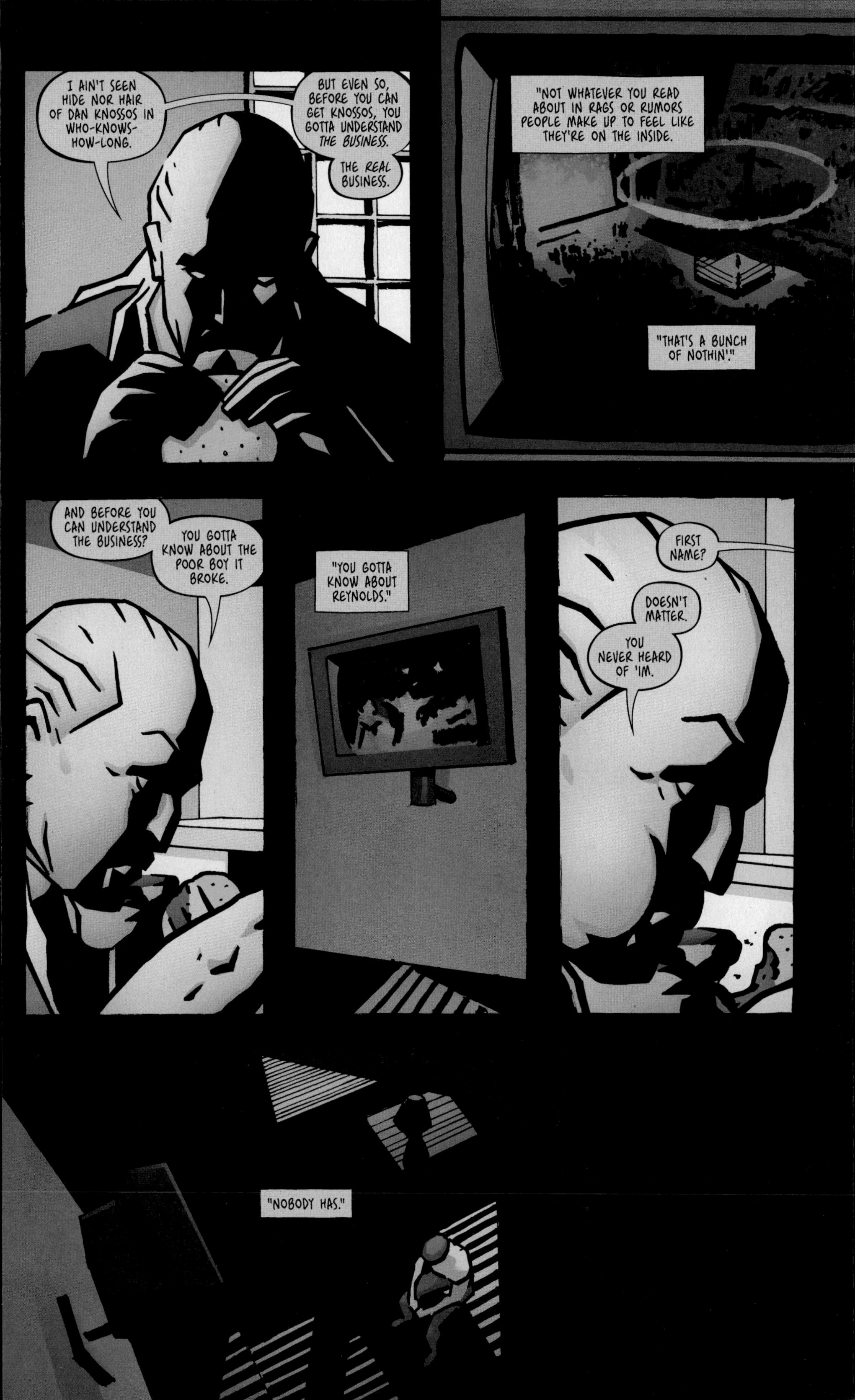
I AIN'T SEEN HIDE NOR HAIR OF DAN KNOSSOS IN WHO-KNOWS-HOW-LONG.
BUT EVEN SO, BEFORE YOU CAN GET KNOSSOS, YOU GOTTA UNDERSTAND *THE BUSINESS.*
THE REAL BUSINESS.
"NOT WHATEVER YOU READ ABOUT IN RAGS OR RUMORS PEOPLE MAKE UP TO FEEL LIKE THEY'RE ON THE INSIDE.
"THAT'S A BUNCH OF NOTHIN'."
AND BEFORE YOU CAN UNDERSTAND THE BUSINESS?
YOU GOTTA KNOW ABOUT THE POOR BOY IT BROKE.
"YOU GOTTA KNOW ABOUT REYNOLDS."
FIRST NAME?
DOESN'T MATTER.
YOU NEVER HEARD OF 'IM.
"NOBODY HAS."

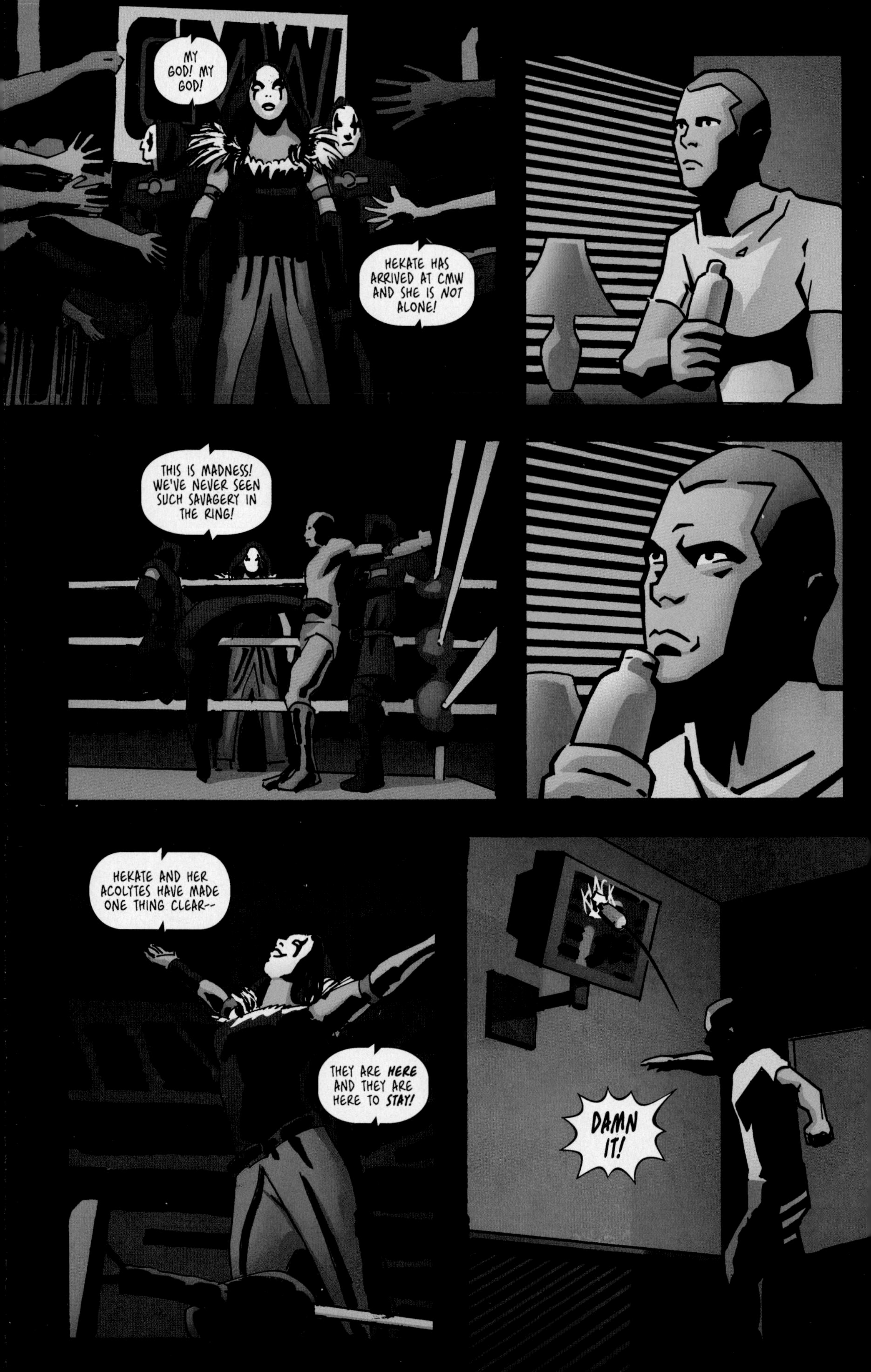
CMW
MY GOD! MY GOD!
HEKATE HAS ARRIVED AT CMW AND SHE IS NOT ALONE!
THIS IS MADNESS! WE'VE NEVER SEEN SUCH SAVAGERY IN THE RING!
HEKATE AND HER ACOLYTES HAVE MADE ONE THING CLEAR--
THEY ARE HERE AND THEY ARE HERE TO STAY!
DAMN IT!

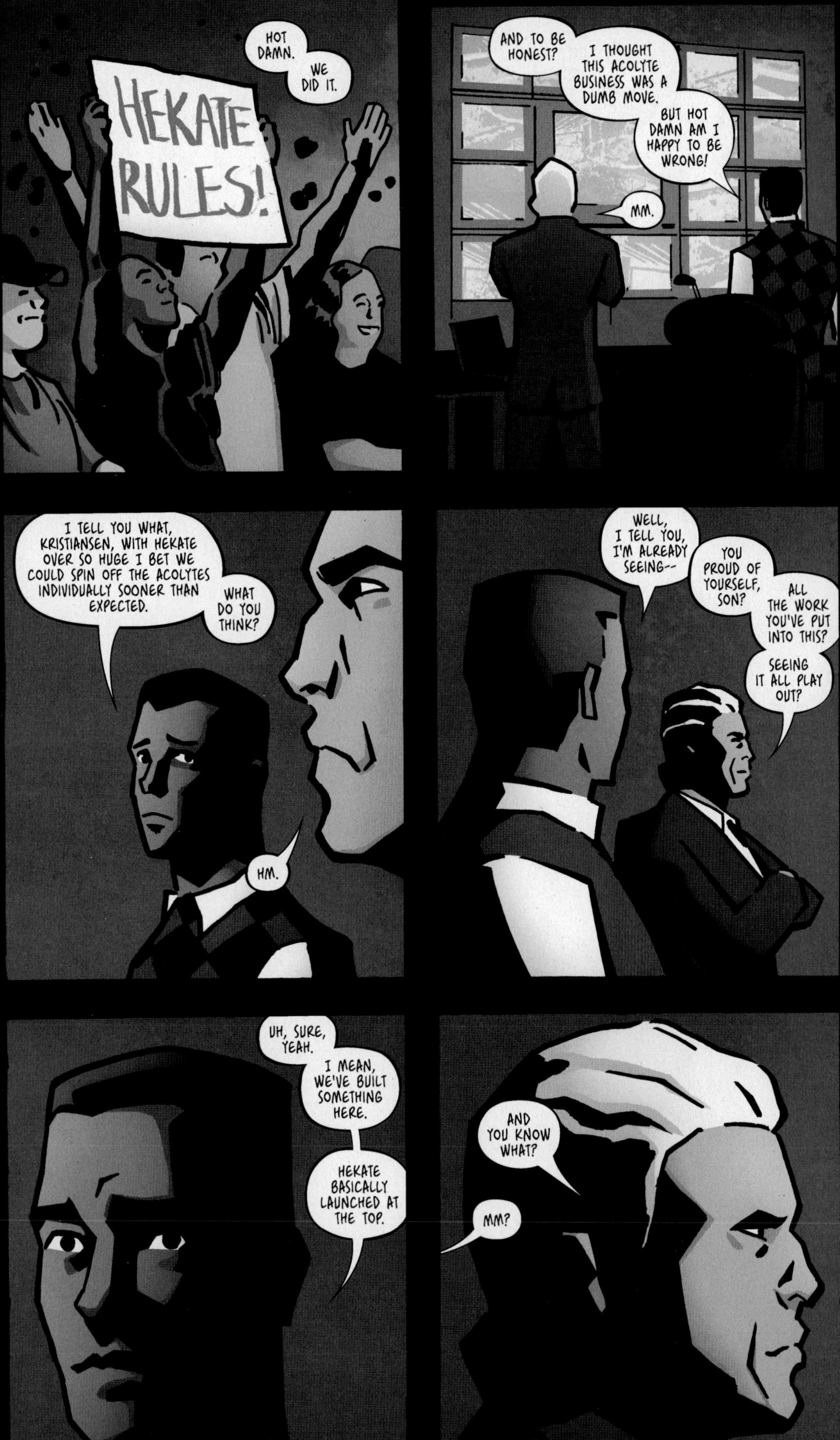
HOT DAMN.
WE DID IT.
HEKATE RULES!
AND TO BE HONEST?
I THOUGHT THIS ACOLYTE BUSINESS WAS A DUMB MOVE.
BUT HOT DAMN AM I HAPPY TO BE WRONG!
MM.
I TELL YOU WHAT, KRISTIANSEN, WITH HEKATE OVER SO HUGE I BET WE COULD SPIN OFF THE ACOLYTES INDIVIDUALLY SOONER THAN EXPECTED.
WHAT DO YOU THINK?
HM.
WELL, I TELL YOU, I'M ALREADY SEEING--
YOU PROUD OF YOURSELF, SON?
ALL THE WORK YOU'VE PUT INTO THIS?
SEEING IT ALL PLAY OUT?
UH, SURE, YEAH.
I MEAN, WE'VE BUILT SOMETHING HERE.
HEKATE BASICALLY LAUNCHED AT THE TOP.
AND YOU KNOW WHAT?
MM?

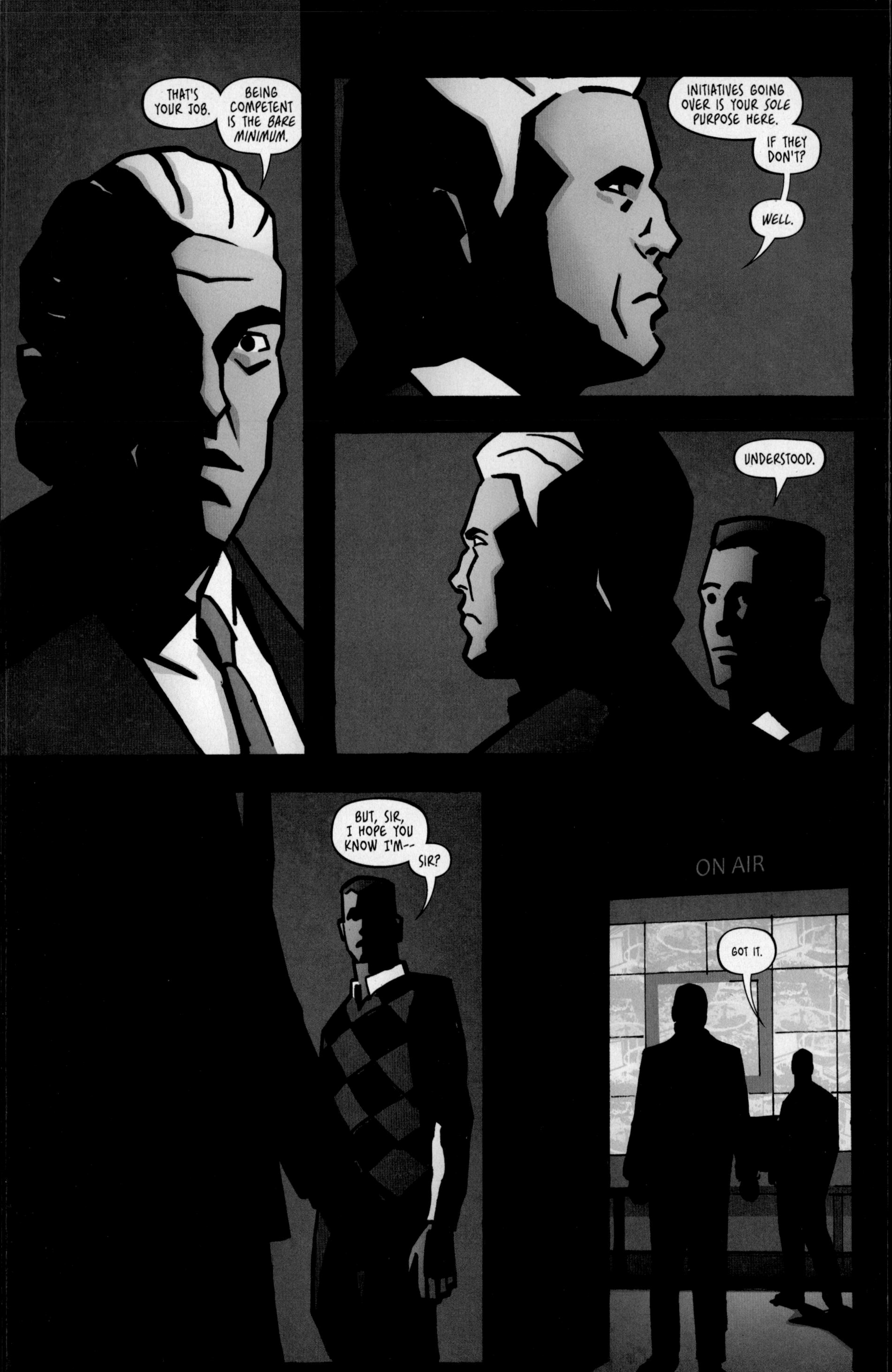
THAT'S YOUR JOB.
BEING COMPETENT IS THE BARE MINIMUM.
INITIATIVES GOING OVER IS YOUR SOLE PURPOSE HERE.
IF THEY DON'T?
WELL.
UNDERSTOOD.
BUT, SIR, I HOPE YOU KNOW I'M--
SIR?
ON AIR
GOT IT.

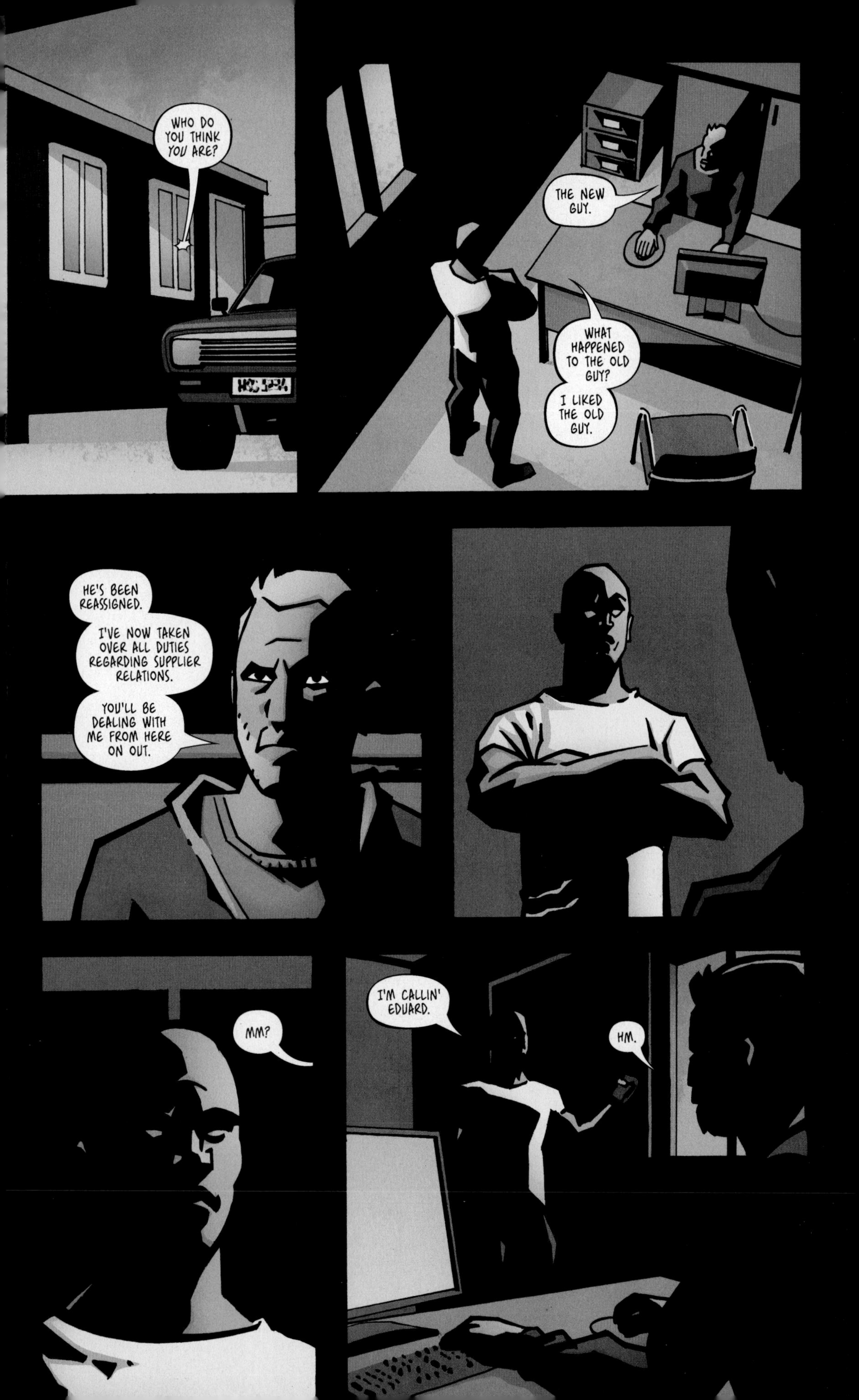
WHO DO YOU THINK YOU ARE?
THE NEW GUY.
WHAT HAPPENED TO THE OLD GUY?
I LIKED THE OLD GUY.
HE'S BEEN REASSIGNED.
I'VE NOW TAKEN OVER ALL DUTIES REGARDING SUPPLIER RELATIONS.
YOU'LL BE DEALING WITH ME FROM HERE ON OUT.
MM?
I'M CALLIN' EDUARD.
HM.

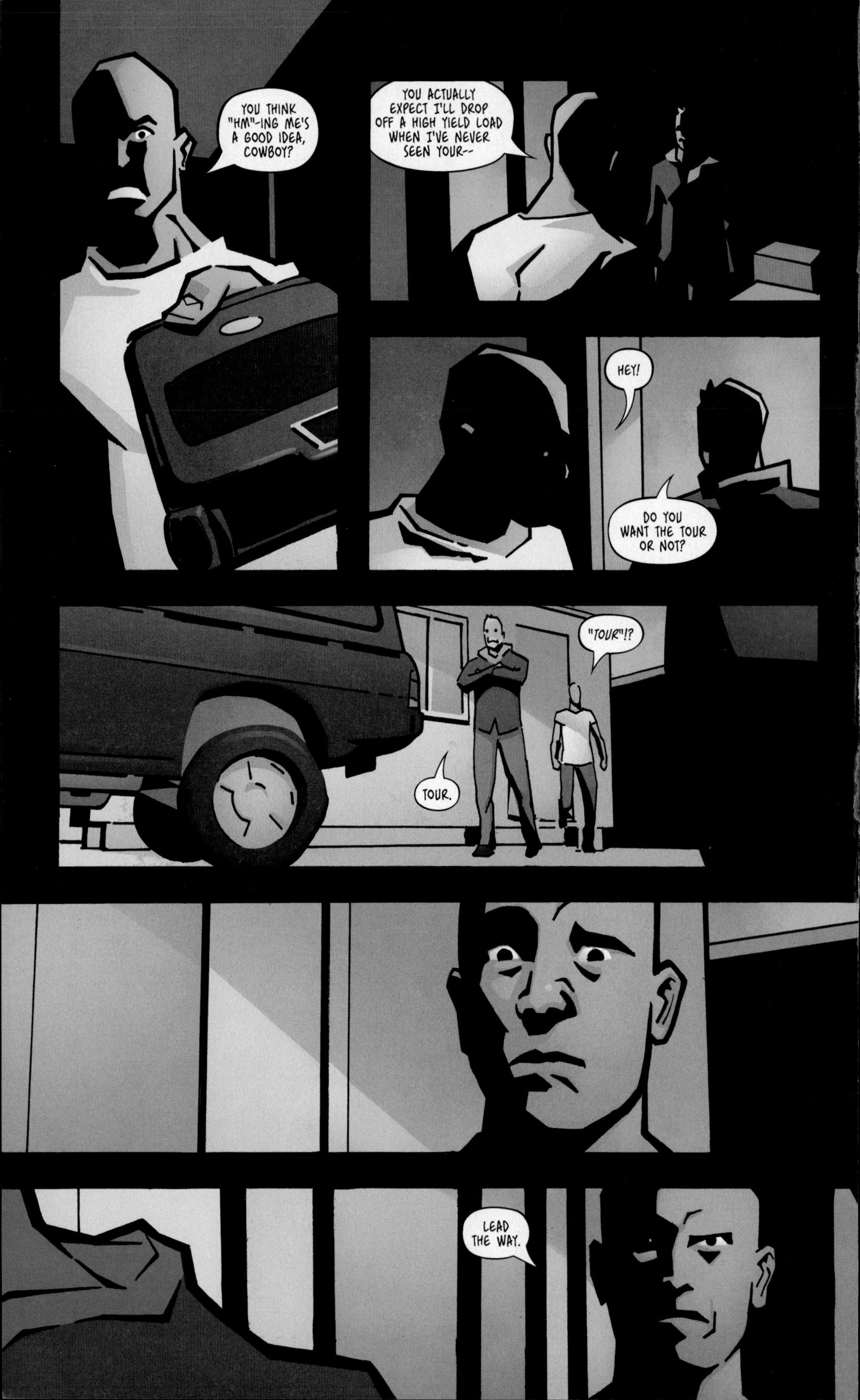
YOU THINK "HM"-ING ME'S A GOOD IDEA, COWBOY?
YOU ACTUALLY EXPECT I'LL DROP OFF A HIGH YIELD LOAD WHEN I'VE NEVER SEEN YOUR--
HEY!
DO YOU WANT THE TOUR OR NOT?
"TOUR"!?
TOUR.
LEAD THE WAY.

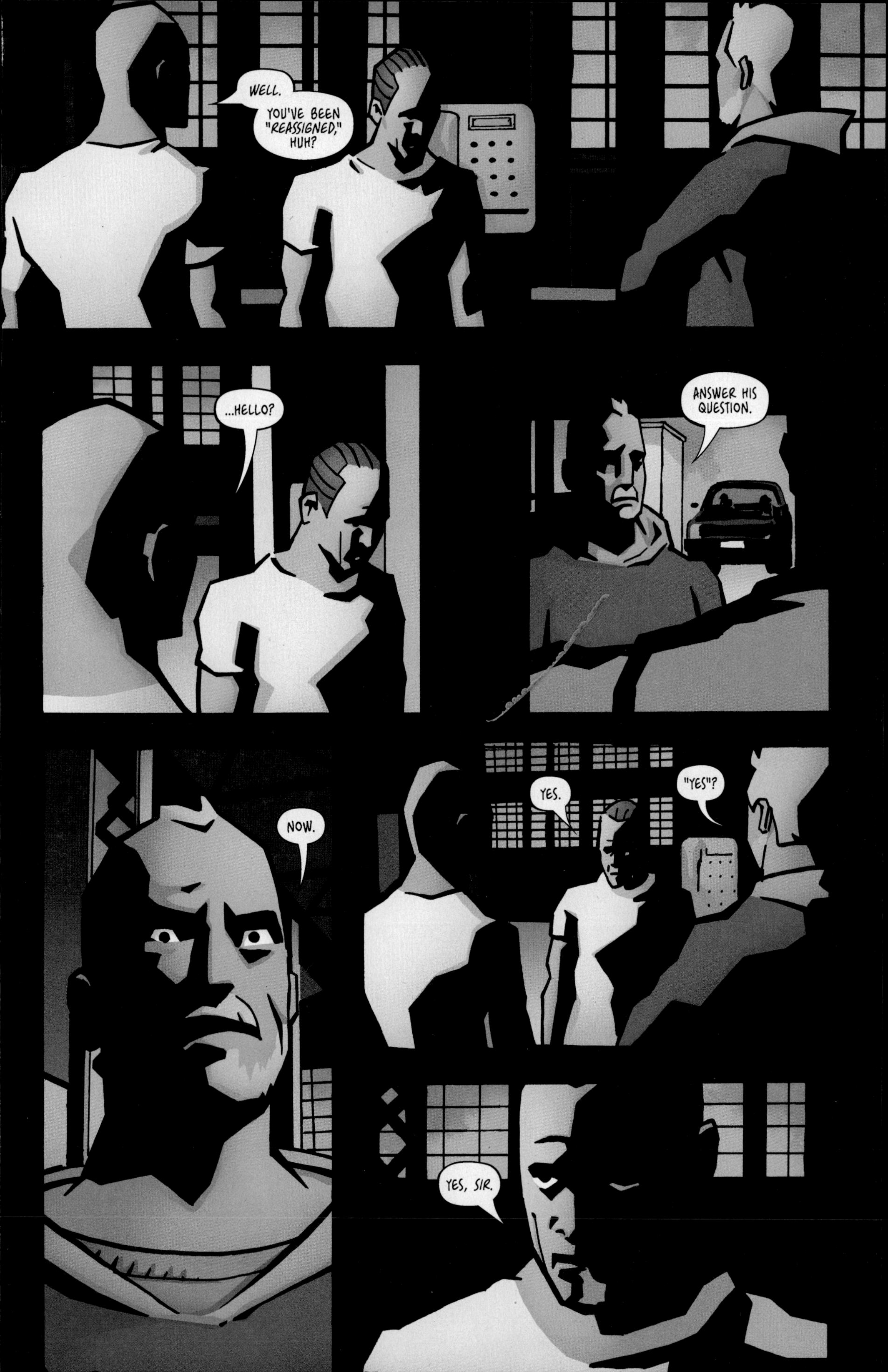
WELL.
YOU'VE BEEN "REASSIGNED," HUH?
...HELLO?
ANSWER HIS QUESTION.
NOW.
YES.
"YES"?
YES, SIR.

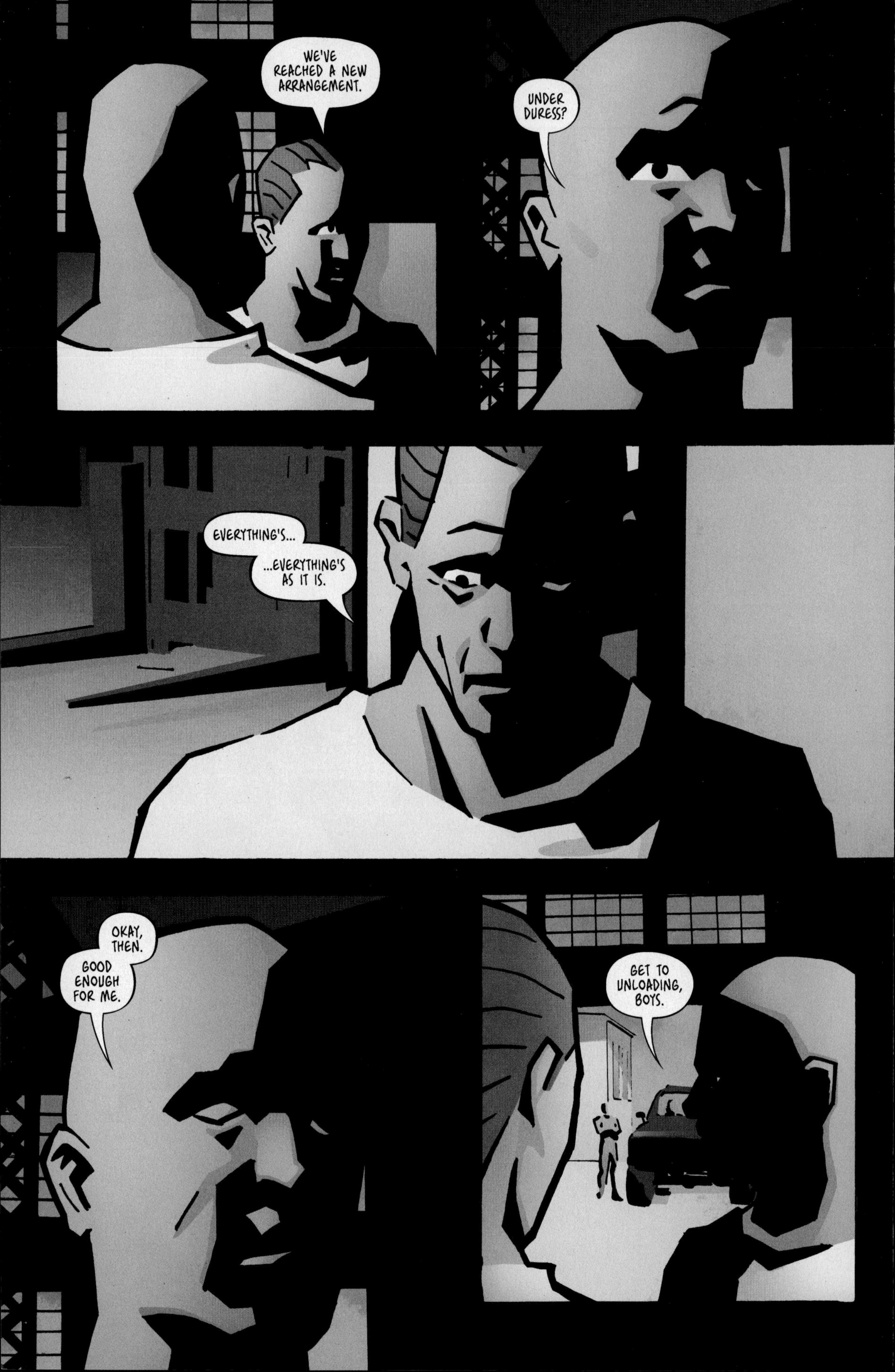
WE'VE REACHED A NEW ARRANGEMENT.
UNDER DURESS?
EVERYTHING'S...
...EVERYTHING'S AS IT IS.
OKAY, THEN.
GOOD ENOUGH FOR ME.
GET TO UNLOADING, BOYS.

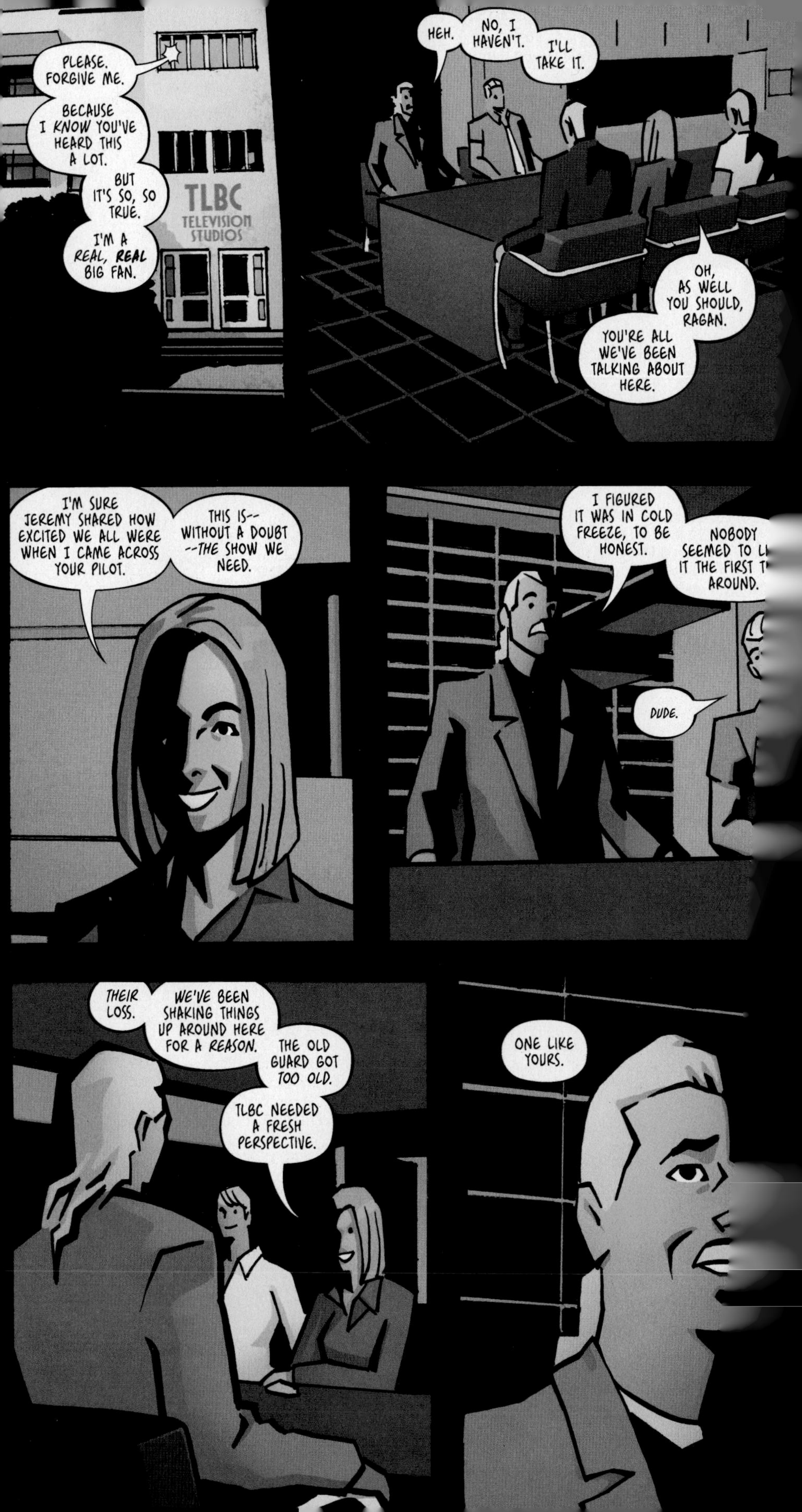
PLEASE. FORGIVE ME.
BECAUSE I KNOW YOU'VE HEARD THIS A LOT.
BUT IT'S SO, SO TRUE.
I'M A REAL, **REAL** BIG FAN.
TLBC TELEVISION STUDIOS
HEH.
NO, I HAVEN'T.
I'LL TAKE IT.
OH, AS WELL YOU SHOULD, RAGAN.
YOU'RE ALL WE'VE BEEN TALKING ABOUT HERE.
I'M SURE JEREMY SHARED HOW EXCITED WE ALL WERE WHEN I CAME ACROSS YOUR PILOT.
THIS IS-- WITHOUT A DOUBT --*THE* SHOW WE NEED.
I FIGURED IT WAS IN COLD FREEZE, TO BE HONEST.
NOBODY SEEMED TO LI IT THE FIRST T AROUND.
DUDE.
THEIR LOSS.
WE'VE BEEN SHAKING THINGS UP AROUND HERE FOR A *REASON.*
THE OLD GUARD GOT *TOO* OLD.
TLBC NEEDED A FRESH PERSPECTIVE.
ONE LIKE YOURS.

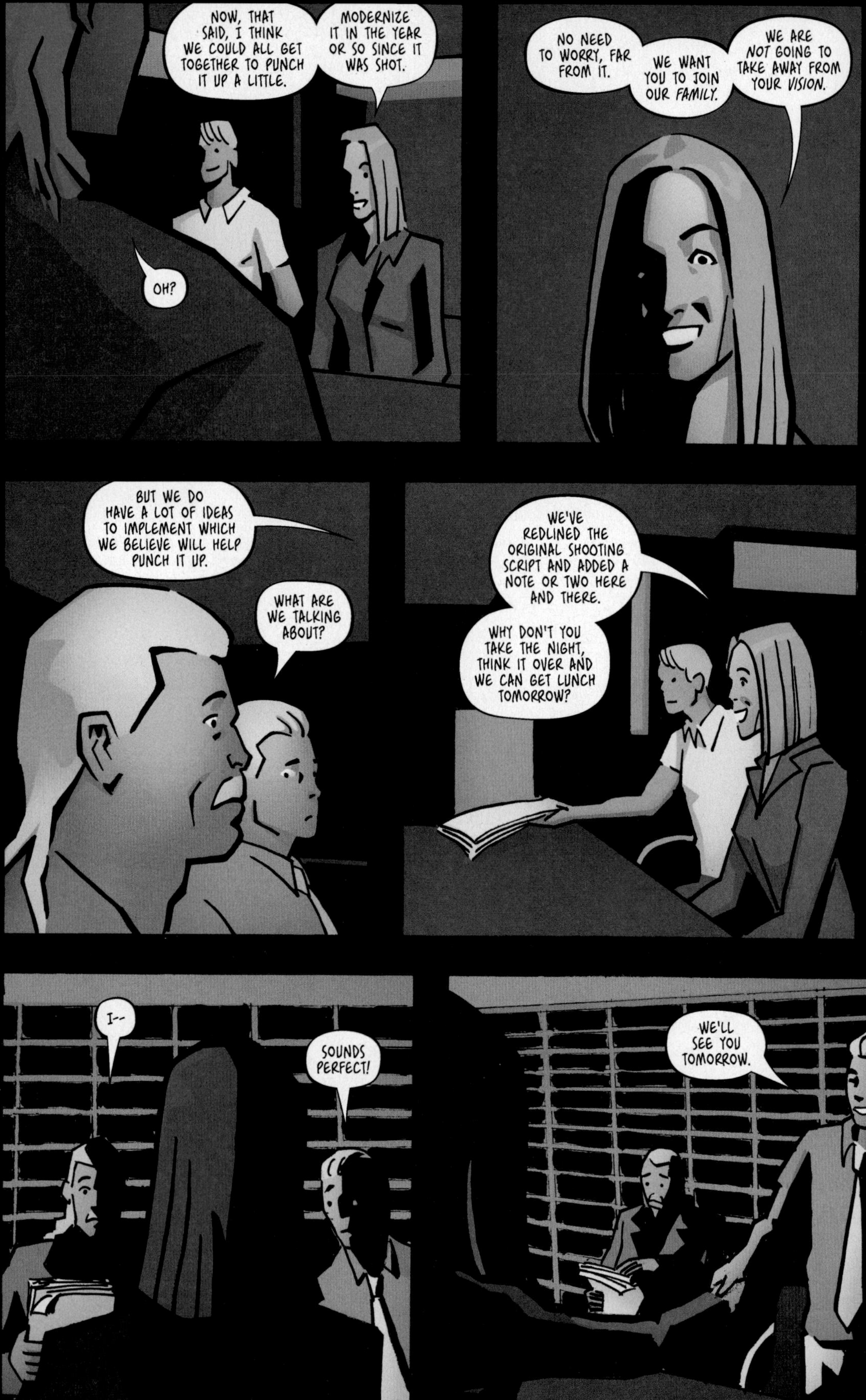
NOW, THAT SAID, I THINK WE COULD ALL GET TOGETHER TO PUNCH IT UP A LITTLE.
MODERNIZE IT IN THE YEAR OR SO SINCE IT WAS SHOT.
OH?
NO NEED TO WORRY, FAR FROM IT.
WE WANT YOU TO JOIN OUR *FAMILY*.
WE ARE *NOT* GOING TO TAKE AWAY FROM YOUR *VISION*.
BUT WE DO HAVE A LOT OF IDEAS TO IMPLEMENT WHICH WE BELIEVE WILL HELP PUNCH IT UP.
WHAT ARE WE TALKING ABOUT?
WE'VE REDLINED THE ORIGINAL SHOOTING SCRIPT AND ADDED A NOTE OR TWO HERE AND THERE.
WHY DON'T YOU TAKE THE NIGHT, THINK IT OVER AND WE CAN GET LUNCH TOMORROW?
I--
SOUNDS PERFECT!
WE'LL SEE YOU TOMORROW.

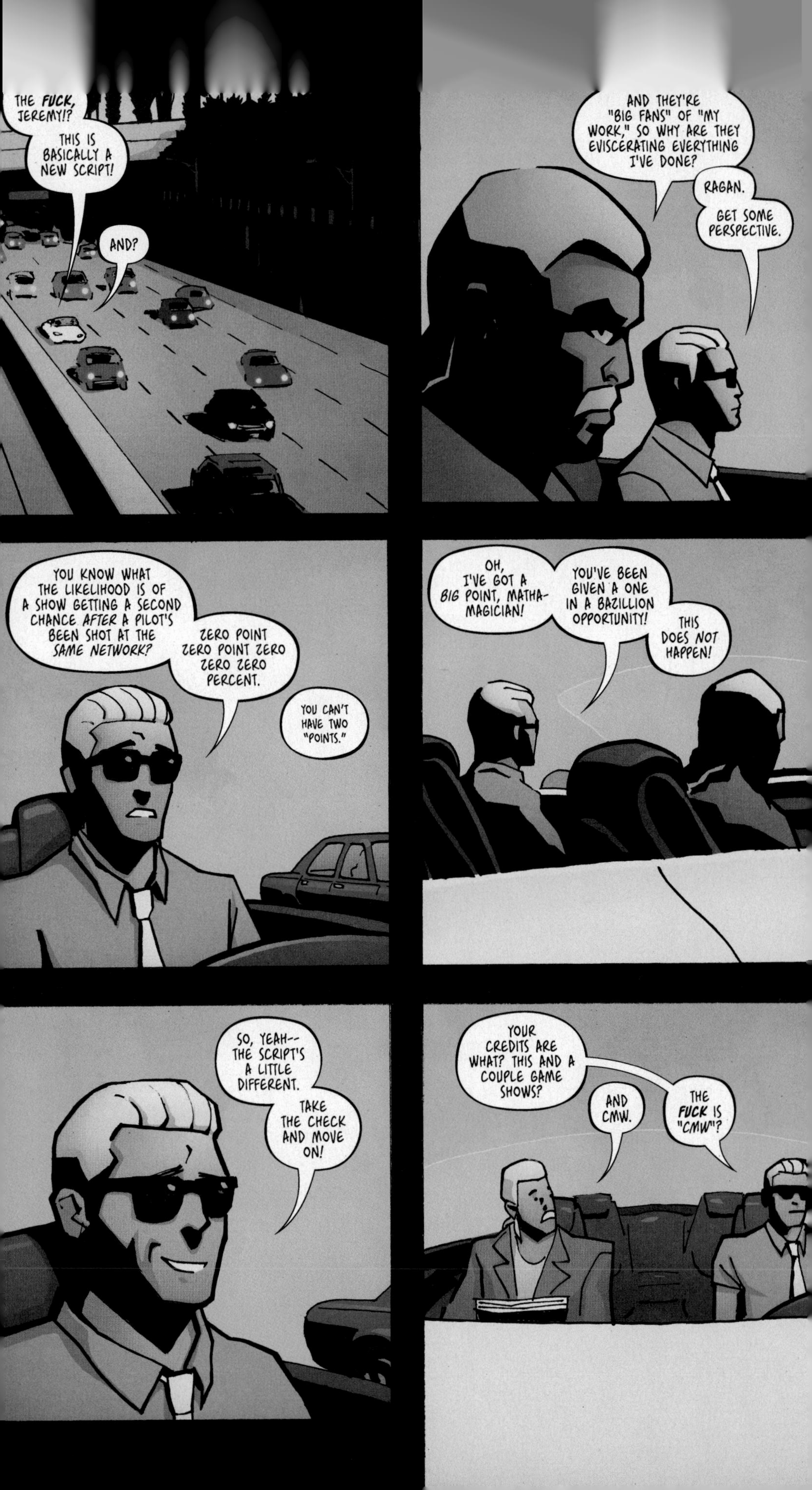
THE FUCK, JEREMY!?
THIS IS BASICALLY A NEW SCRIPT!
AND?
AND THEY'RE "BIG FANS" OF "MY WORK," SO WHY ARE THEY EVISCERATING EVERYTHING I'VE DONE?
RAGAN.
GET SOME PERSPECTIVE.
YOU KNOW WHAT THE LIKELIHOOD IS OF A SHOW GETTING A SECOND CHANCE AFTER A PILOT'S BEEN SHOT AT THE SAME NETWORK?
ZERO POINT ZERO POINT ZERO ZERO ZERO PERCENT.
YOU CAN'T HAVE TWO "POINTS."
OH, I'VE GOT A BIG POINT, MATHA-MAGICIAN!
YOU'VE BEEN GIVEN A ONE IN A BAZILLION OPPORTUNITY!
THIS DOES NOT HAPPEN!
SO, YEAH-- THE SCRIPT'S A LITTLE DIFFERENT.
TAKE THE CHECK AND MOVE ON!
YOUR CREDITS ARE WHAT? THIS AND A COUPLE GAME SHOWS?
AND CMW.
THE FUCK IS "CMW"?

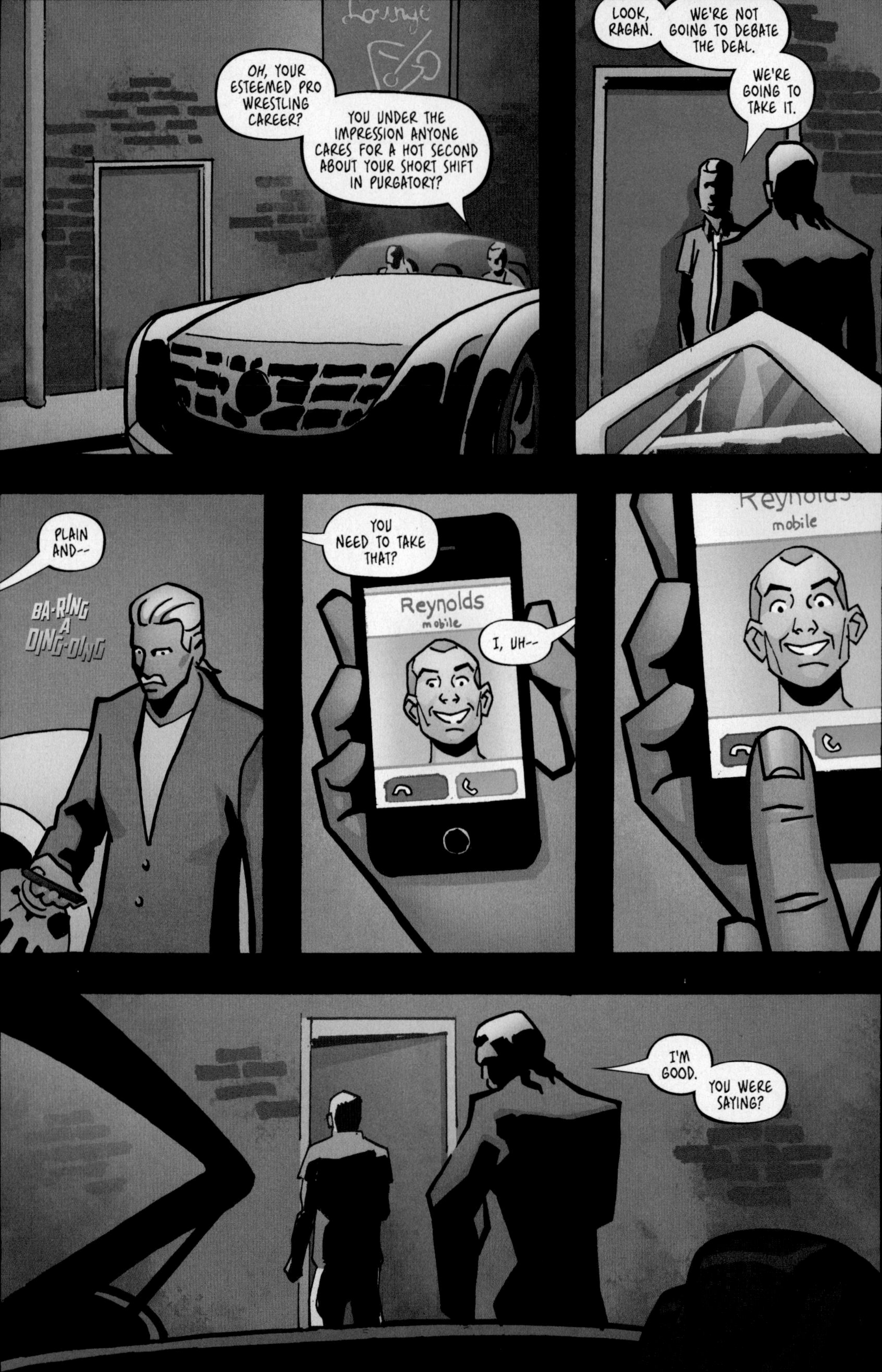
Lounge
OH, YOUR ESTEEMED PRO WRESTLING CAREER?
YOU UNDER THE IMPRESSION ANYONE CARES FOR A HOT SECOND ABOUT YOUR SHORT SHIFT IN PURGATORY?
LOOK, RAGAN.
WE'RE NOT GOING TO DEBATE THE DEAL.
WE'RE GOING TO TAKE IT.
PLAIN AND--
BA-RING A DING-DING
YOU NEED TO TAKE THAT?
Reynolds
mobile
I, UH--
Reynolds
mobile
I'M GOOD.
YOU WERE SAYING?

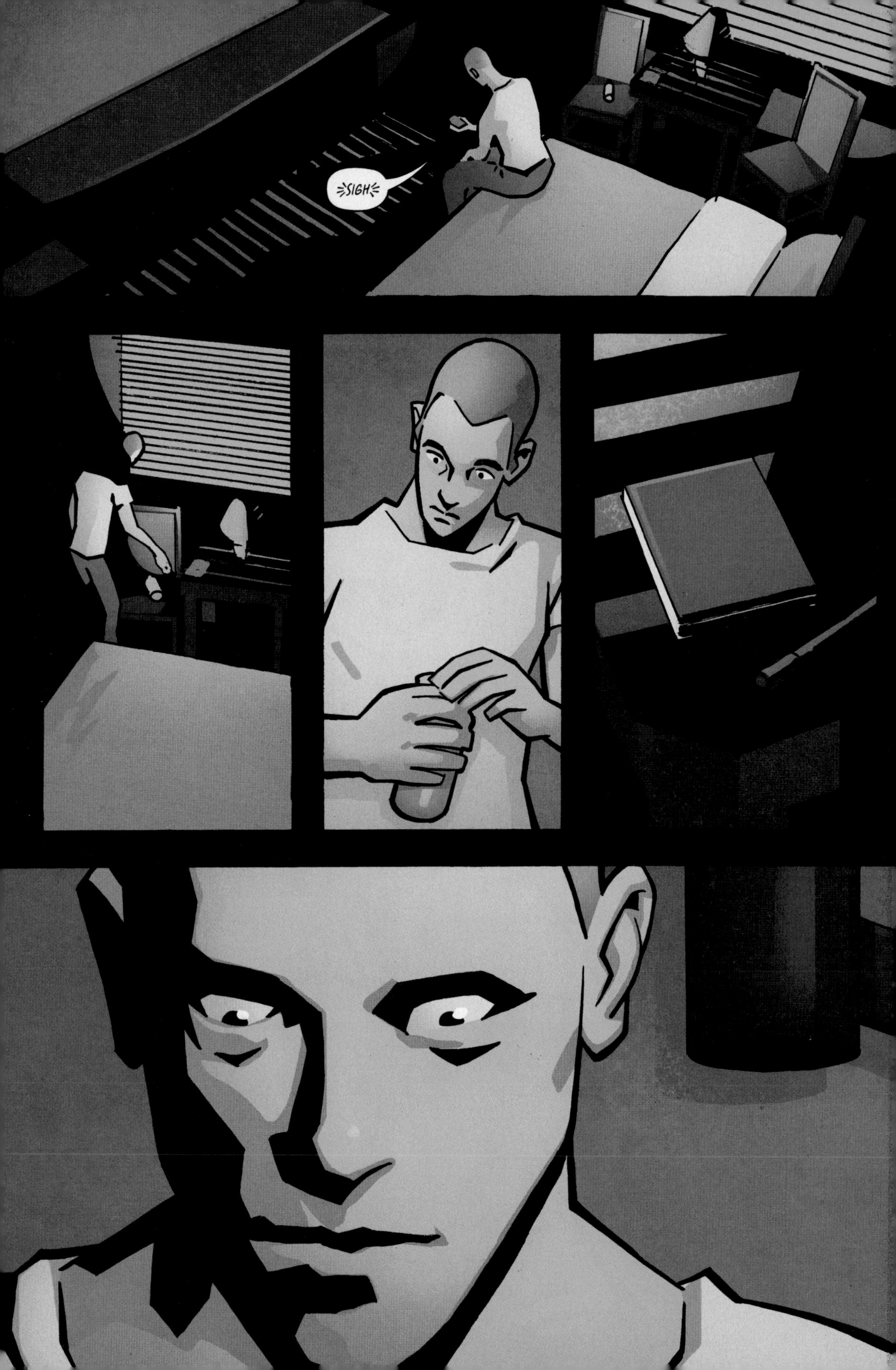
SIGH

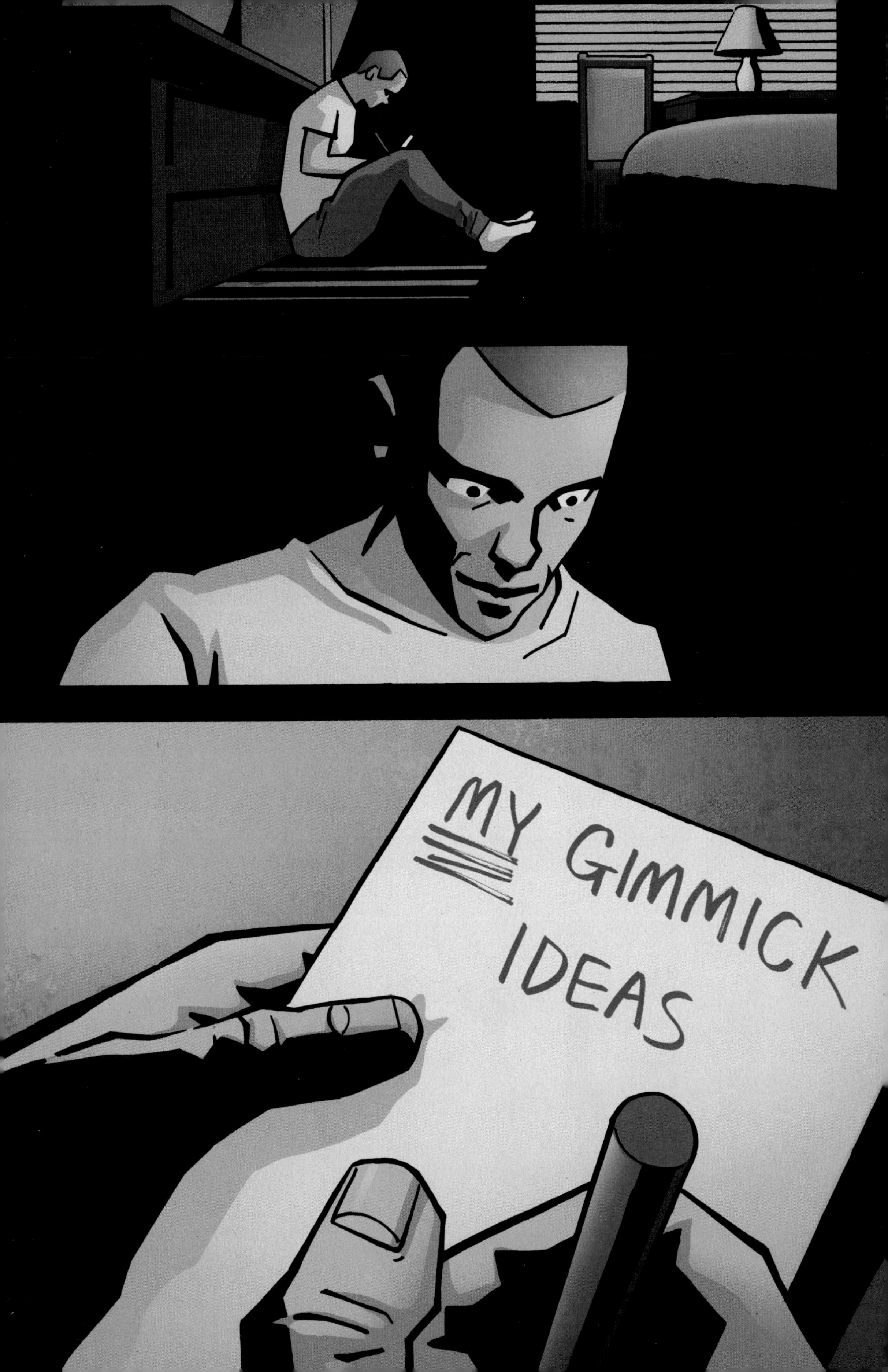
MY GIMMICK IDEAS

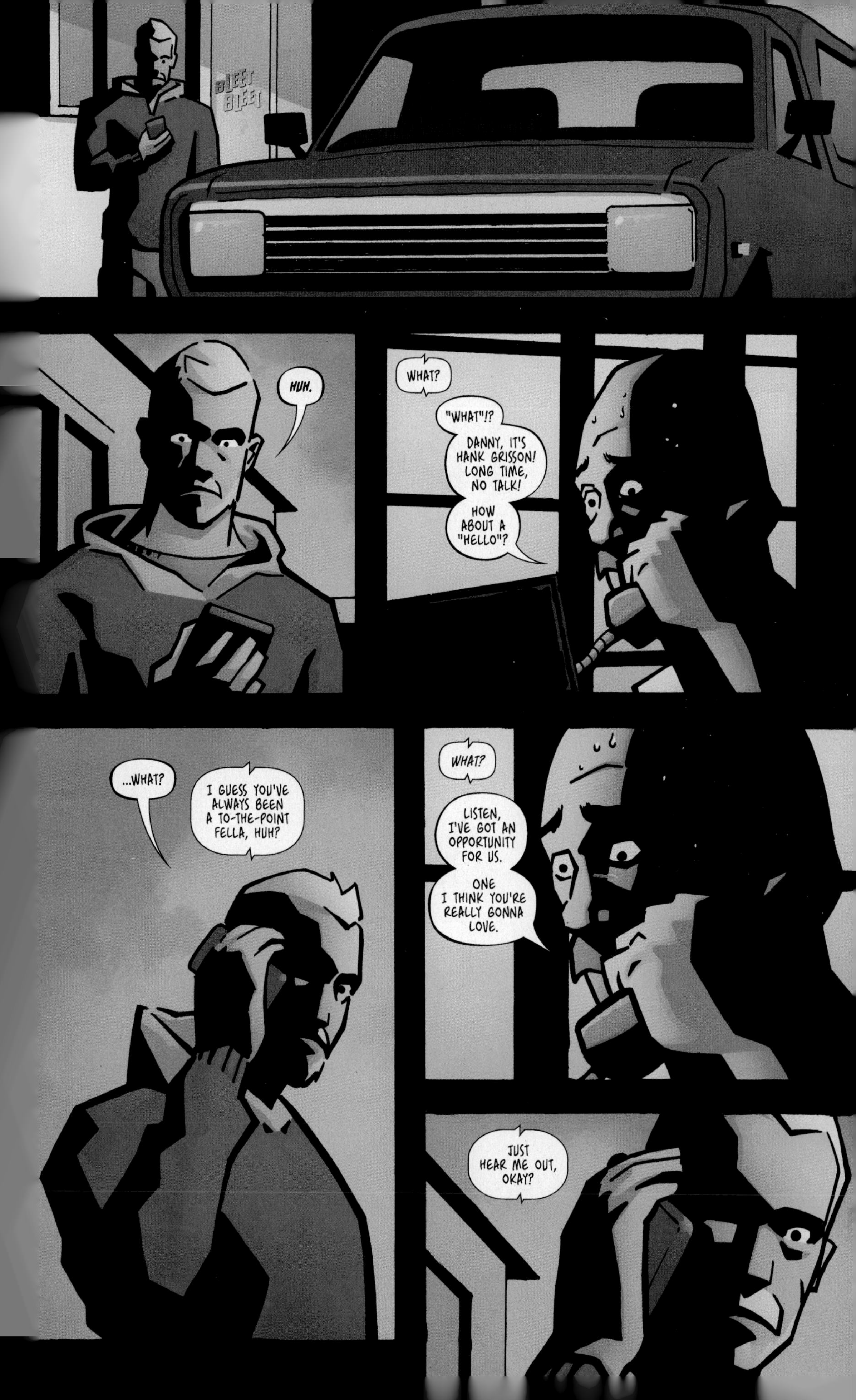
BLEET BLEET
HUH.
WHAT?
"WHAT"!?
DANNY, IT'S HANK GRISSON! LONG TIME, NO TALK!
HOW ABOUT A "HELLO"?
...WHAT?
I GUESS YOU'VE ALWAYS BEEN A TO-THE-POINT FELLA, HUH?
WHAT?
LISTEN, I'VE GOT AN OPPORTUNITY FOR US.
ONE I THINK YOU'RE REALLY GONNA LOVE.
JUST HEAR ME OUT, OKAY?

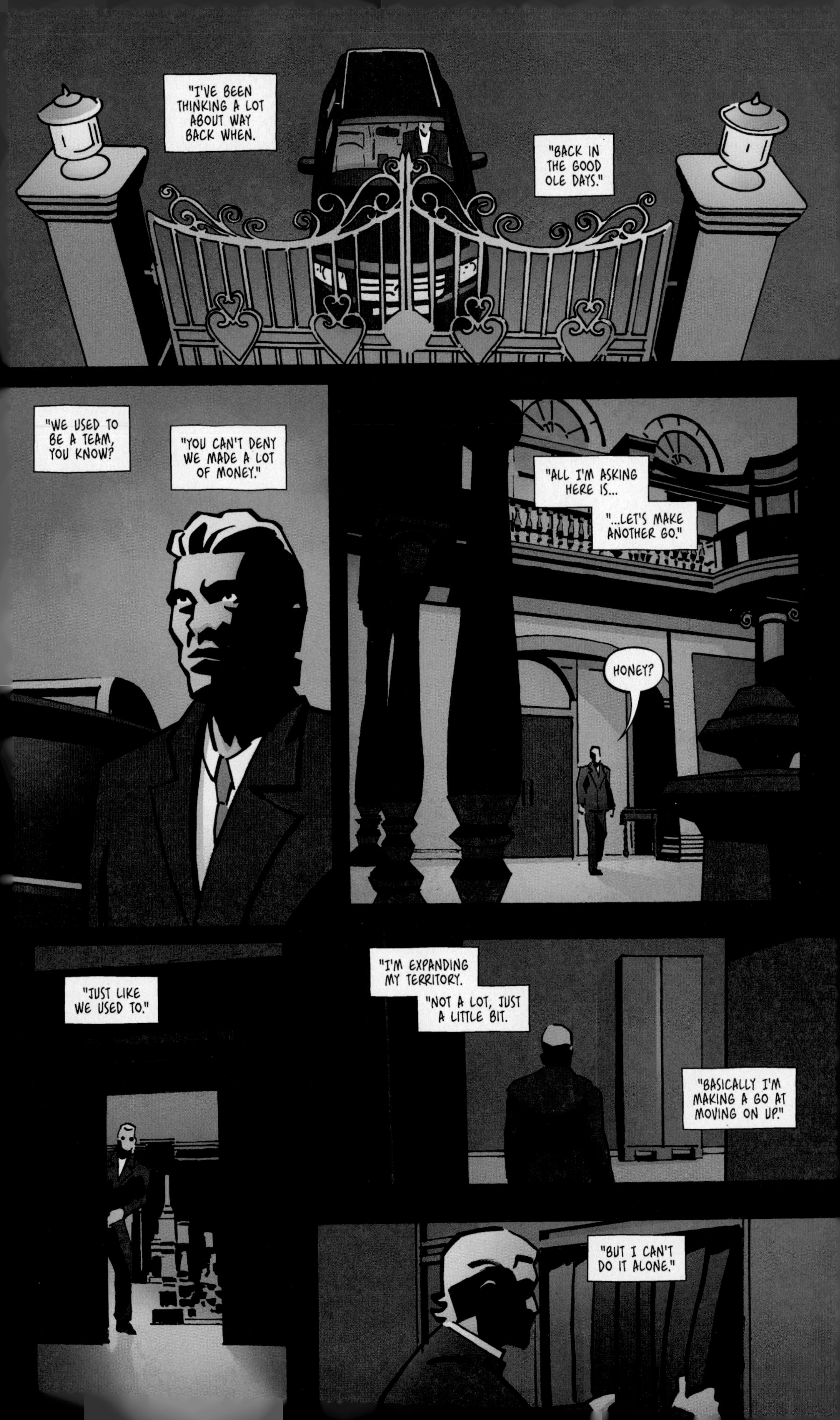
"I'VE BEEN THINKING A LOT ABOUT WAY BACK WHEN.
"BACK IN THE GOOD OLE DAYS."
"WE USED TO BE A TEAM, YOU KNOW?
"YOU CAN'T DENY WE MADE A LOT OF MONEY."
"ALL I'M ASKING HERE IS...
"...LET'S MAKE ANOTHER GO."
HONEY?
"JUST LIKE WE USED TO."
"I'M EXPANDING MY TERRITORY.
"NOT A LOT, JUST A LITTLE BIT.
"BASICALLY I'M MAKING A GO AT MOVING ON UP."
"BUT I CAN'T DO IT ALONE."

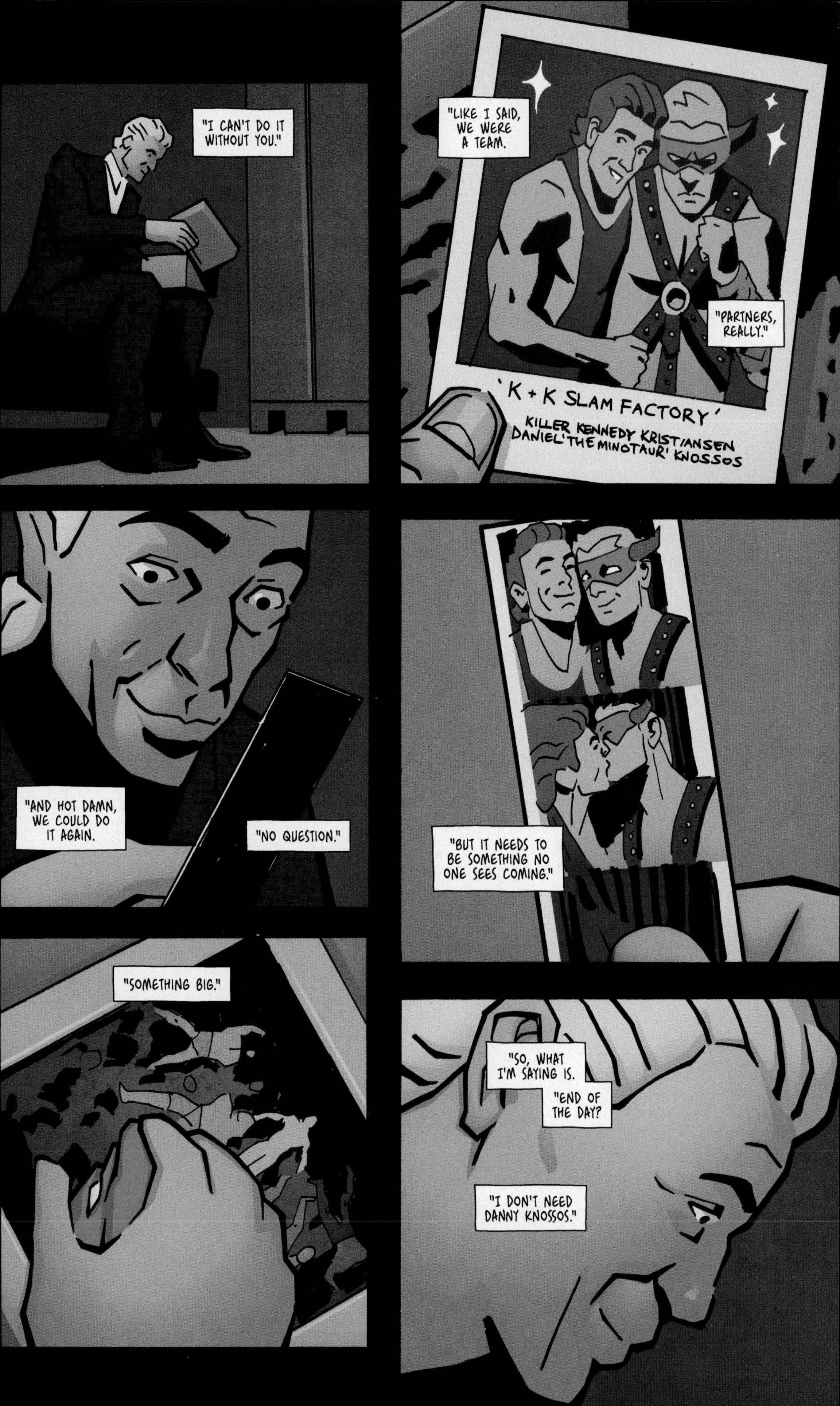
"I CAN'T DO IT WITHOUT YOU."
"LIKE I SAID, WE WERE A TEAM.
"PARTNERS, REALLY."
'K + K SLAM FACTORY'
KILLER KENNEDY KRISTIANSEN
DANIEL 'THE MINOTAUR' KNOSSOS
"AND HOT DAMN, WE COULD DO IT AGAIN.
"NO QUESTION."
"BUT IT NEEDS TO BE SOMETHING NO ONE SEES COMING."
"SOMETHING BIG."
"SO, WHAT I'M SAYING IS.
"END OF THE DAY?
"I DON'T NEED DANNY KNOSSOS."

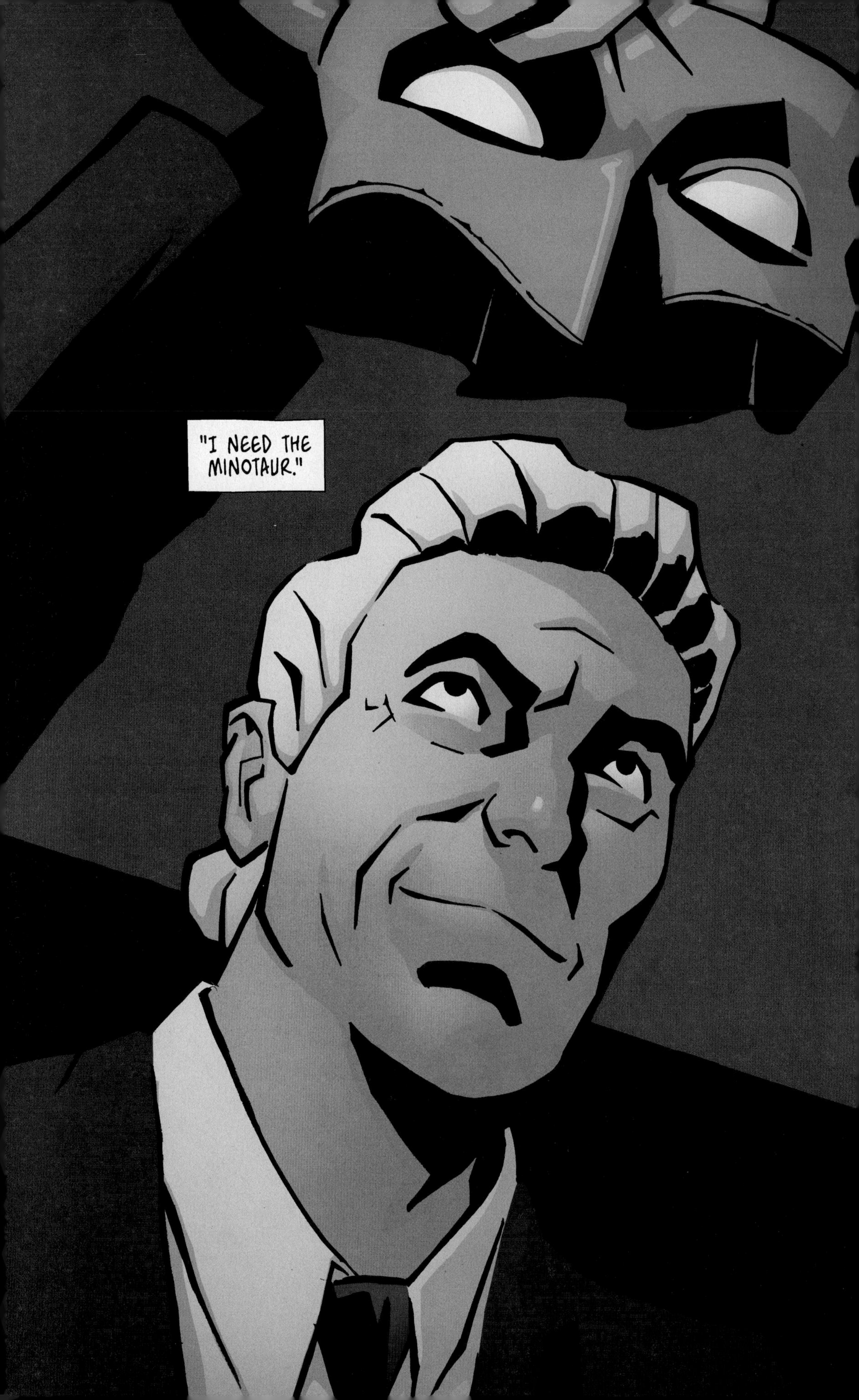
"I NEED THE MINOTAUR."

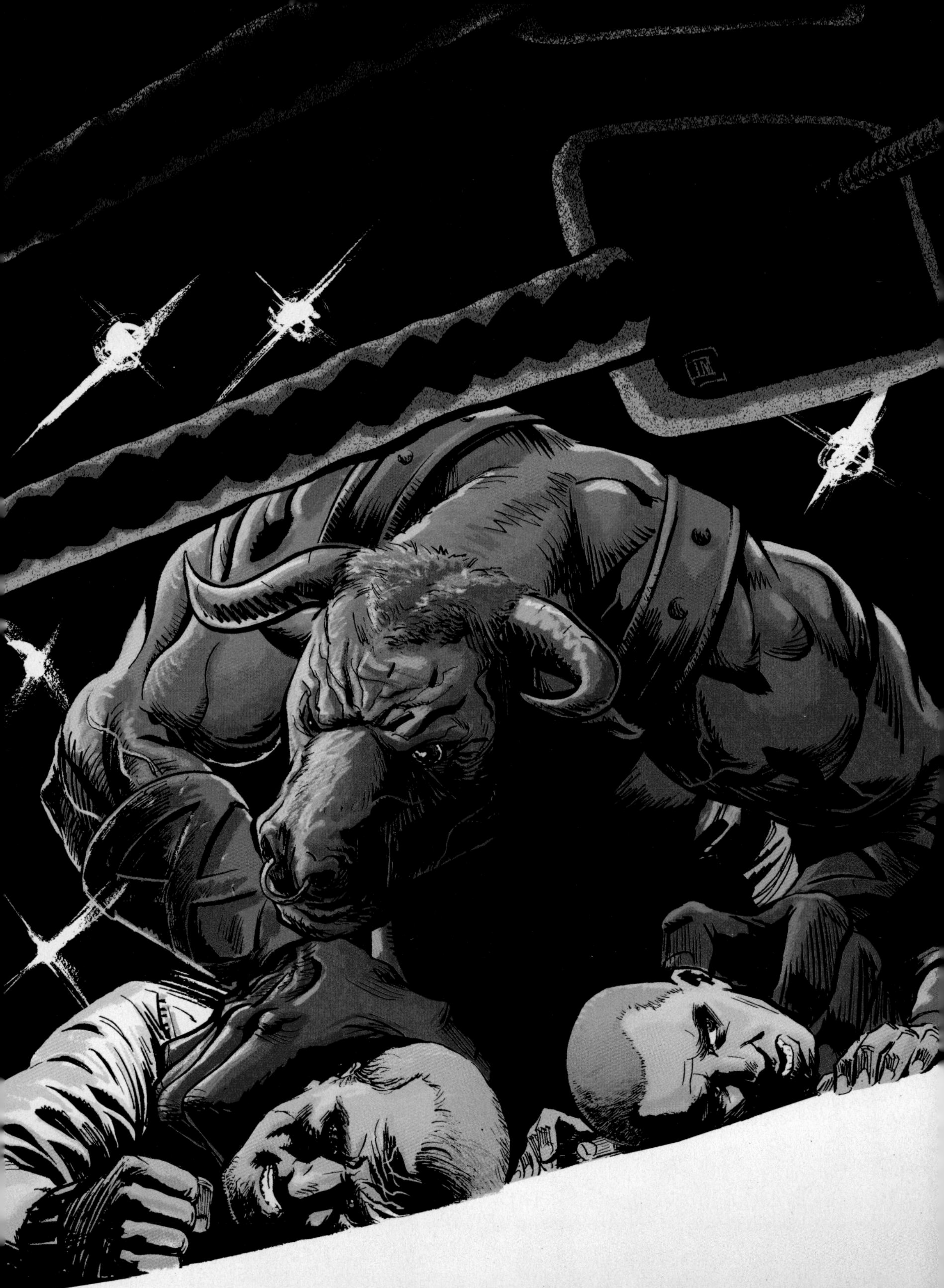

CHAPTER TWELVE

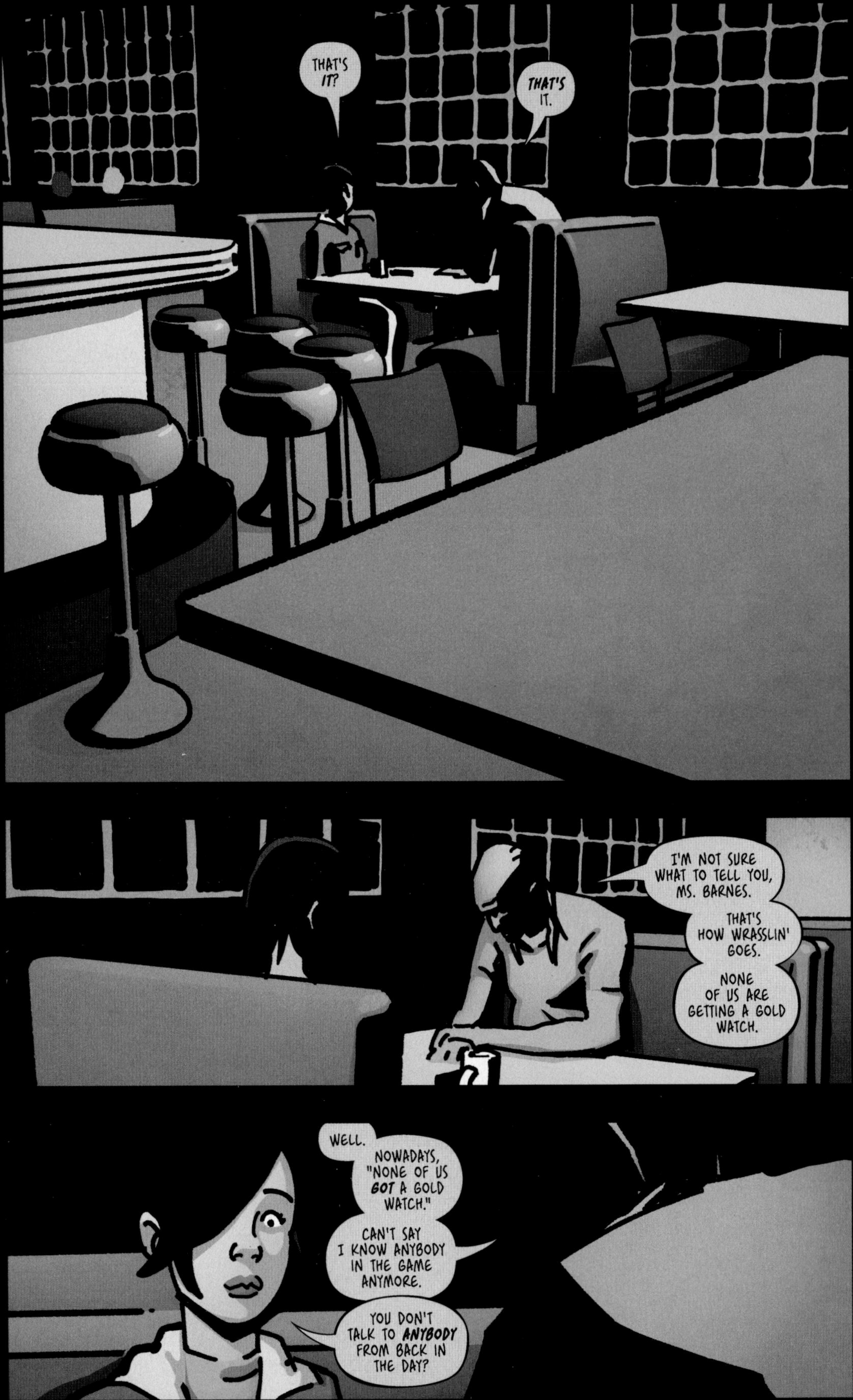
THAT'S IT?
THAT'S IT.
I'M NOT SURE WHAT TO TELL YOU, MS. BARNES.
THAT'S HOW WRASSLIN' GOES.
NONE OF US ARE GETTING A GOLD WATCH.
WELL.
NOWADAYS, "NONE OF US GOT A GOLD WATCH."
CAN'T SAY I KNOW ANYBODY IN THE GAME ANYMORE.
YOU DON'T TALK TO ANYBODY FROM BACK IN THE DAY?

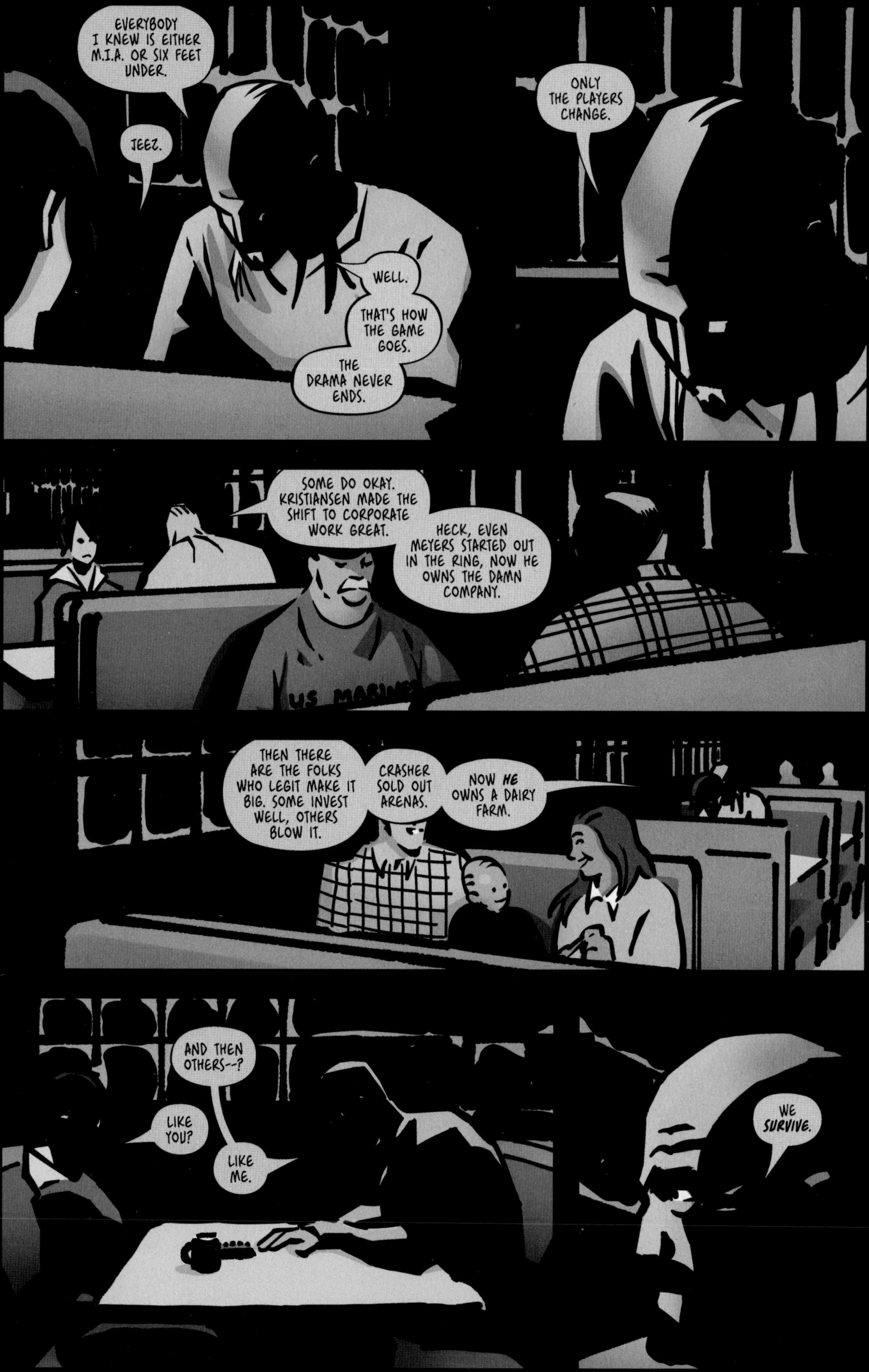
EVERYBODY I KNEW IS EITHER M.I.A. OR SIX FEET UNDER.
JEEZ.
WELL.
THAT'S HOW THE GAME GOES.
THE DRAMA NEVER ENDS.
ONLY THE PLAYERS CHANGE.
SOME DO OKAY. KRISTIANSEN MADE THE SHIFT TO CORPORATE WORK GREAT.
HECK, EVEN MEYERS STARTED OUT IN THE RING, NOW HE OWNS THE DAMN COMPANY.
US MARINES
THEN THERE ARE THE FOLKS WHO LEGIT MAKE IT BIG. SOME INVEST WELL, OTHERS BLOW IT.
CRASHER SOLD OUT ARENAS.
NOW *HE* OWNS A DAIRY FARM.
AND THEN OTHERS--?
LIKE YOU?
LIKE ME.
WE *SURVIVE*.

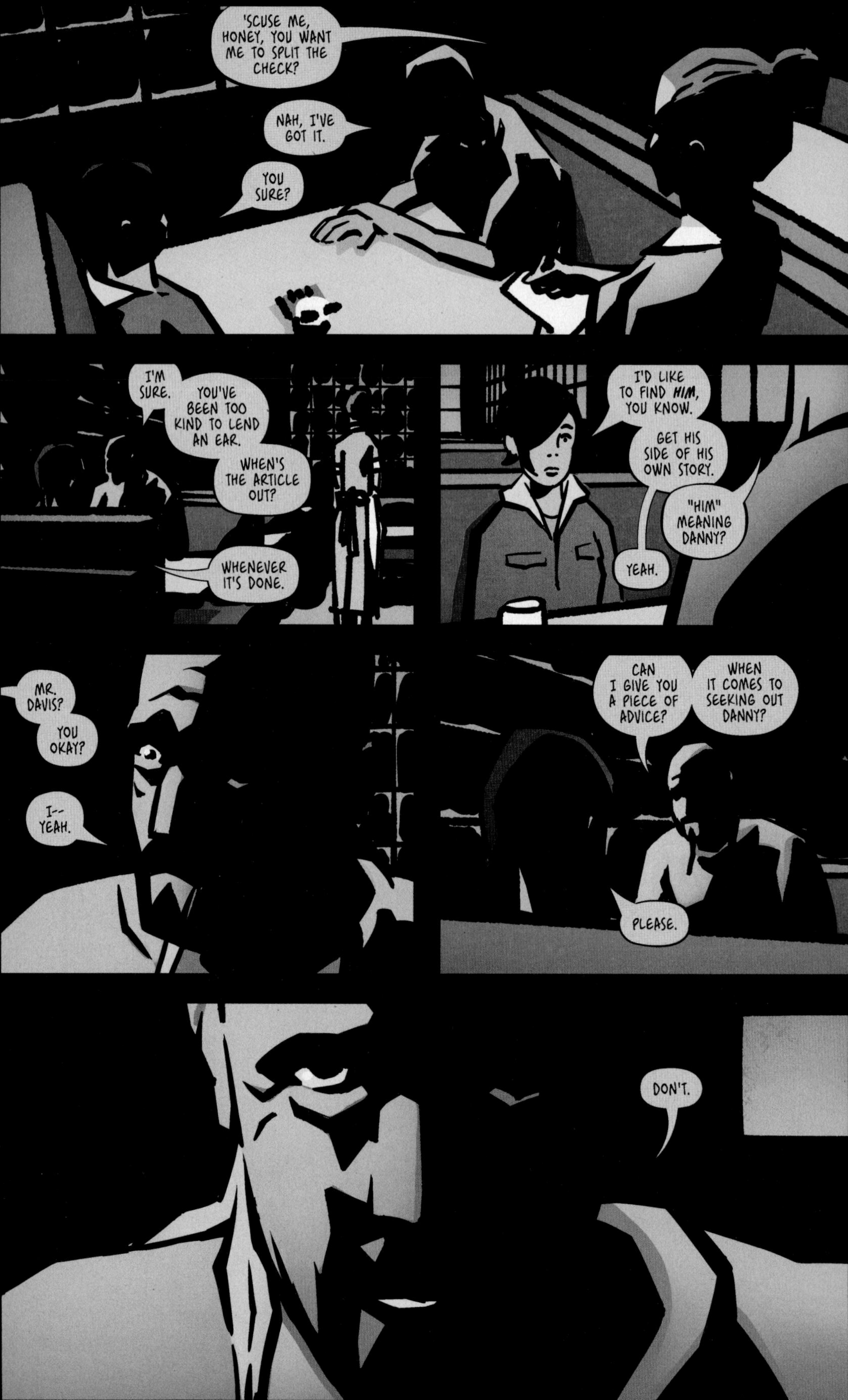
'SCUSE ME, HONEY, YOU WANT ME TO SPLIT THE CHECK?
NAH, I'VE GOT IT.
YOU SURE?
I'M SURE.
YOU'VE BEEN TOO KIND TO LEND AN EAR.
WHEN'S THE ARTICLE OUT?
WHENEVER IT'S DONE.
I'D LIKE TO FIND HIM, YOU KNOW.
GET HIS SIDE OF HIS OWN STORY.
"HIM" MEANING DANNY?
YEAH.
MR. DAVIS?
YOU OKAY?
I-- YEAH.
CAN I GIVE YOU A PIECE OF ADVICE?
WHEN IT COMES TO SEEKING OUT DANNY?
PLEASE.
DON'T.

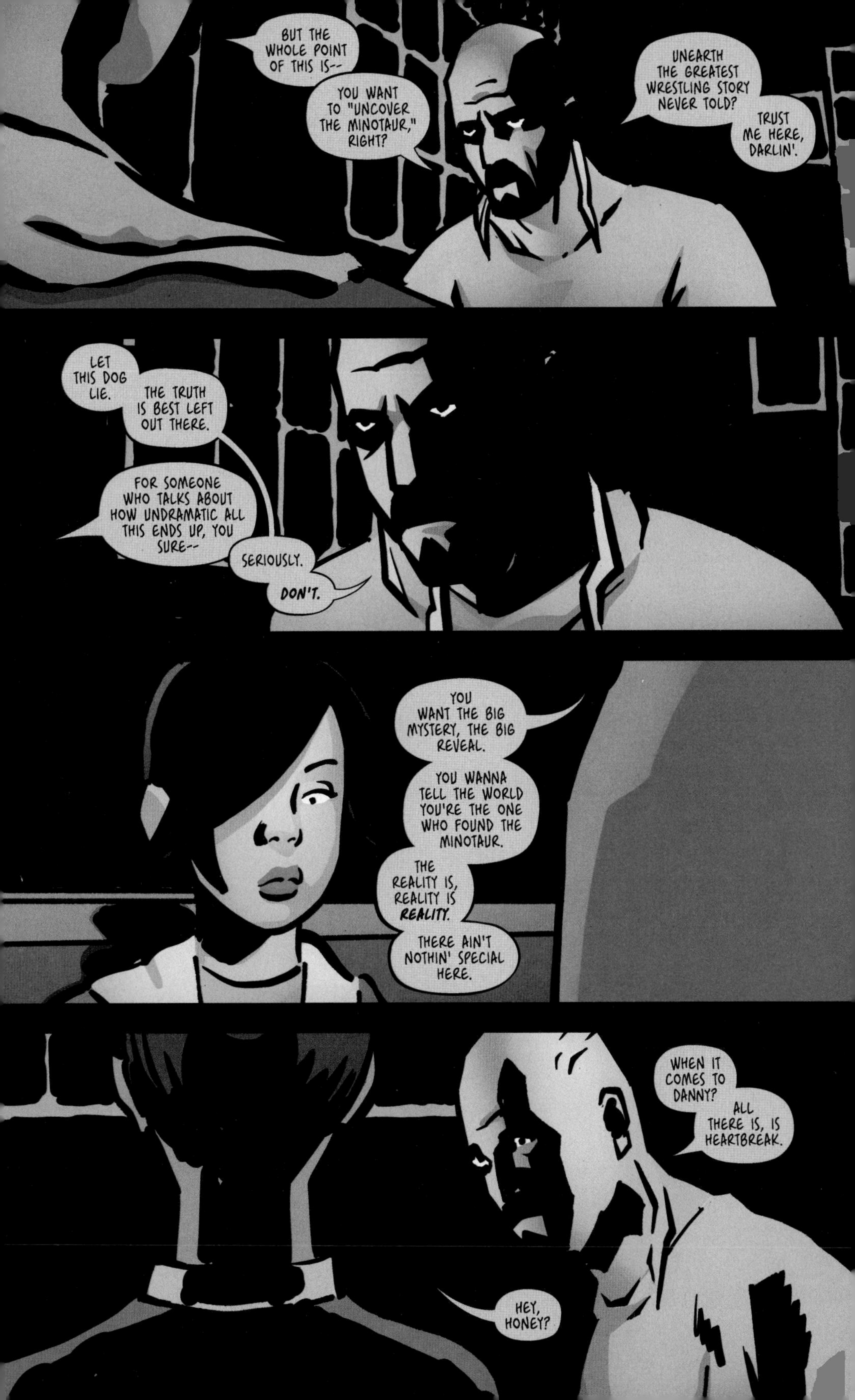
BUT THE WHOLE POINT OF THIS IS--
YOU WANT TO "UNCOVER THE MINOTAUR," RIGHT?
UNEARTH THE GREATEST WRESTLING STORY NEVER TOLD?
TRUST ME HERE, DARLIN'.
LET THIS DOG LIE.
THE TRUTH IS BEST LEFT OUT THERE.
FOR SOMEONE WHO TALKS ABOUT HOW UNDRAMATIC ALL THIS ENDS UP, YOU SURE--
SERIOUSLY.
DON'T.
YOU WANT THE BIG MYSTERY, THE BIG REVEAL.
YOU WANNA TELL THE WORLD YOU'RE THE ONE WHO FOUND THE MINOTAUR.
THE REALITY IS, REALITY IS REALITY.
THERE AIN'T NOTHIN' SPECIAL HERE.
WHEN IT COMES TO DANNY?
ALL THERE IS, IS HEARTBREAK.
HEY, HONEY?

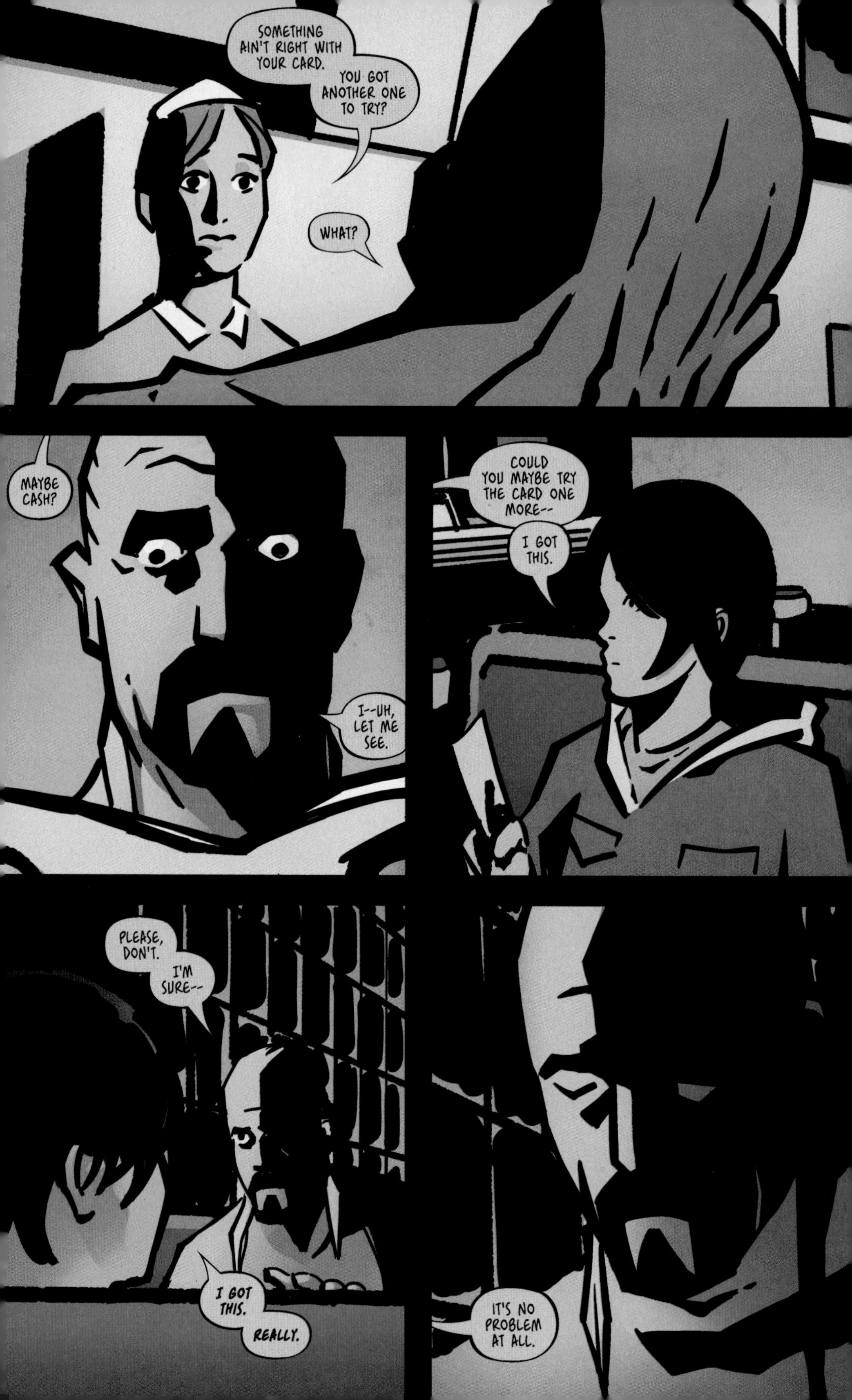
SOMETHING AIN'T RIGHT WITH YOUR CARD.
YOU GOT ANOTHER ONE TO TRY?
WHAT?
MAYBE CASH?
I--UH, LET ME SEE.
COULD YOU MAYBE TRY THE CARD ONE MORE--
I GOT THIS.
PLEASE, DON'T.
I'M SURE--
I GOT THIS.
REALLY.
IT'S NO PROBLEM AT ALL.

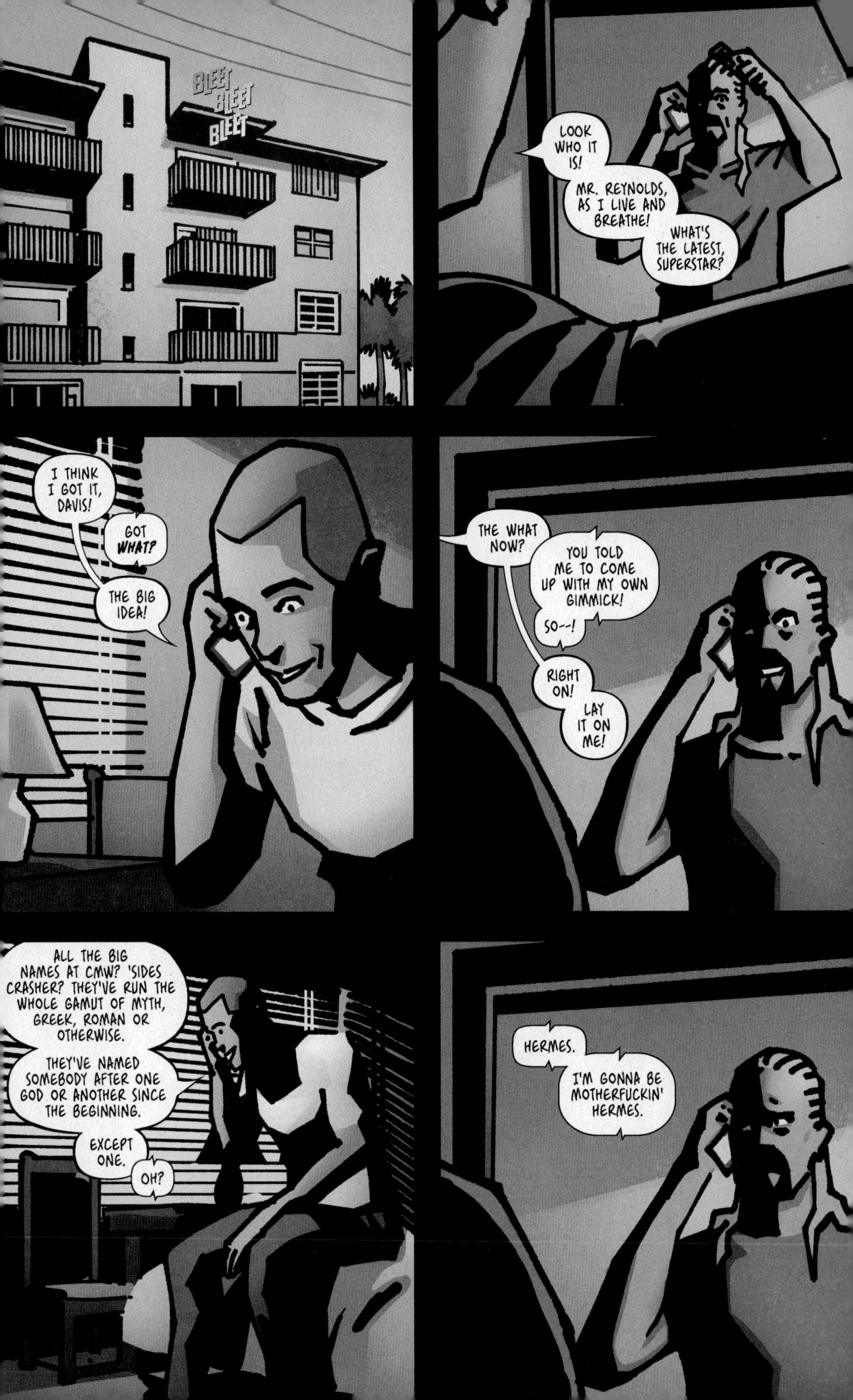
BLEET BLEET BLEET
LOOK WHO IT IS!
MR. REYNOLDS, AS I LIVE AND BREATHE!
WHAT'S THE LATEST, SUPERSTAR?
I THINK I GOT IT, DAVIS!
GOT WHAT?
THE BIG IDEA!
THE WHAT NOW?
YOU TOLD ME TO COME UP WITH MY OWN GIMMICK!
SO--!
RIGHT ON!
LAY IT ON ME!
ALL THE BIG NAMES AT CMW? 'SIDES CRASHER? THEY'VE RUN THE WHOLE GAMUT OF MYTH, GREEK, ROMAN OR OTHERWISE.
THEY'VE NAMED SOMEBODY AFTER ONE GOD OR ANOTHER SINCE THE BEGINNING.
EXCEPT ONE.
OH?
HERMES.
I'M GONNA BE MOTHERFUCKIN' HERMES.

NO.

WHAT DO YOU MEAN "NO"!?

DUDE, YOU SERIOUS?

HECK YEAH! WHAT'S THE MATTER?

REHASHING THE SAME GENERAL SCHTICK THE COMPANY'S BEEN PULLING FOR *DECADES*? THAT'S THE BIG IDEA?

BUDDY, WHAT'S YOUR GOAL HERE?

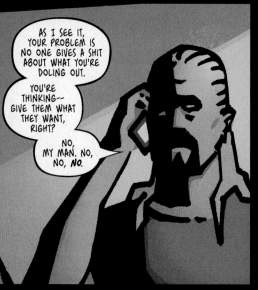

AS I SEE IT, YOUR PROBLEM IS NO ONE GIVES A SHIT ABOUT WHAT YOU'RE DOLING OUT.

YOU'RE THINKING-- GIVE THEM WHAT THEY WANT, RIGHT?

NO, MY MAN. NO, NO, *NO.*

YOU WANT TO STICK OUT? GET ATTENTION?

THEN STICK OUT. GET ATTENTION.

YOU'RE NOT GOING TO DO THAT BY GIVING THEM MORE OF THE SAME.

YOU'VE GOTTA GET ANOTHER ANGLE, KID.

A BETTER ANGLE.

SOMETHING CLEVER.

SOMETHING *DIFFERENT.*

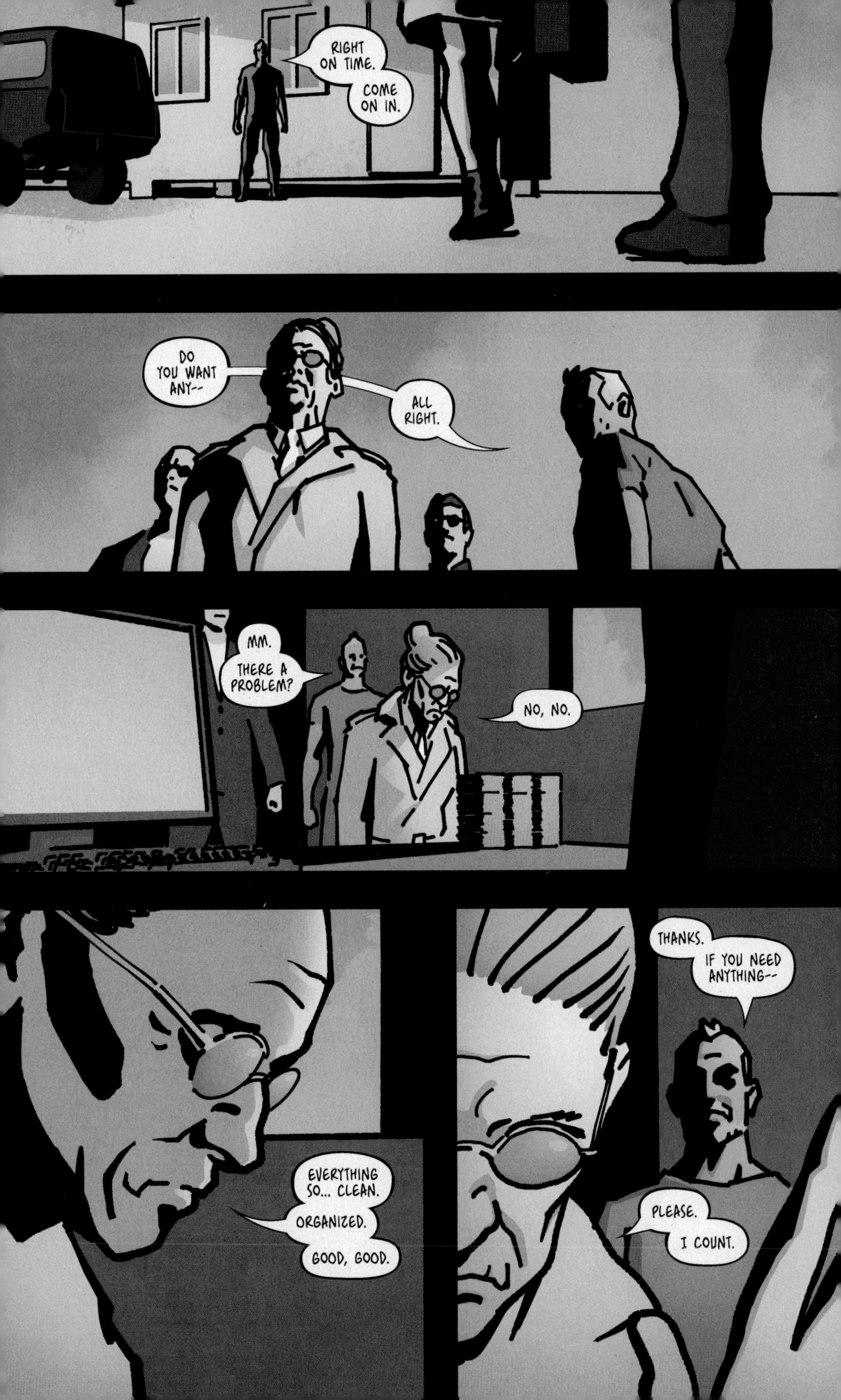
RIGHT ON TIME.
COME ON IN.
DO YOU WANT ANY--
ALL RIGHT.
MM.
THERE A PROBLEM?
NO, NO.
EVERYTHING SO... CLEAN.
ORGANIZED.
GOOD, GOOD.
THANKS.
IF YOU NEED ANYTHING--
PLEASE.
I COUNT.

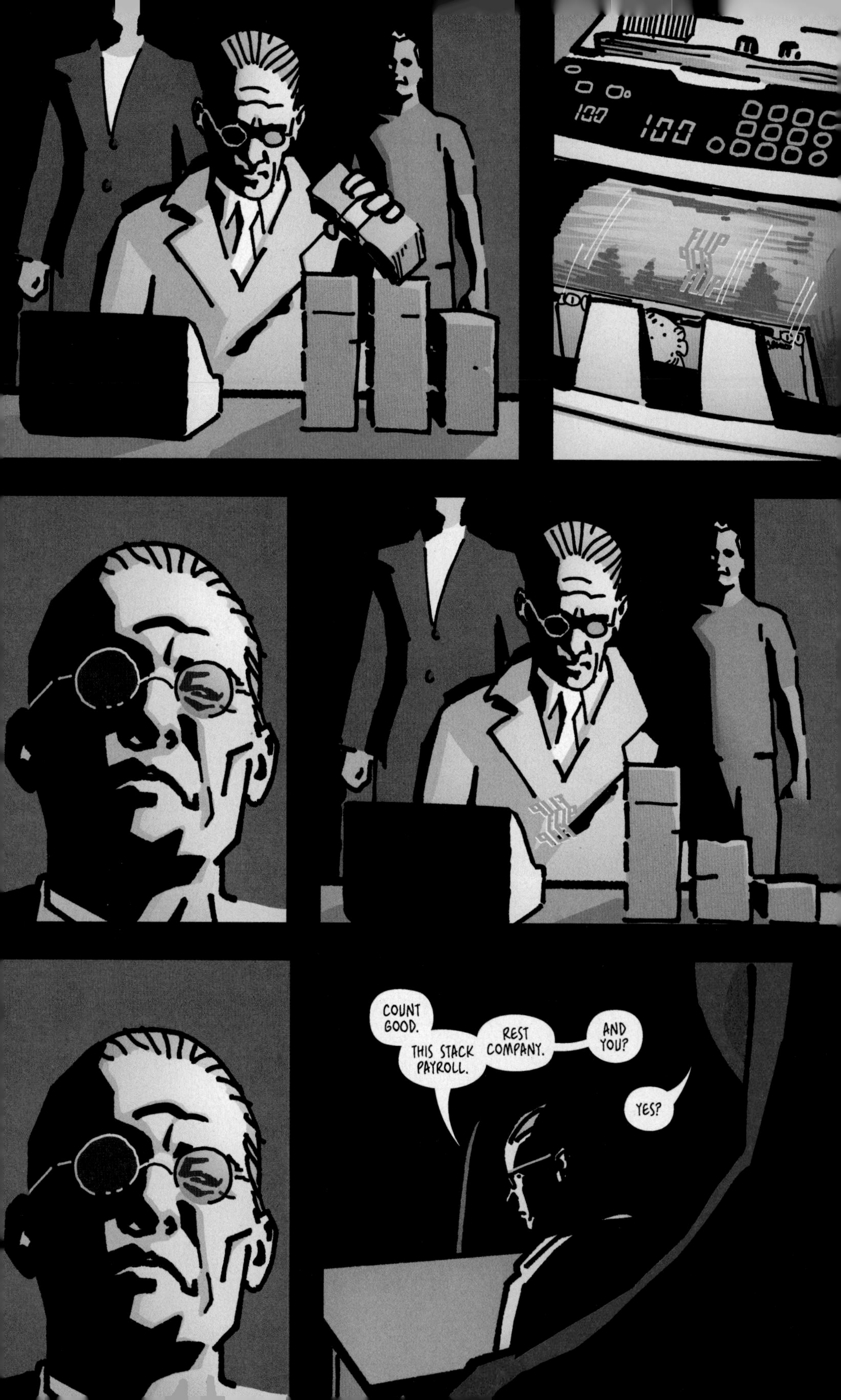
100
100
COUNT GOOD.
THIS STACK PAYROLL.
REST COMPANY.
AND YOU?
YES?

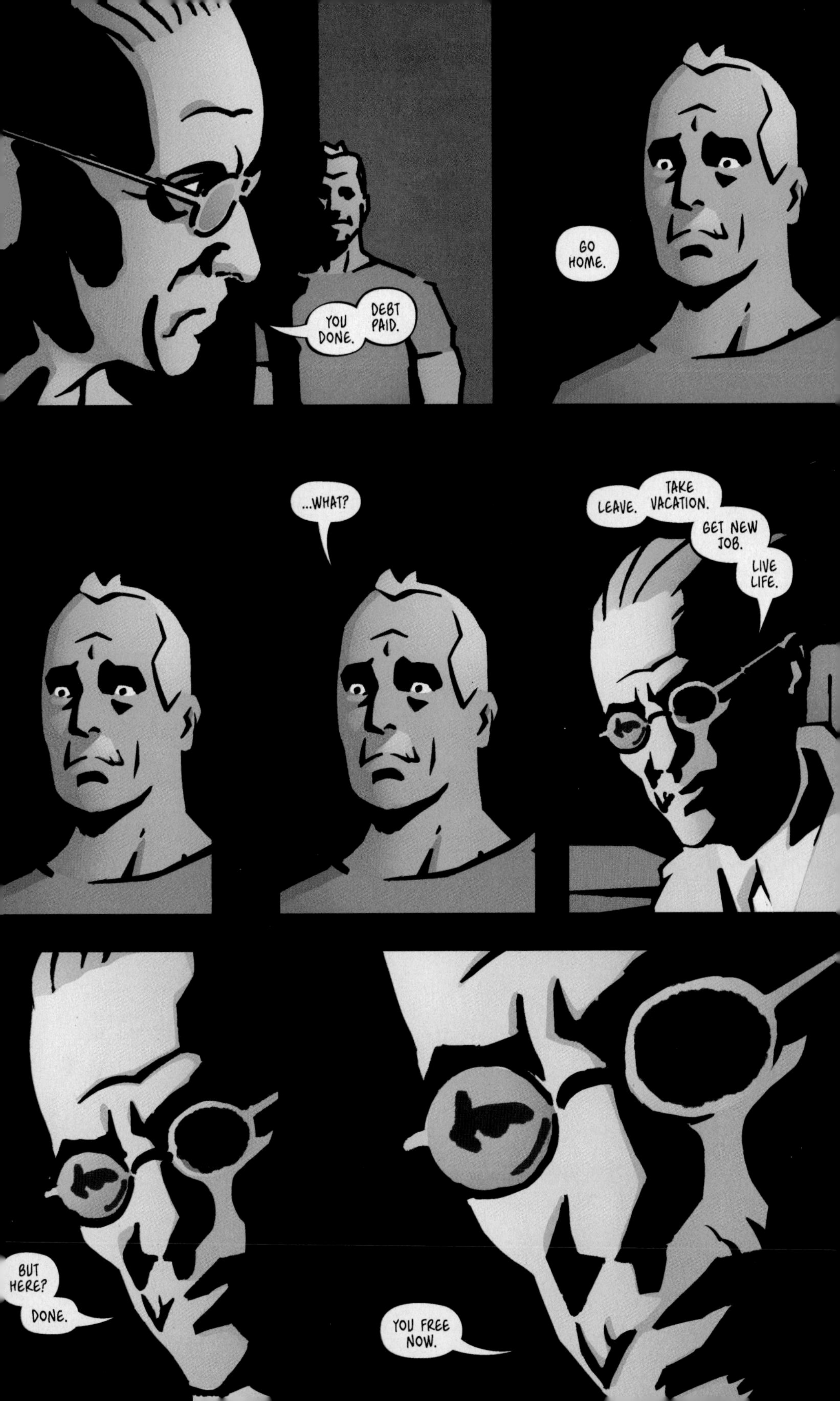
YOU DONE.
DEBT PAID.
GO HOME.
...WHAT?
LEAVE.
TAKE VACATION.
GET NEW JOB.
LIVE LIFE.
BUT HERE?
DONE.
YOU FREE NOW.

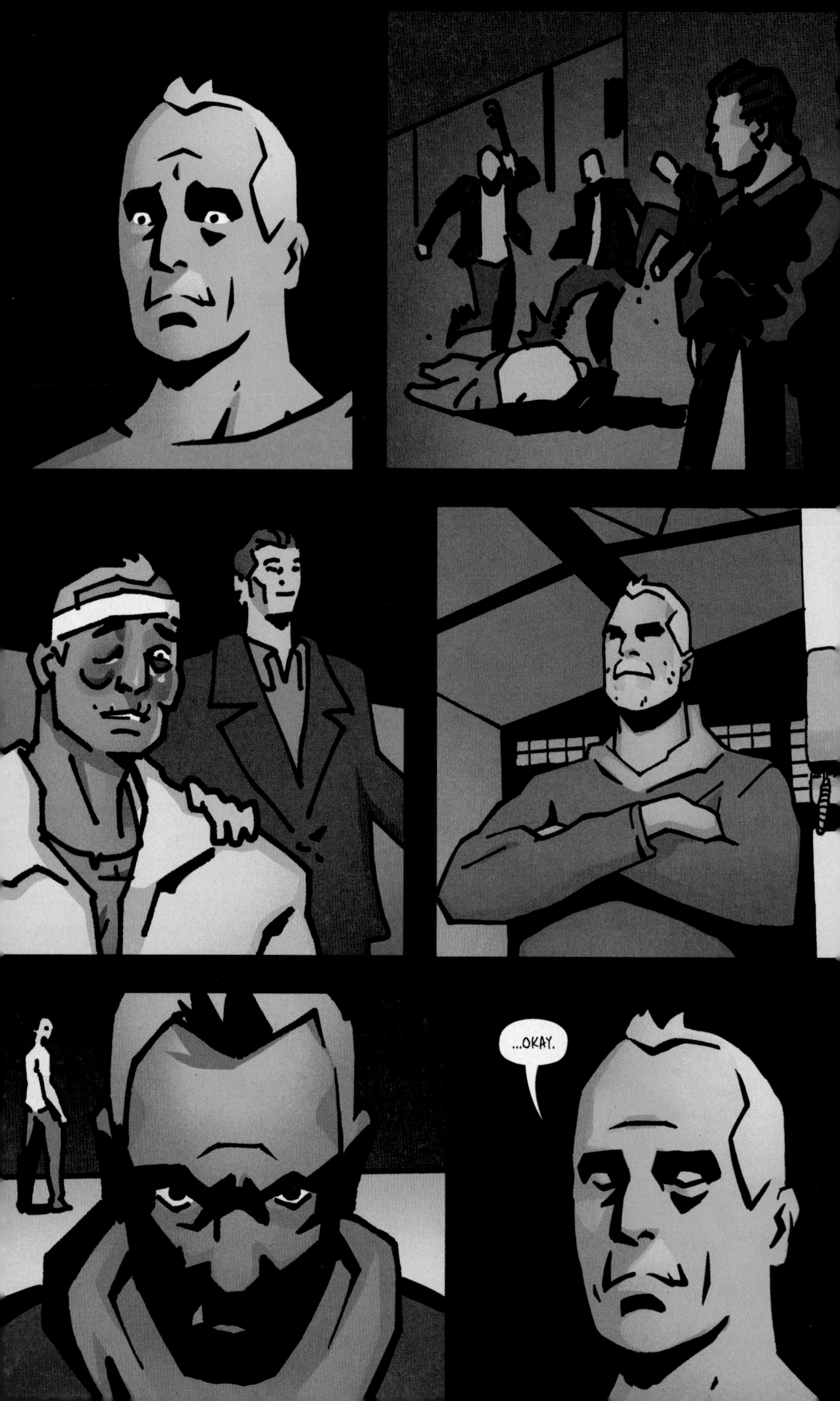
...OKAY.

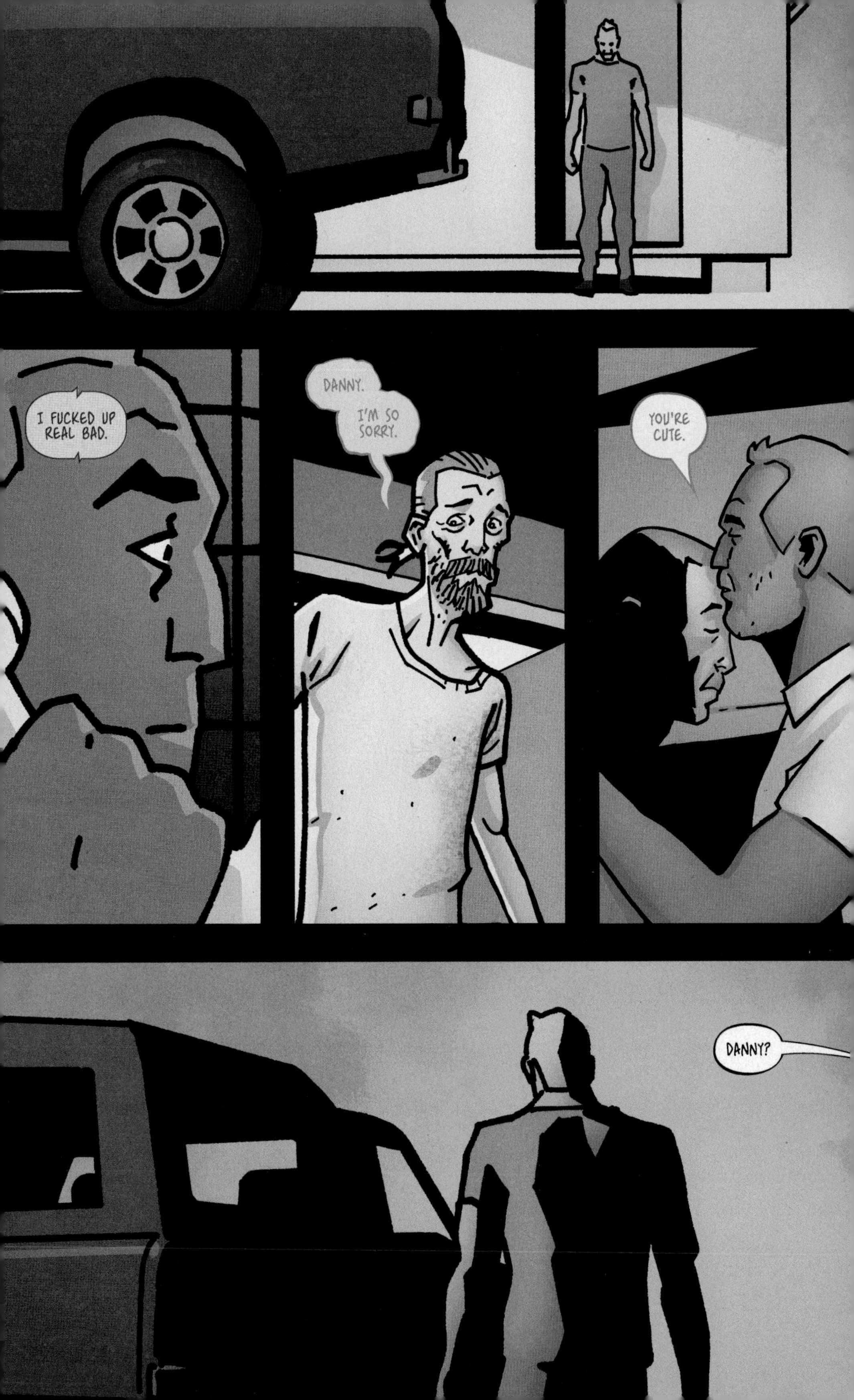
I FUCKED UP REAL BAD.
DANNY.
I'M SO SORRY.
YOU'RE CUTE.
DANNY?

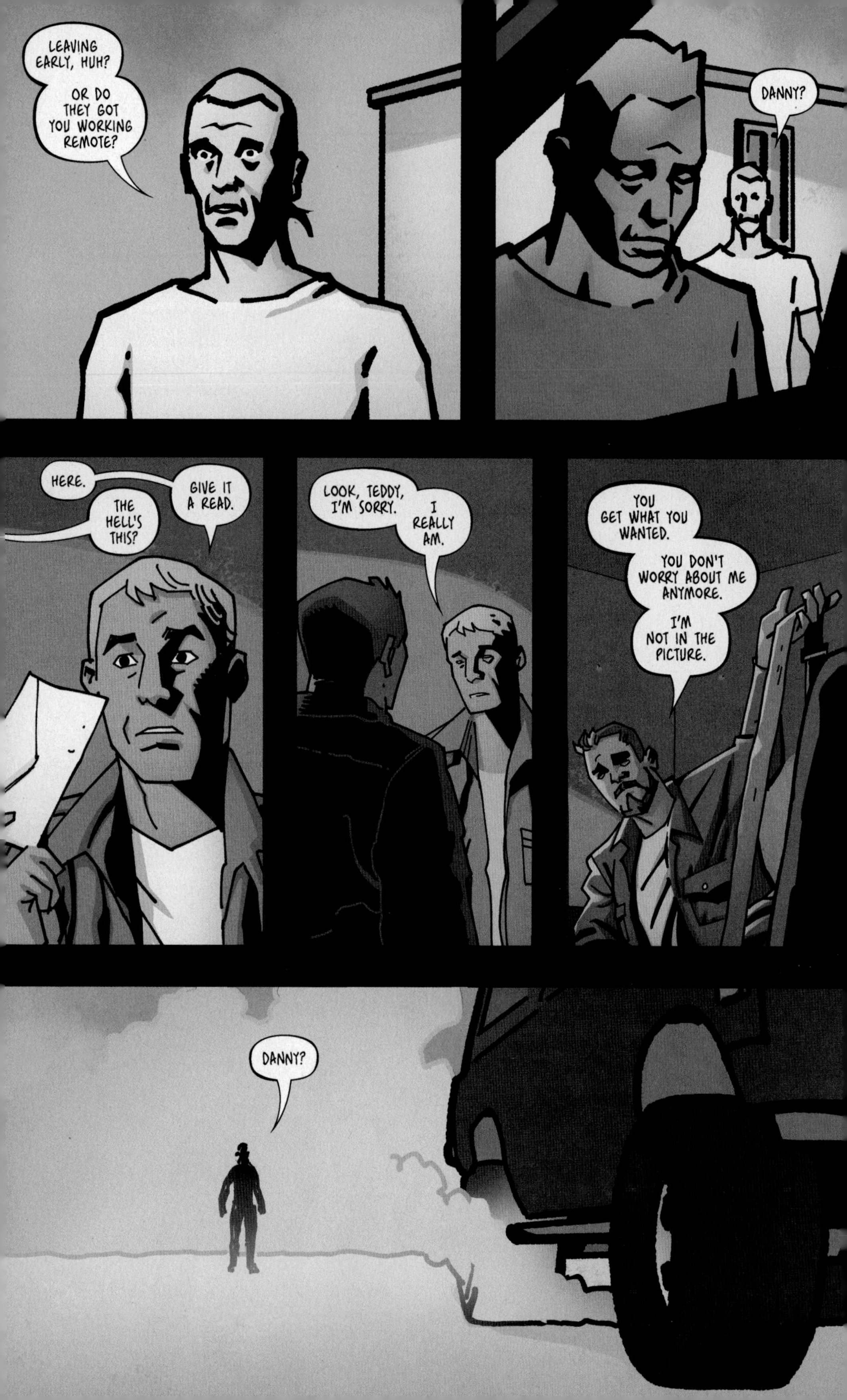
LEAVING EARLY, HUH?
OR DO THEY GOT YOU WORKING REMOTE?
DANNY?
HERE.
THE HELL'S THIS?
GIVE IT A READ.
LOOK, TEDDY, I'M SORRY.
I REALLY AM.
YOU GET WHAT YOU WANTED.
YOU DON'T WORRY ABOUT ME ANYMORE.
I'M NOT IN THE PICTURE.
DANNY?

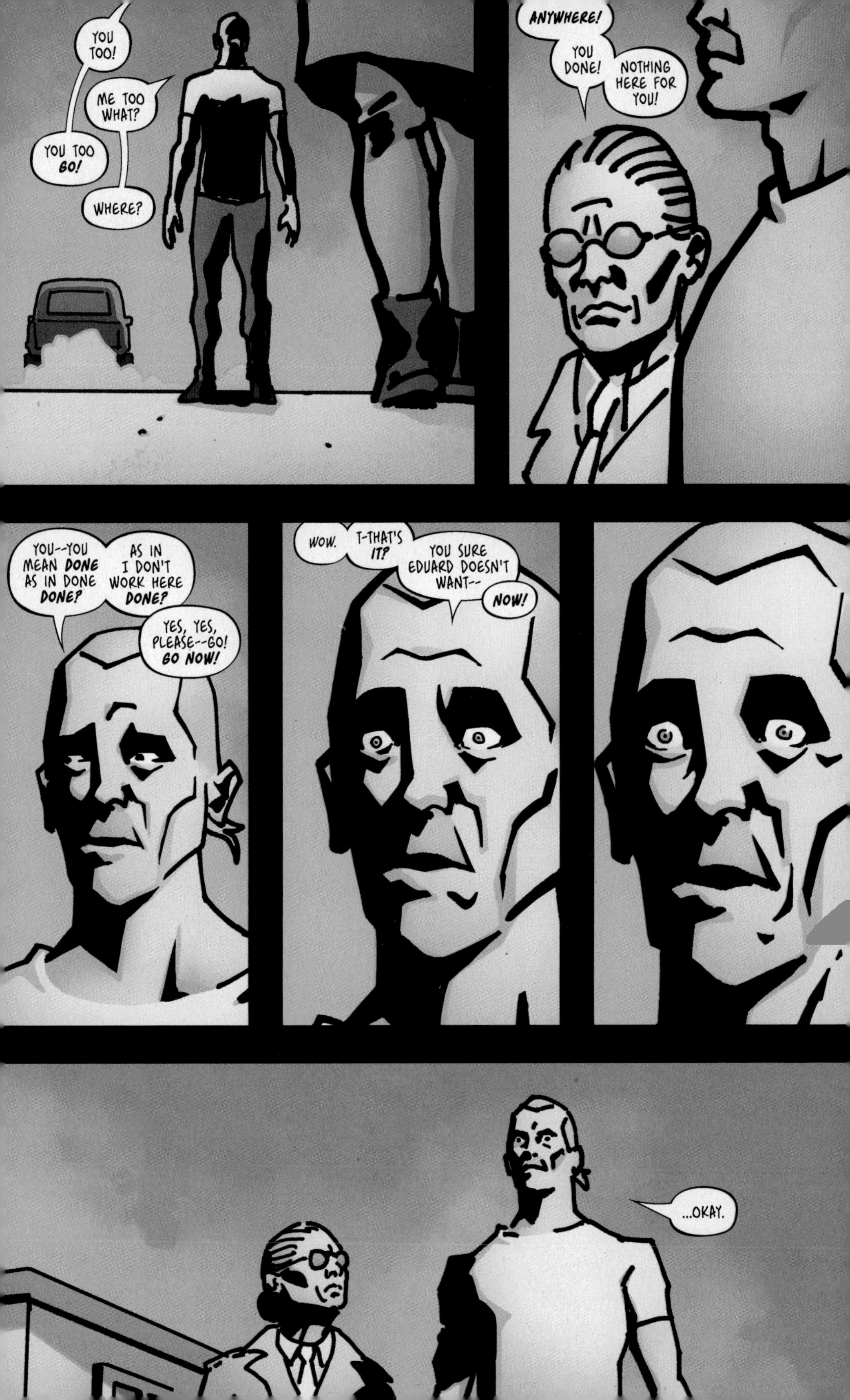
YOU TOO!
ME TOO WHAT?
YOU TOO GO!
WHERE?
ANYWHERE!
YOU DONE!
NOTHING HERE FOR YOU!
YOU--YOU MEAN DONE AS IN DONE DONE?
AS IN I DON'T WORK HERE DONE?
YES, YES, PLEASE--GO! GO NOW!
WOW.
T-THAT'S IT?
YOU SURE EDUARD DOESN'T WANT--
NOW!
...OKAY.

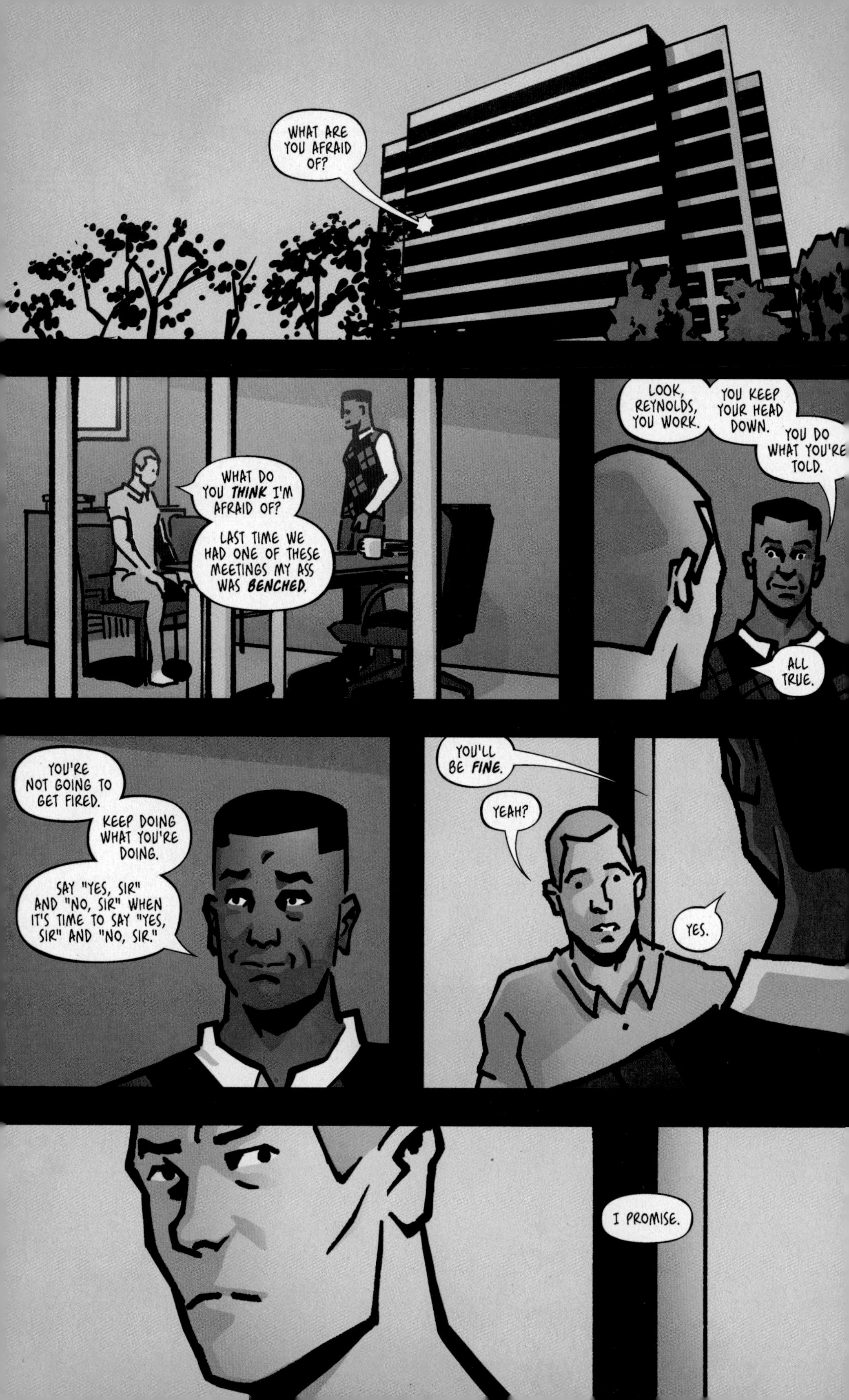
WHAT ARE YOU AFRAID OF?
WHAT DO YOU *THINK* I'M AFRAID OF?
LAST TIME WE HAD ONE OF THESE MEETINGS MY ASS WAS *BENCHED*.
LOOK, REYNOLDS, YOU WORK.
YOU KEEP YOUR HEAD DOWN.
YOU DO WHAT YOU'RE TOLD.
ALL TRUE.
YOU'RE NOT GOING TO GET FIRED.
KEEP DOING WHAT YOU'RE DOING.
SAY "YES, SIR" AND "NO, SIR" WHEN IT'S TIME TO SAY "YES, SIR" AND "NO, SIR."
YOU'LL BE *FINE*.
YEAH?
YES.
I PROMISE.

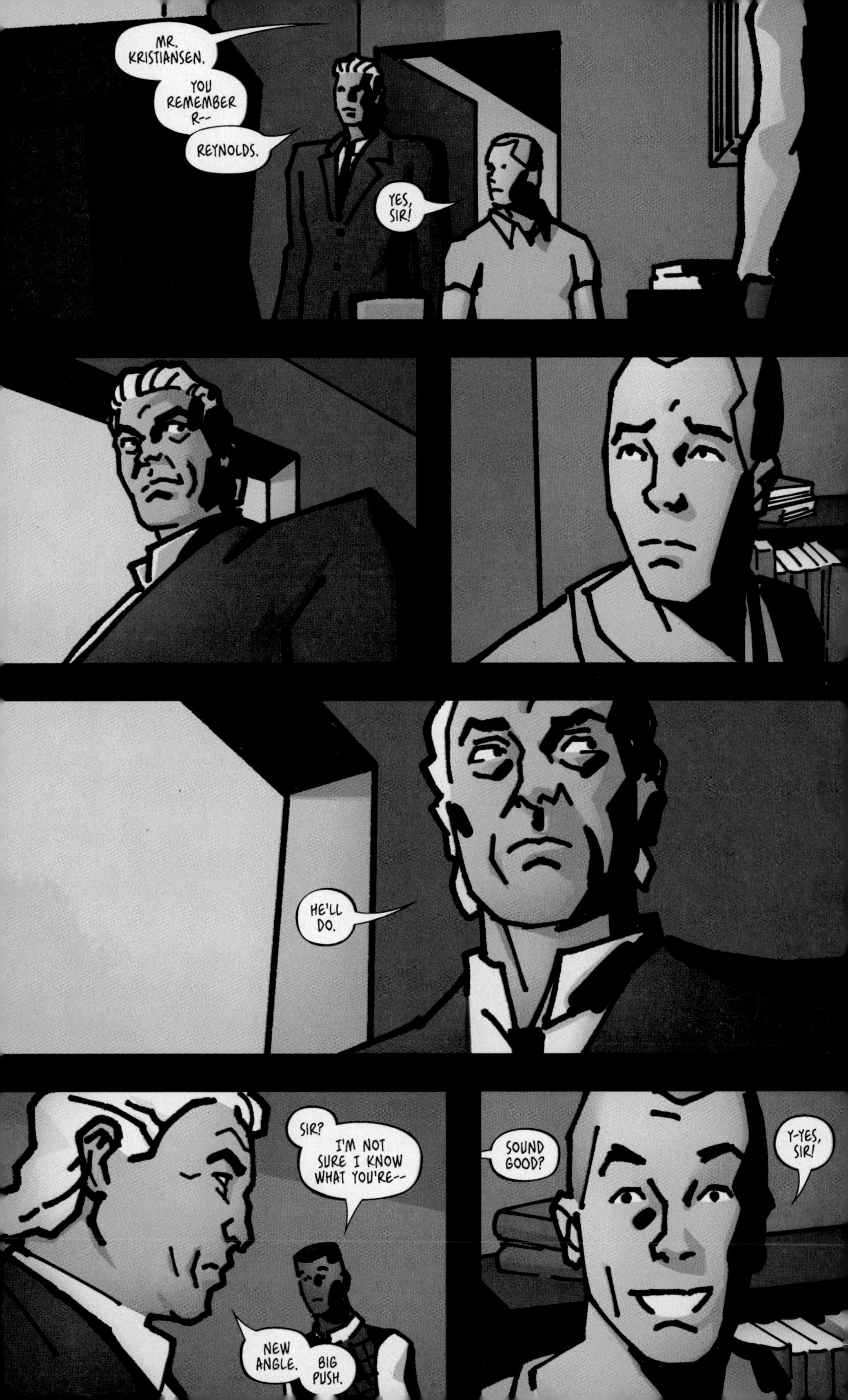
MR. KRISTIANSEN.
YOU REMEMBER R--
REYNOLDS.
YES, SIR!
HE'LL DO.
SIR?
I'M NOT SURE I KNOW WHAT YOU'RE--
NEW ANGLE.
BIG PUSH.
SOUND GOOD?
Y-YES, SIR!

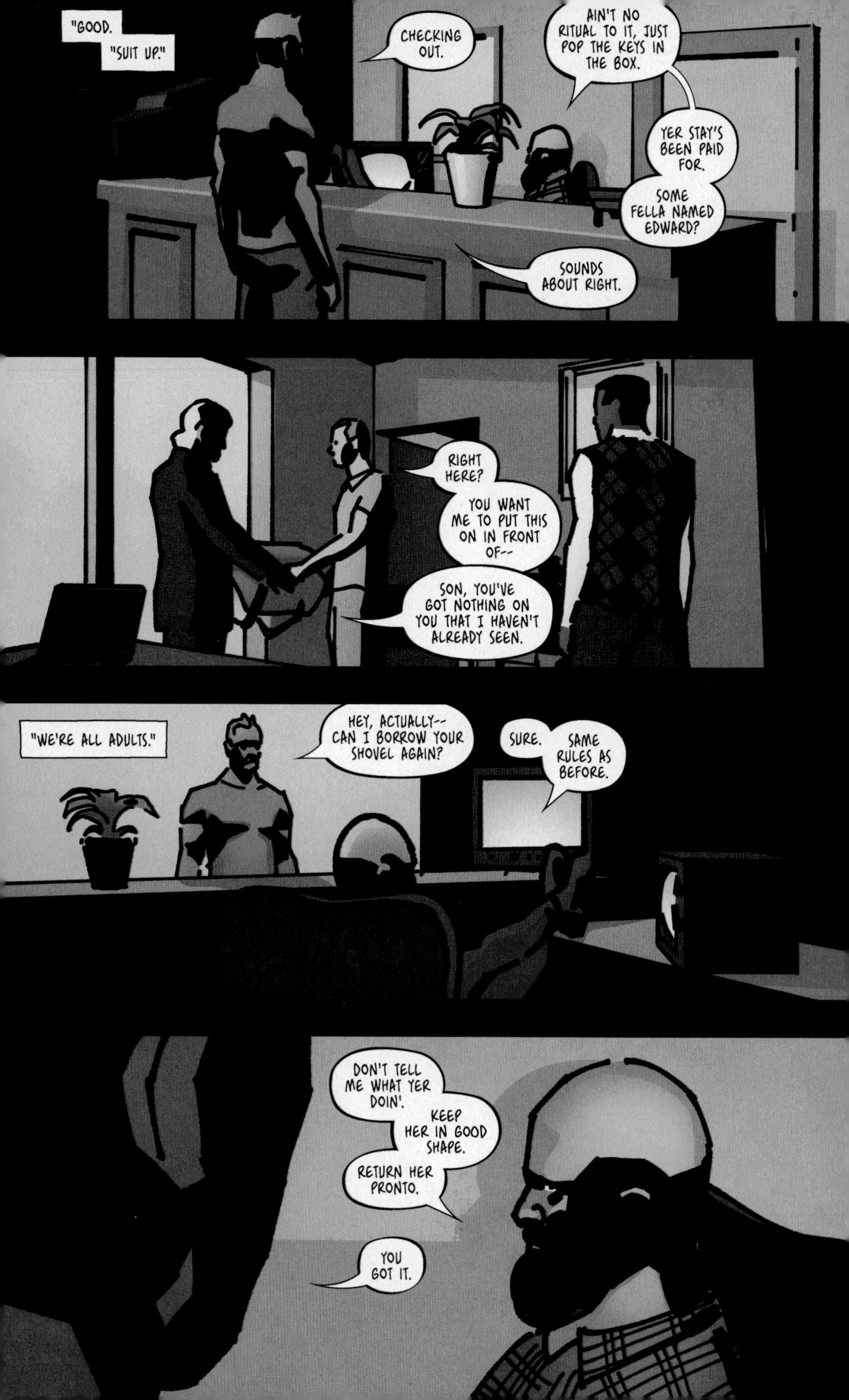
"GOOD.
"SUIT UP."
CHECKING OUT.
AIN'T NO RITUAL TO IT, JUST POP THE KEYS IN THE BOX.
YER STAY'S BEEN PAID FOR.
SOME FELLA NAMED EDWARD?
SOUNDS ABOUT RIGHT.
RIGHT HERE?
YOU WANT ME TO PUT THIS ON IN FRONT OF--
SON, YOU'VE GOT NOTHING ON YOU THAT I HAVEN'T ALREADY SEEN.
"WE'RE ALL ADULTS."
HEY, ACTUALLY-- CAN I BORROW YOUR SHOVEL AGAIN?
SURE.
SAME RULES AS BEFORE.
DON'T TELL ME WHAT YER DOIN'.
KEEP HER IN GOOD SHAPE.
RETURN HER PRONTO.
YOU GOT IT.

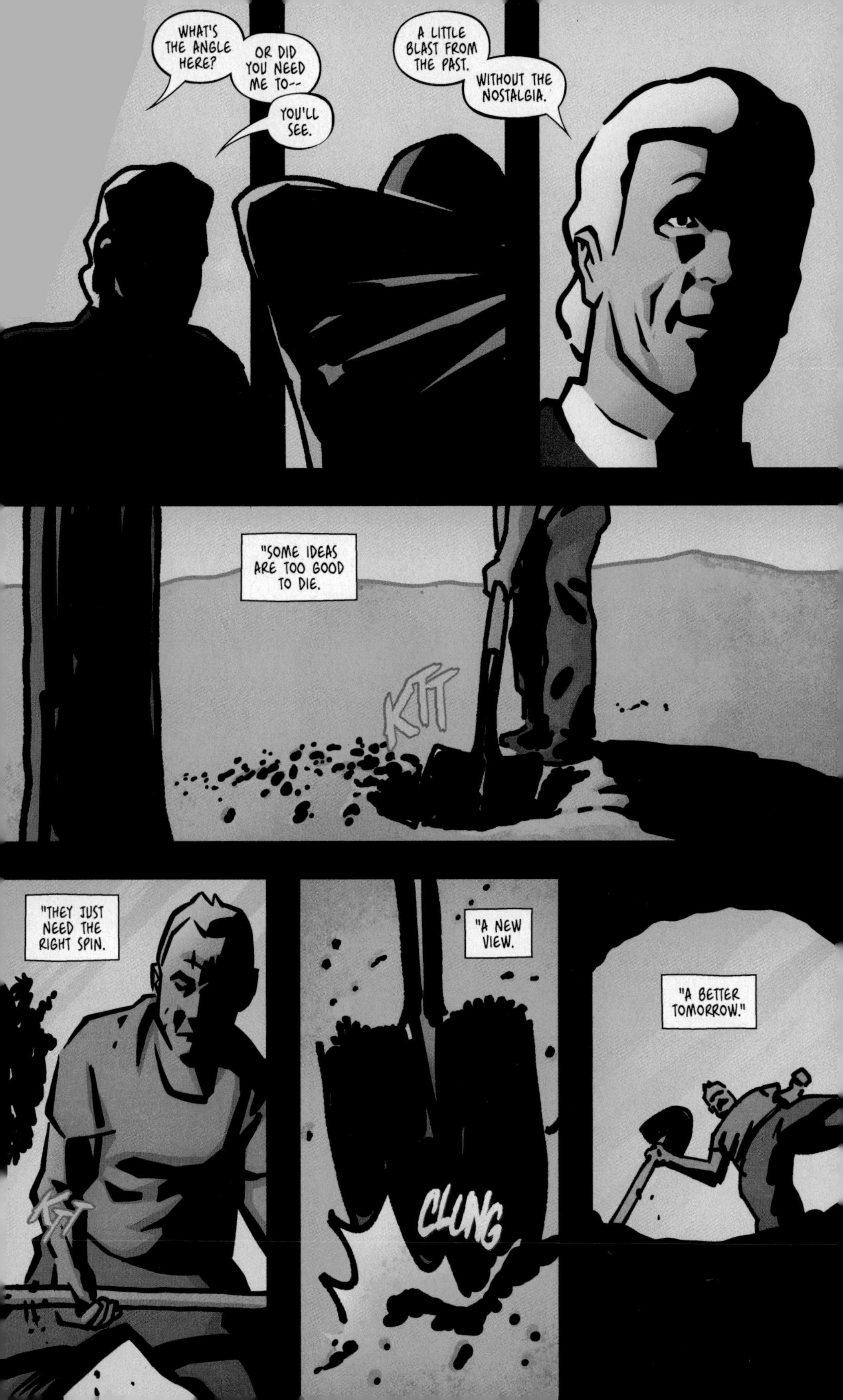
WHAT'S THE ANGLE HERE?
OR DID YOU NEED ME TO--
YOU'LL SEE.
A LITTLE BLAST FROM THE PAST.
WITHOUT THE NOSTALGIA.
"SOME IDEAS ARE TOO GOOD TO DIE.
KTT
"THEY JUST NEED THE RIGHT SPIN.
KTT
"A NEW VIEW.
CLUNG
"A BETTER TOMORROW."

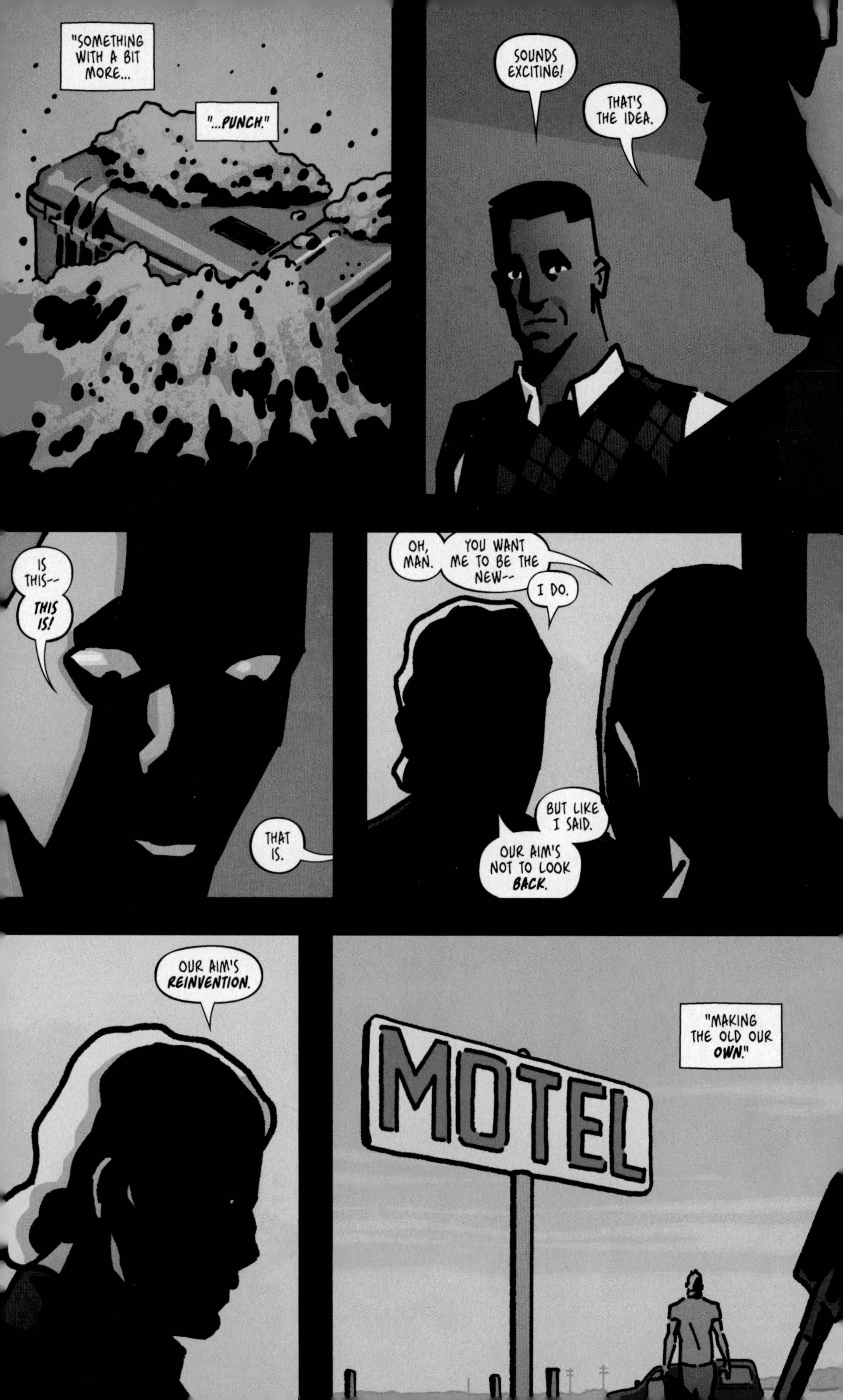
"SOMETHING WITH A BIT MORE...
"...PUNCH."
SOUNDS EXCITING!
THAT'S THE IDEA.
IS THIS--
THIS IS!
THAT IS.
OH, MAN.
YOU WANT ME TO BE THE NEW--
I DO.
BUT LIKE I SAID.
OUR AIM'S NOT TO LOOK BACK.
OUR AIM'S REINVENTION.
MOTEL
"MAKING THE OLD OUR OWN."

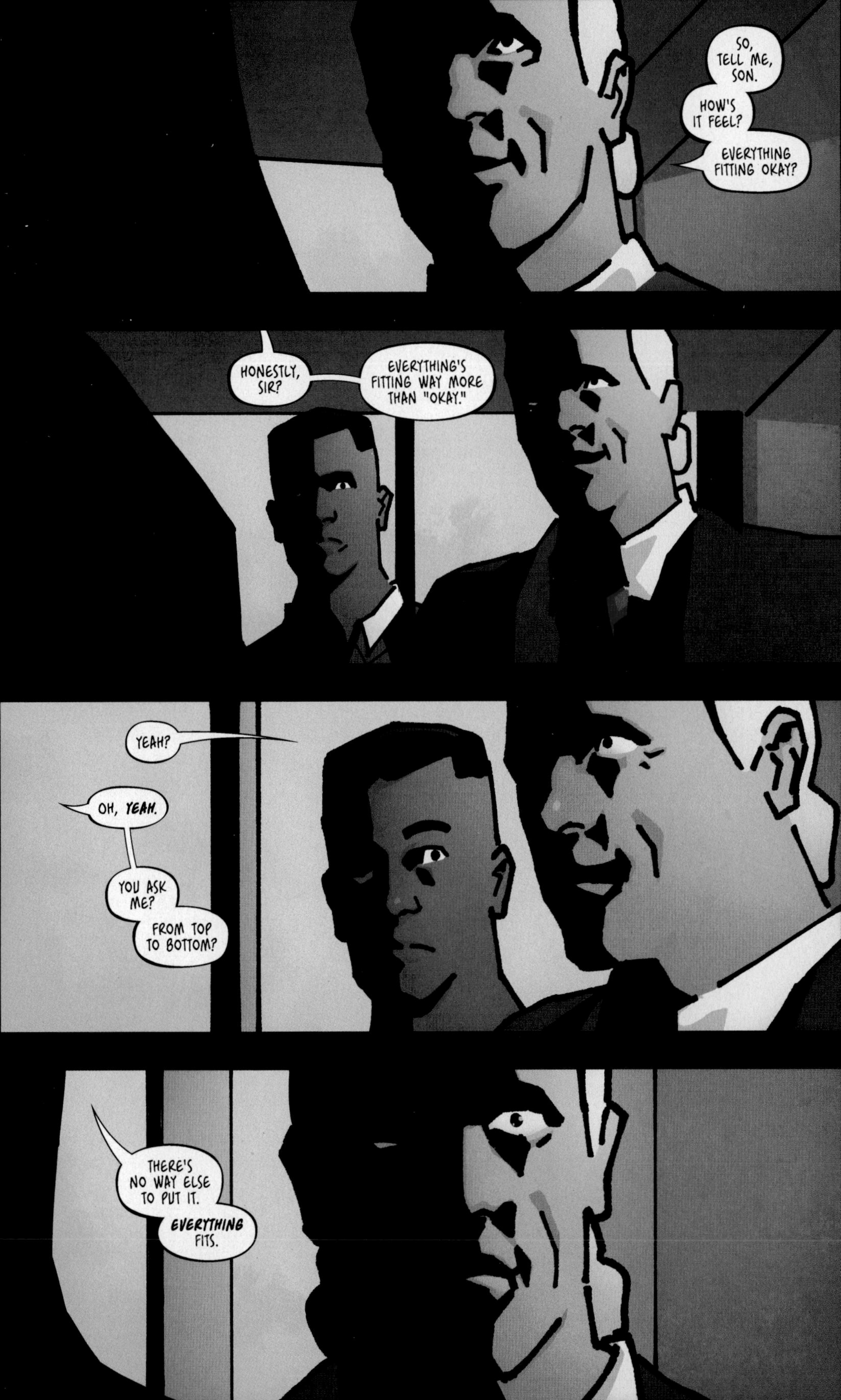
SO, TELL ME, SON.
HOW'S IT FEEL?
EVERYTHING FITTING OKAY?
HONESTLY, SIR?
EVERYTHING'S FITTING WAY MORE THAN "OKAY."
YEAH?
OH, YEAH.
YOU ASK ME?
FROM TOP TO BOTTOM?
THERE'S NO WAY ELSE TO PUT IT.
EVERYTHING FITS.

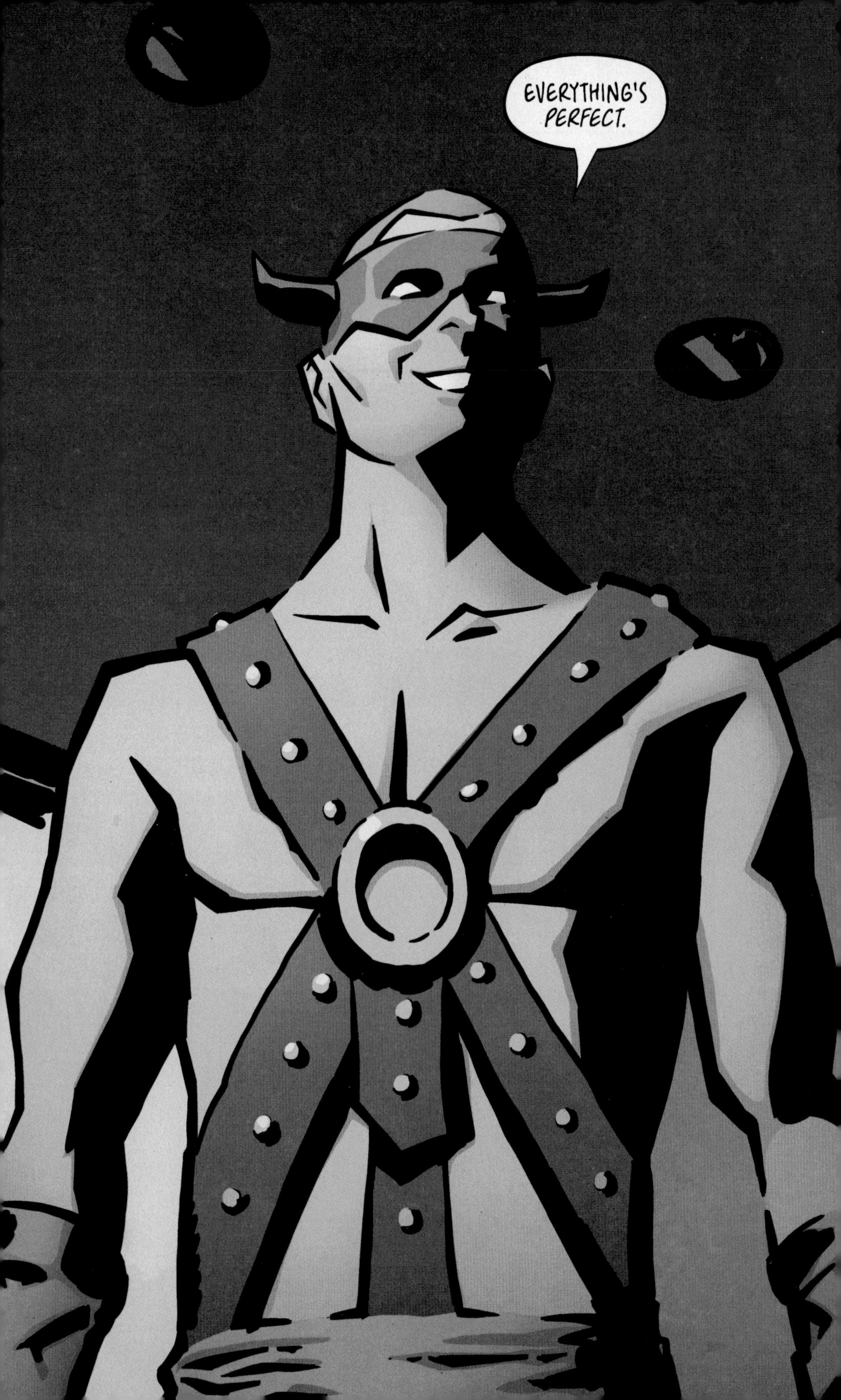
EVERYTHING'S PERFECT.

CHAPTER THIRTEEN

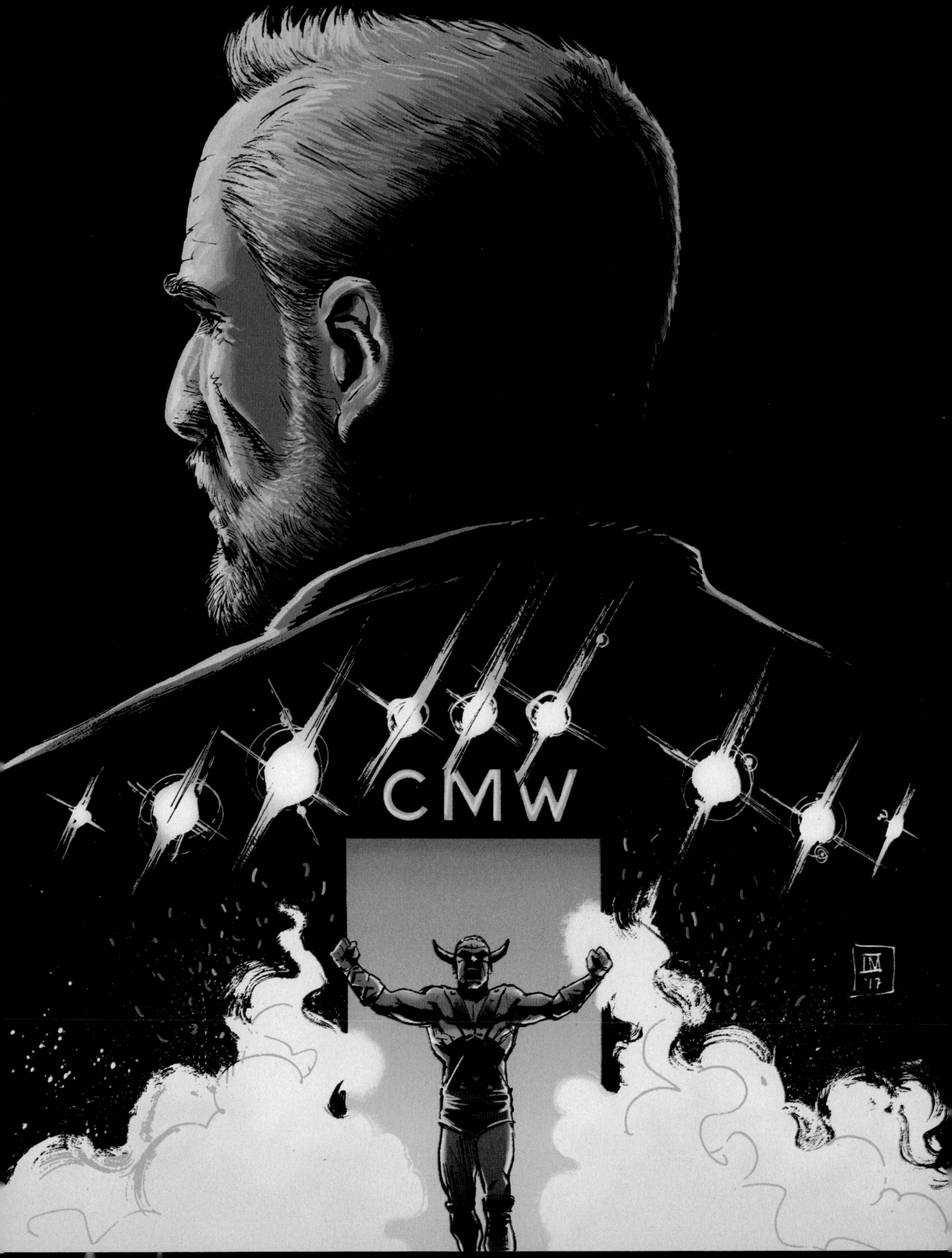
CMW

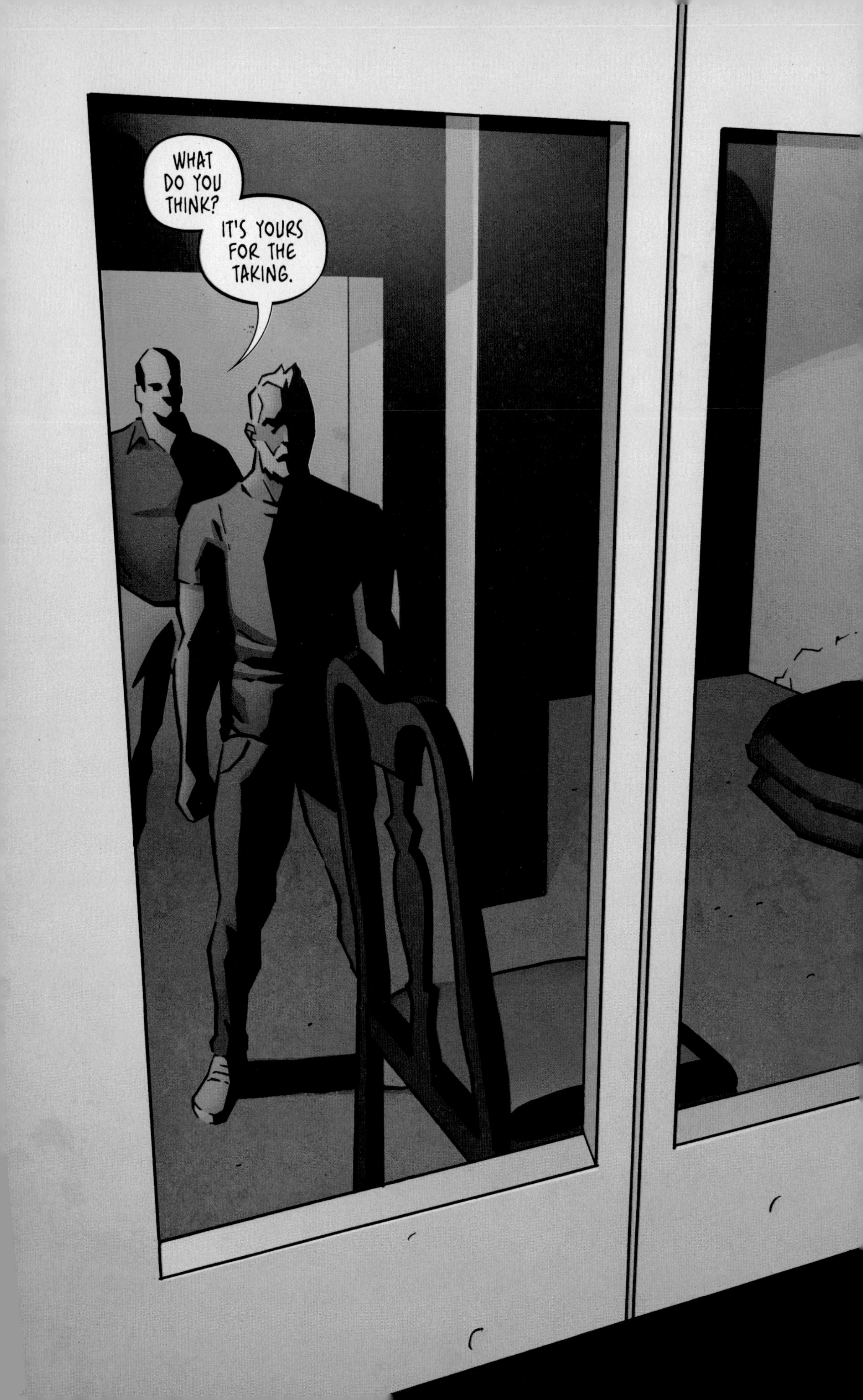
WHAT DO YOU THINK?
IT'S YOURS FOR THE TAKING.

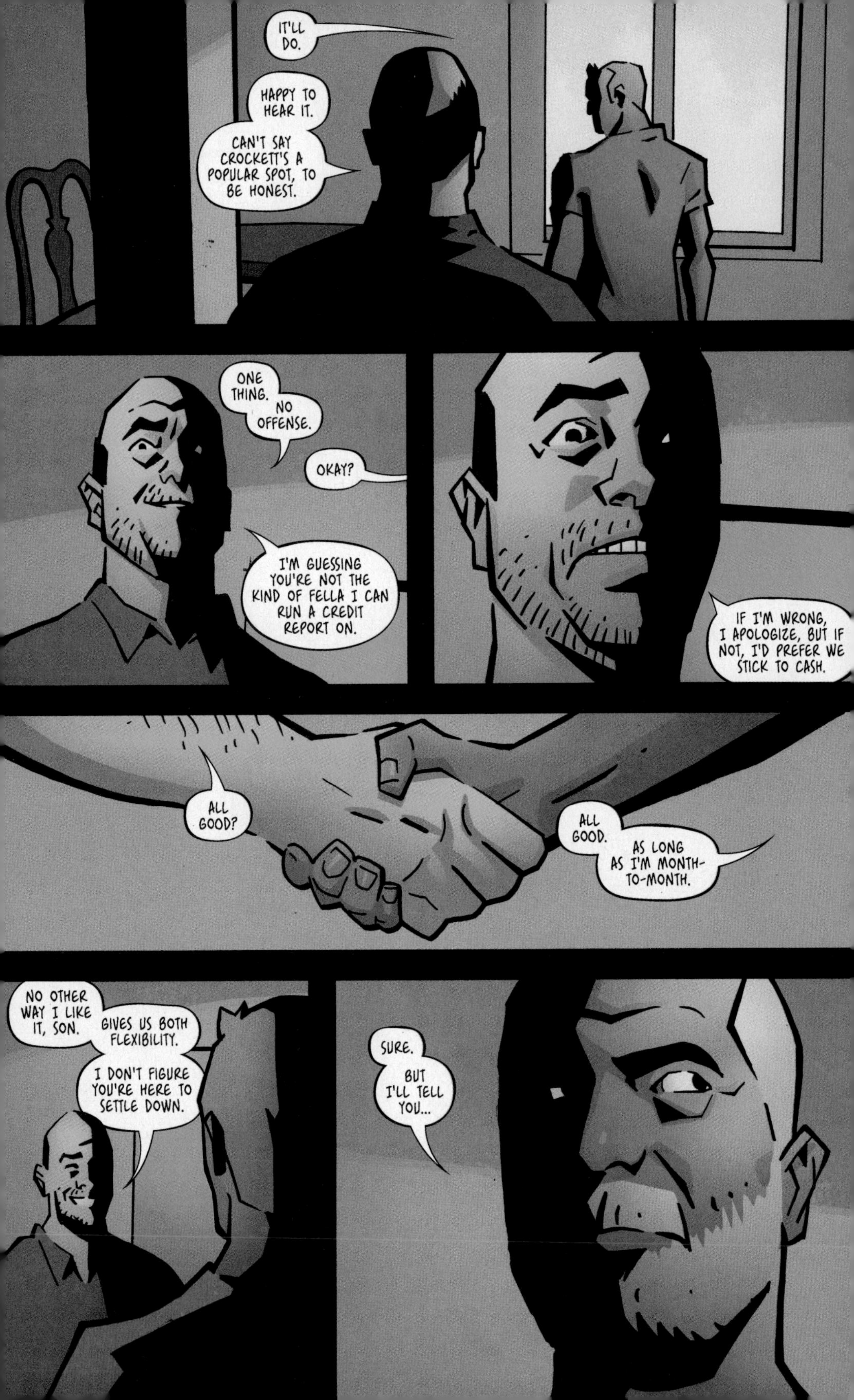
IT'LL DO.
HAPPY TO HEAR IT.
CAN'T SAY CROCKETT'S A POPULAR SPOT, TO BE HONEST.
ONE THING.
NO OFFENSE.
OKAY?
I'M GUESSING YOU'RE NOT THE KIND OF FELLA I CAN RUN A CREDIT REPORT ON.
IF I'M WRONG, I APOLOGIZE, BUT IF NOT, I'D PREFER WE STICK TO CASH.
ALL GOOD?
ALL GOOD.
AS LONG AS I'M MONTH-TO-MONTH.
NO OTHER WAY I LIKE IT, SON.
GIVES US BOTH FLEXIBILITY.
I DON'T FIGURE YOU'RE HERE TO SETTLE DOWN.
SURE.
BUT I'LL TELL YOU...

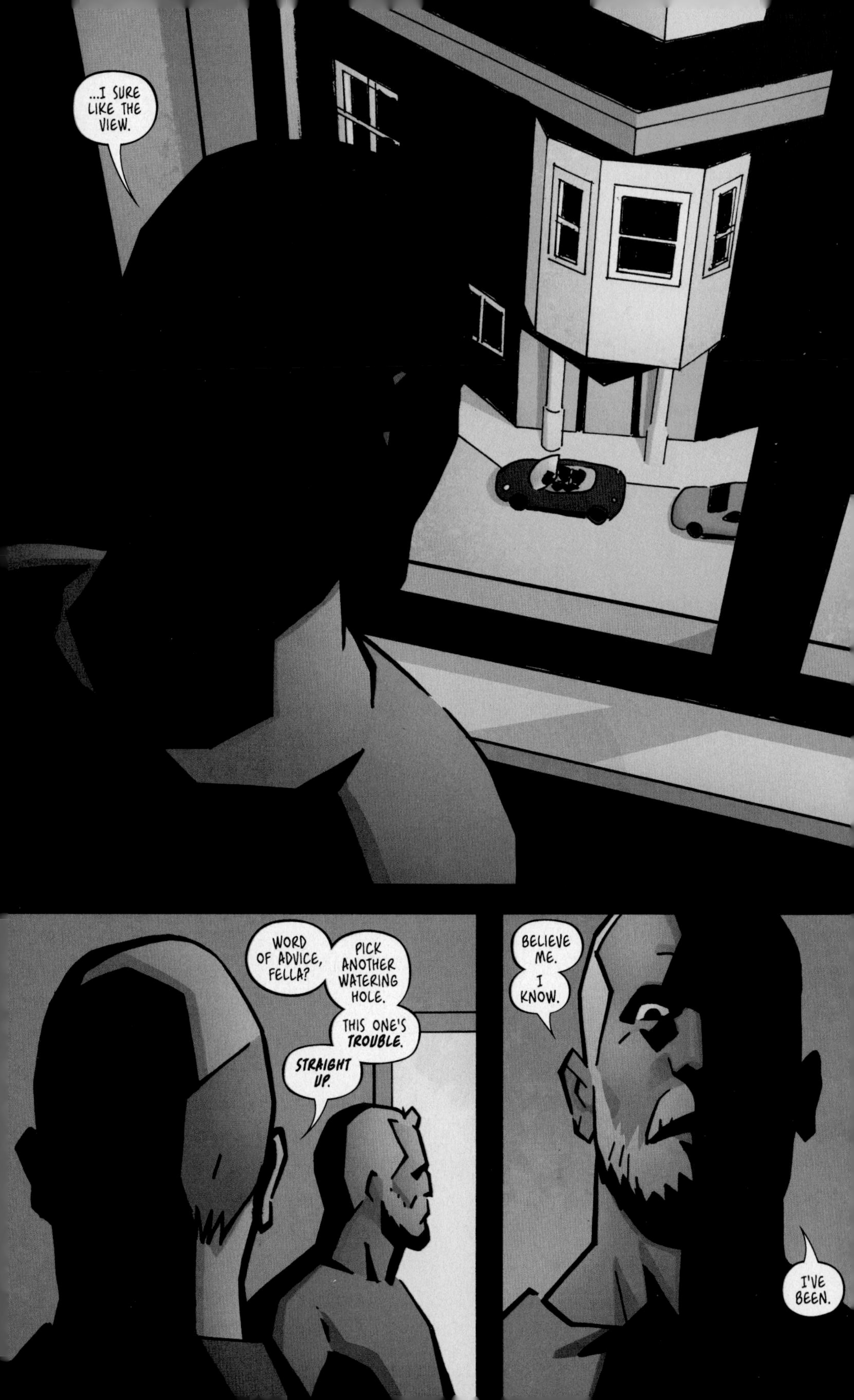
...I SURE LIKE THE VIEW.
WORD OF ADVICE, FELLA?
PICK ANOTHER WATERING HOLE.
THIS ONE'S TROUBLE.
STRAIGHT UP.
BELIEVE ME.
I KNOW.
I'VE BEEN.

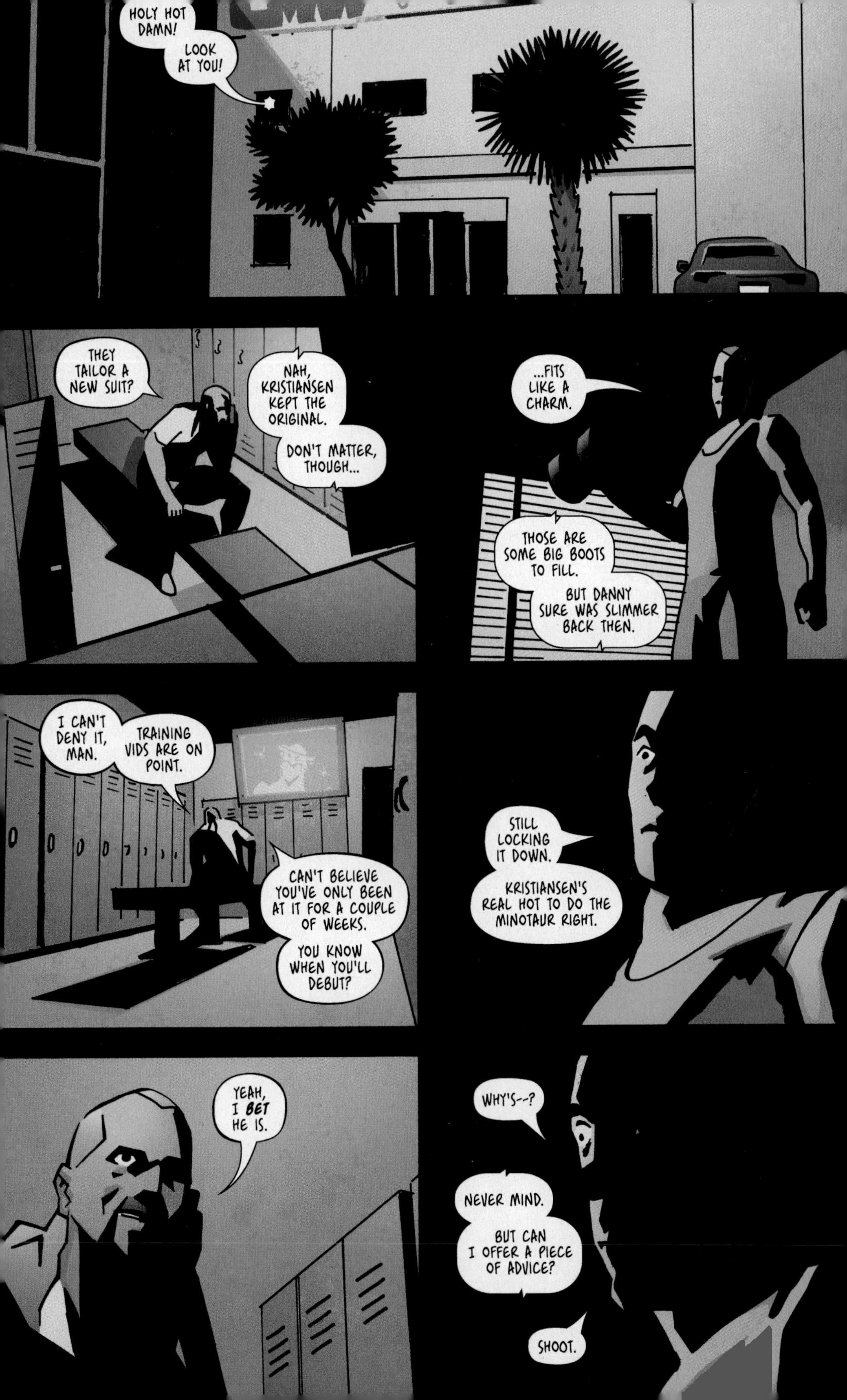
HOLY HOT DAMN!
LOOK AT YOU!
THEY TAILOR A NEW SUIT?
NAH, KRISTIANSEN KEPT THE ORIGINAL.
DON'T MATTER, THOUGH...
...FITS LIKE A CHARM.
THOSE ARE SOME BIG BOOTS TO FILL.
BUT DANNY SURE WAS SLIMMER BACK THEN.
I CAN'T DENY IT, MAN.
TRAINING VIDS ARE ON POINT.
CAN'T BELIEVE YOU'VE ONLY BEEN AT IT FOR A COUPLE OF WEEKS.
YOU KNOW WHEN YOU'LL DEBUT?
STILL LOCKING IT DOWN.
KRISTIANSEN'S REAL HOT TO DO THE MINOTAUR RIGHT.
YEAH, I BET HE IS.
WHY'S--?
NEVER MIND.
BUT CAN I OFFER A PIECE OF ADVICE?
SHOOT.

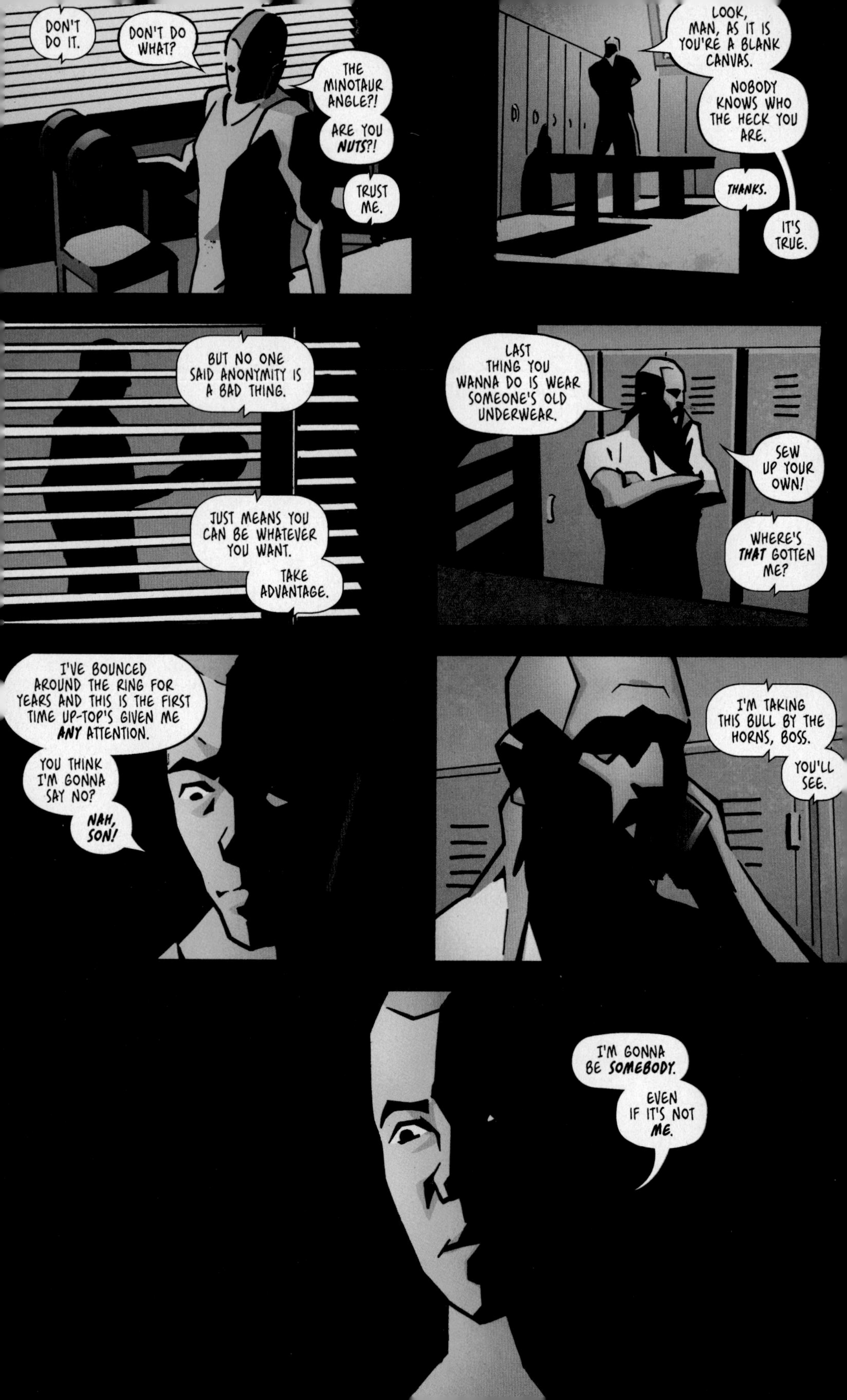
DON'T DO IT.
DON'T DO WHAT?
THE MINOTAUR ANGLE?!
ARE YOU **NUTS**?!
TRUST ME.
LOOK, MAN, AS IT IS YOU'RE A BLANK CANVAS.
NOBODY KNOWS WHO THE HECK YOU ARE.
THANKS.
IT'S TRUE.
BUT NO ONE SAID ANONYMITY IS A BAD THING.
JUST MEANS YOU CAN BE WHATEVER YOU WANT.
TAKE ADVANTAGE.
LAST THING YOU WANNA DO IS WEAR SOMEONE'S OLD UNDERWEAR.
SEW UP YOUR OWN!
WHERE'S **THAT** GOTTEN ME?
I'VE BOUNCED AROUND THE RING FOR YEARS AND THIS IS THE FIRST TIME UP-TOP'S GIVEN ME **ANY** ATTENTION.
YOU THINK I'M GONNA SAY NO?
NAH, SON!
I'M TAKING THIS BULL BY THE HORNS, BOSS.
YOU'LL SEE.
I'M GONNA BE **SOMEBODY.**
EVEN IF IT'S NOT **ME.**

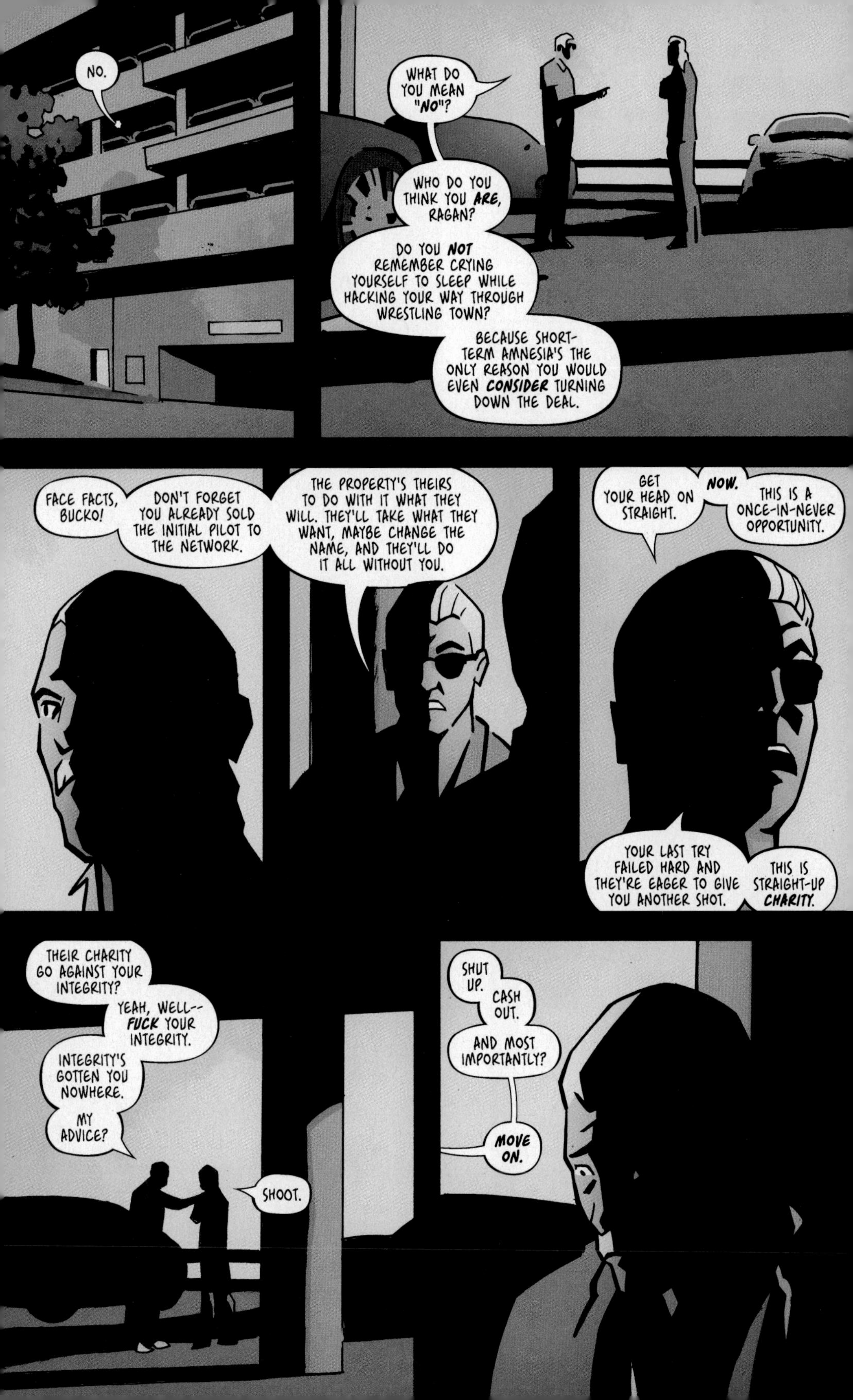
NO.
WHAT DO YOU MEAN "NO"?
WHO DO YOU THINK YOU ARE, RAGAN?
DO YOU NOT REMEMBER CRYING YOURSELF TO SLEEP WHILE HACKING YOUR WAY THROUGH WRESTLING TOWN?
BECAUSE SHORT-TERM AMNESIA'S THE ONLY REASON YOU WOULD EVEN CONSIDER TURNING DOWN THE DEAL.
FACE FACTS, BUCKO!
DON'T FORGET YOU ALREADY SOLD THE INITIAL PILOT TO THE NETWORK.
THE PROPERTY'S THEIRS TO DO WITH IT WHAT THEY WILL. THEY'LL TAKE WHAT THEY WANT, MAYBE CHANGE THE NAME, AND THEY'LL DO IT ALL WITHOUT YOU.
GET YOUR HEAD ON STRAIGHT.
NOW.
THIS IS A ONCE-IN-NEVER OPPORTUNITY.
YOUR LAST TRY FAILED HARD AND THEY'RE EAGER TO GIVE YOU ANOTHER SHOT.
THIS IS STRAIGHT-UP CHARITY.
THEIR CHARITY GO AGAINST YOUR INTEGRITY?
YEAH, WELL--FUCK YOUR INTEGRITY.
INTEGRITY'S GOTTEN YOU NOWHERE.
MY ADVICE?
SHOOT.
SHUT UP.
CASH OUT.
AND MOST IMPORTANTLY?
MOVE ON.

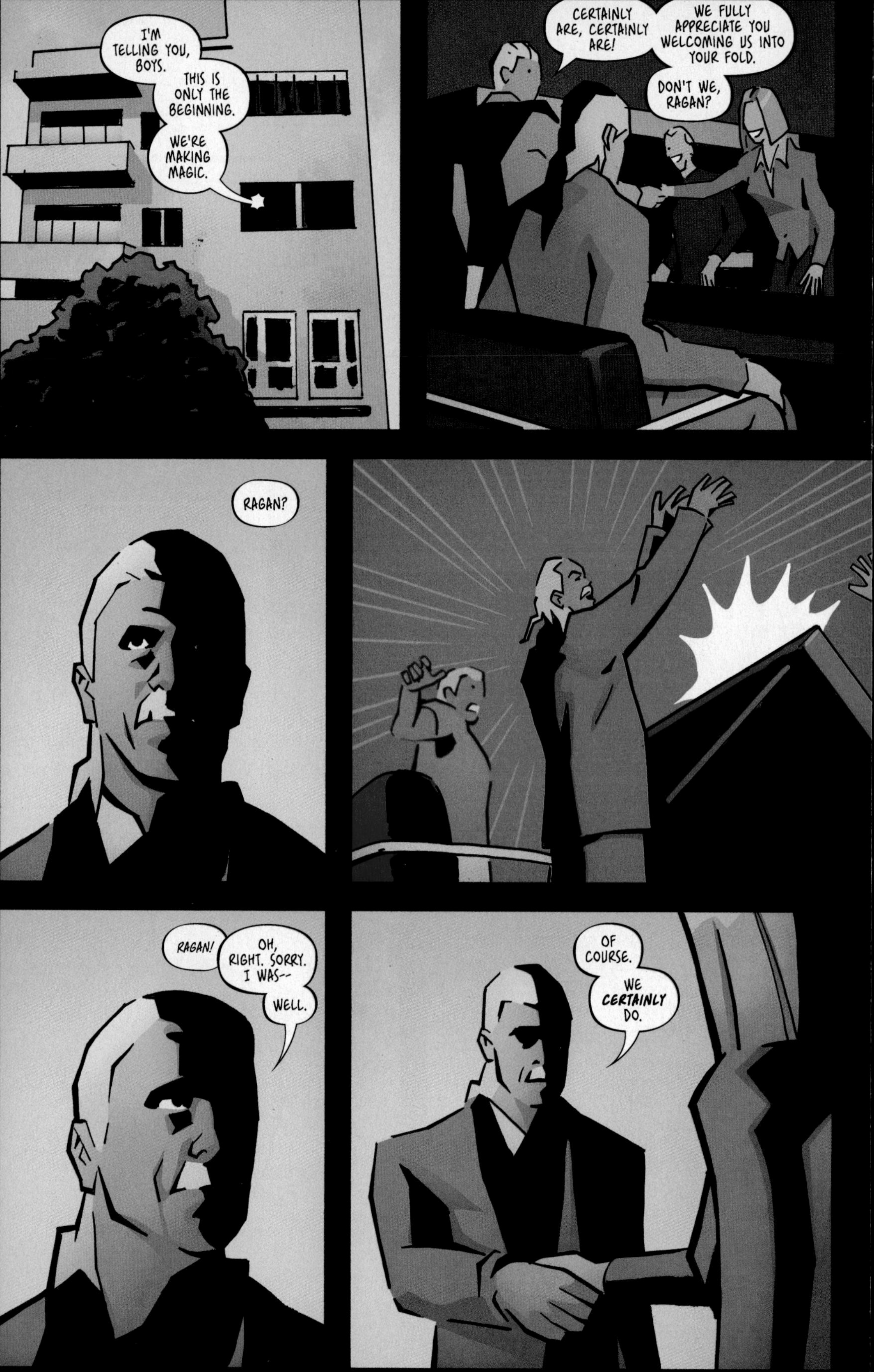
I'M TELLING YOU, BOYS.
THIS IS ONLY THE BEGINNING.
WE'RE MAKING MAGIC.
CERTAINLY ARE, CERTAINLY ARE!
WE FULLY APPRECIATE YOU WELCOMING US INTO YOUR FOLD.
DON'T WE, RAGAN?
RAGAN?
RAGAN!
OH, RIGHT. SORRY. I WAS--
WELL.
OF COURSE.
WE CERTAINLY DO.

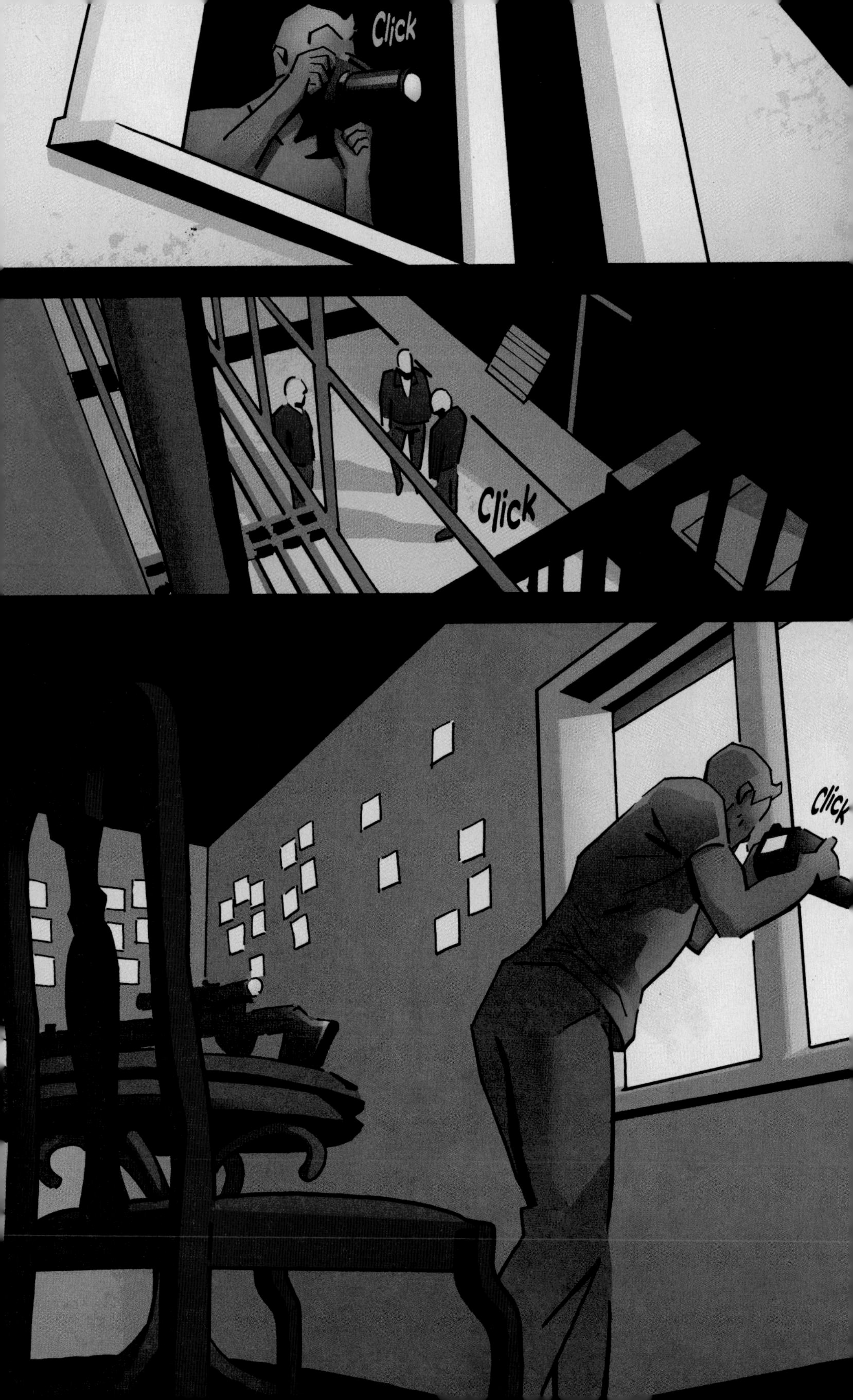
Click
Click
Click

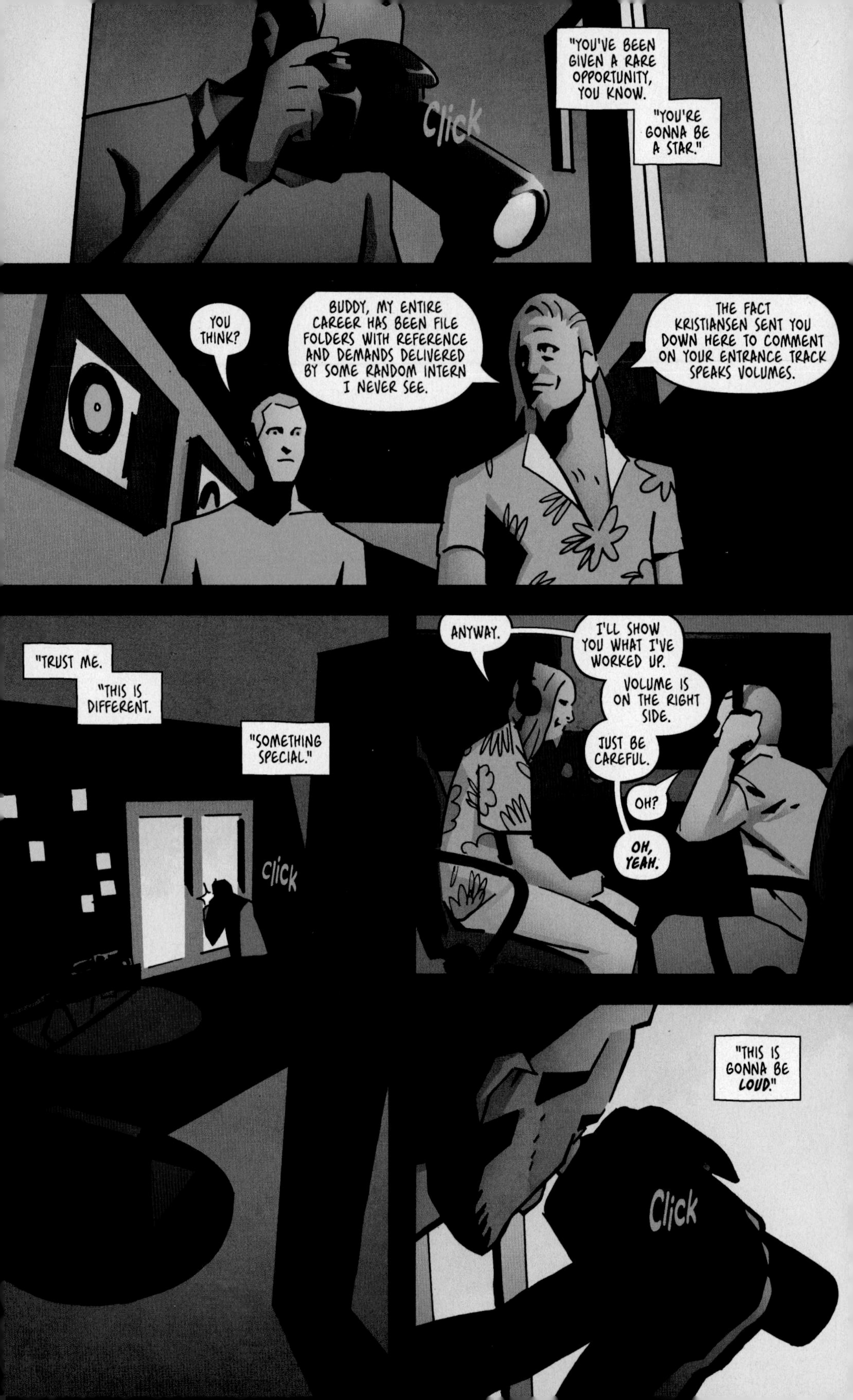
"YOU'VE BEEN GIVEN A RARE OPPORTUNITY, YOU KNOW.
"YOU'RE GONNA BE A STAR."
Click
YOU THINK?
BUDDY, MY ENTIRE CAREER HAS BEEN FILE FOLDERS WITH REFERENCE AND DEMANDS DELIVERED BY SOME RANDOM INTERN I NEVER SEE.
THE FACT KRISTIANSEN SENT YOU DOWN HERE TO COMMENT ON YOUR ENTRANCE TRACK SPEAKS VOLUMES.
"TRUST ME.
"THIS IS DIFFERENT.
"SOMETHING SPECIAL."
Click
ANYWAY.
I'LL SHOW YOU WHAT I'VE WORKED UP.
VOLUME IS ON THE RIGHT SIDE.
JUST BE CAREFUL.
OH?
OH, YEAH.
"THIS IS GONNA BE LOUD."
Click

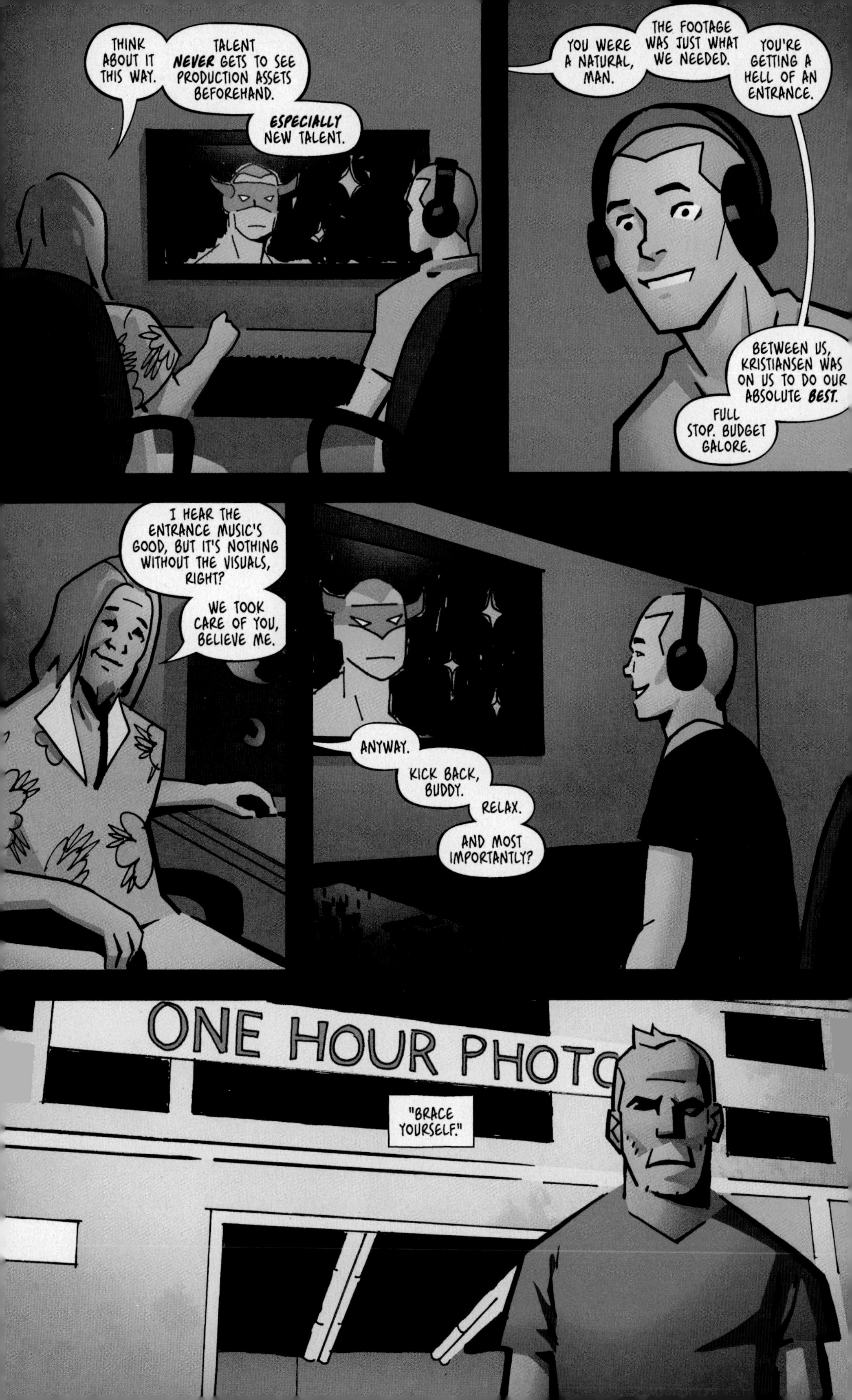
THINK ABOUT IT THIS WAY.
TALENT **NEVER** GETS TO SEE PRODUCTION ASSETS BEFOREHAND.
ESPECIALLY NEW TALENT.
YOU WERE A NATURAL, MAN.
THE FOOTAGE WAS JUST WHAT WE NEEDED.
YOU'RE GETTING A HELL OF AN ENTRANCE.
BETWEEN US, KRISTIANSEN WAS ON US TO DO OUR ABSOLUTE **BEST**.
FULL STOP. BUDGET GALORE.
I HEAR THE ENTRANCE MUSIC'S GOOD, BUT IT'S NOTHING WITHOUT THE VISUALS, RIGHT?
WE TOOK CARE OF YOU, BELIEVE ME.
ANYWAY.
KICK BACK, BUDDY.
RELAX.
AND MOST IMPORTANTLY?
ONE HOUR PHOTO
"BRACE YOURSELF."

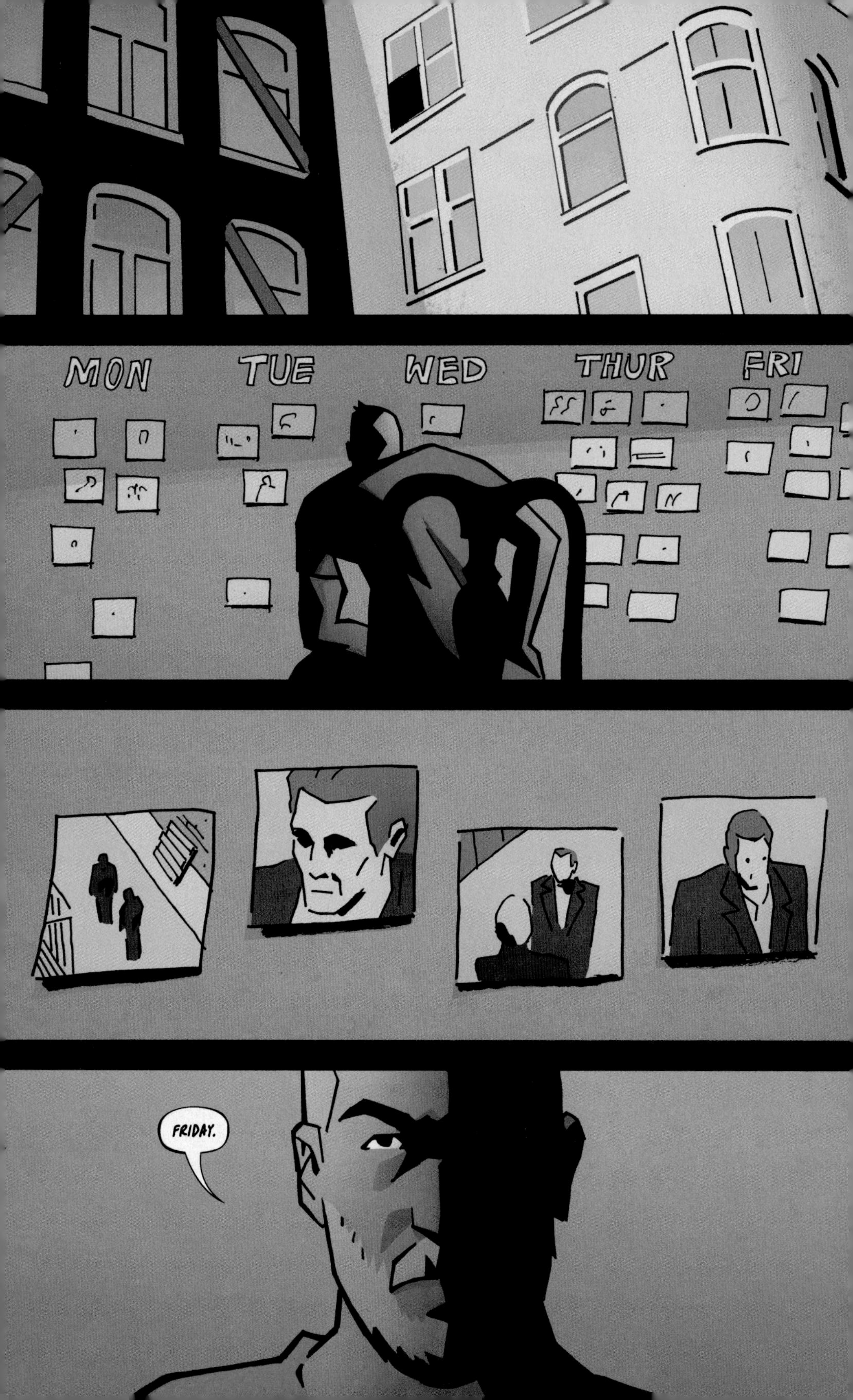
MON
TUE
WED
THUR
FRI
FRIDAY.

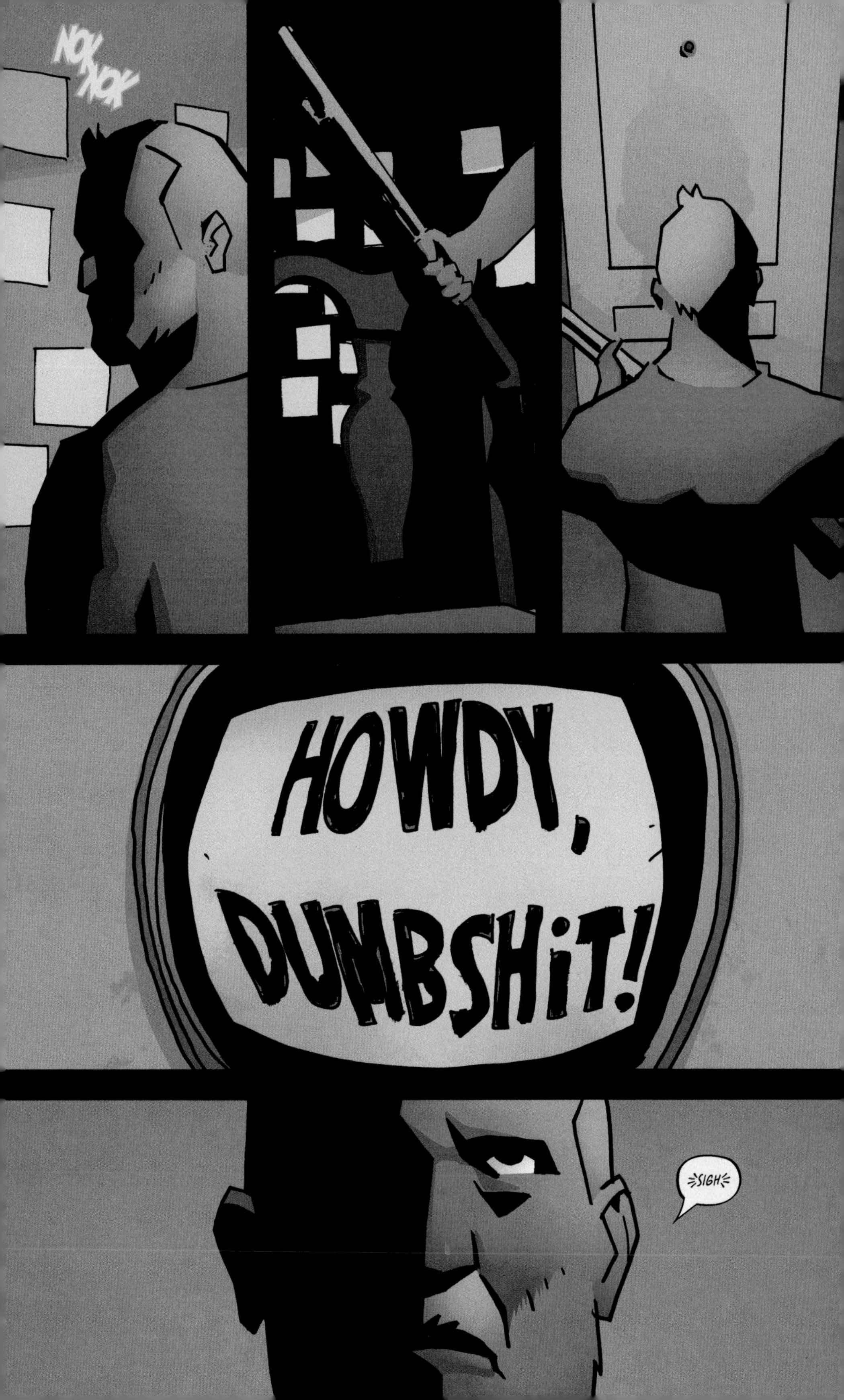
NOK NOK
HOWDY, DUMBSHiT!
SIGH

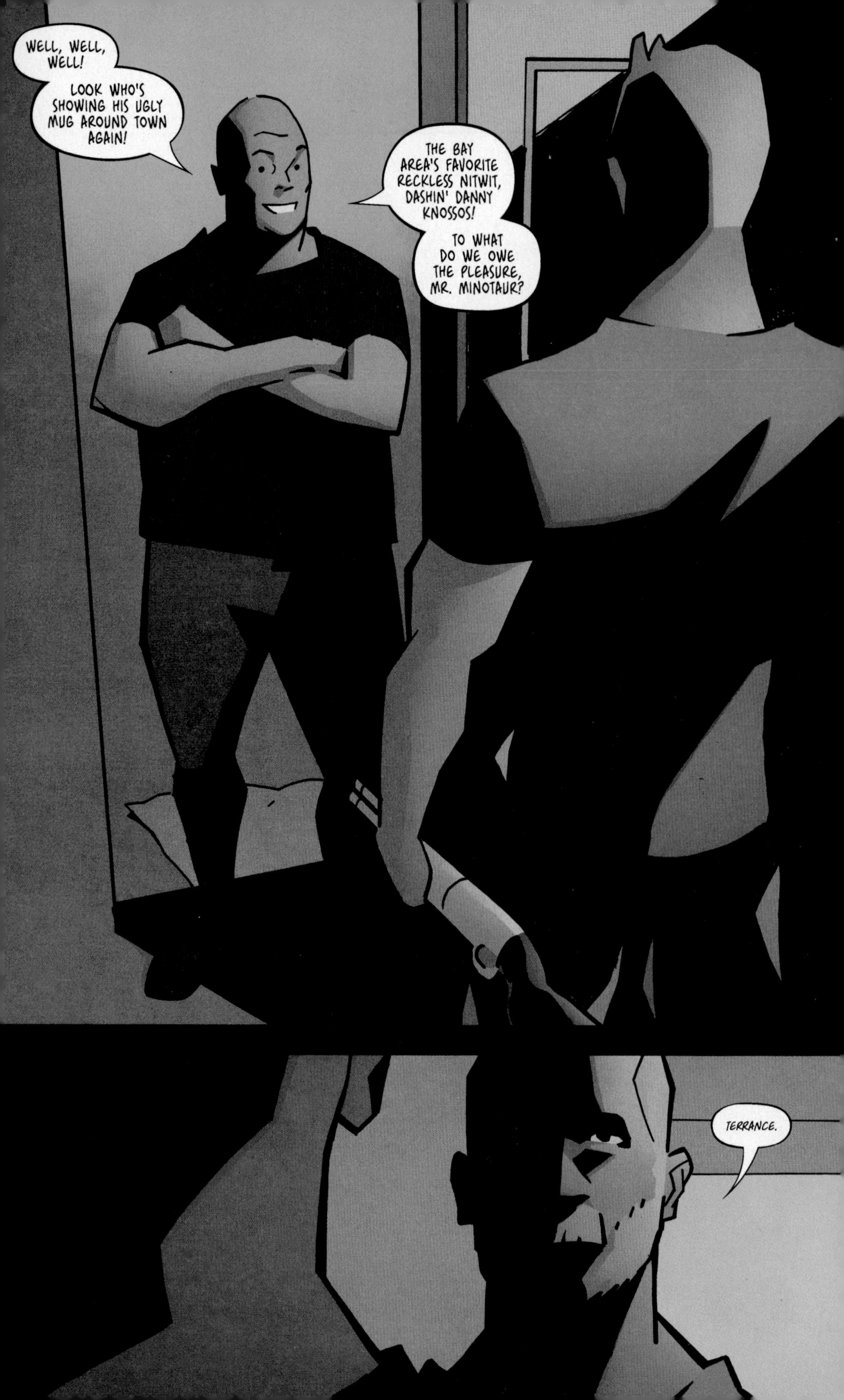
WELL, WELL, WELL!
LOOK WHO'S SHOWING HIS UGLY MUG AROUND TOWN AGAIN!
THE BAY AREA'S FAVORITE RECKLESS NITWIT, DASHIN' DANNY KNOSSOS!
TO WHAT DO WE OWE THE PLEASURE, MR. MINOTAUR?
TERRANCE.

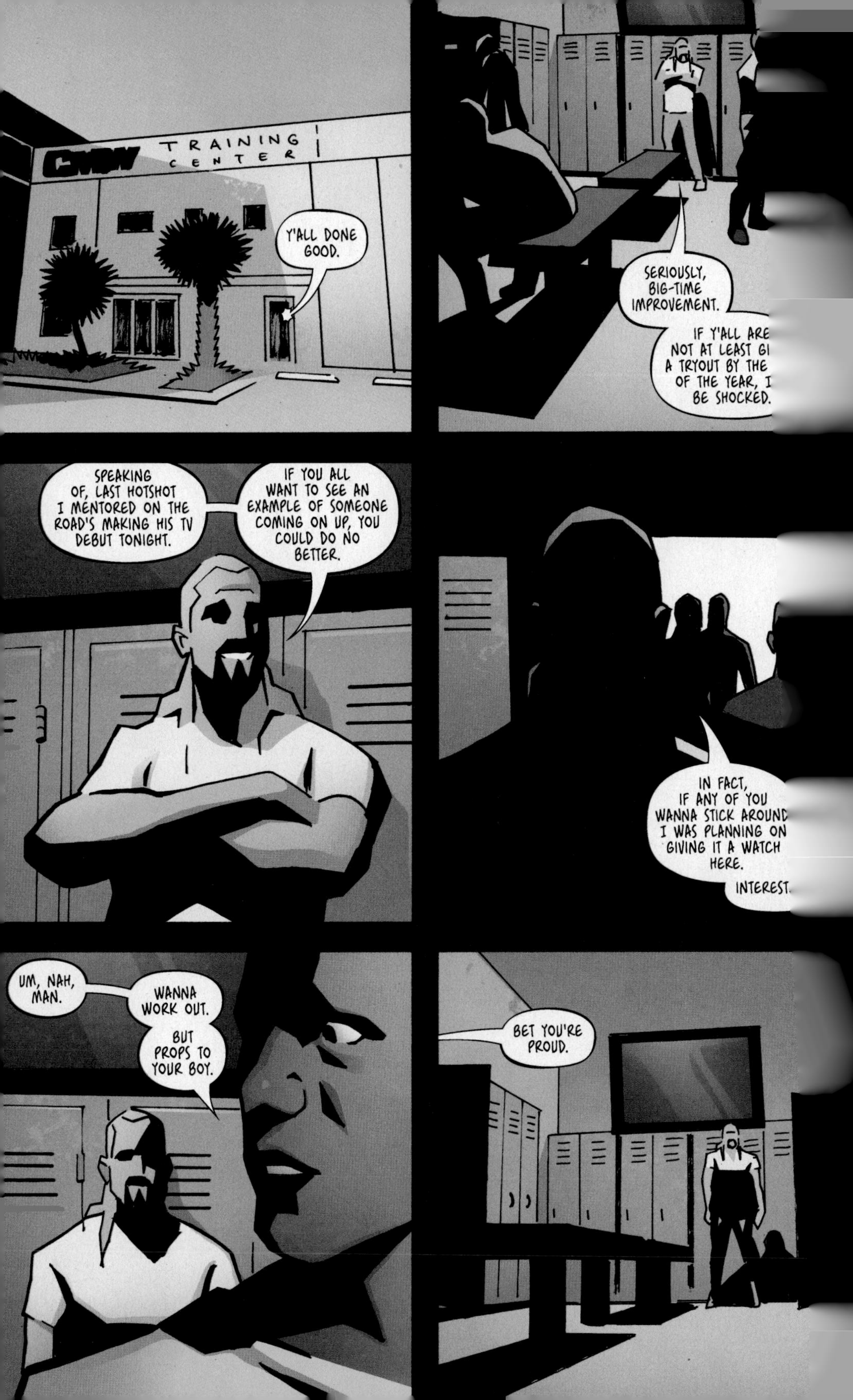
TRAINING CENTER
Y'ALL DONE GOOD.
SERIOUSLY, BIG-TIME IMPROVEMENT.
IF Y'ALL ARE NOT AT LEAST GI A TRYOUT BY THE OF THE YEAR, I BE SHOCKED.
SPEAKING OF, LAST HOTSHOT I MENTORED ON THE ROAD'S MAKING HIS TV DEBUT TONIGHT.
IF YOU ALL WANT TO SEE AN EXAMPLE OF SOMEONE COMING ON UP, YOU COULD DO NO BETTER.
IN FACT, IF ANY OF YOU WANNA STICK AROUND I WAS PLANNING ON GIVING IT A WATCH HERE.
INTEREST
UM, NAH, MAN.
WANNA WORK OUT.
BUT PROPS TO YOUR BOY.
BET YOU'RE PROUD.

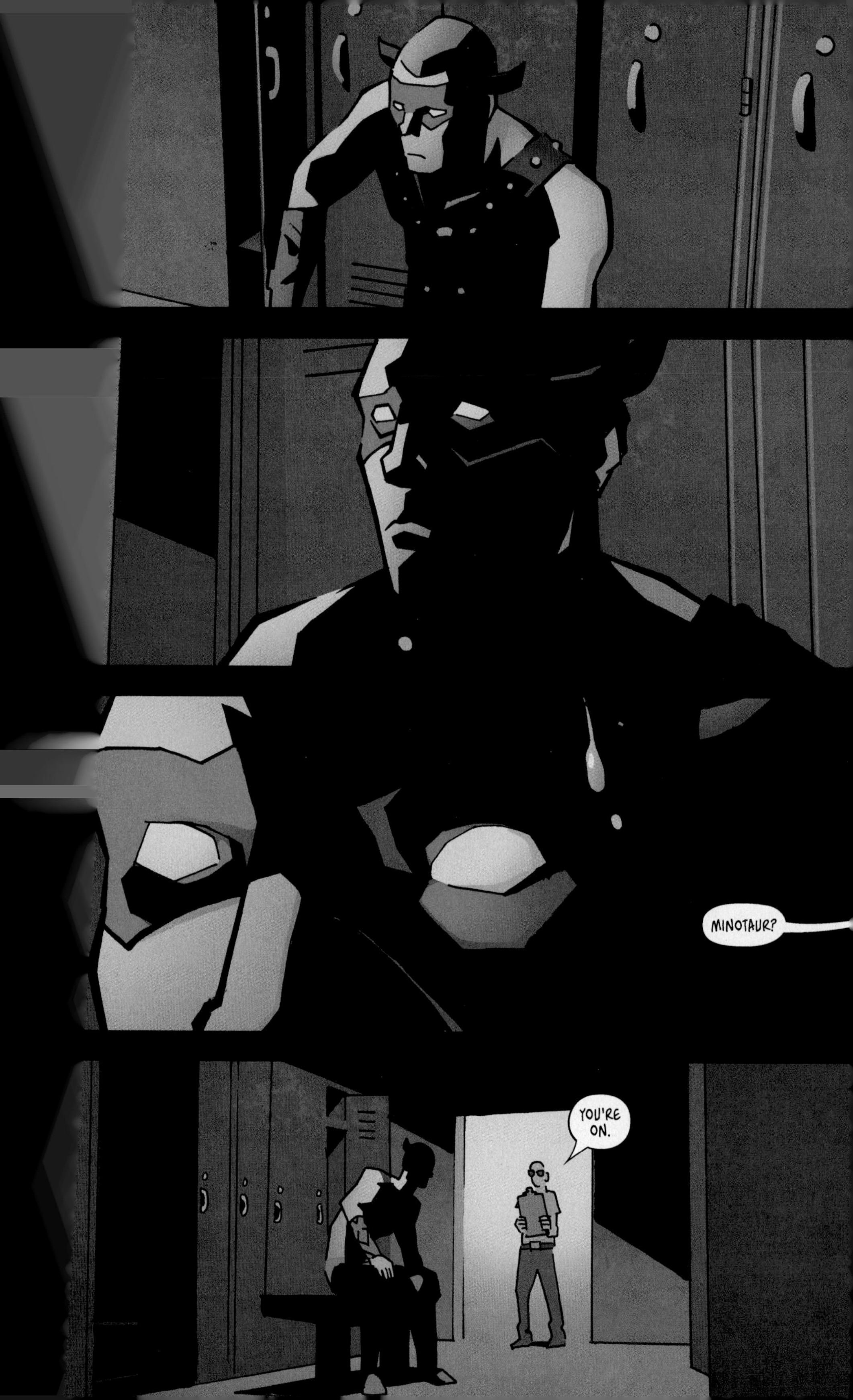
MINOTAUR?
YOU'RE ON.

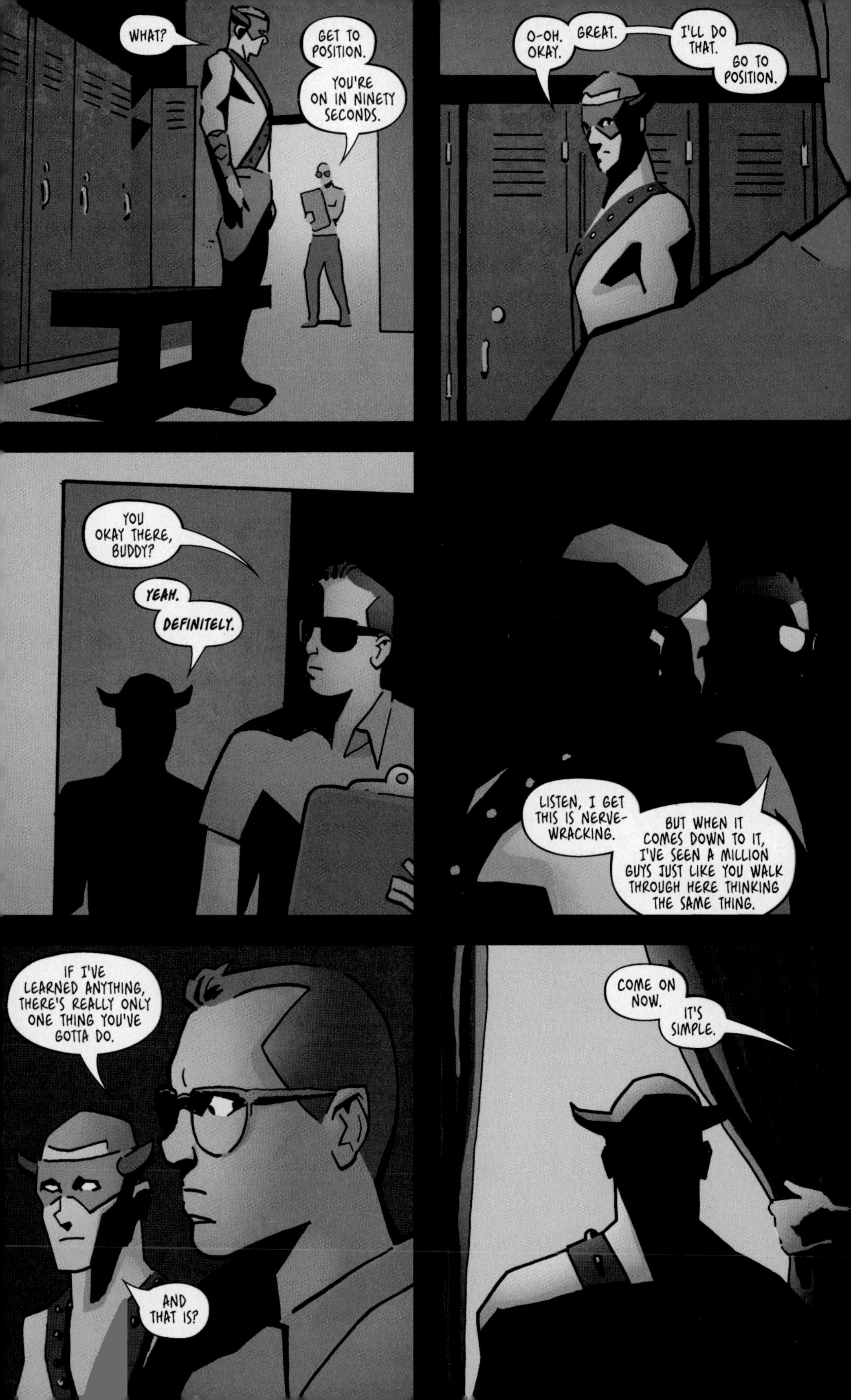
WHAT?
GET TO POSITION.
YOU'RE ON IN NINETY SECONDS.
O-OH. OKAY.
GREAT.
I'LL DO THAT.
GO TO POSITION.
YOU OKAY THERE, BUDDY?
YEAH.
DEFINITELY.
LISTEN, I GET THIS IS NERVE-WRACKING.
BUT WHEN IT COMES DOWN TO IT, I'VE SEEN A MILLION GUYS JUST LIKE YOU WALK THROUGH HERE THINKING THE SAME THING.
IF I'VE LEARNED ANYTHING, THERE'S REALLY ONLY ONE THING YOU'VE GOTTA DO.
AND THAT IS?
COME ON NOW.
IT'S SIMPLE.

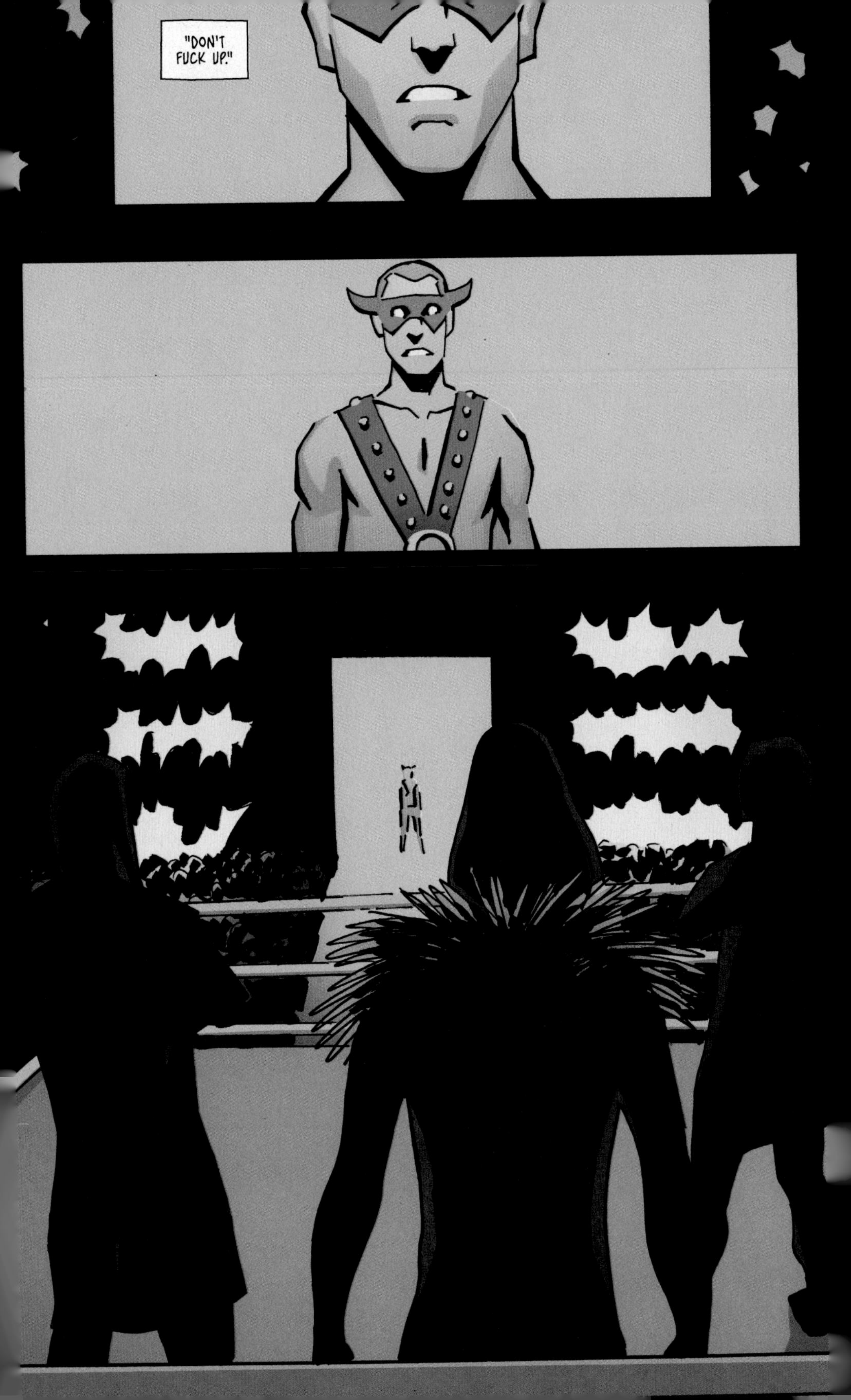
"DON'T
FUCK UP."

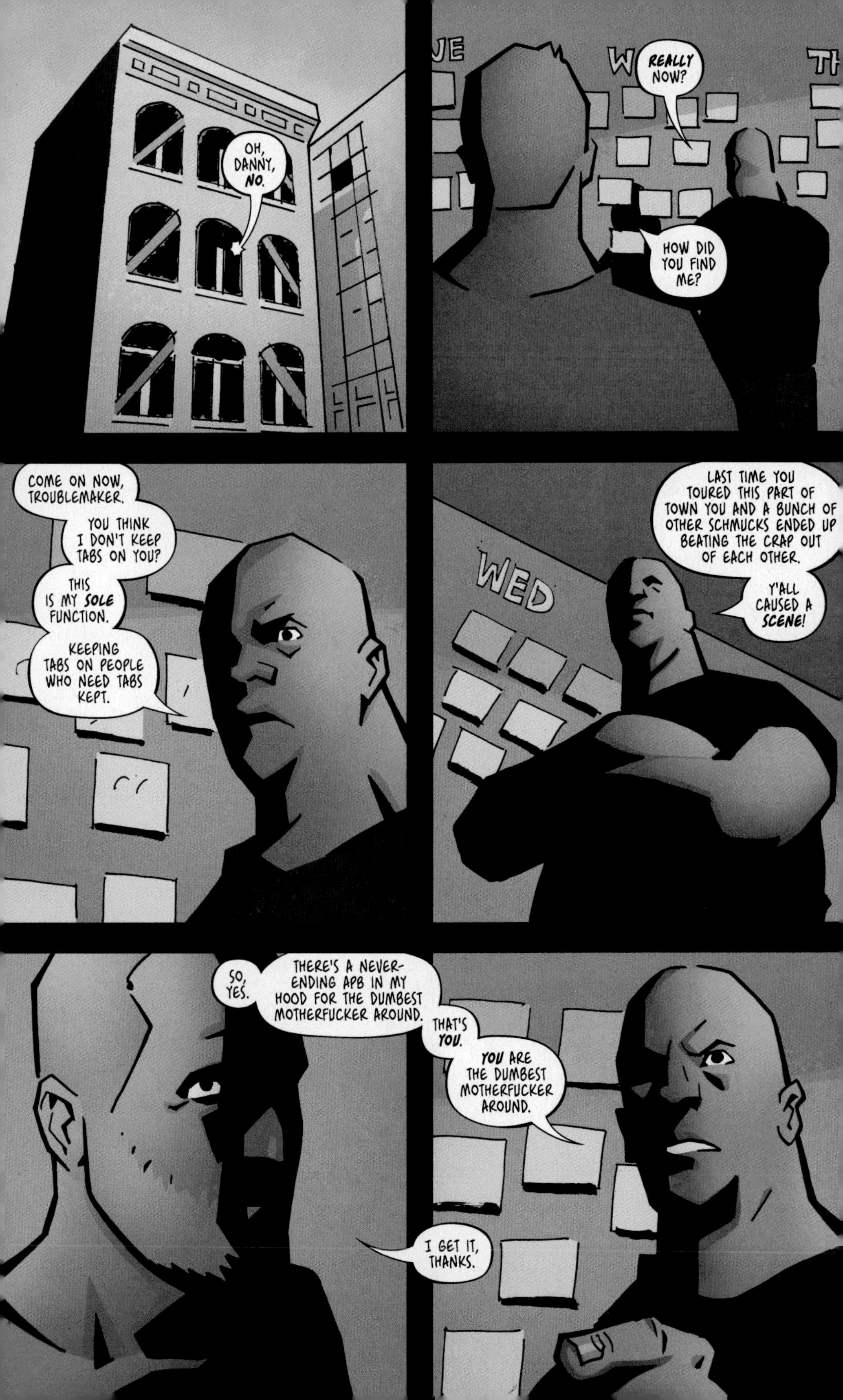
OH, DANNY, NO.
REALLY NOW?
HOW DID YOU FIND ME?
COME ON NOW, TROUBLEMAKER.
YOU THINK I DON'T KEEP TABS ON YOU?
THIS IS MY SOLE FUNCTION.
KEEPING TABS ON PEOPLE WHO NEED TABS KEPT.
WED
LAST TIME YOU TOURED THIS PART OF TOWN YOU AND A BUNCH OF OTHER SCHMUCKS ENDED UP BEATING THE CRAP OUT OF EACH OTHER.
Y'ALL CAUSED A SCENE!
SO, YES.
THERE'S A NEVER-ENDING APB IN MY HOOD FOR THE DUMBEST MOTHERFUCKER AROUND.
THAT'S YOU.
YOU ARE THE DUMBEST MOTHERFUCKER AROUND.
I GET IT, THANKS.

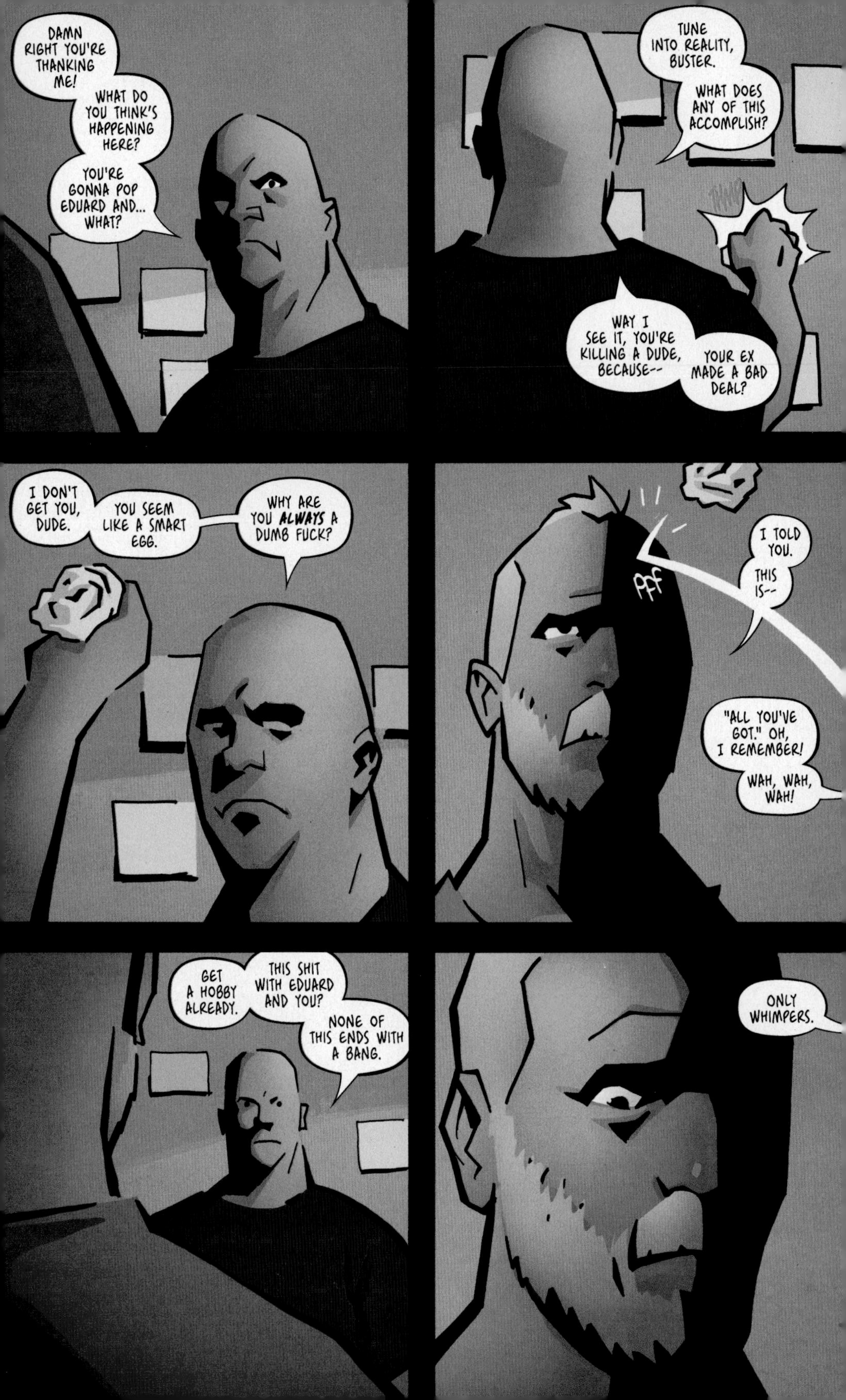
DAMN RIGHT YOU'RE THANKING ME!
WHAT DO YOU THINK'S HAPPENING HERE?
YOU'RE GONNA POP EDUARD AND... WHAT?
TUNE INTO REALITY, BUSTER.
WHAT DOES ANY OF THIS ACCOMPLISH?
WAY I SEE IT, YOU'RE KILLING A DUDE, BECAUSE--
YOUR EX MADE A BAD DEAL?
I DON'T GET YOU, DUDE.
YOU SEEM LIKE A SMART EGG.
WHY ARE YOU **ALWAYS** A DUMB FUCK?
PFF
I TOLD YOU.
THIS IS--
"ALL YOU'VE GOT." OH, I REMEMBER!
WAH, WAH, WAH!
GET A HOBBY ALREADY.
THIS SHIT WITH EDUARD AND YOU?
NONE OF THIS ENDS WITH A BANG.
ONLY WHIMPERS.

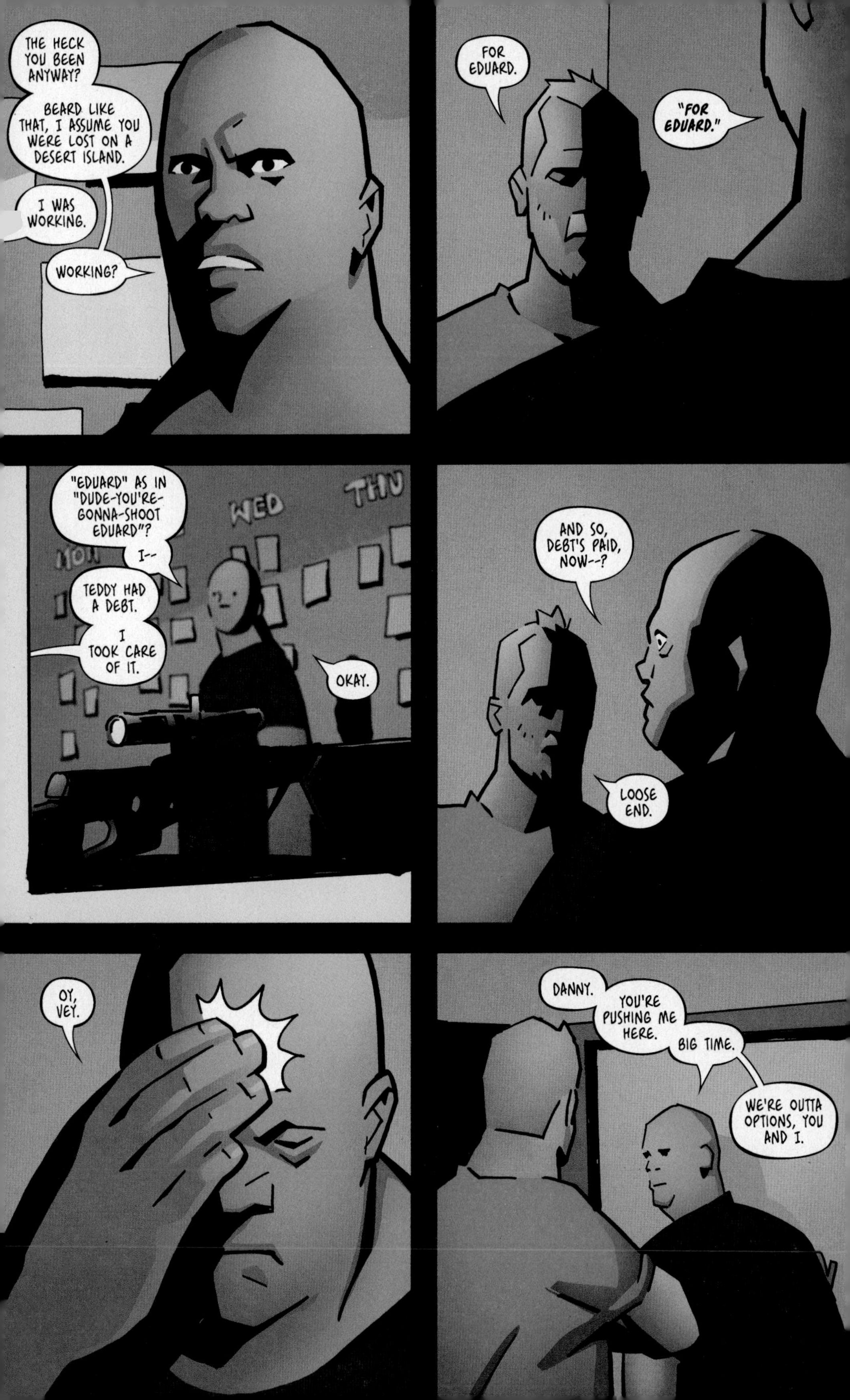
THE HECK YOU BEEN ANYWAY?
BEARD LIKE THAT, I ASSUME YOU WERE LOST ON A DESERT ISLAND.
I WAS WORKING.
WORKING?
FOR EDUARD.
"FOR EDUARD."
"EDUARD" AS IN "DUDE-YOU'RE-GONNA-SHOOT EDUARD"?
I--
TEDDY HAD A DEBT.
I TOOK CARE OF IT.
WED
THU
OKAY.
AND SO, DEBT'S PAID, NOW--?
LOOSE END.
OY, VEY.
DANNY.
YOU'RE PUSHING ME HERE.
BIG TIME.
WE'RE OUTTA OPTIONS, YOU AND I.

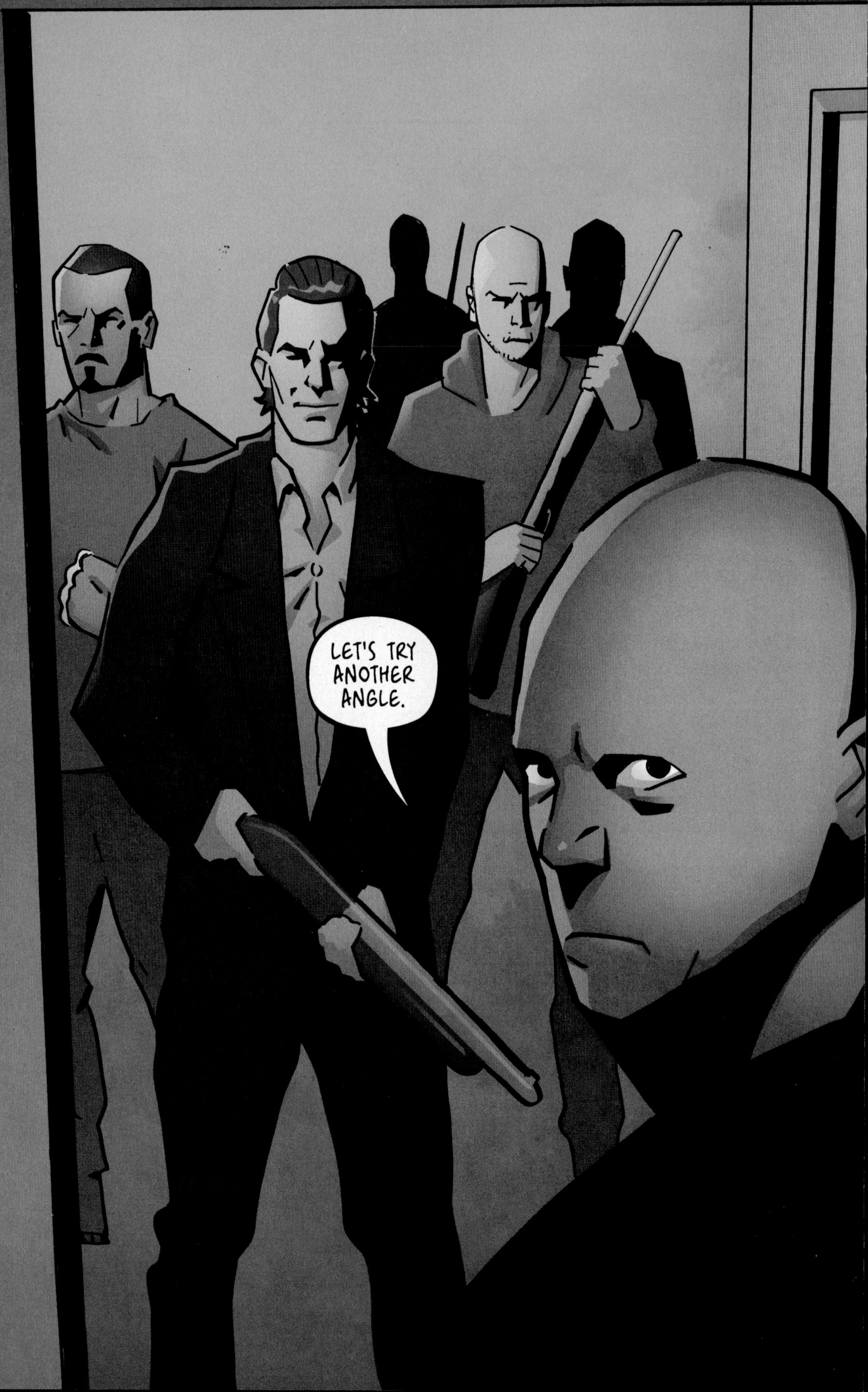
LET'S TRY ANOTHER ANGLE.

CHAPTER FOURTEEN

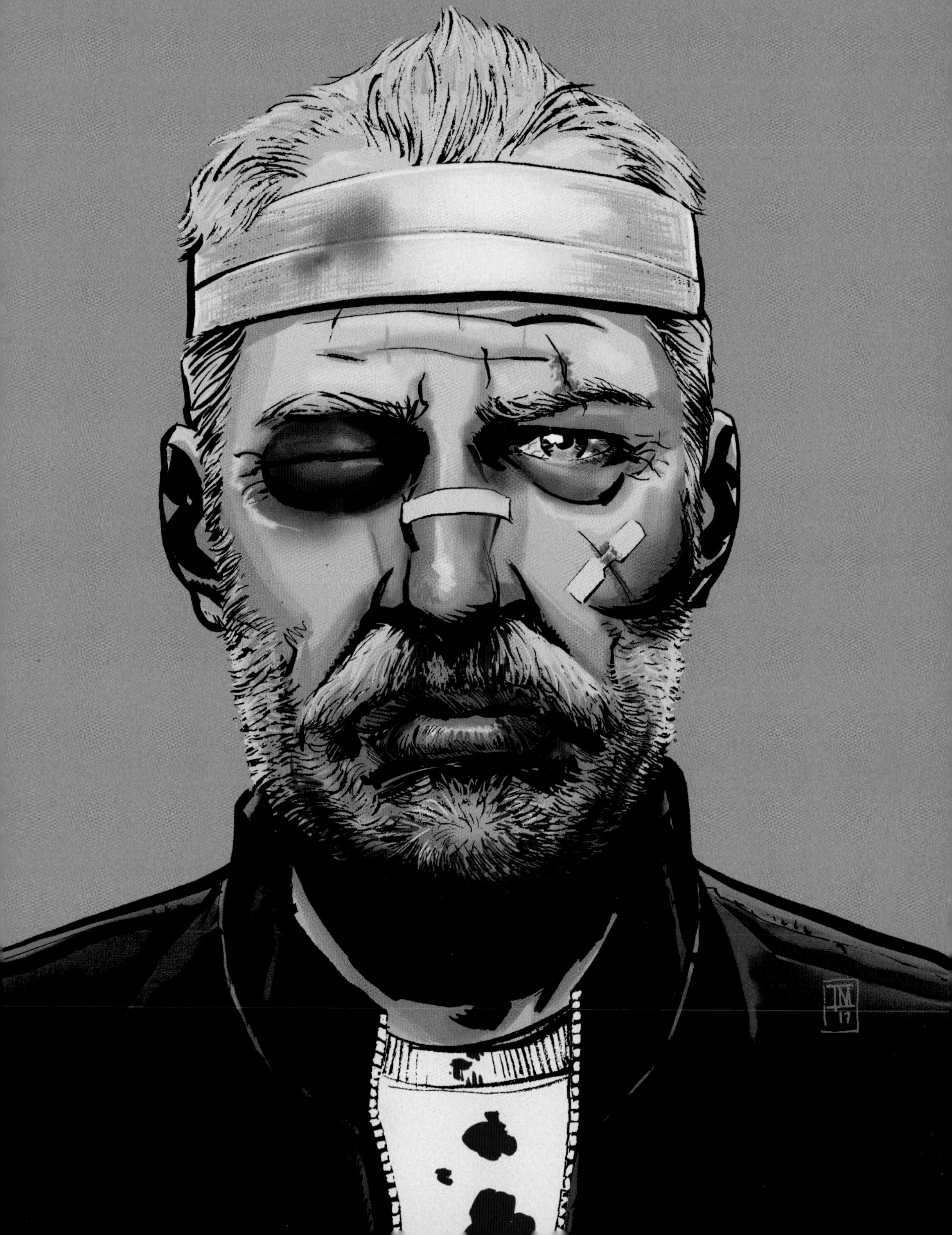

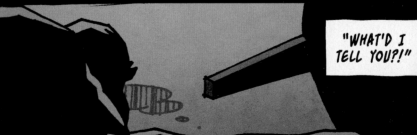

"WHAT'D I TELL YOU?!"

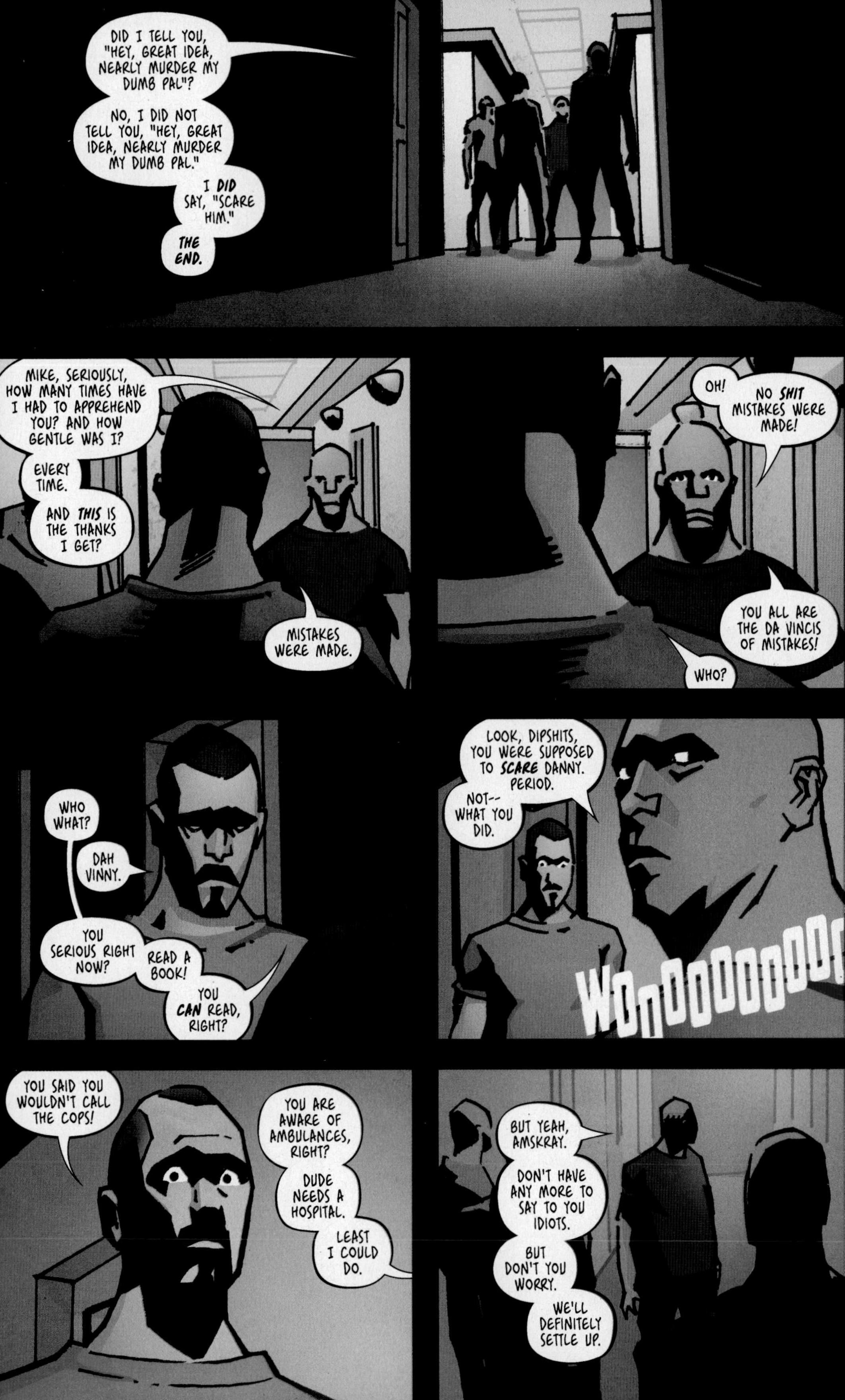
DID I TELL YOU, "HEY, GREAT IDEA, NEARLY MURDER MY DUMB PAL"?
NO, I DID NOT TELL YOU, "HEY, GREAT IDEA, NEARLY MURDER MY DUMB PAL."
I DID SAY, "SCARE HIM."
THE END.
MIKE, SERIOUSLY, HOW MANY TIMES HAVE I HAD TO APPREHEND YOU? AND HOW GENTLE WAS I?
EVERY TIME.
AND THIS IS THE THANKS I GET?
MISTAKES WERE MADE.
OH!
NO SHIT MISTAKES WERE MADE!
YOU ALL ARE THE DA VINCIS OF MISTAKES!
WHO?
WHO WHAT?
DAH VINNY.
YOU SERIOUS RIGHT NOW?
READ A BOOK!
YOU CAN READ, RIGHT?
LOOK, DIPSHITS, YOU WERE SUPPOSED TO SCARE DANNY. PERIOD.
NOT-- WHAT YOU DID.
WOOOOOOOOOO
YOU SAID YOU WOULDN'T CALL THE COPS!
YOU ARE AWARE OF AMBULANCES, RIGHT?
DUDE NEEDS A HOSPITAL.
LEAST I COULD DO.
BUT YEAH, AMSKRAY.
DON'T HAVE ANY MORE TO SAY TO YOU IDIOTS.
BUT DON'T YOU WORRY.
WE'LL DEFINITELY SETTLE UP.

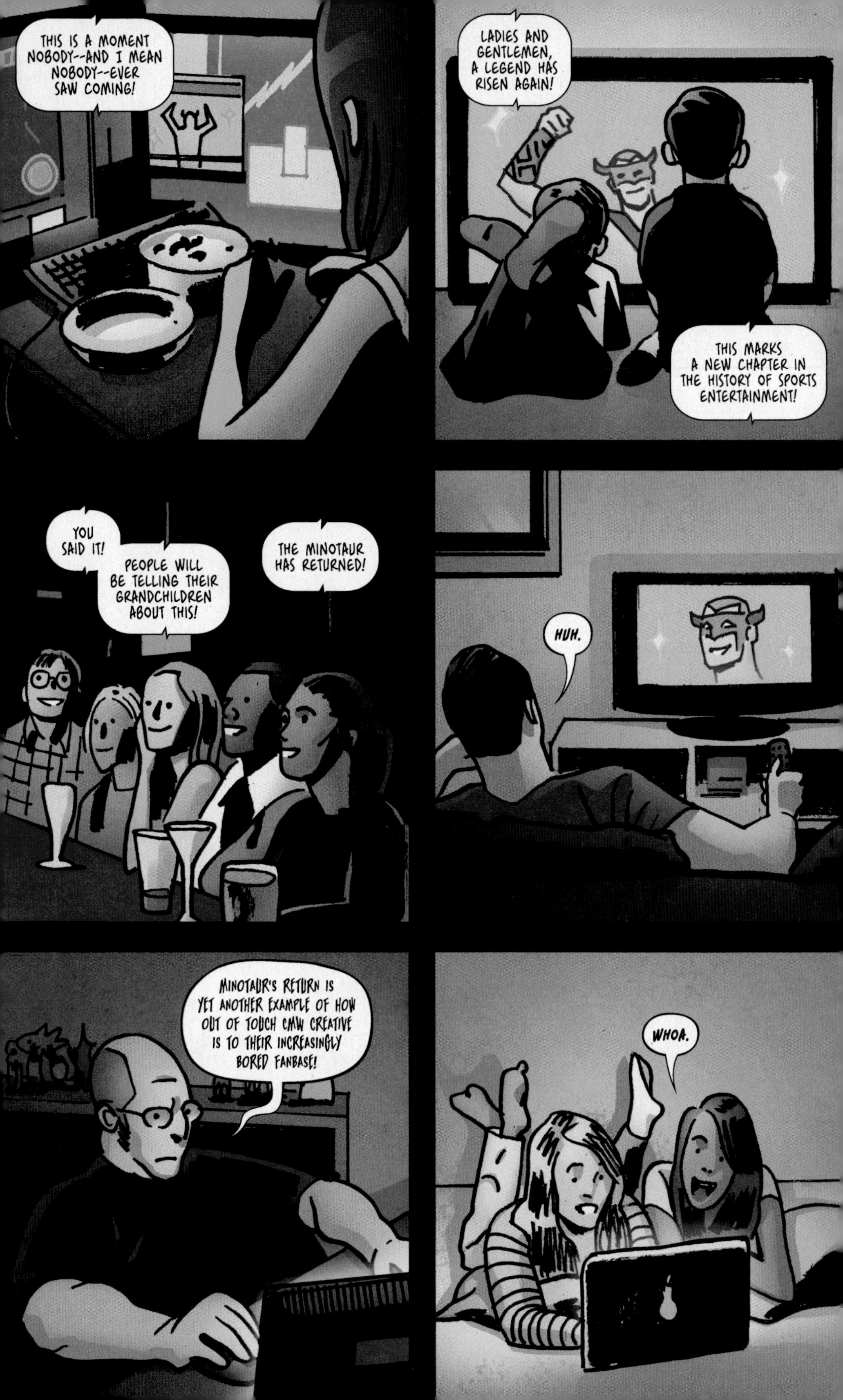
THIS IS A MOMENT NOBODY--AND I MEAN NOBODY--EVER SAW COMING!
LADIES AND GENTLEMEN, A LEGEND HAS RISEN AGAIN!
THIS MARKS A NEW CHAPTER IN THE HISTORY OF SPORTS ENTERTAINMENT!
YOU SAID IT!
PEOPLE WILL BE TELLING THEIR GRANDCHILDREN ABOUT THIS!
THE MINOTAUR HAS RETURNED!
HUH.
MINOTAUR'S RETURN IS YET ANOTHER EXAMPLE OF HOW OUT OF TOUCH CMW CREATIVE IS TO THEIR INCREASINGLY BORED FANBASE!
WHOA.

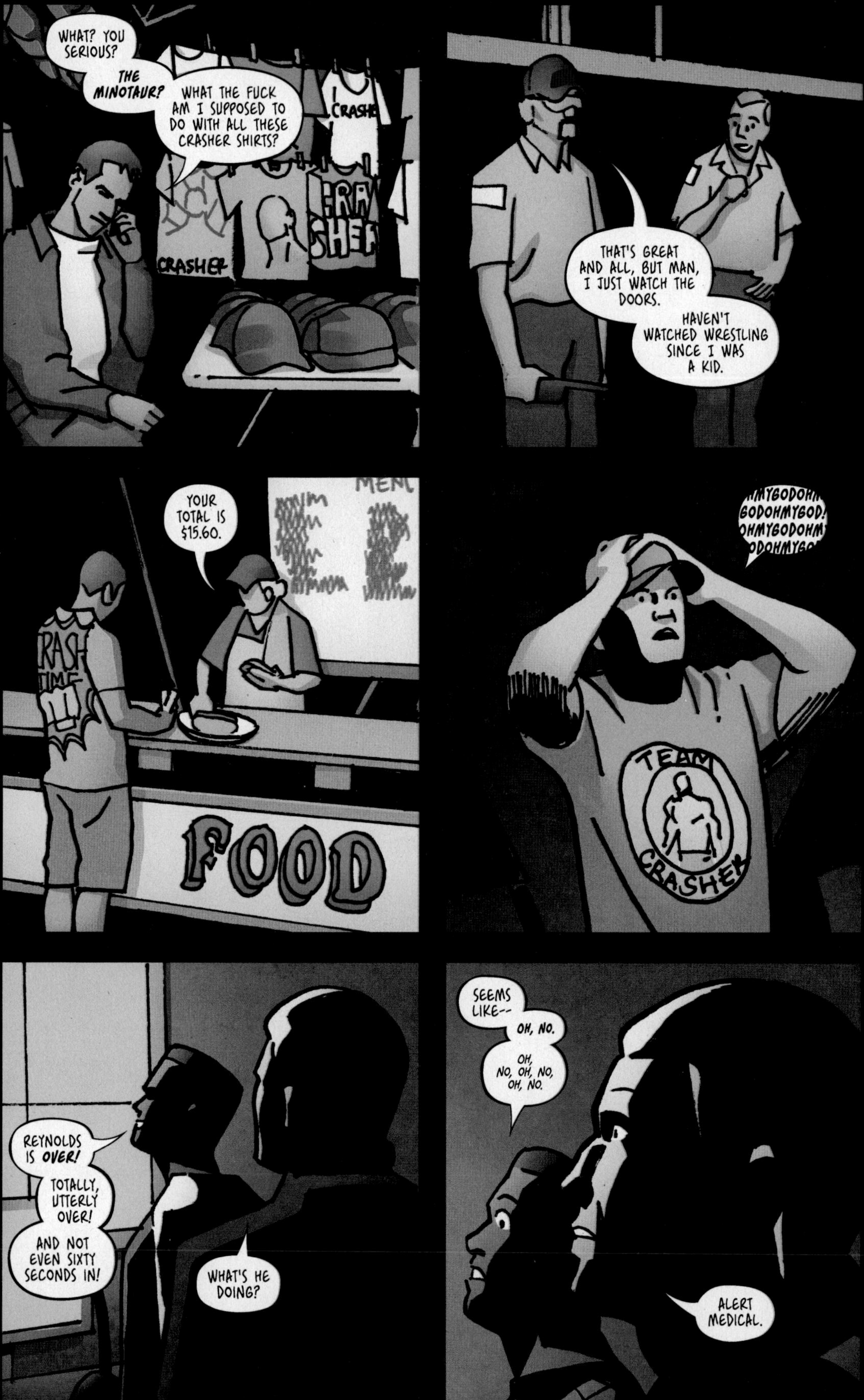
WHAT? YOU SERIOUS?
THE MINOTAUR?
WHAT THE FUCK AM I SUPPOSED TO DO WITH ALL THESE CRASHER SHIRTS?
THAT'S GREAT AND ALL, BUT MAN, I JUST WATCH THE DOORS.
HAVEN'T WATCHED WRESTLING SINCE I WAS A KID.
YOUR TOTAL IS $15.60.
FOOD
OHMYGODOHMYGODOHMYGOD!
TEAM CRASHER
REYNOLDS IS OVER!
TOTALLY, UTTERLY OVER!
AND NOT EVEN SIXTY SECONDS IN!
WHAT'S HE DOING?
SEEMS LIKE--
OH, NO.
OH, NO, OH, NO, OH, NO.
ALERT MEDICAL.

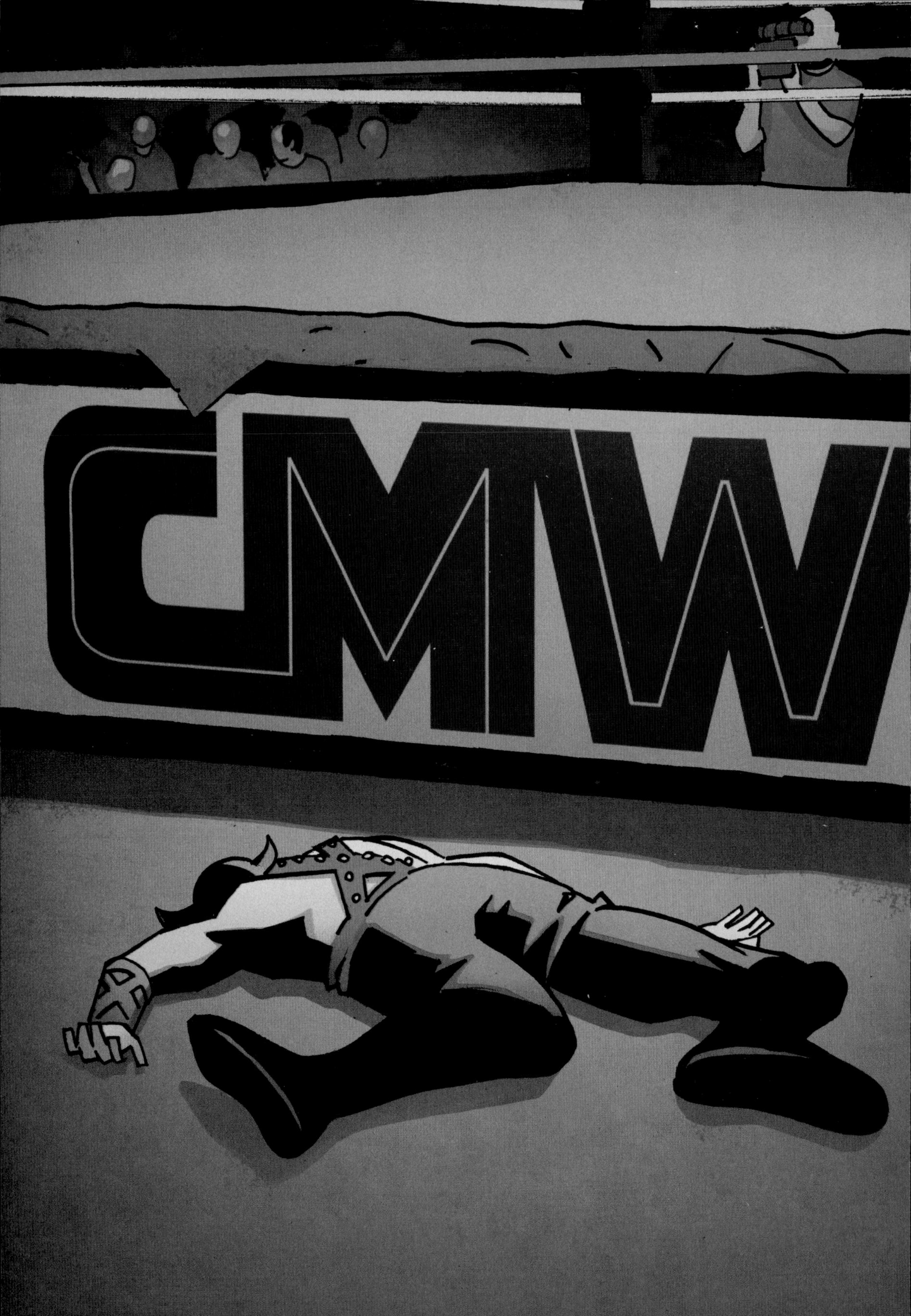
CMW

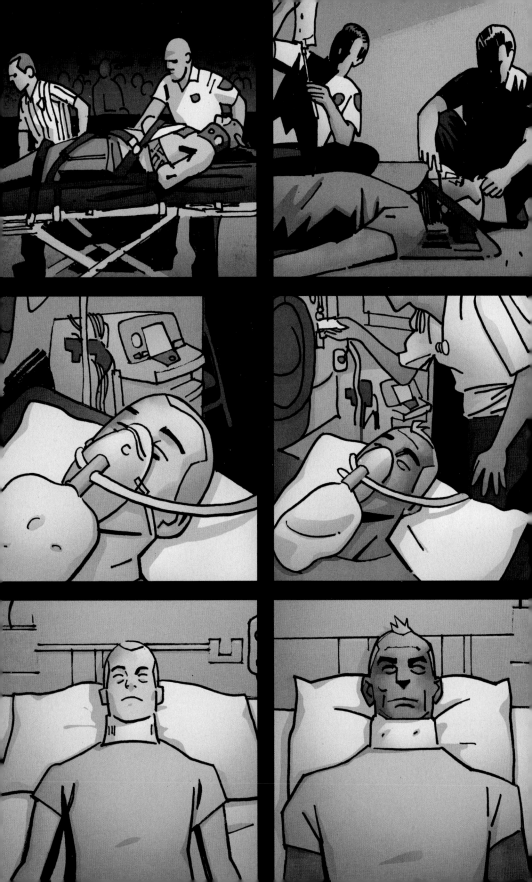

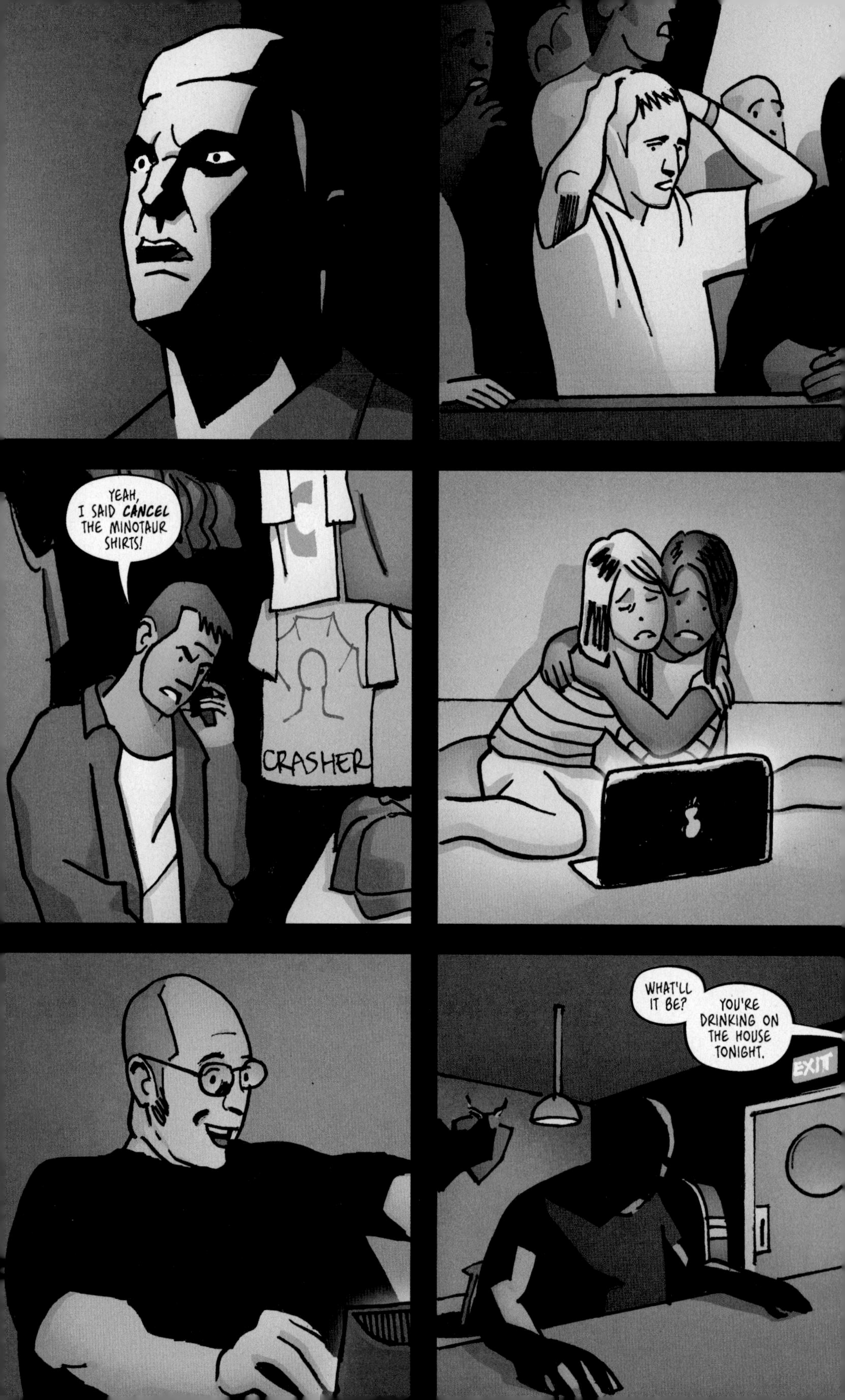
YEAH, I SAID CANCEL THE MINOTAUR SHIRTS!
CRASHER
WHAT'LL IT BE?
YOU'RE DRINKING ON THE HOUSE TONIGHT.
EXIT

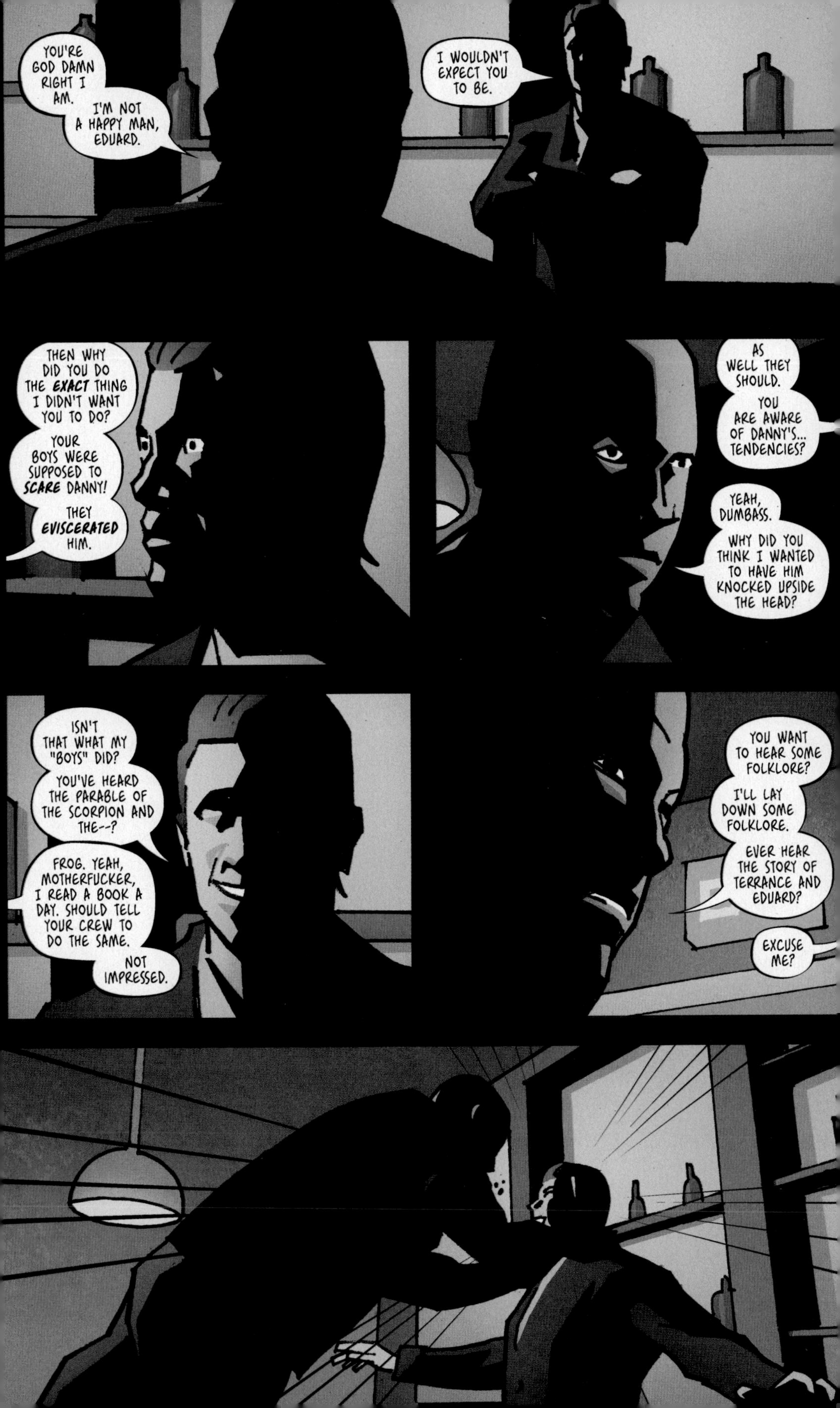
YOU'RE GOD DAMN RIGHT I AM.
I'M NOT A HAPPY MAN, EDUARD.
I WOULDN'T EXPECT YOU TO BE.
THEN WHY DID YOU DO THE EXACT THING I DIDN'T WANT YOU TO DO?
YOUR BOYS WERE SUPPOSED TO SCARE DANNY!
THEY EVISCERATED HIM.
AS WELL THEY SHOULD.
YOU ARE AWARE OF DANNY'S... TENDENCIES?
YEAH, DUMBASS.
WHY DID YOU THINK I WANTED TO HAVE HIM KNOCKED UPSIDE THE HEAD?
ISN'T THAT WHAT MY "BOYS" DID?
YOU'VE HEARD THE PARABLE OF THE SCORPION AND THE--?
FROG. YEAH, MOTHERFUCKER, I READ A BOOK A DAY. SHOULD TELL YOUR CREW TO DO THE SAME.
NOT IMPRESSED.
YOU WANT TO HEAR SOME FOLKLORE?
I'LL LAY DOWN SOME FOLKLORE.
EVER HEAR THE STORY OF TERRANCE AND EDUARD?
EXCUSE ME?

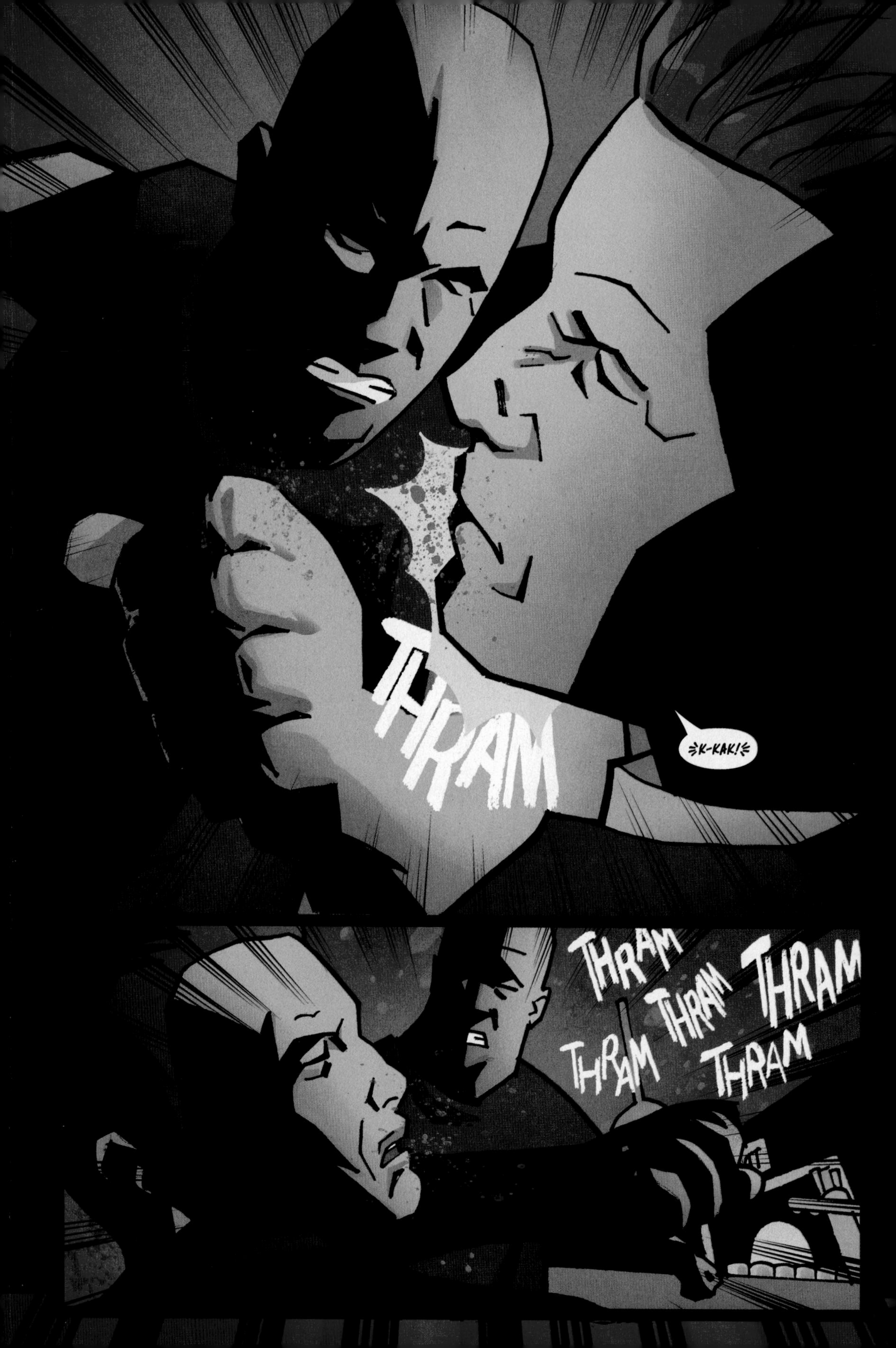
THRAM
K-KAK!
THRAM
THRAM
THRAM
THRAM
THRAM

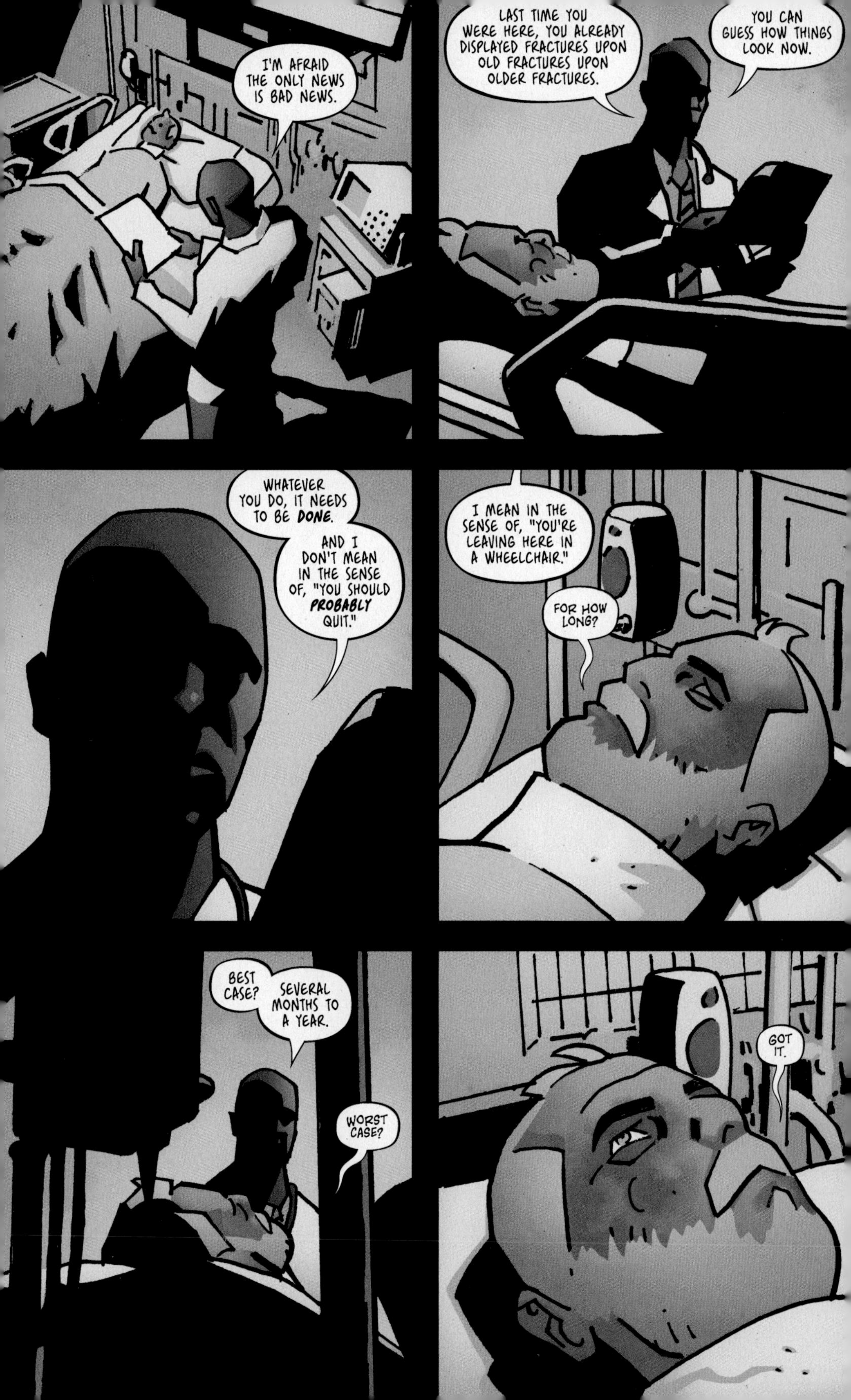
I'M AFRAID THE ONLY NEWS IS BAD NEWS.
LAST TIME YOU WERE HERE, YOU ALREADY DISPLAYED FRACTURES UPON OLD FRACTURES UPON OLDER FRACTURES.
YOU CAN GUESS HOW THINGS LOOK NOW.
WHATEVER YOU DO, IT NEEDS TO BE **DONE**.
AND I DON'T MEAN IN THE SENSE OF, "YOU SHOULD ***PROBABLY*** QUIT."
I MEAN IN THE SENSE OF, "YOU'RE LEAVING HERE IN A WHEELCHAIR."
FOR HOW LONG?
BEST CASE?
SEVERAL MONTHS TO A YEAR.
WORST CASE?
GOT IT.

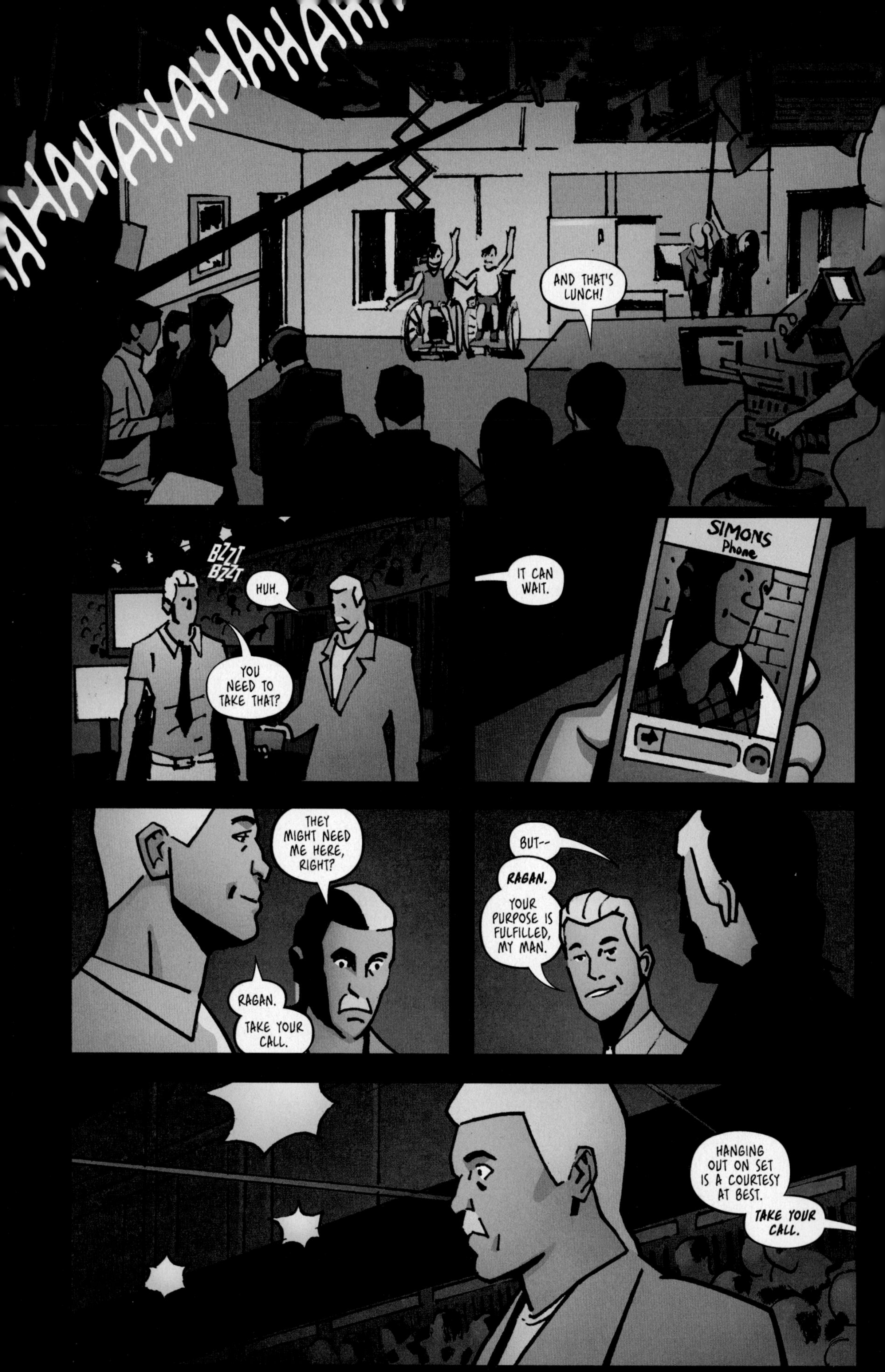
AHAHAHAHAHAHAH
AND THAT'S LUNCH!
BZZT BZZT
HUH.
YOU NEED TO TAKE THAT?
IT CAN WAIT.
SIMONS Phone
THEY MIGHT NEED ME HERE, RIGHT?
RAGAN.
TAKE YOUR CALL.
BUT--
RAGAN.
YOUR PURPOSE IS FULFILLED, MY MAN.
HANGING OUT ON SET IS A COURTESY AT BEST.
TAKE YOUR CALL.

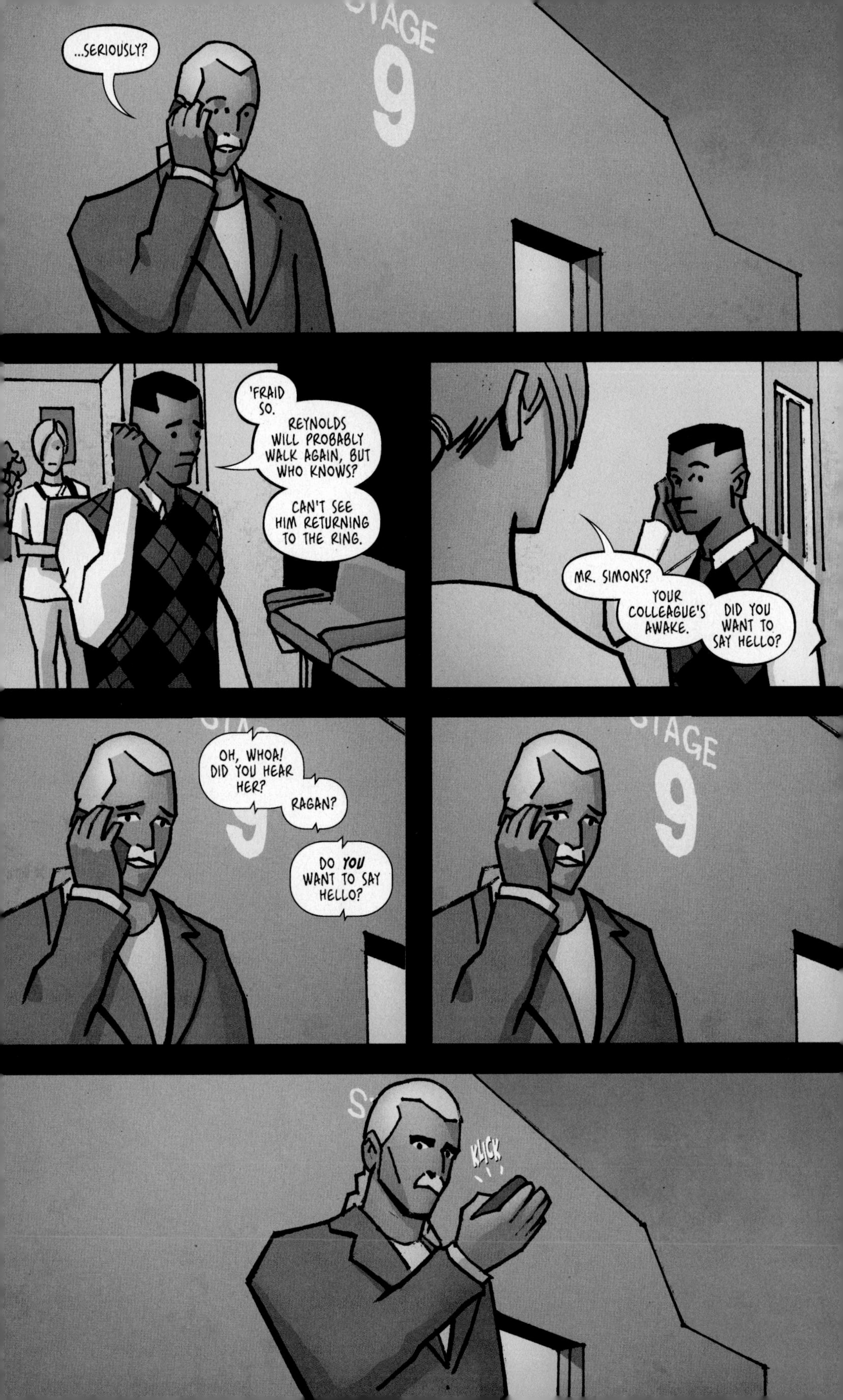
STAGE
9
...SERIOUSLY?
'FRAID SO.
REYNOLDS WILL PROBABLY WALK AGAIN, BUT WHO KNOWS?
CAN'T SEE HIM RETURNING TO THE RING.
MR. SIMONS?
YOUR COLLEAGUE'S AWAKE.
DID YOU WANT TO SAY HELLO?
OH, WHOA! DID YOU HEAR HER?
RAGAN?
DO YOU WANT TO SAY HELLO?
STAGE
9
KLICK

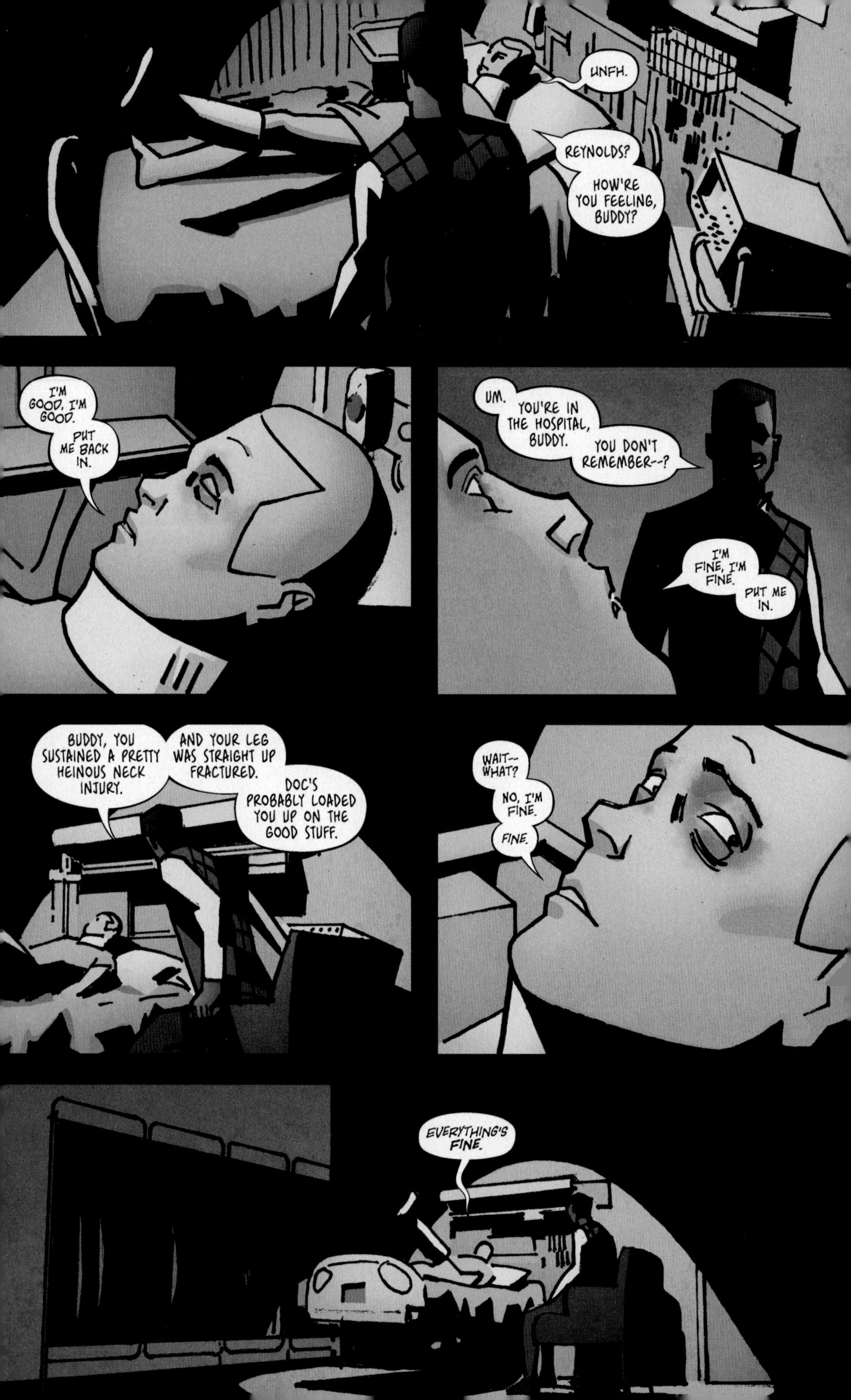
UNFH.
REYNOLDS?
HOW'RE YOU FEELING, BUDDY?
I'M GOOD, I'M GOOD.
PUT ME BACK IN.
UM.
YOU'RE IN THE HOSPITAL, BUDDY.
YOU DON'T REMEMBER--?
I'M FINE, I'M FINE.
PUT ME IN.
BUDDY, YOU SUSTAINED A PRETTY HEINOUS NECK INJURY.
AND YOUR LEG WAS STRAIGHT UP FRACTURED.
DOC'S PROBABLY LOADED YOU UP ON THE GOOD STUFF.
WAIT-- WHAT?
NO, I'M FINE.
FINE.
EVERYTHING'S FINE.

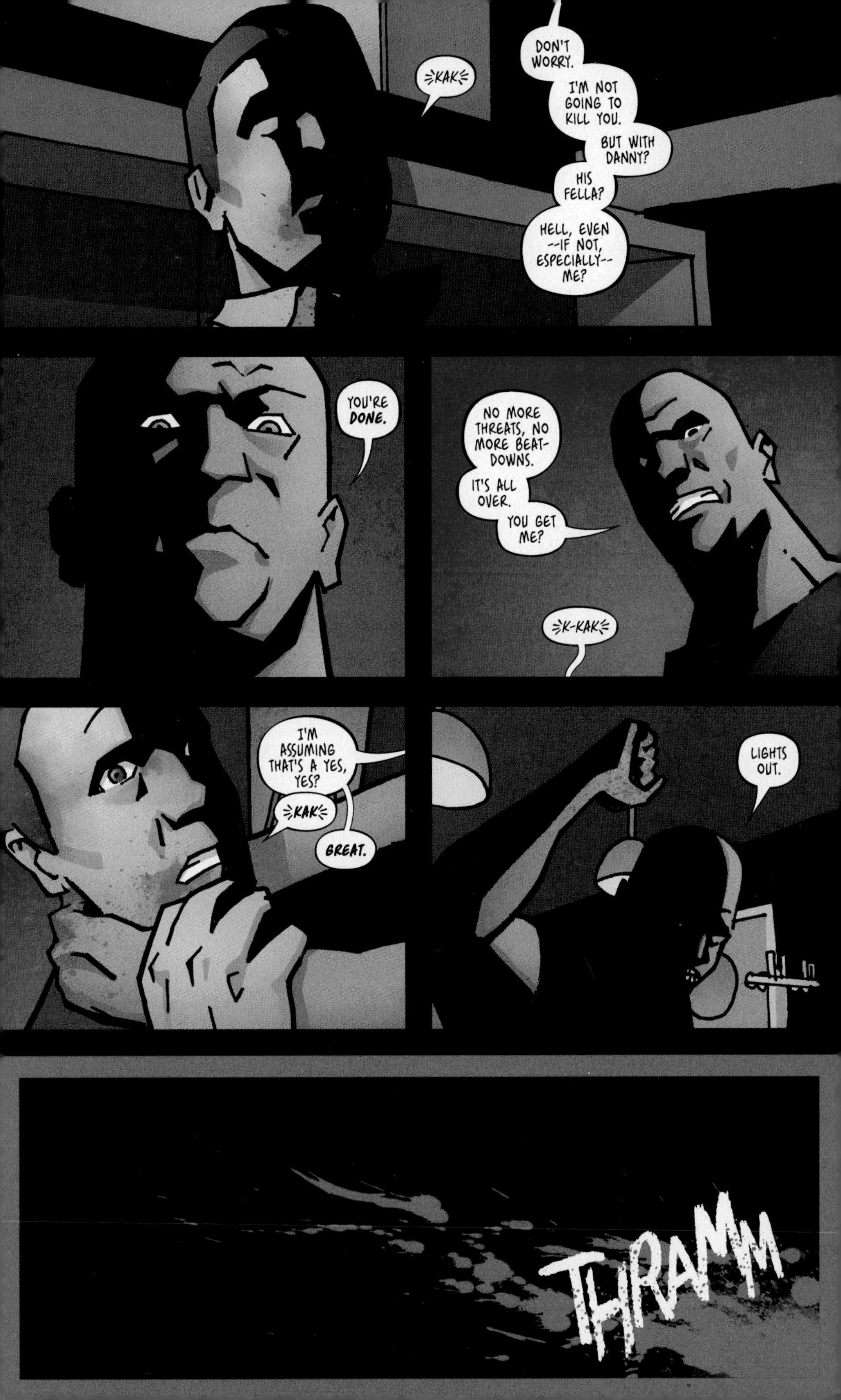
DON'T WORRY.
I'M NOT GOING TO KILL YOU.
BUT WITH DANNY?
HIS FELLA?
HELL, EVEN --IF NOT, ESPECIALLY-- ME?
KAK
YOU'RE **DONE.**
NO MORE THREATS, NO MORE BEAT-DOWNS.
IT'S ALL OVER.
YOU GET ME?
K-KAK
I'M ASSUMING THAT'S A YES, YES?
KAK
GREAT.
LIGHTS OUT.
THRAMM

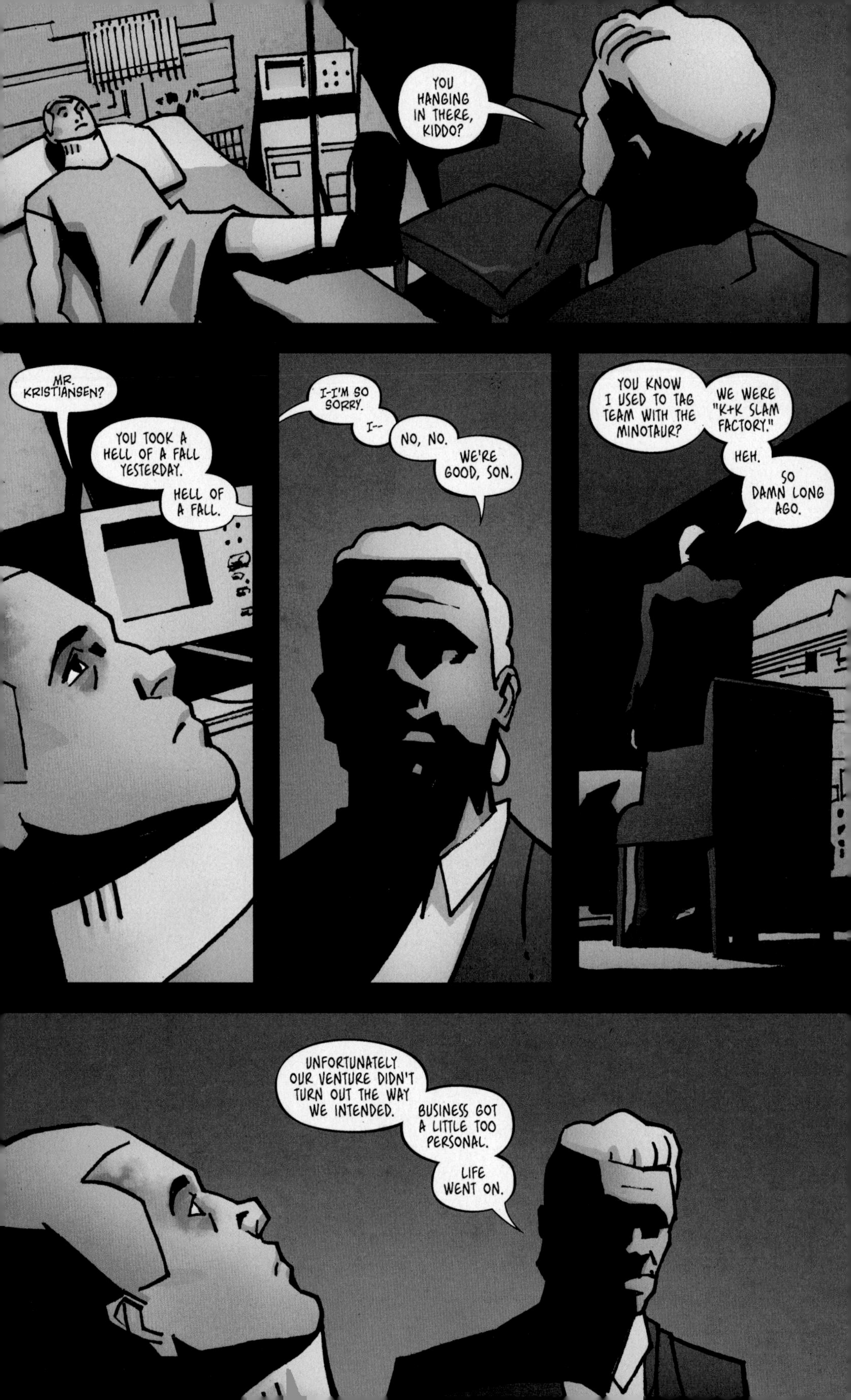
YOU HANGING IN THERE, KIDDO?
MR. KRISTIANSEN?
YOU TOOK A HELL OF A FALL YESTERDAY.
HELL OF A FALL.
I-I'M SO SORRY.
I--
NO, NO.
WE'RE GOOD, SON.
YOU KNOW I USED TO TAG TEAM WITH THE MINOTAUR?
WE WERE "K+K SLAM FACTORY."
HEH.
SO DAMN LONG AGO.
UNFORTUNATELY OUR VENTURE DIDN'T TURN OUT THE WAY WE INTENDED.
BUSINESS GOT A LITTLE TOO PERSONAL.
LIFE WENT ON.

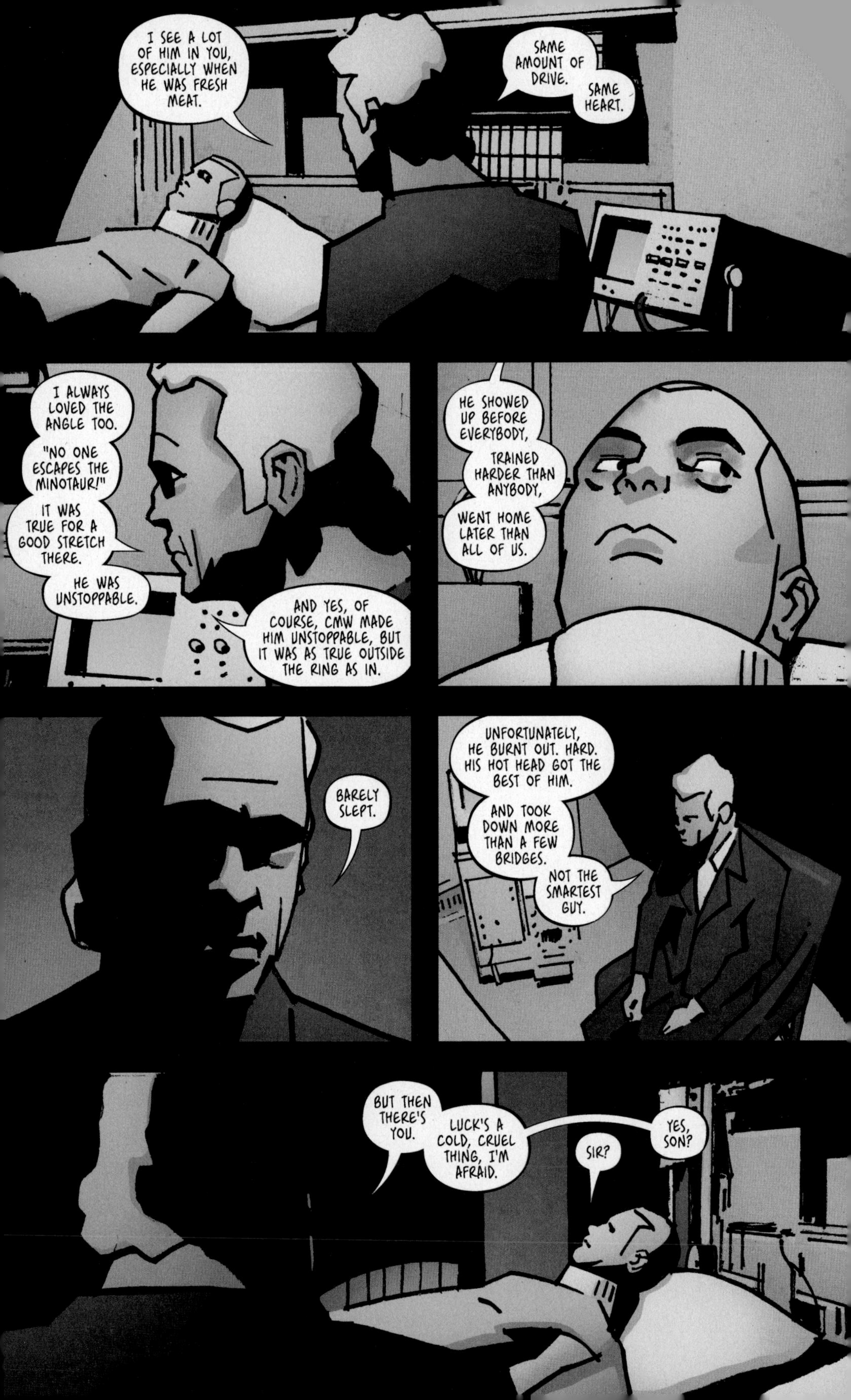
I SEE A LOT OF HIM IN YOU, ESPECIALLY WHEN HE WAS FRESH MEAT.
SAME AMOUNT OF DRIVE.
SAME HEART.
I ALWAYS LOVED THE ANGLE TOO.
"NO ONE ESCAPES THE MINOTAUR!"
IT WAS TRUE FOR A GOOD STRETCH THERE.
HE WAS UNSTOPPABLE.
AND YES, OF COURSE, CMW MADE HIM UNSTOPPABLE, BUT IT WAS AS TRUE OUTSIDE THE RING AS IN.
HE SHOWED UP BEFORE EVERYBODY,
TRAINED HARDER THAN ANYBODY,
WENT HOME LATER THAN ALL OF US.
BARELY SLEPT.
UNFORTUNATELY, HE BURNT OUT. HARD. HIS HOT HEAD GOT THE BEST OF HIM.
AND TOOK DOWN MORE THAN A FEW BRIDGES.
NOT THE SMARTEST GUY.
BUT THEN THERE'S YOU.
LUCK'S A COLD, CRUEL THING, I'M AFRAID.
SIR?
YES, SON?

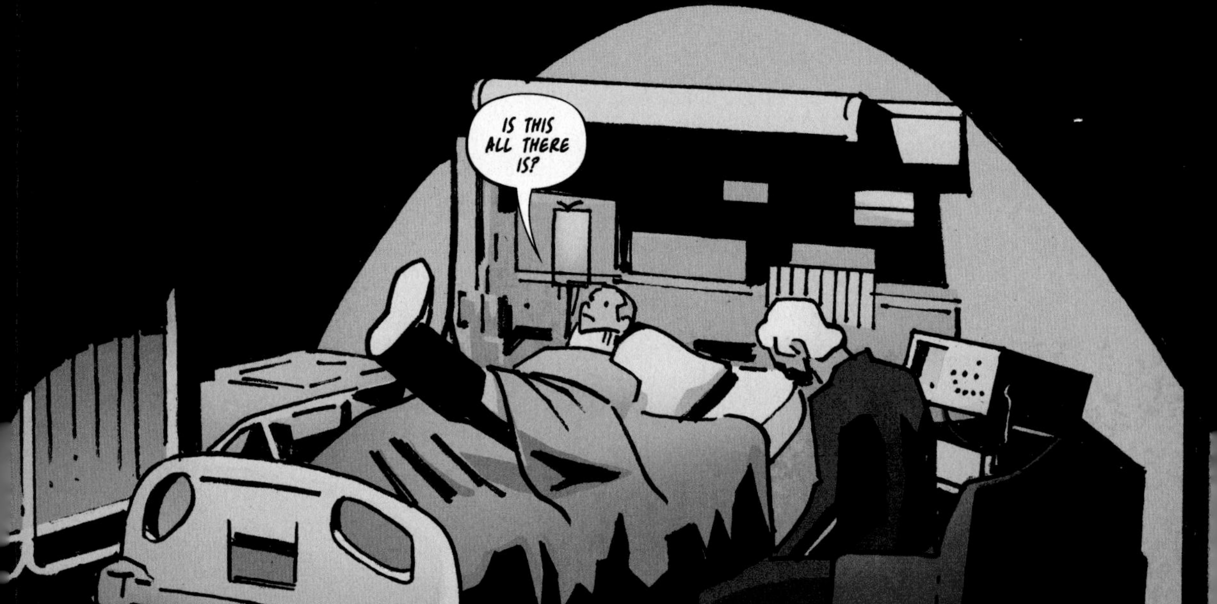
IS THIS ALL THERE IS?

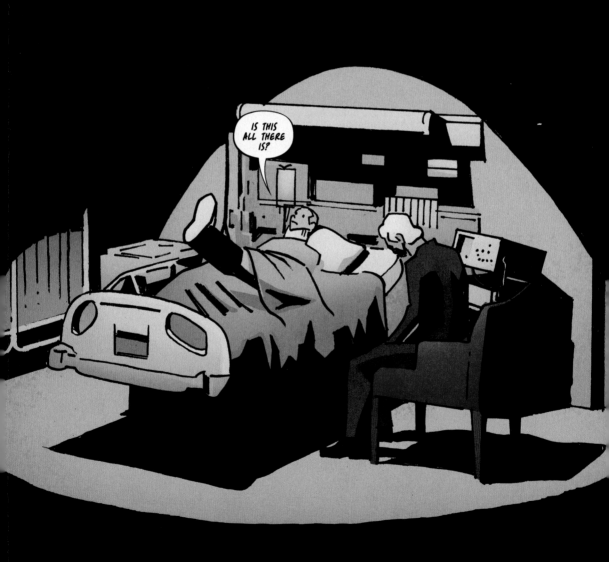

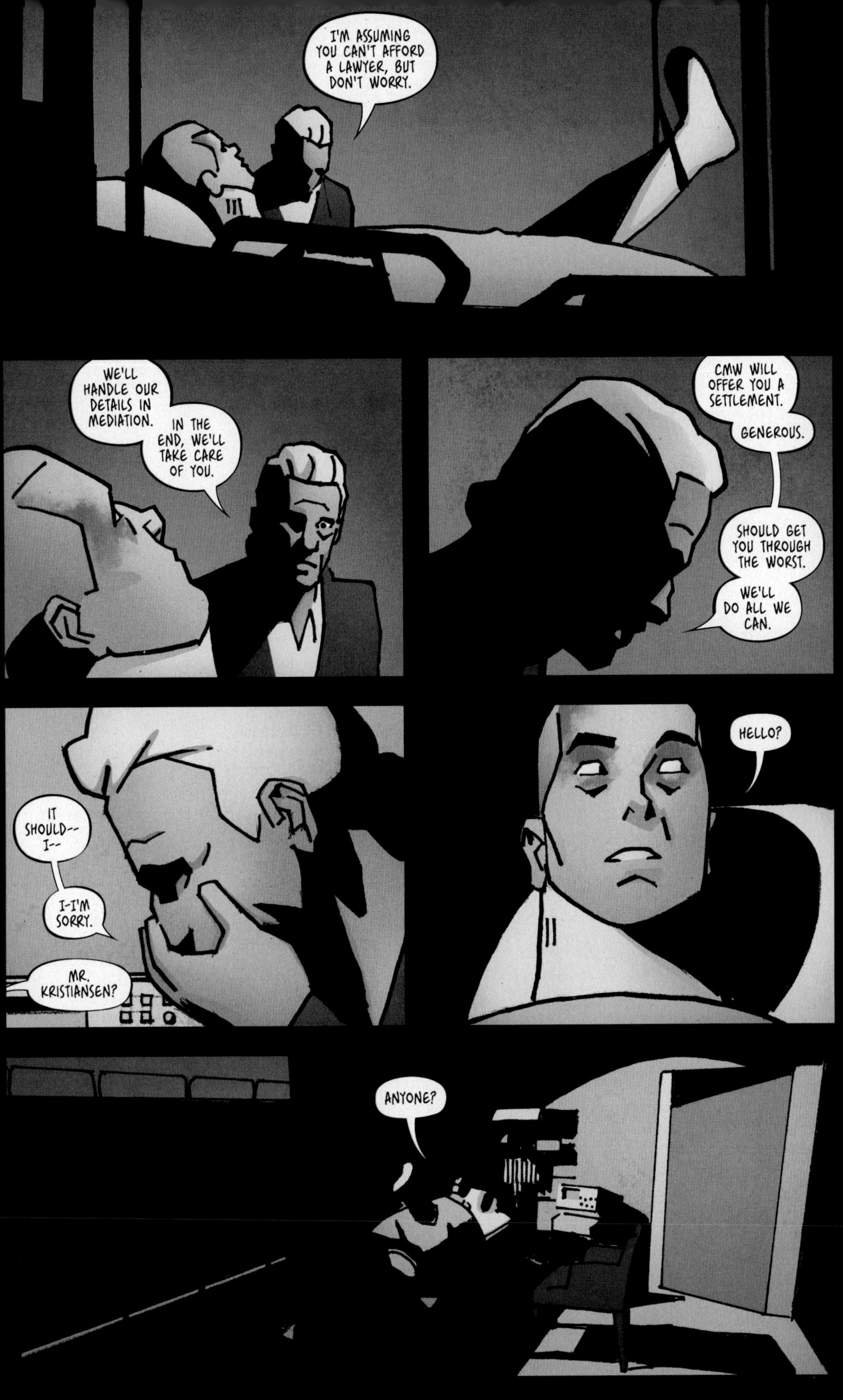
I'M ASSUMING YOU CAN'T AFFORD A LAWYER, BUT DON'T WORRY.
WE'LL HANDLE OUR DETAILS IN MEDIATION.
IN THE END, WE'LL TAKE CARE OF YOU.
CMW WILL OFFER YOU A SETTLEMENT.
GENEROUS.
SHOULD GET YOU THROUGH THE WORST.
WE'LL DO ALL WE CAN.
IT SHOULD-- I--
I-I'M SORRY.
MR. KRISTIANSEN?
HELLO?
ANYONE?

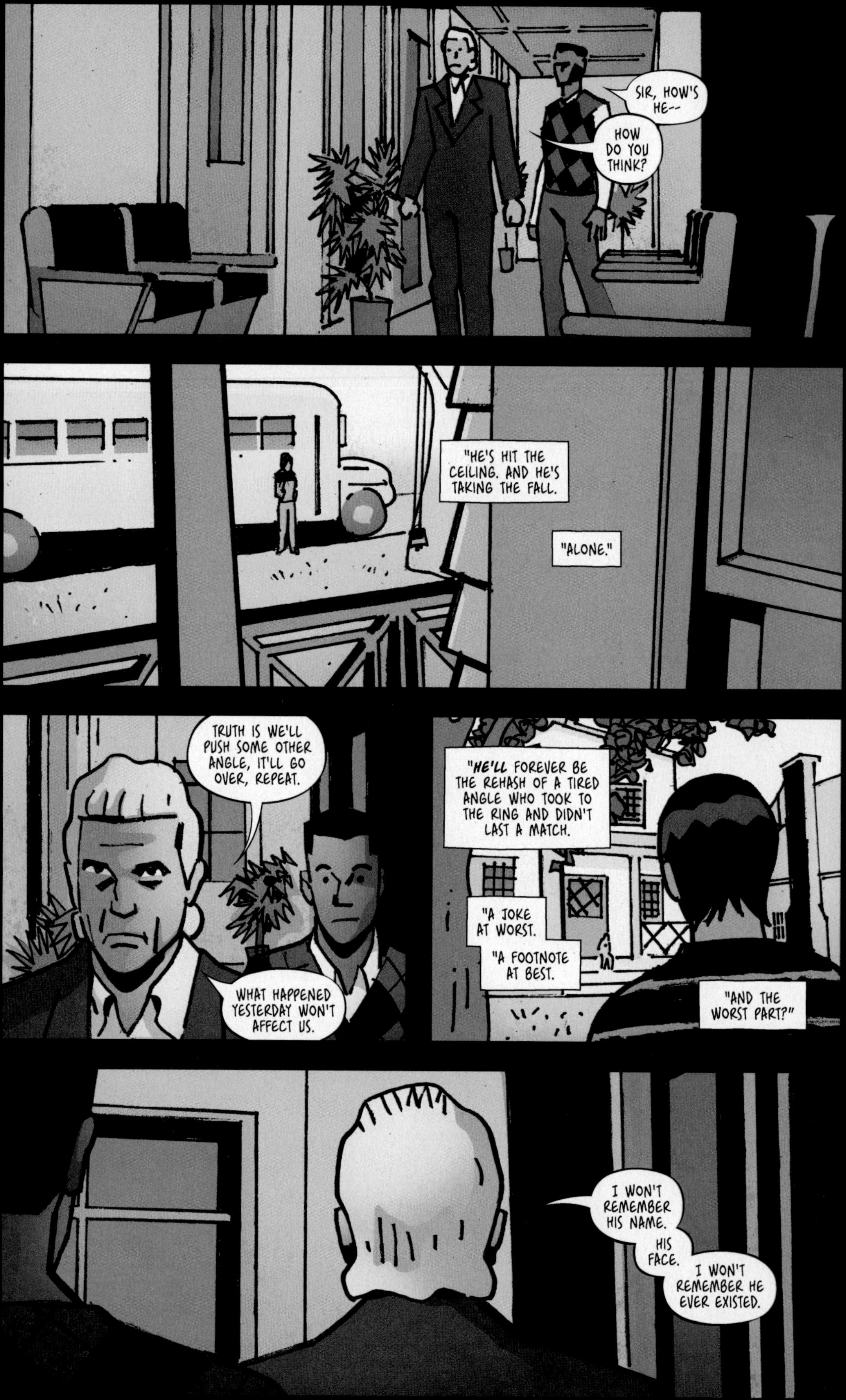
SIR, HOW'S HE--
HOW DO YOU THINK?
"HE'S HIT THE CEILING. AND HE'S TAKING THE FALL.
"ALONE."
TRUTH IS WE'LL PUSH SOME OTHER ANGLE, IT'LL GO OVER, REPEAT.
WHAT HAPPENED YESTERDAY WON'T AFFECT US.
"HE'LL FOREVER BE THE REHASH OF A TIRED ANGLE WHO TOOK TO THE RING AND DIDN'T LAST A MATCH.
"A JOKE AT WORST.
"A FOOTNOTE AT BEST.
"AND THE WORST PART?"
I WON'T REMEMBER HIS NAME.
HIS FACE.
I WON'T REMEMBER HE EVER EXISTED.

"NEITHER WILL YOU."

EXCUSE ME? IS YOUR DAD HOME?

"NO ONE WILL."

DAAAADD!!

"WE'LL MOVE ON."

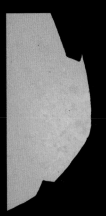

"LIKE IT NEVER HAPPENED."

UM!

HELLO!

HI!

CAN I HELP YOU?

HI, YEAH, I'M RILEY-- I CALLED ABOUT--

DANNY.

≈SIGH≈ COME ON IN.

I'M SORRY, SIR. I DIDN'T MEAN TO--

IT'S NOT YOU.

SOME MEMORIES ARE...*SOME MEMORIES.*

AND PLEASE DON'T "SIR" ME.

I KNOW I'M OLD, BUT EVEN STILL...

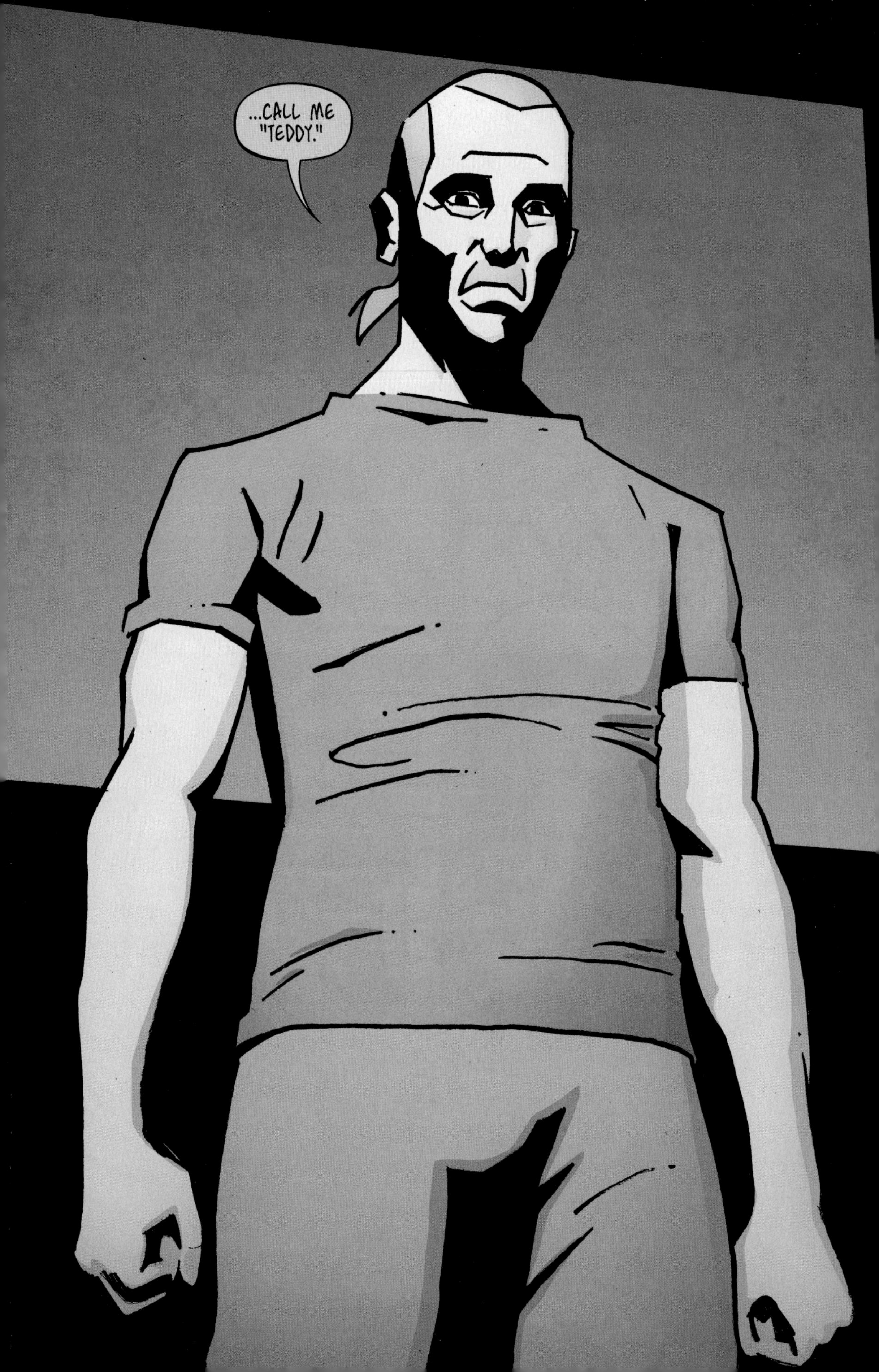
...CALL ME "TEDDY."

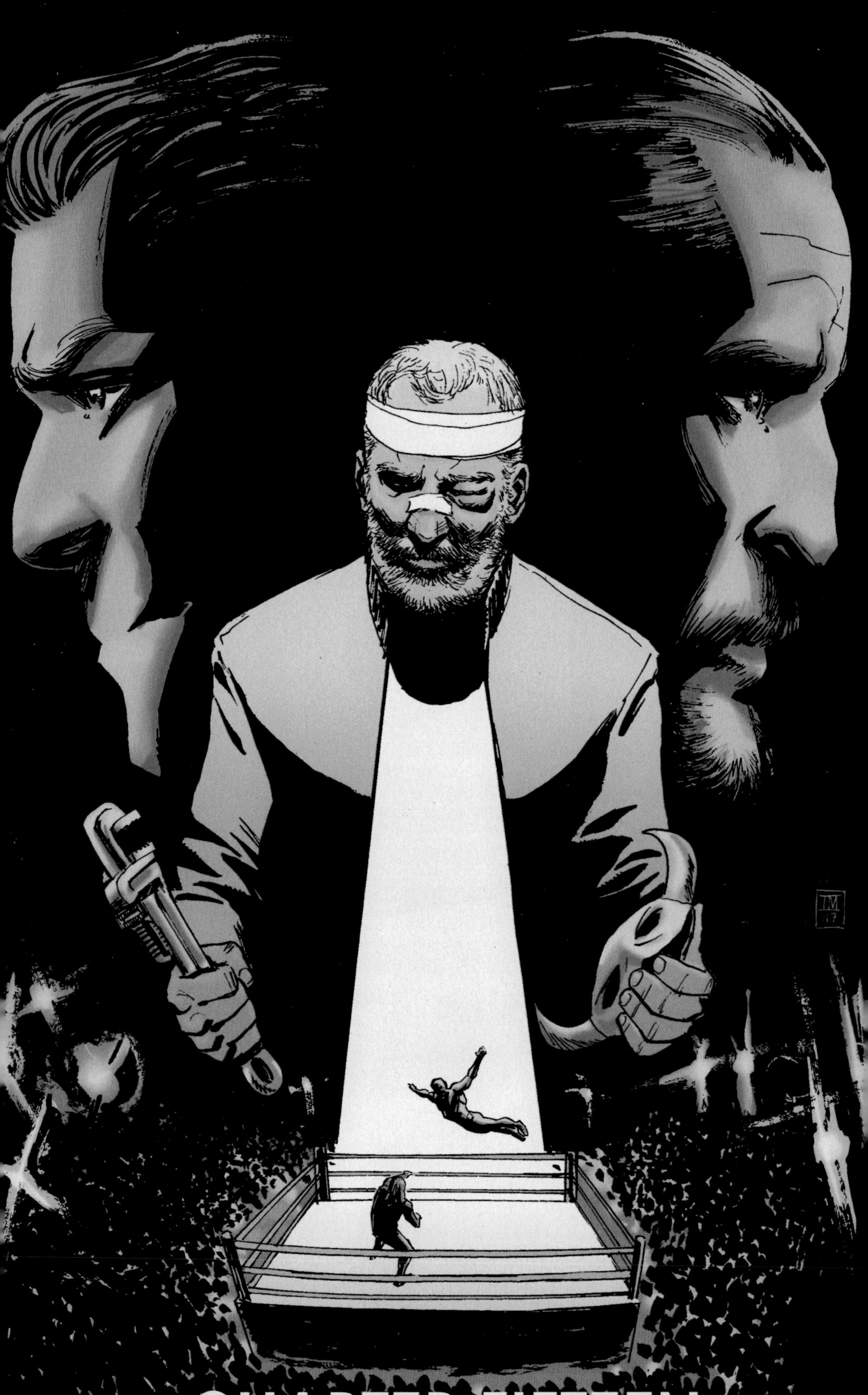

CHAPTER FIFTEEN

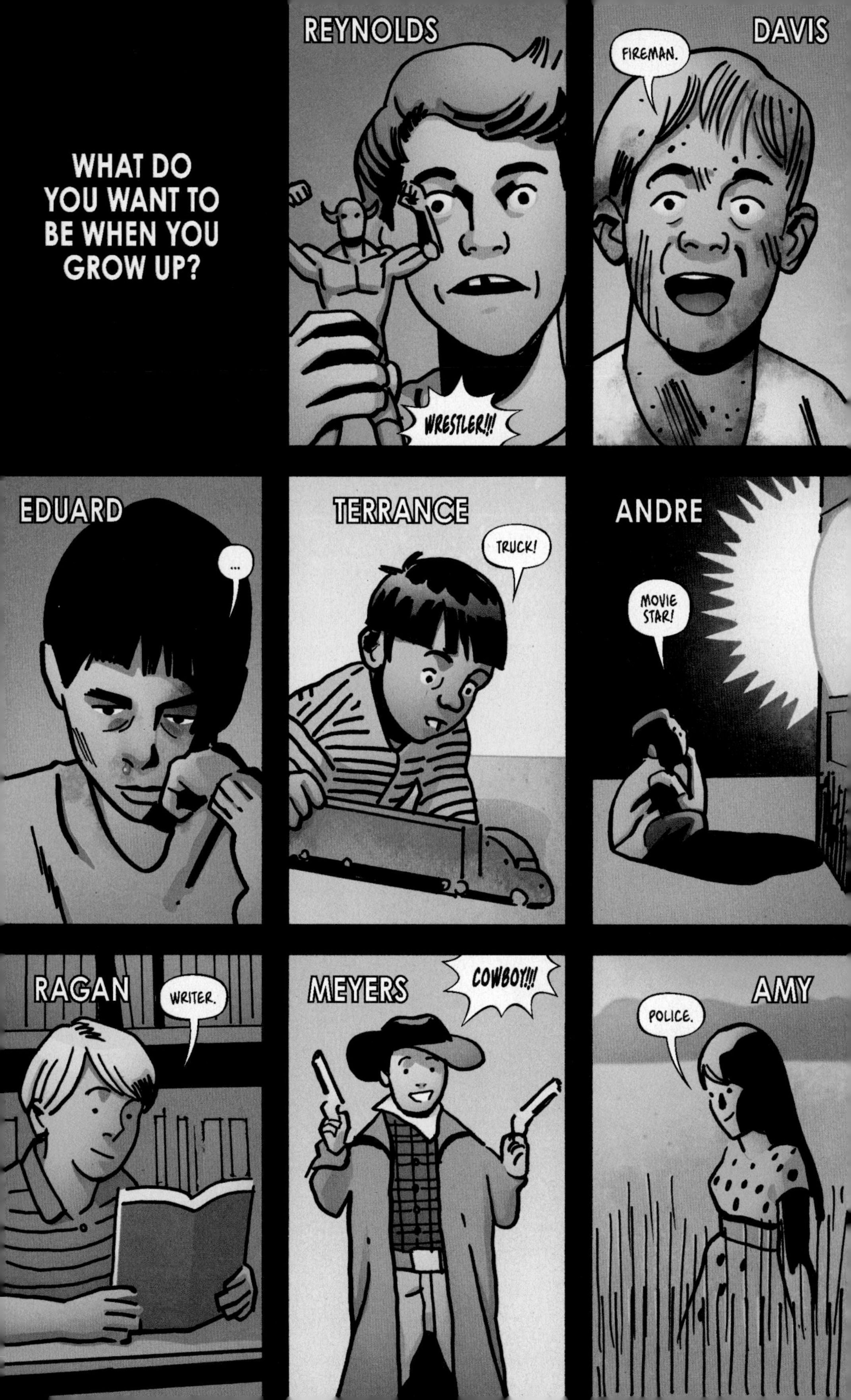
WHAT DO YOU WANT TO BE WHEN YOU GROW UP?
REYNOLDS
WRESTLER!!!
DAVIS
FIREMAN.
EDUARD
...
TERRANCE
TRUCK!
ANDRE
MOVIE STAR!
RAGAN
WRITER.
MEYERS
COWBOY!!!
AMY
POLICE.

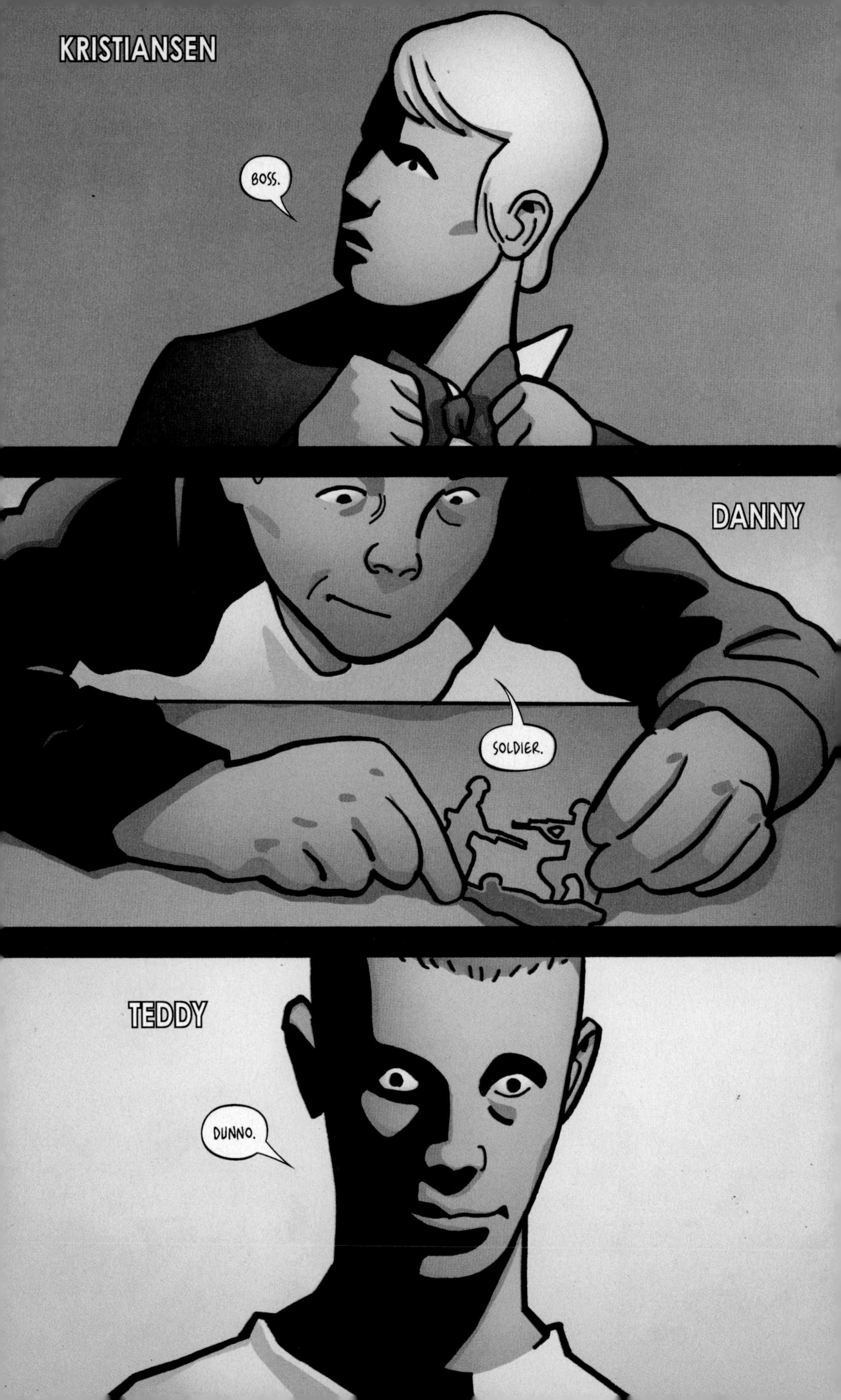
KRISTIANSEN
BOSS.
DANNY
SOLDIER.
TEDDY
DUNNO.

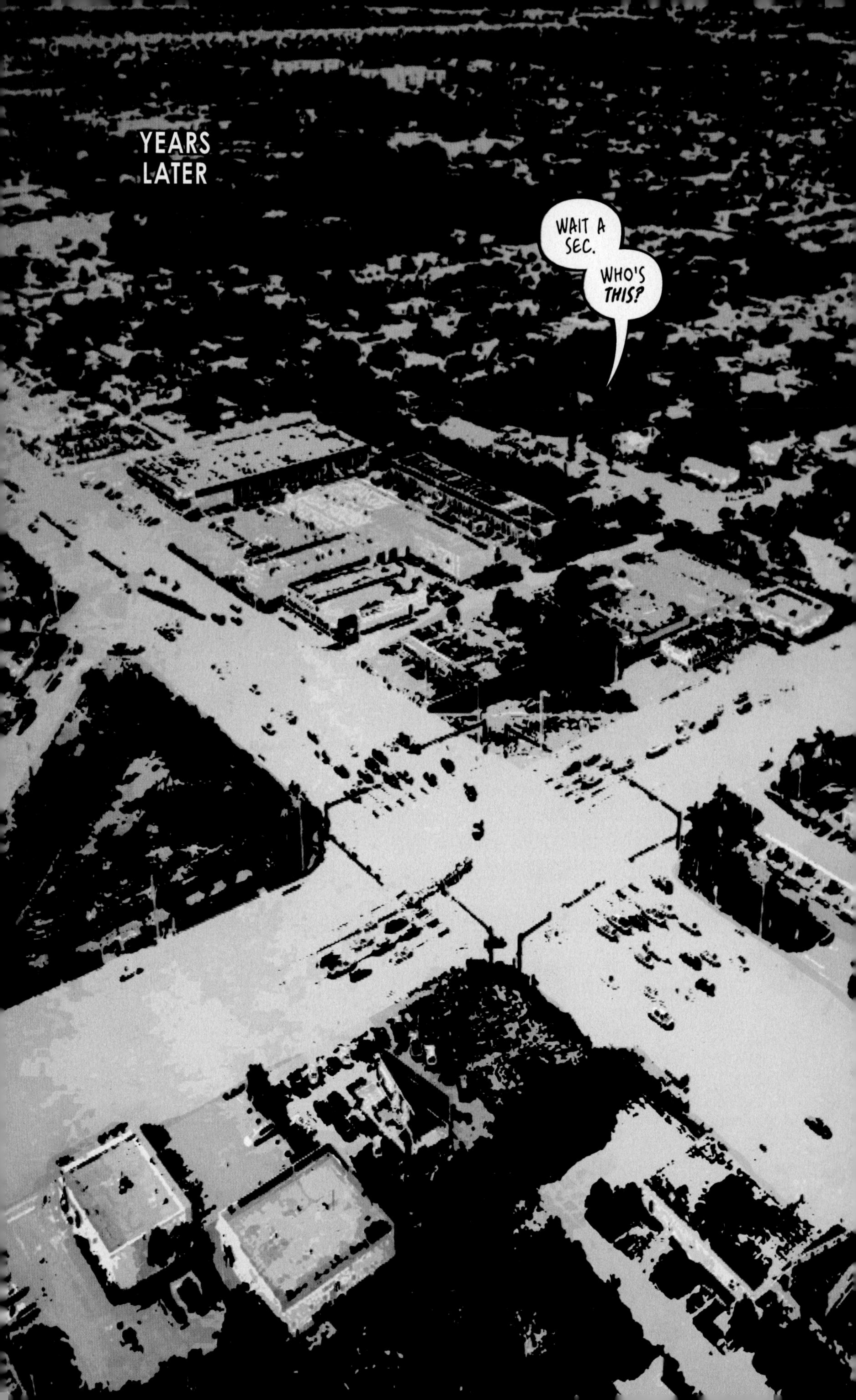
YEARS LATER
WAIT A SEC.
WHO'S THIS?

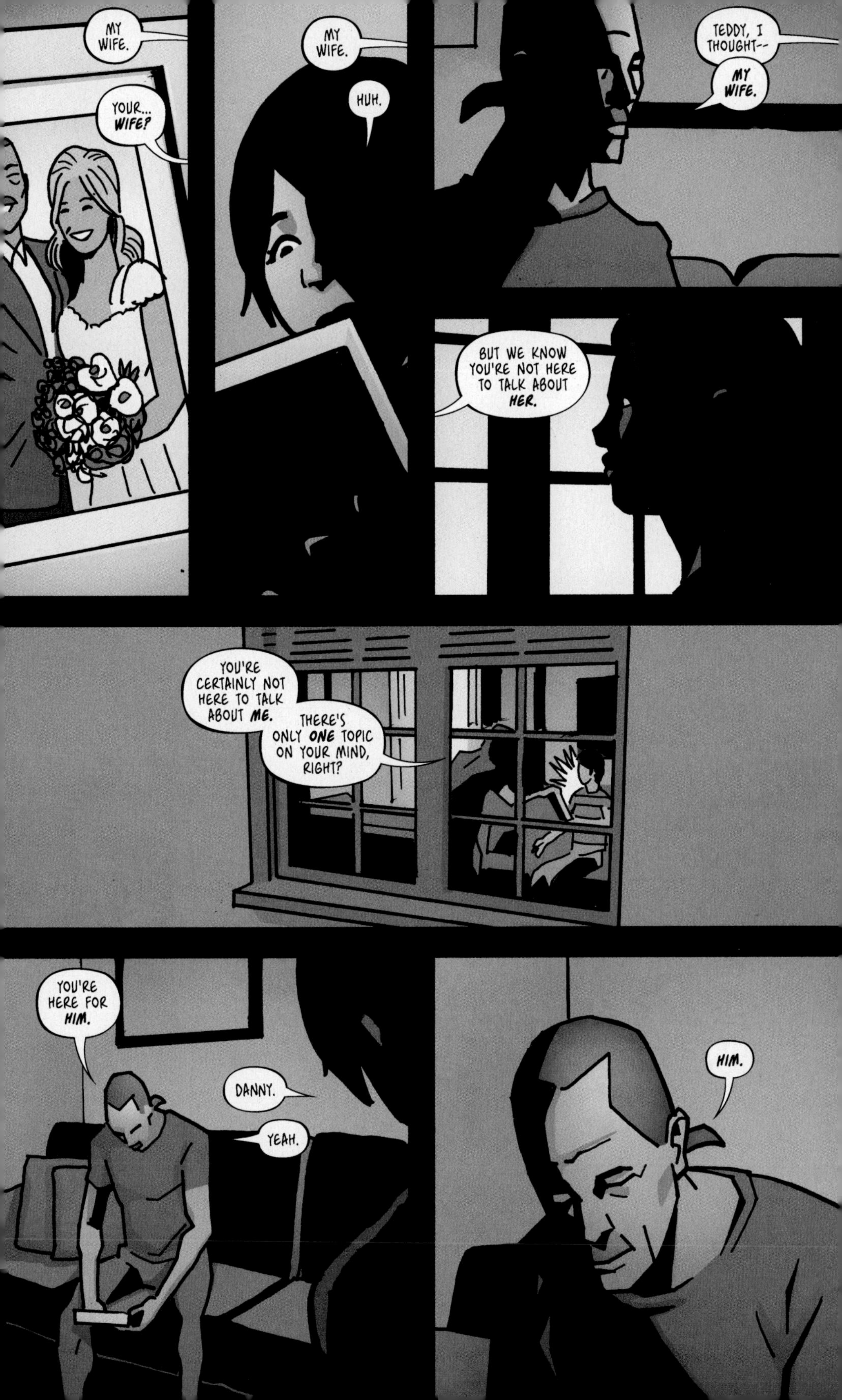
MY WIFE.
YOUR... WIFE?
MY WIFE.
HUH.
TEDDY, I THOUGHT--
MY WIFE.
BUT WE KNOW YOU'RE NOT HERE TO TALK ABOUT HER.
YOU'RE CERTAINLY NOT HERE TO TALK ABOUT ME.
THERE'S ONLY ONE TOPIC ON YOUR MIND, RIGHT?
YOU'RE HERE FOR HIM.
DANNY.
YEAH.
HIM.

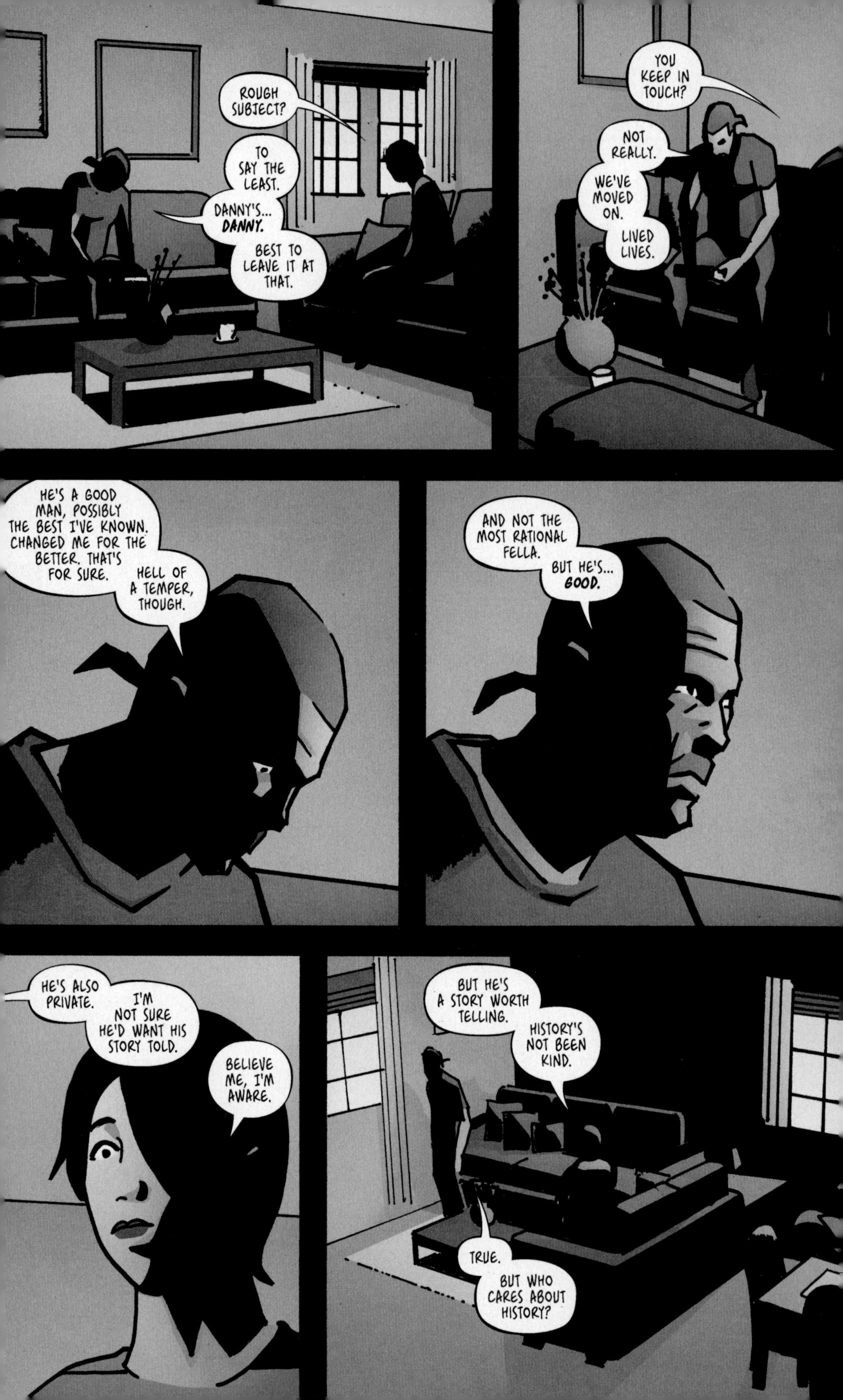
ROUGH SUBJECT?
TO SAY THE LEAST.
DANNY'S... DANNY.
BEST TO LEAVE IT AT THAT.
YOU KEEP IN TOUCH?
NOT REALLY.
WE'VE MOVED ON.
LIVED LIVES.
HE'S A GOOD MAN, POSSIBLY THE BEST I'VE KNOWN. CHANGED ME FOR THE BETTER. THAT'S FOR SURE.
HELL OF A TEMPER, THOUGH.
AND NOT THE MOST RATIONAL FELLA.
BUT HE'S... GOOD.
HE'S ALSO PRIVATE.
I'M NOT SURE HE'D WANT HIS STORY TOLD.
BELIEVE ME, I'M AWARE.
BUT HE'S A STORY WORTH TELLING.
HISTORY'S NOT BEEN KIND.
TRUE.
BUT WHO CARES ABOUT HISTORY?

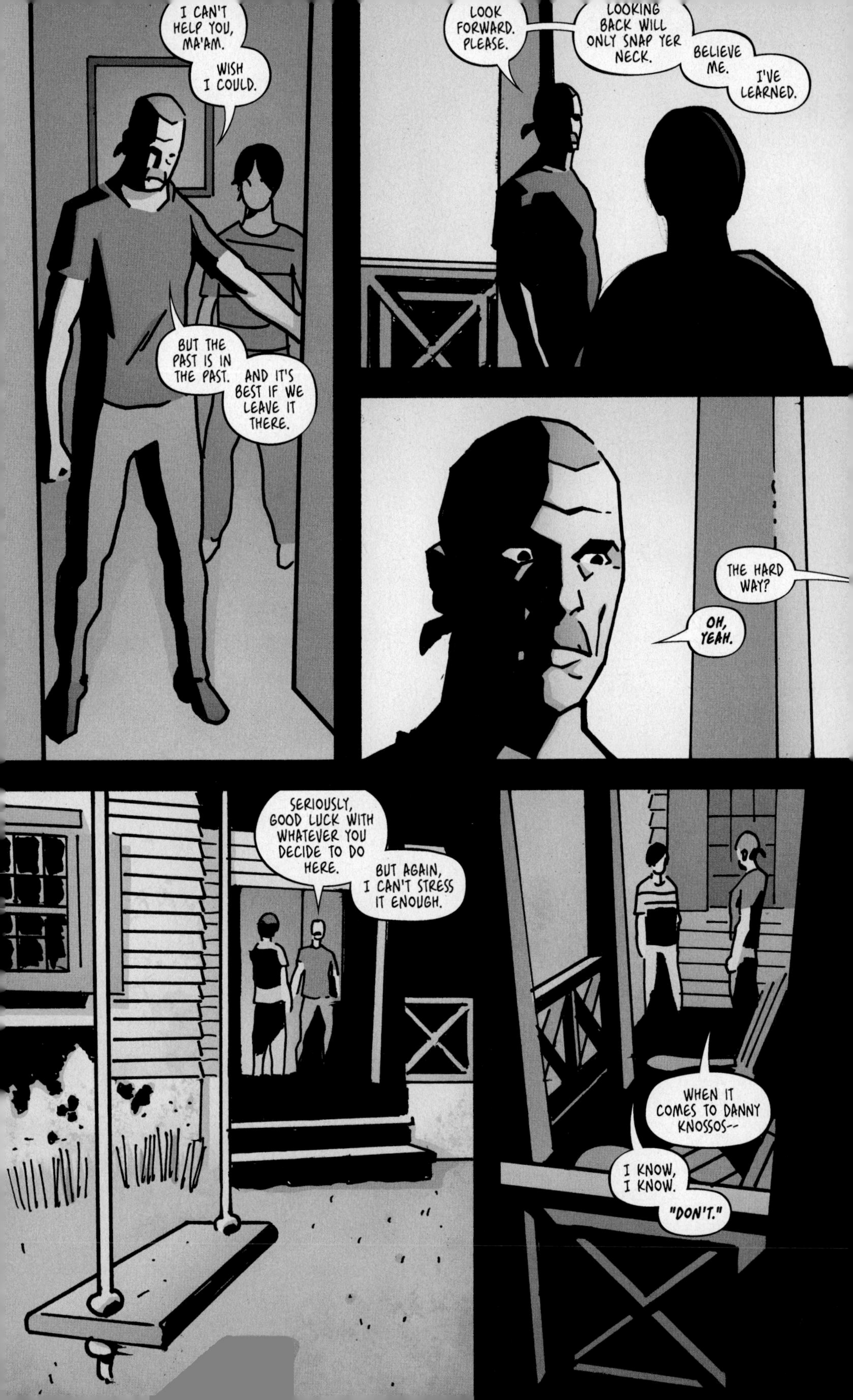
I CAN'T HELP YOU, MA'AM.
WISH I COULD.
BUT THE PAST IS IN THE PAST.
AND IT'S BEST IF WE LEAVE IT THERE.
LOOK FORWARD. PLEASE.
LOOKING BACK WILL ONLY SNAP YER NECK.
BELIEVE ME.
I'VE LEARNED.
THE HARD WAY?
OH, YEAH.
SERIOUSLY, GOOD LUCK WITH WHATEVER YOU DECIDE TO DO HERE.
BUT AGAIN, I CAN'T STRESS IT ENOUGH.
WHEN IT COMES TO DANNY KNOSSOS--
I KNOW, I KNOW.
"DON'T."

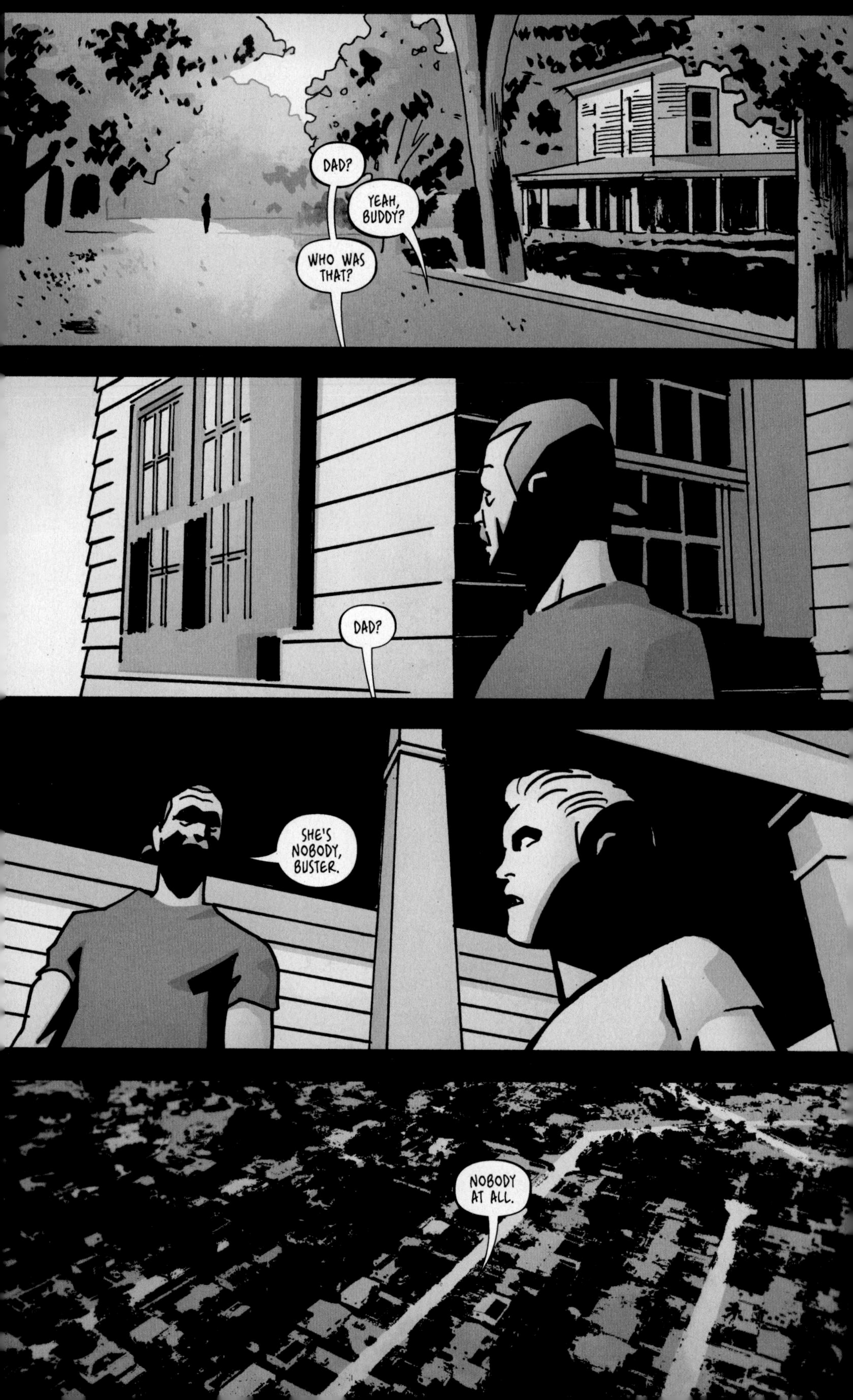
DAD?
YEAH, BUDDY?
WHO WAS THAT?
DAD?
SHE'S NOBODY, BUSTER.
NOBODY AT ALL.

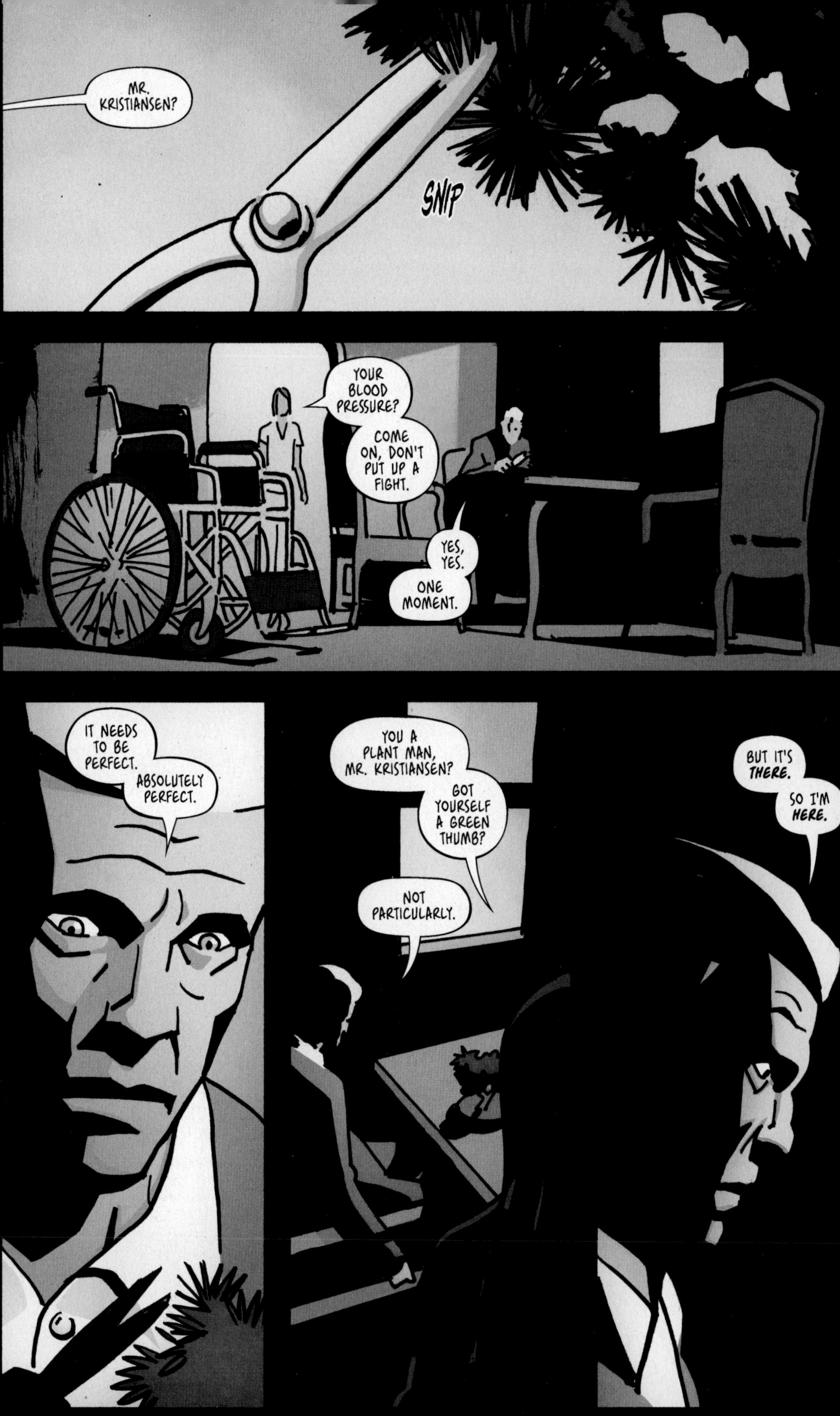
MR. KRISTIANSEN?
SNIP
YOUR BLOOD PRESSURE?
COME ON, DON'T PUT UP A FIGHT.
YES, YES.
ONE MOMENT.
IT NEEDS TO BE PERFECT.
ABSOLUTELY PERFECT.
YOU A PLANT MAN, MR. KRISTIANSEN?
GOT YOURSELF A GREEN THUMB?
NOT PARTICULARLY.
BUT IT'S *THERE.*
SO I'M *HERE.*

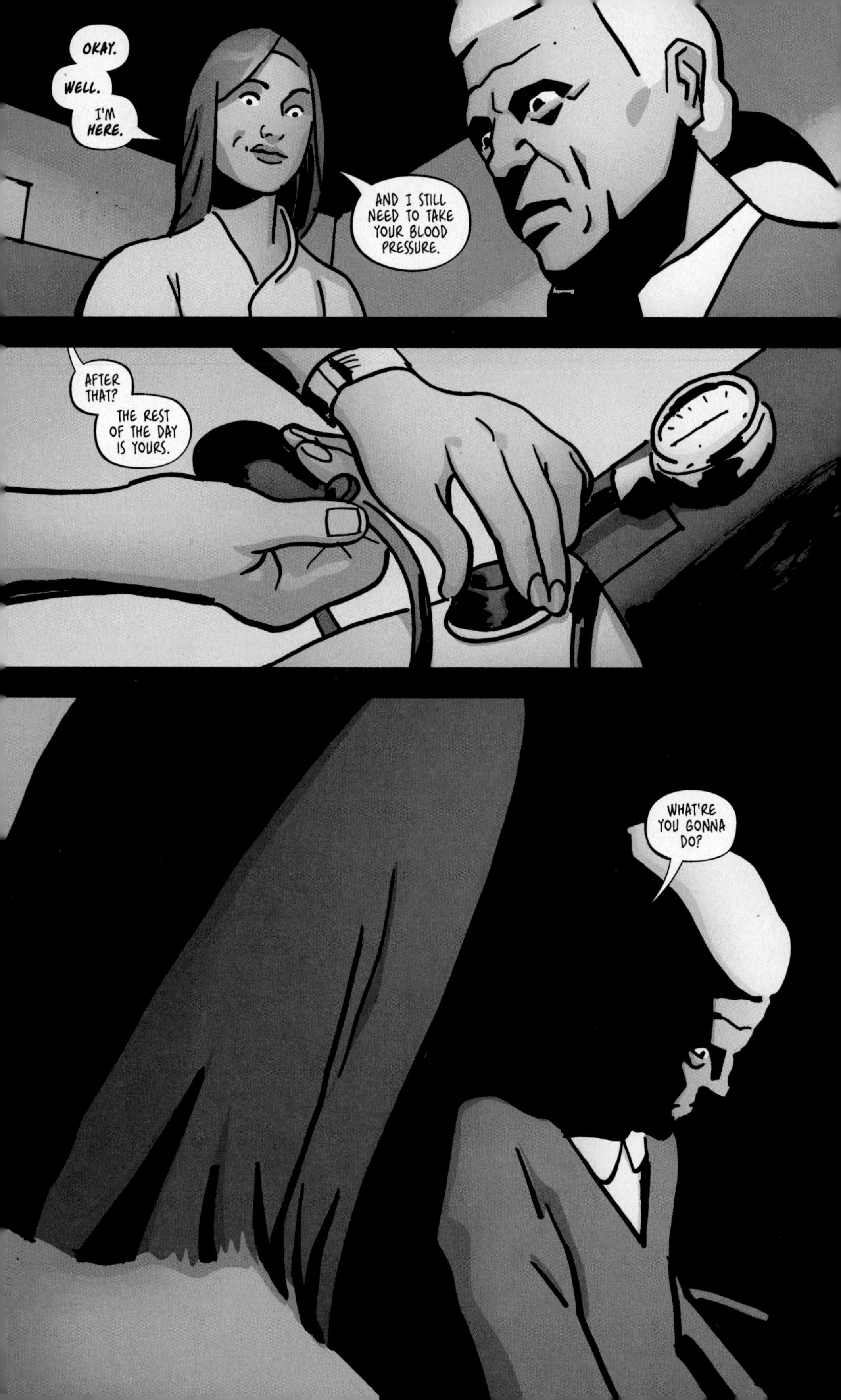
OKAY.
WELL.
I'M HERE.
AND I STILL NEED TO TAKE YOUR BLOOD PRESSURE.
AFTER THAT?
THE REST OF THE DAY IS YOURS.
WHAT'RE YOU GONNA DO?

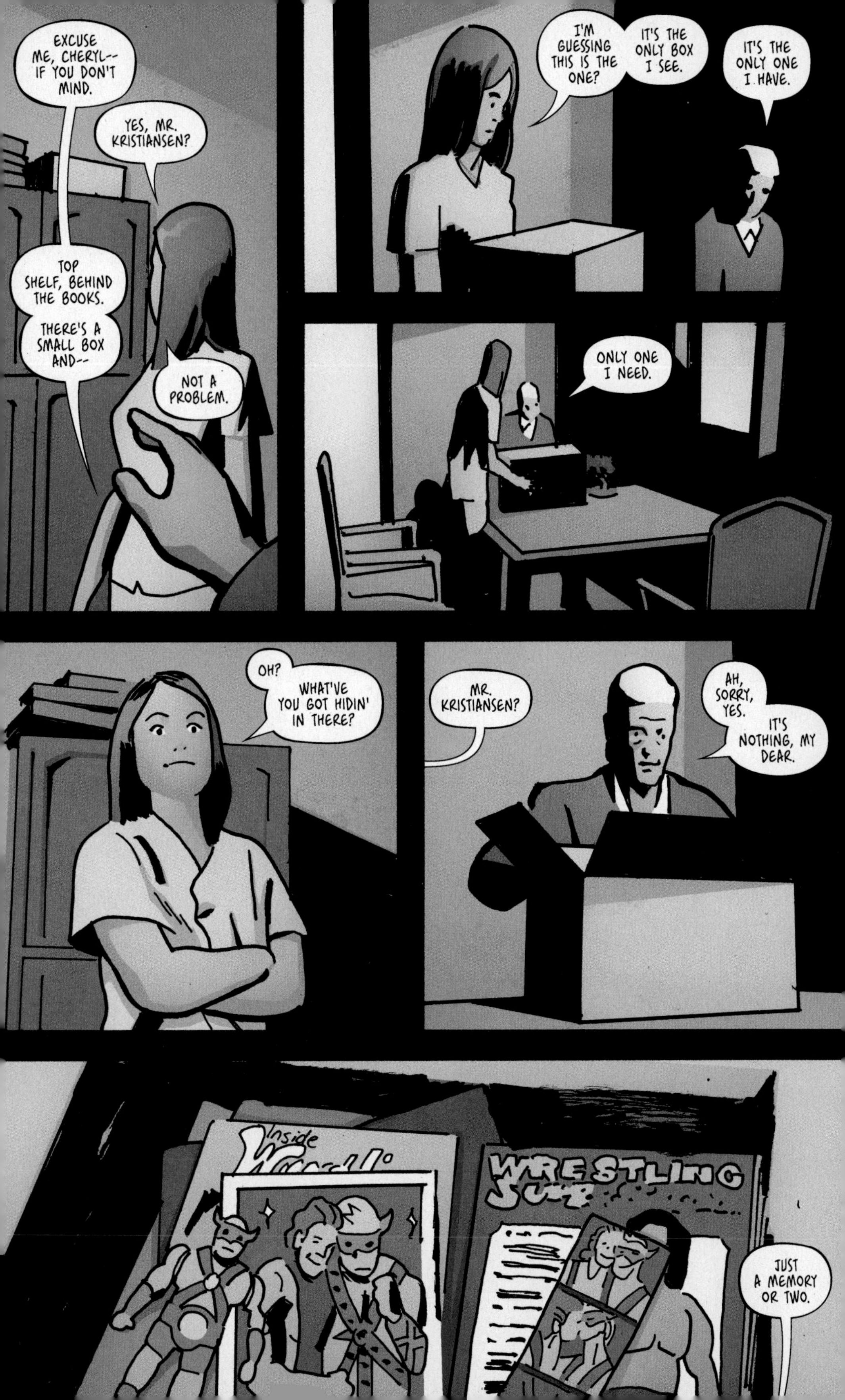
EXCUSE ME, CHERYL-- IF YOU DON'T MIND.
YES, MR. KRISTIANSEN?
TOP SHELF, BEHIND THE BOOKS.
THERE'S A SMALL BOX AND--
NOT A PROBLEM.
I'M GUESSING THIS IS THE ONE?
IT'S THE ONLY BOX I SEE.
IT'S THE ONLY ONE I HAVE.
ONLY ONE I NEED.
OH?
WHAT'VE YOU GOT HIDIN' IN THERE?
MR. KRISTIANSEN?
AH, SORRY, YES.
IT'S NOTHING, MY DEAR.
Inside
WRESTLING
JUST A MEMORY OR TWO.

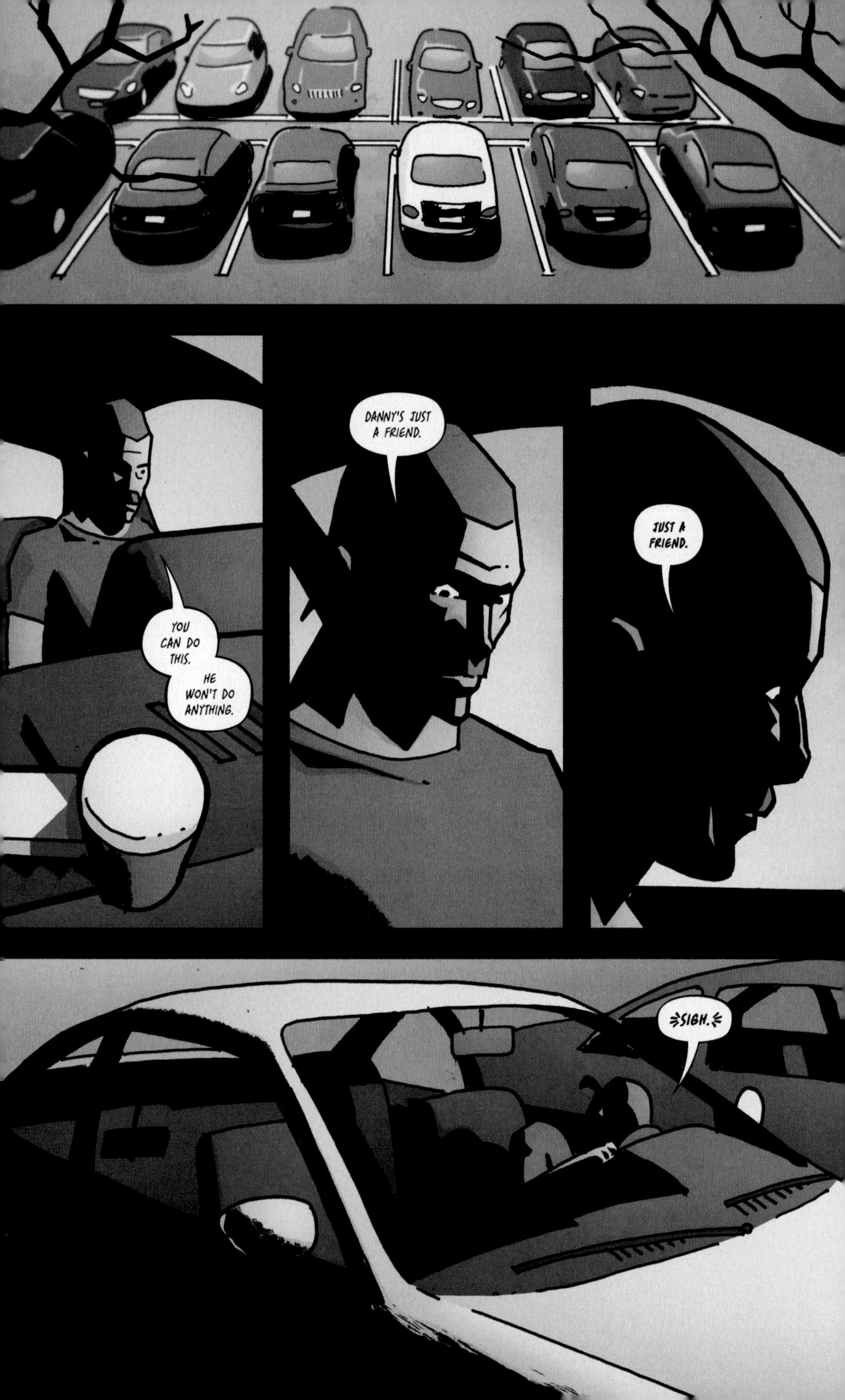
YOU CAN DO THIS.
HE WON'T DO ANYTHING.
DANNY'S JUST A FRIEND.
JUST A FRIEND.
SIGH.

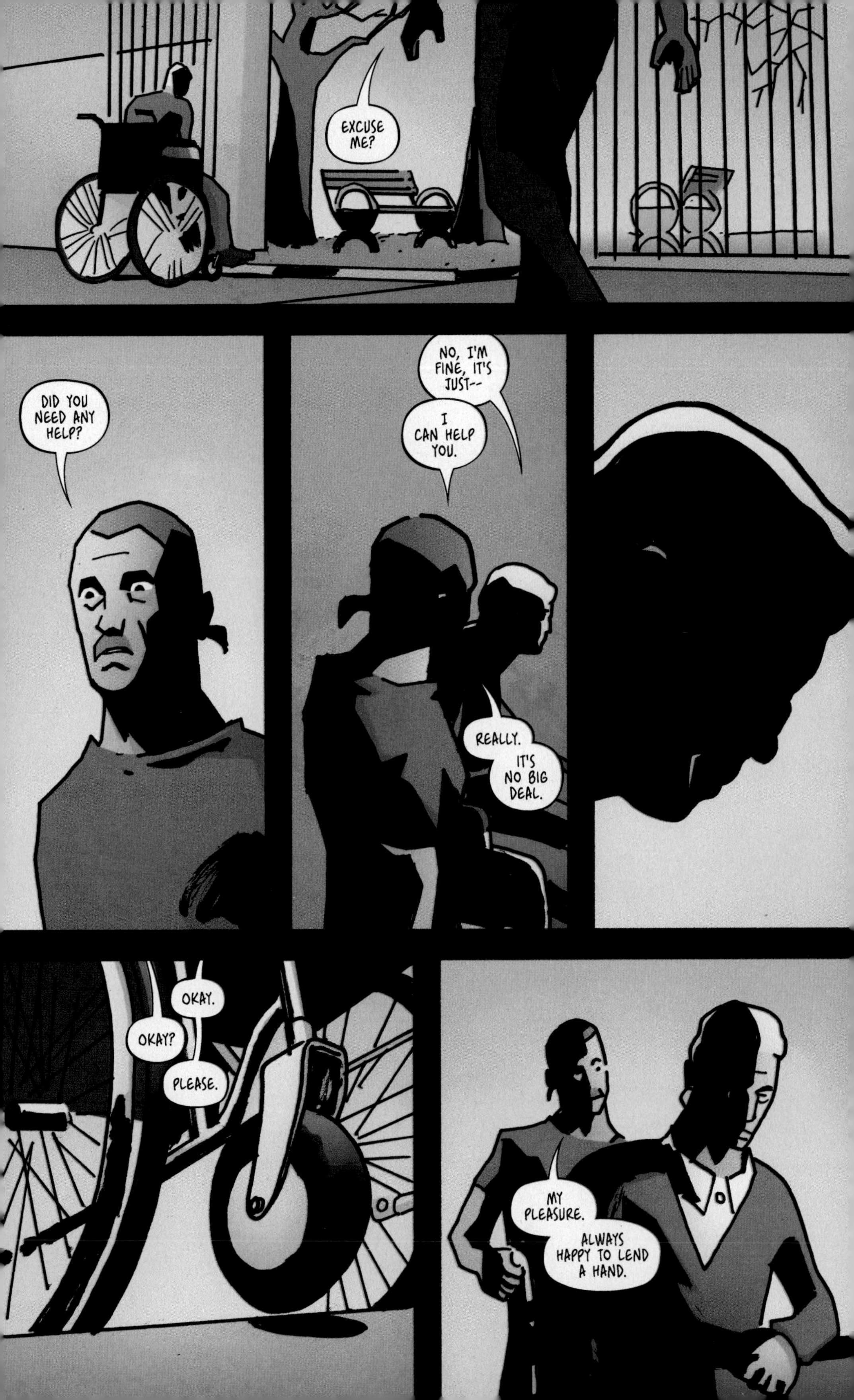
EXCUSE ME?
DID YOU NEED ANY HELP?
NO, I'M FINE, IT'S JUST--
I CAN HELP YOU.
REALLY.
IT'S NO BIG DEAL.
OKAY?
OKAY.
PLEASE.
MY PLEASURE.
ALWAYS HAPPY TO LEND A HAND.

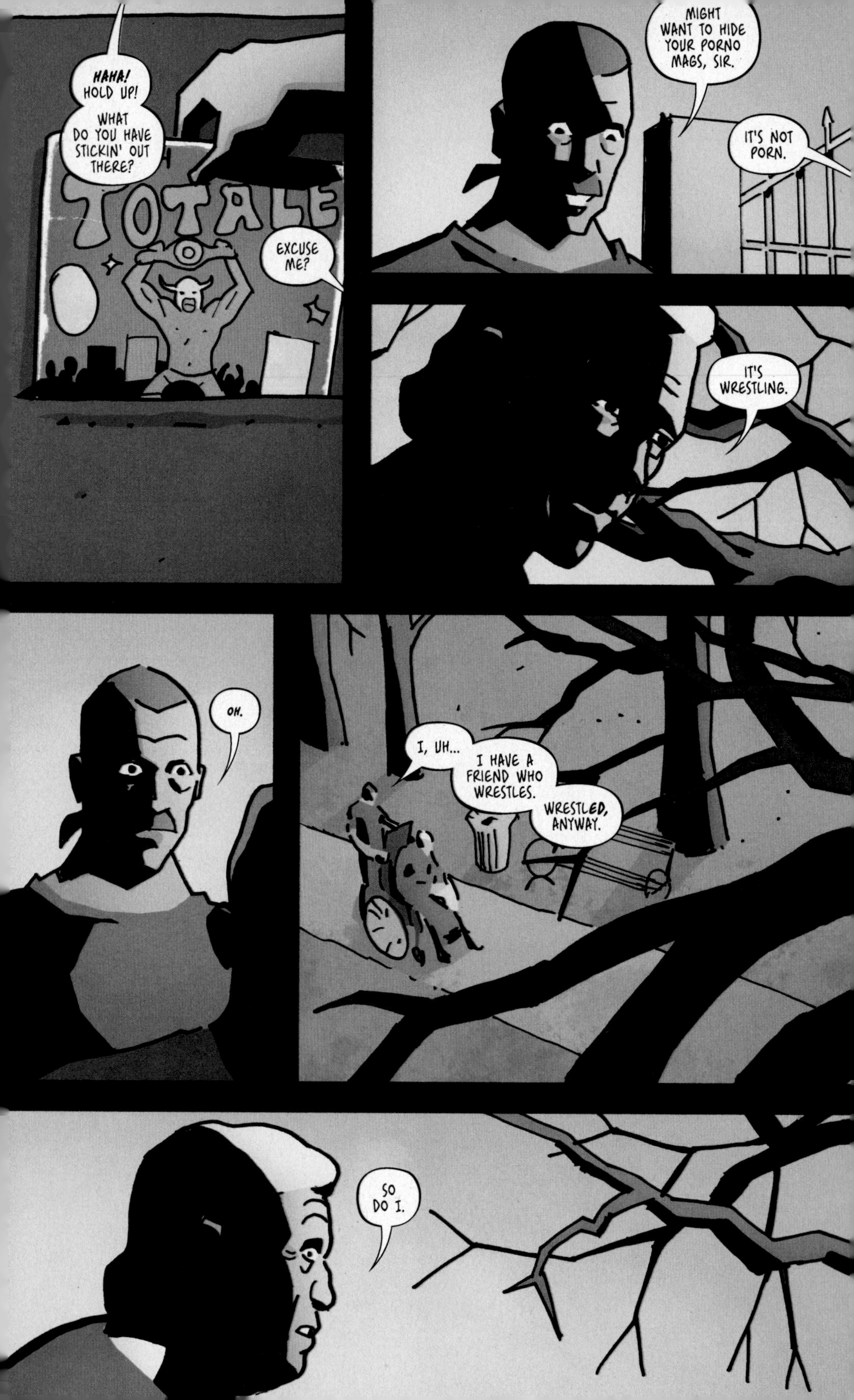
HAHA! HOLD UP!
WHAT DO YOU HAVE STICKIN' OUT THERE?
TOTALE
EXCUSE ME?
MIGHT WANT TO HIDE YOUR PORNO MAGS, SIR.
IT'S NOT PORN.
IT'S WRESTLING.
OH.
I, UH...
I HAVE A FRIEND WHO WRESTLES.
WRESTLED, ANYWAY.
SO DO I.

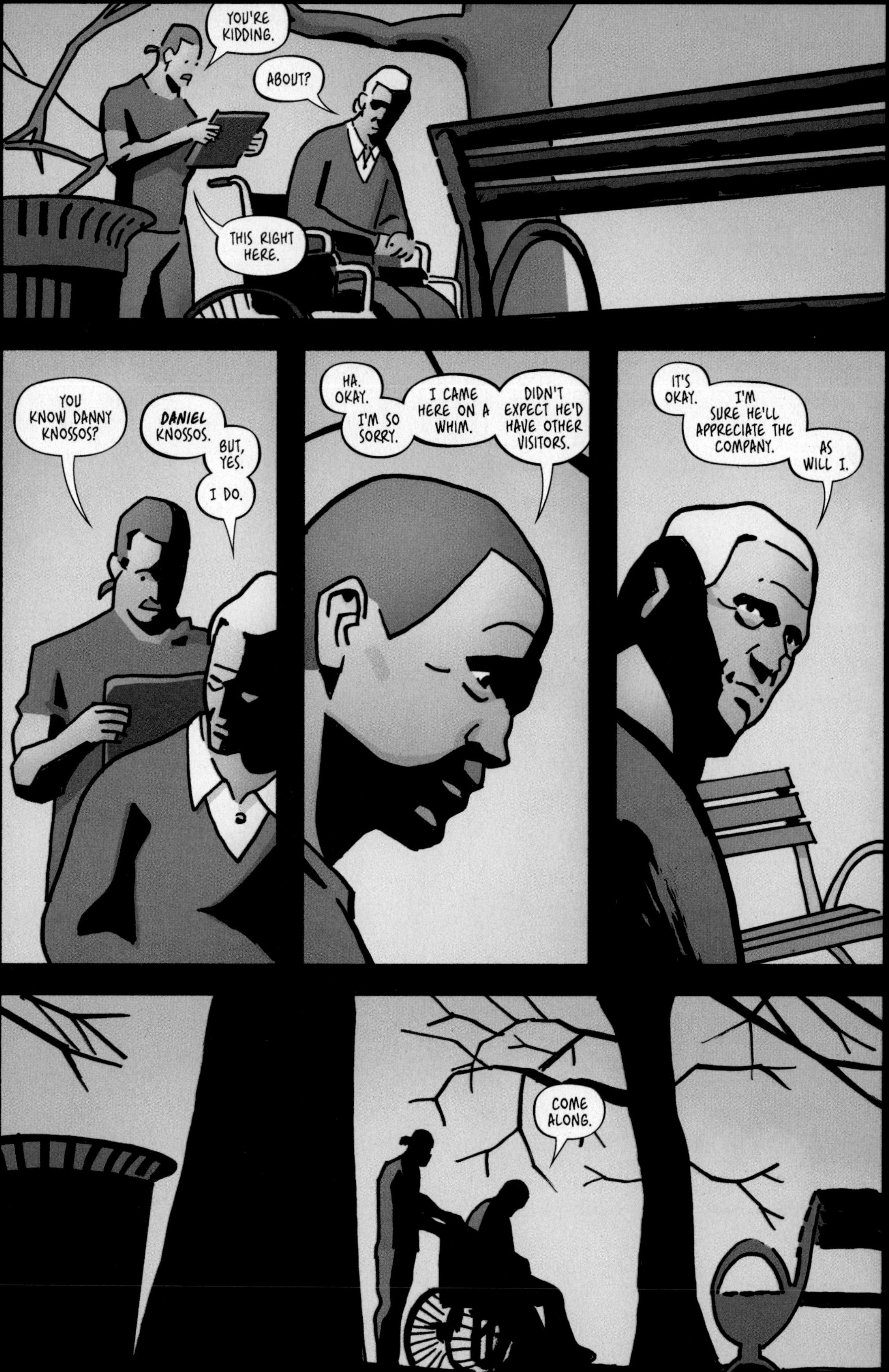
YOU'RE KIDDING.
ABOUT?
THIS RIGHT HERE.
YOU KNOW DANNY KNOSSOS?
DANIEL KNOSSOS.
BUT, YES.
I DO.
HA. OKAY.
I'M SO SORRY.
I CAME HERE ON A WHIM.
DIDN'T EXPECT HE'D HAVE OTHER VISITORS.
IT'S OKAY.
I'M SURE HE'LL APPRECIATE THE COMPANY.
AS WILL I.
COME ALONG.

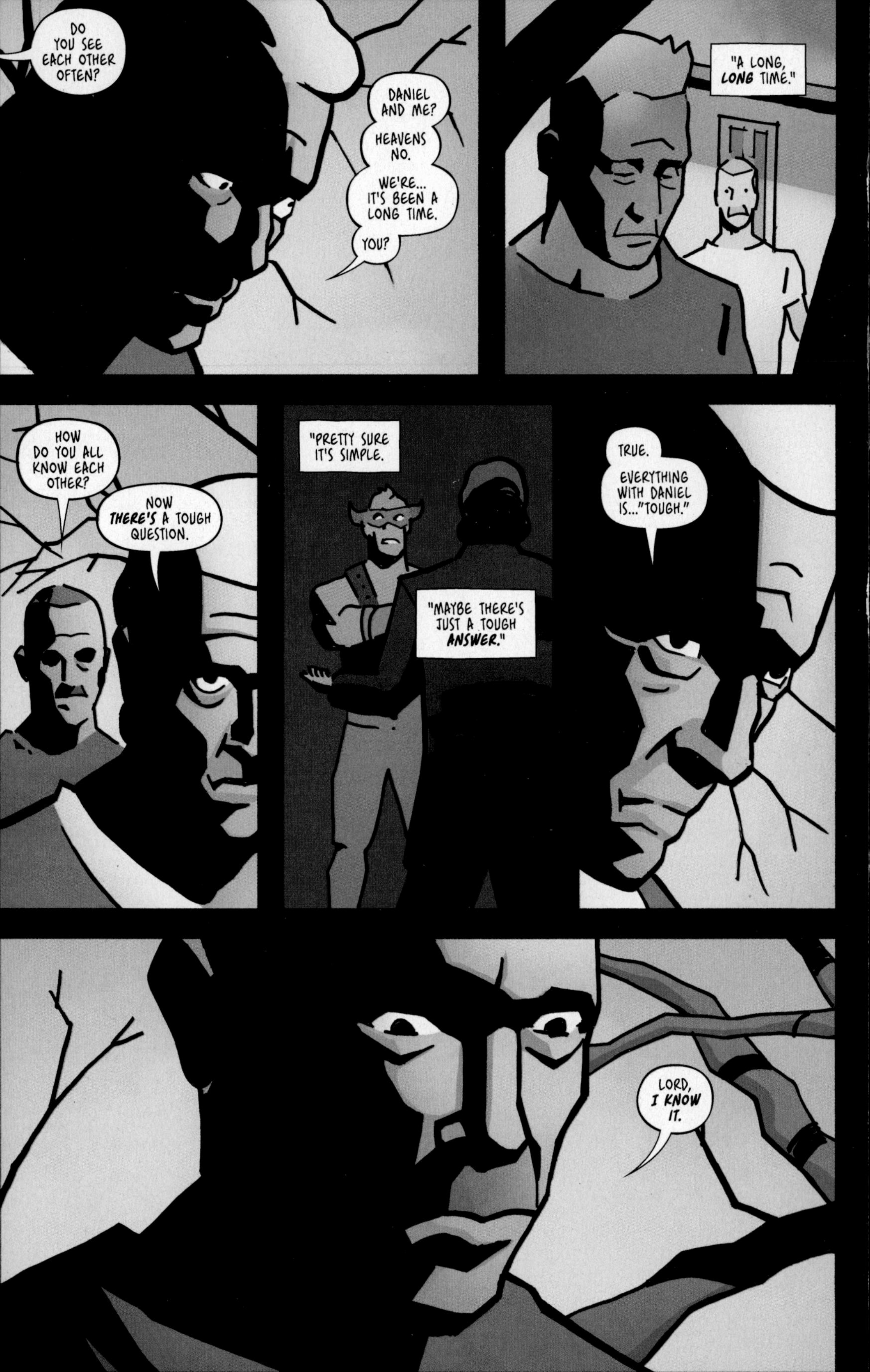
DO YOU SEE EACH OTHER OFTEN?
DANIEL AND ME?
HEAVENS NO.
WE'RE... IT'S BEEN A LONG TIME.
YOU?
"A LONG, **LONG** TIME."
HOW DO YOU ALL KNOW EACH OTHER?
NOW **THERE'S** A TOUGH QUESTION.
"PRETTY SURE IT'S SIMPLE.
"MAYBE THERE'S JUST A TOUGH **ANSWER.**"
TRUE.
EVERYTHING WITH DANIEL IS..."TOUGH."
LORD, **I KNOW IT.**

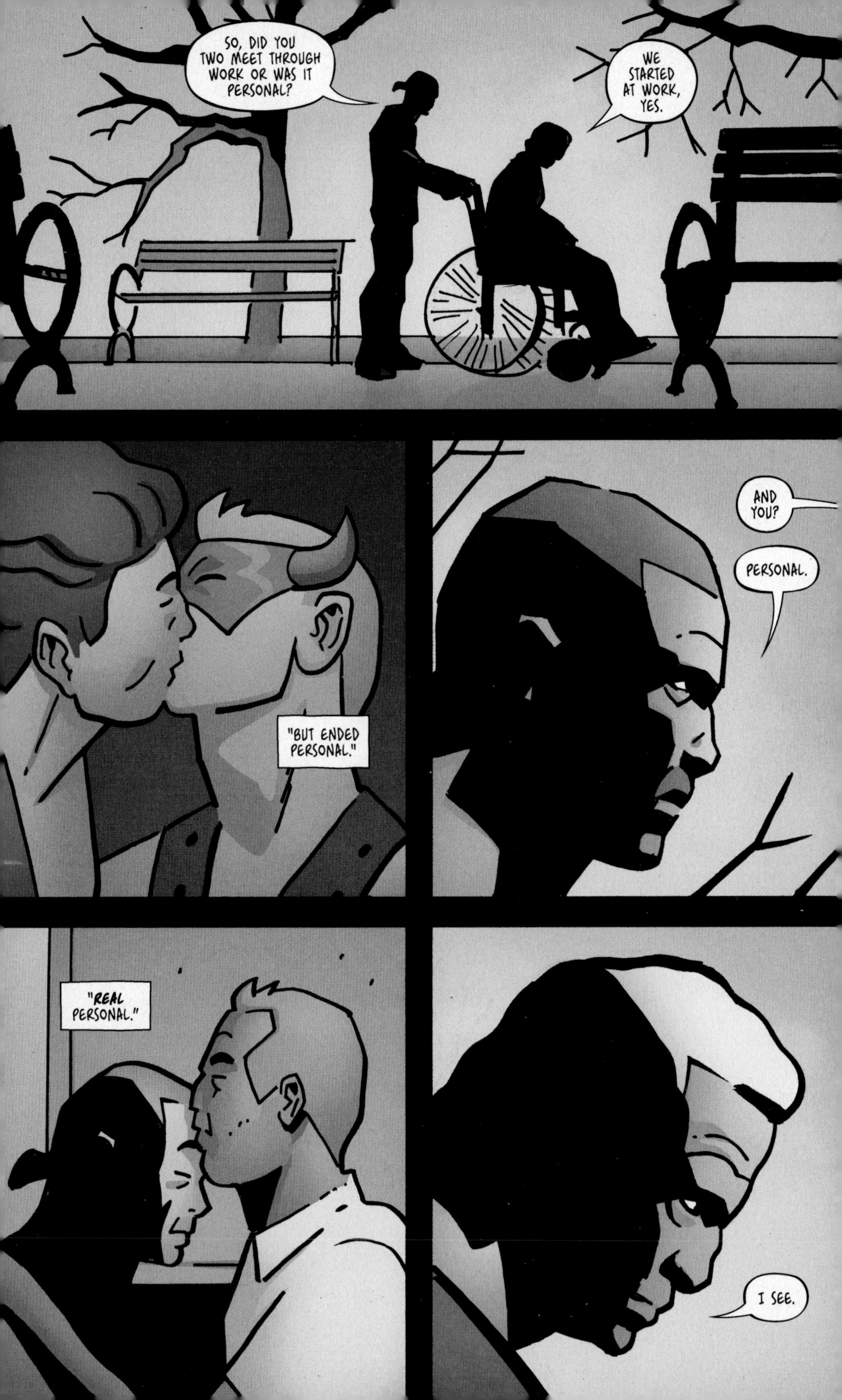
SO, DID YOU TWO MEET THROUGH WORK OR WAS IT PERSONAL?
WE STARTED AT WORK, YES.
"BUT ENDED PERSONAL."
AND YOU?
PERSONAL.
"REAL PERSONAL."
I SEE.

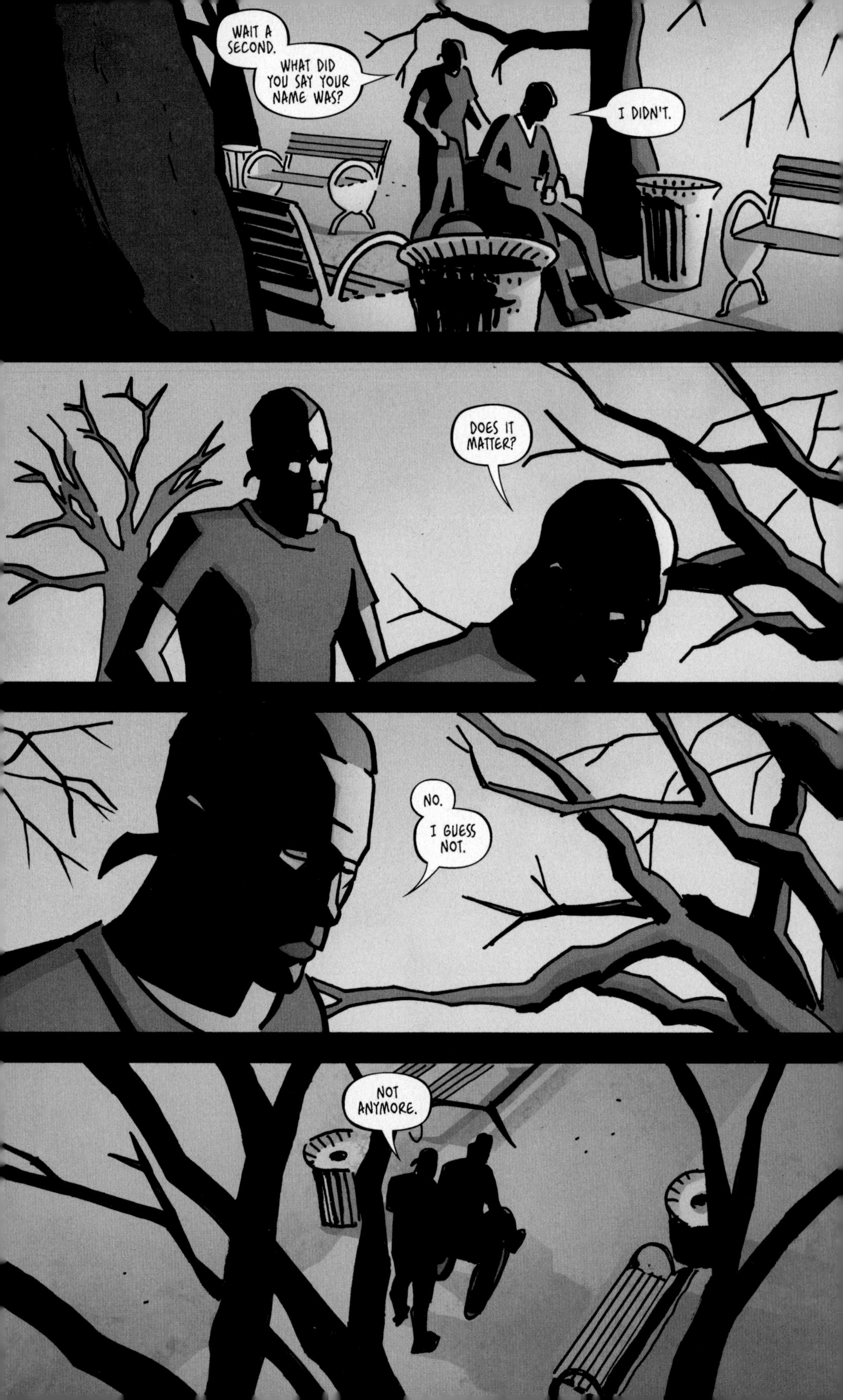
WAIT A SECOND.
WHAT DID YOU SAY YOUR NAME WAS?
I DIDN'T.
DOES IT MATTER?
NO.
I GUESS NOT.
NOT ANYMORE.

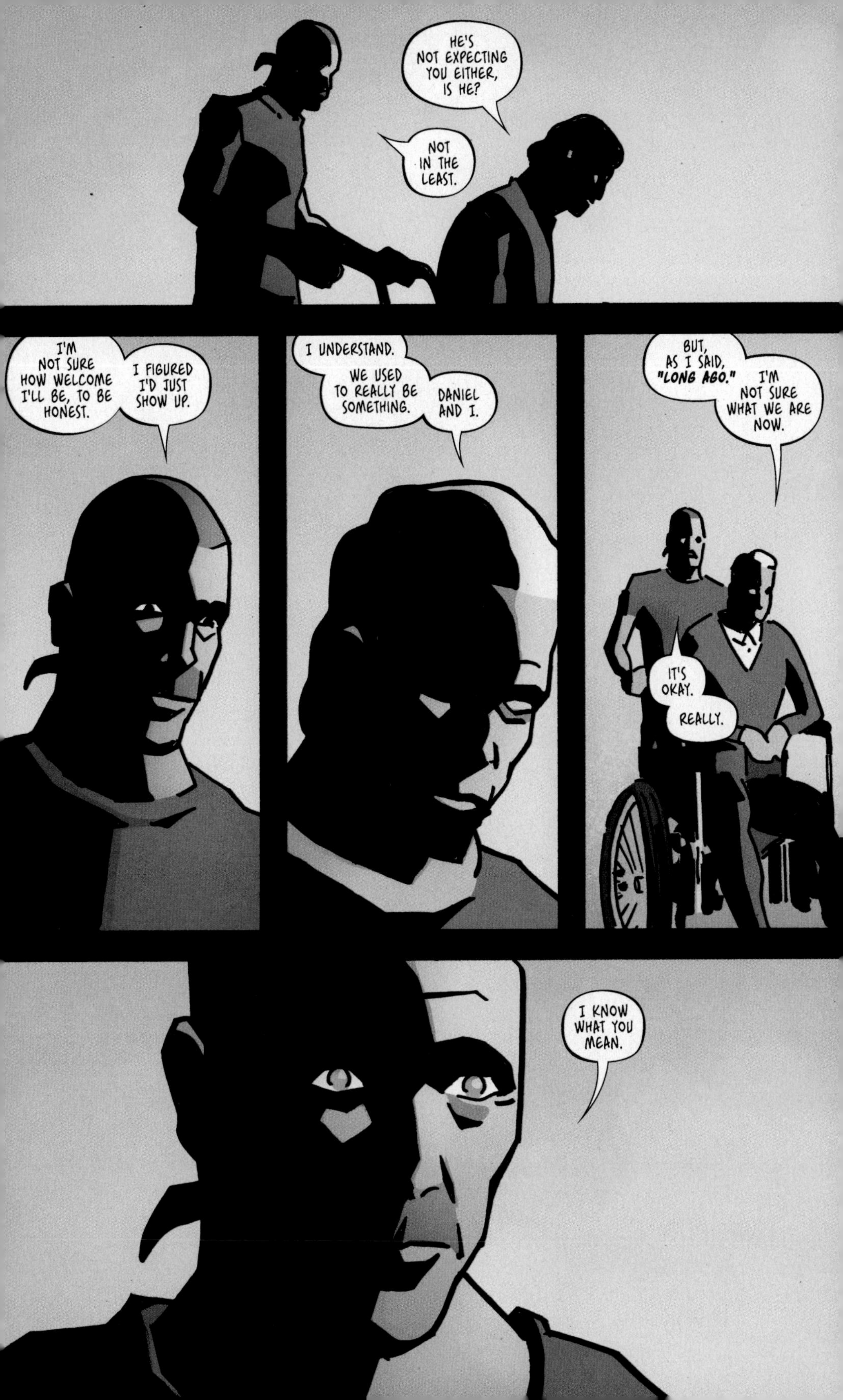
HE'S NOT EXPECTING YOU EITHER, IS HE?
NOT IN THE LEAST.
I'M NOT SURE HOW WELCOME I'LL BE, TO BE HONEST.
I FIGURED I'D JUST SHOW UP.
I UNDERSTAND.
WE USED TO REALLY BE SOMETHING.
DANIEL AND I.
BUT, AS I SAID, "LONG AGO."
I'M NOT SURE WHAT WE ARE NOW.
IT'S OKAY.
REALLY.
I KNOW WHAT YOU MEAN.

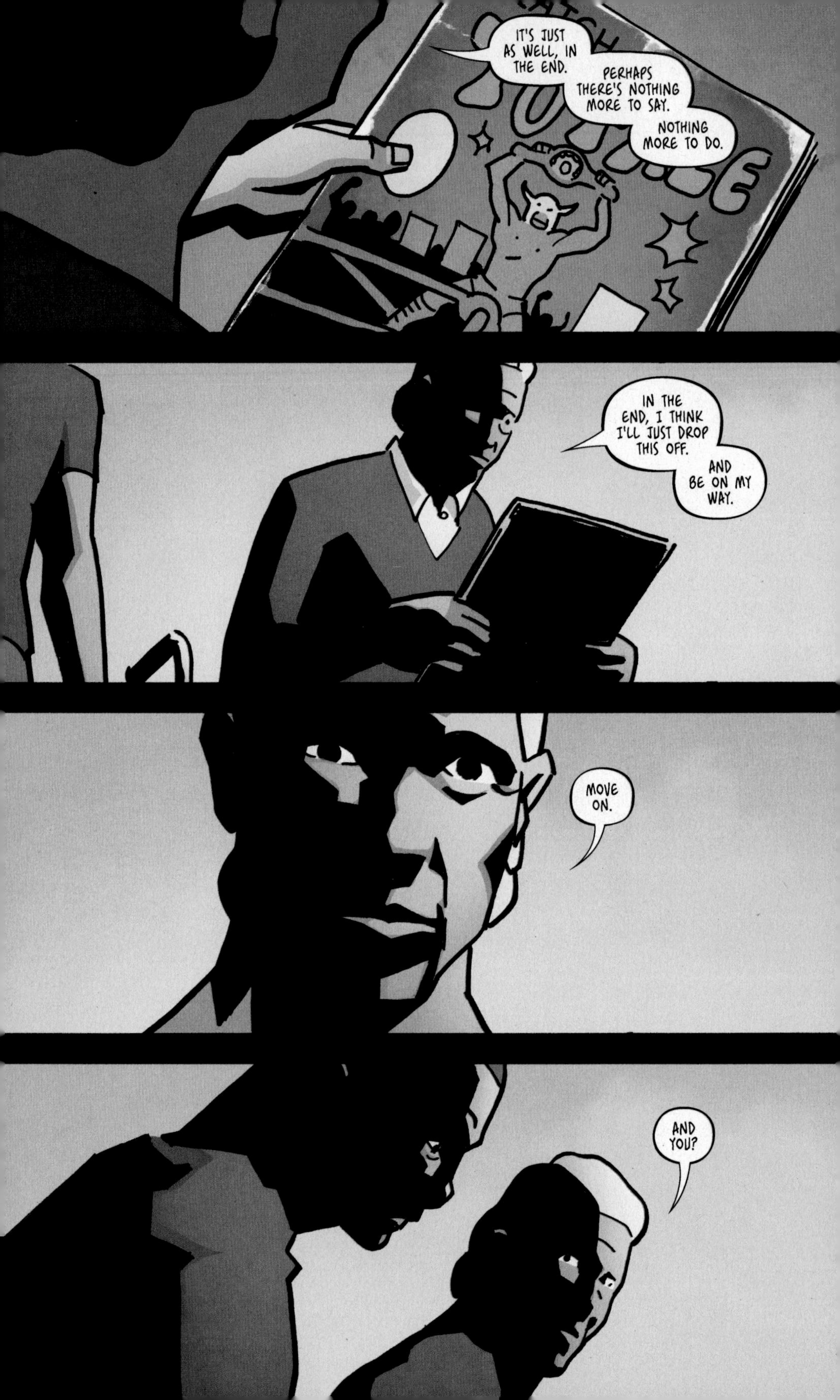
IT'S JUST AS WELL, IN THE END.
PERHAPS THERE'S NOTHING MORE TO SAY.
NOTHING MORE TO DO.
IN THE END, I THINK I'LL JUST DROP THIS OFF.
AND BE ON MY WAY.
MOVE ON.
AND YOU?

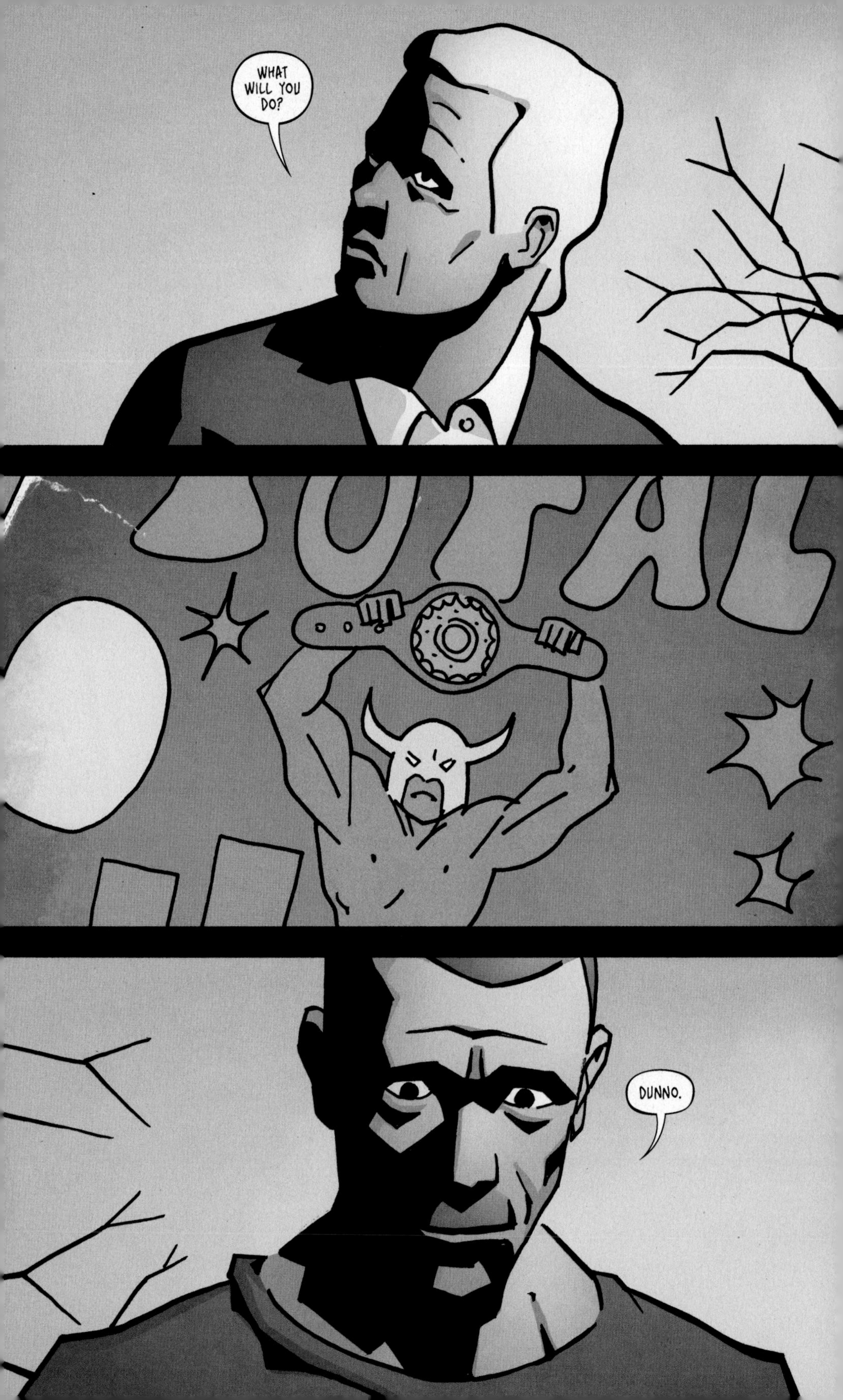
WHAT WILL YOU DO?
DUNNO.

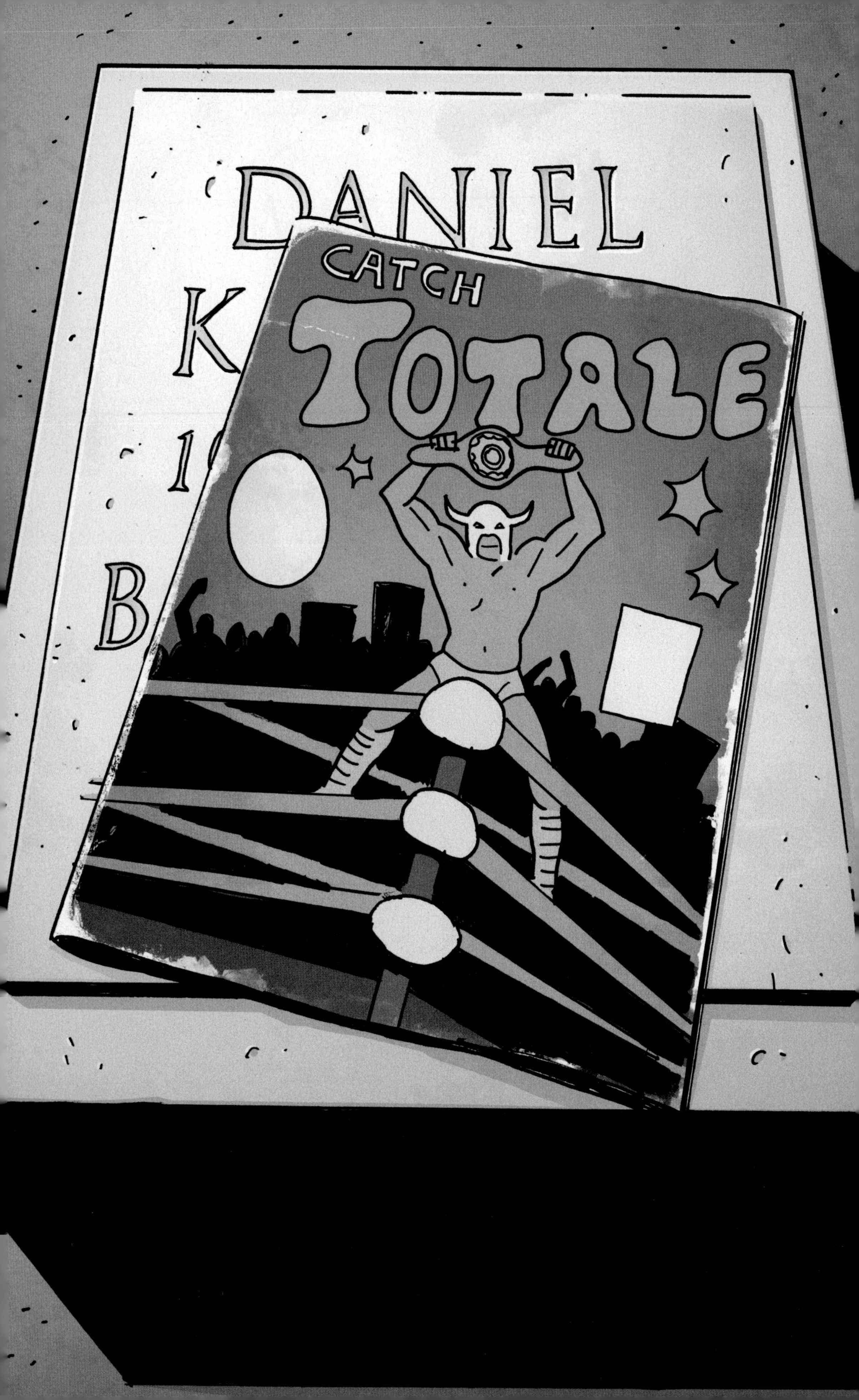
DANIEL
CATCH
TOTALE

THE END.

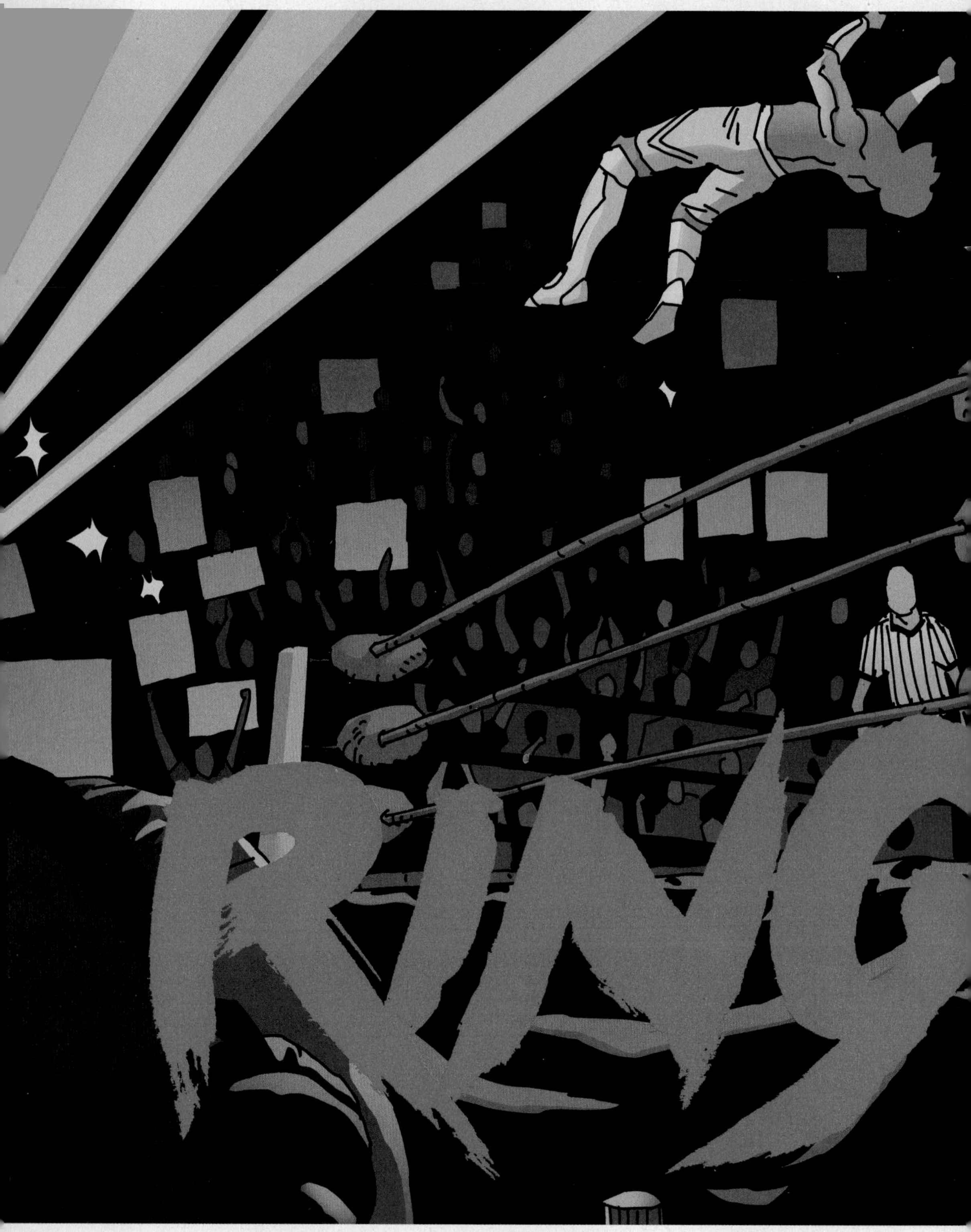
RING

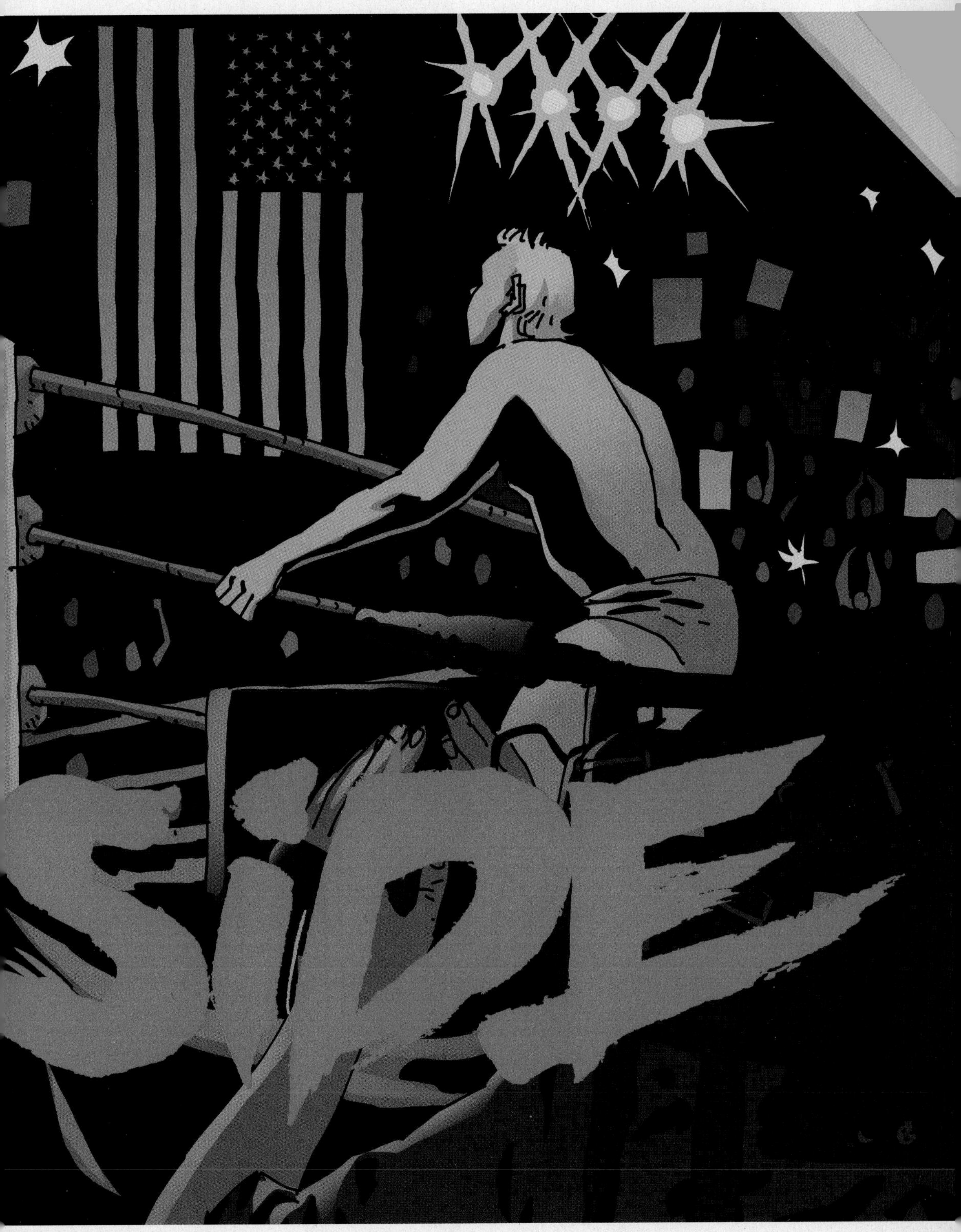
SIDE

PROCESS GALLERY

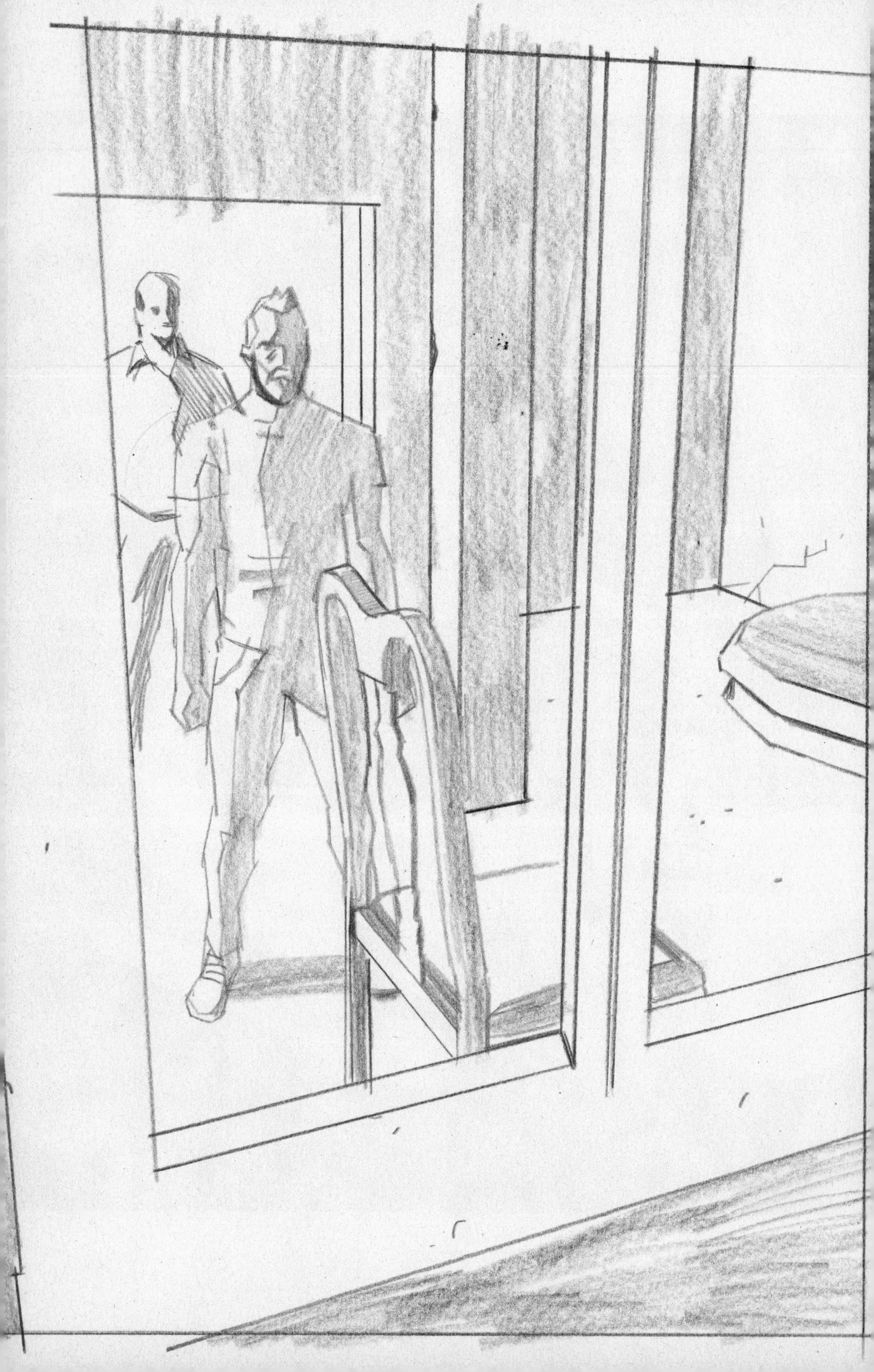

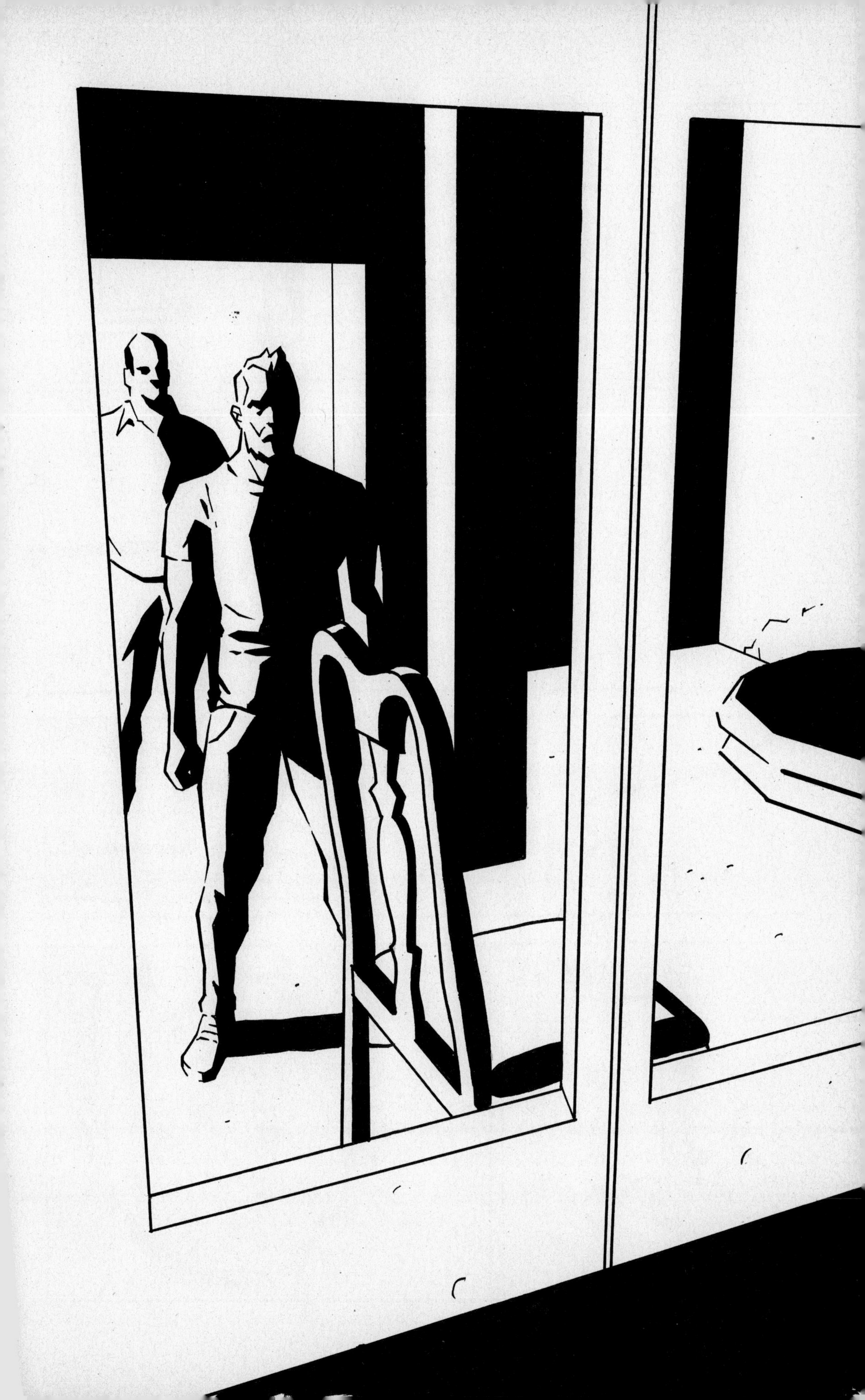

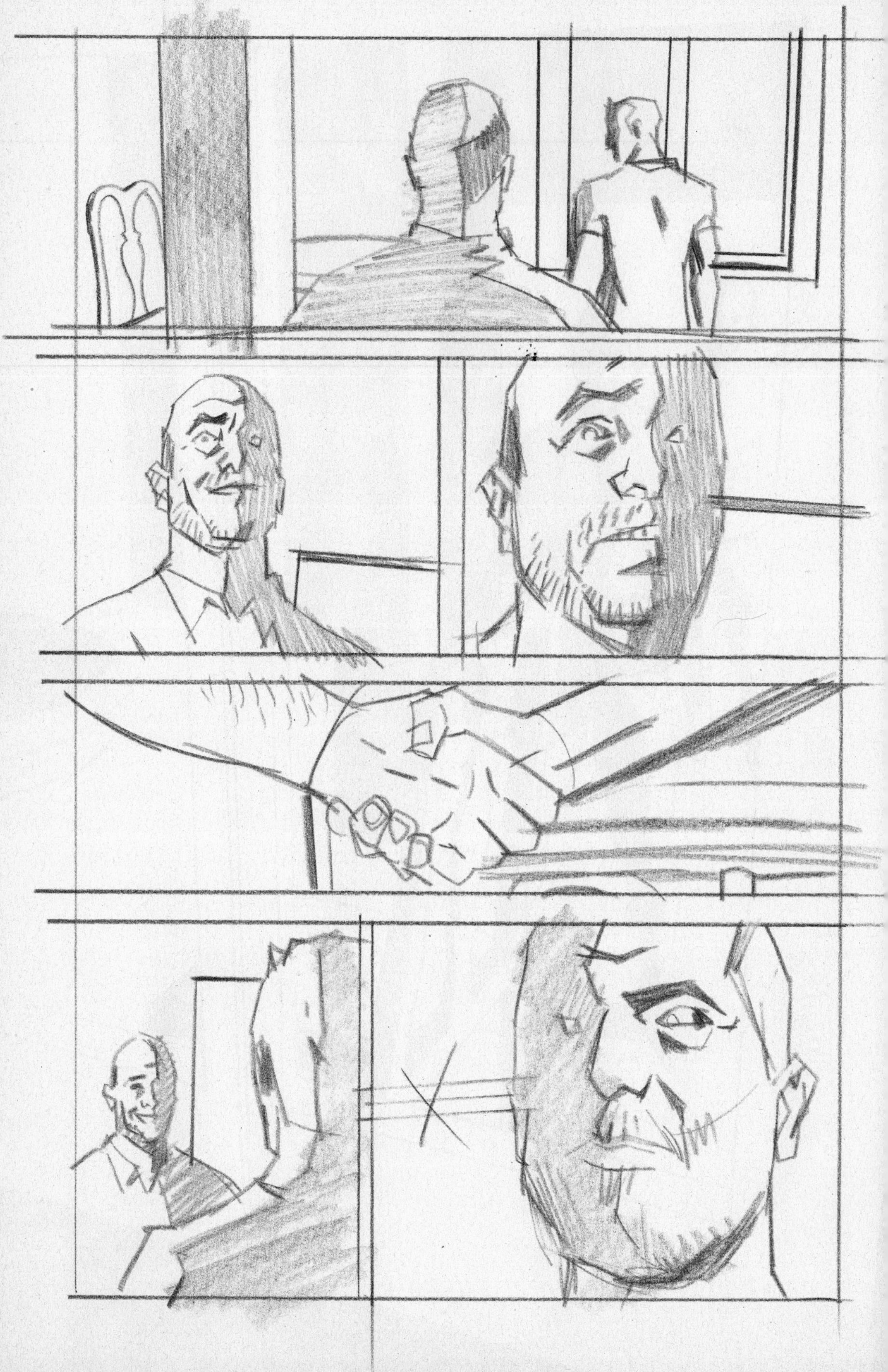

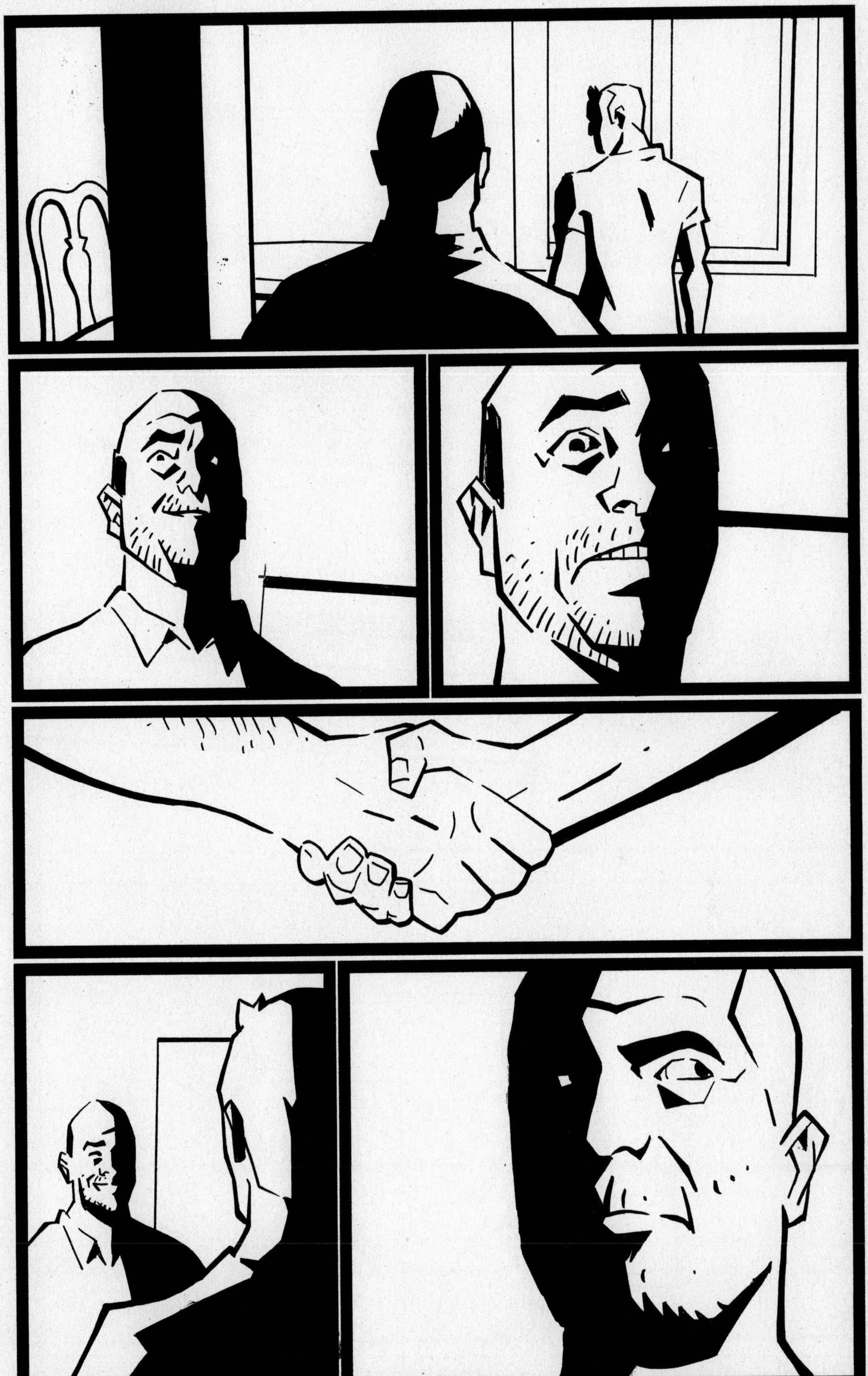

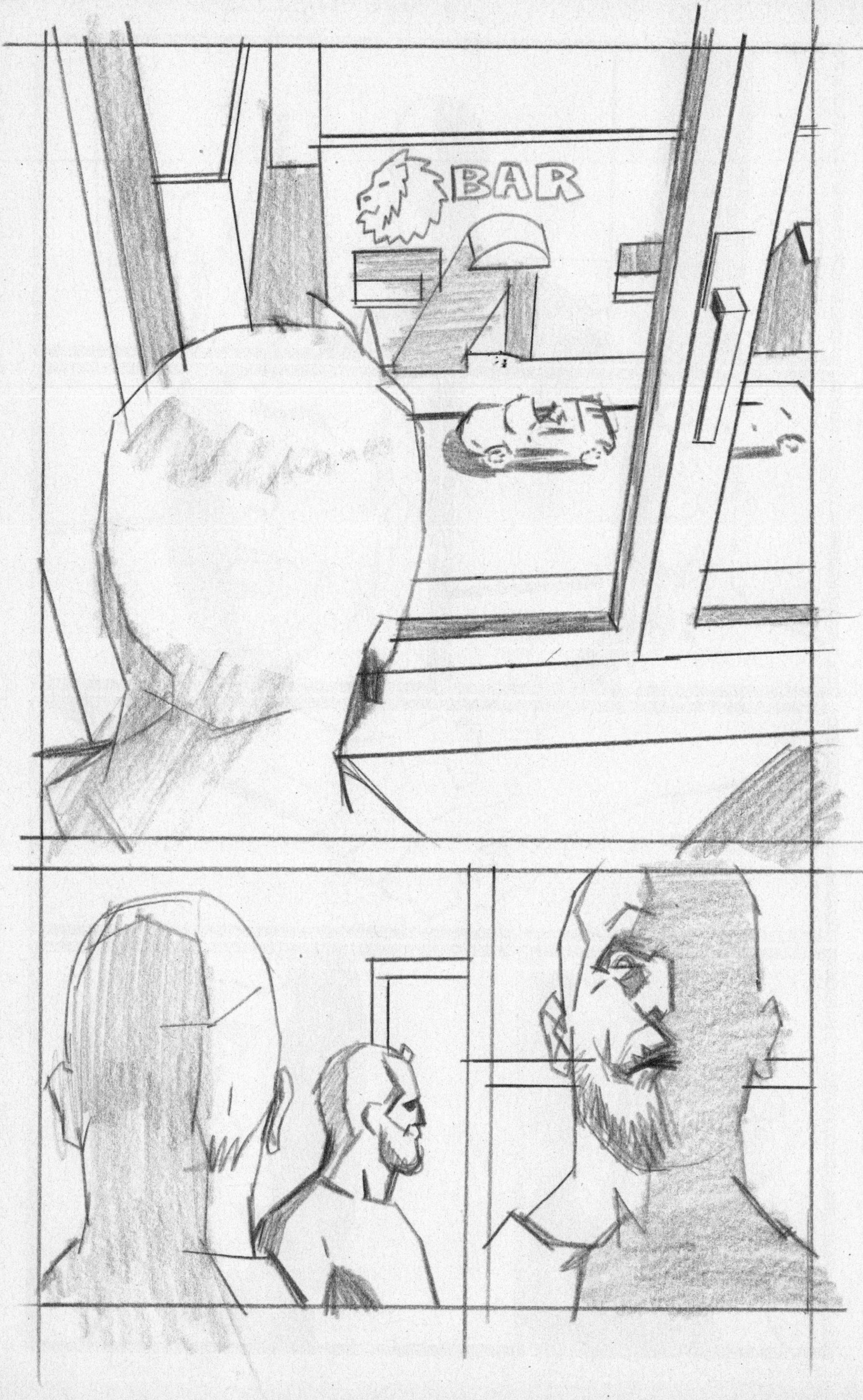
BAR

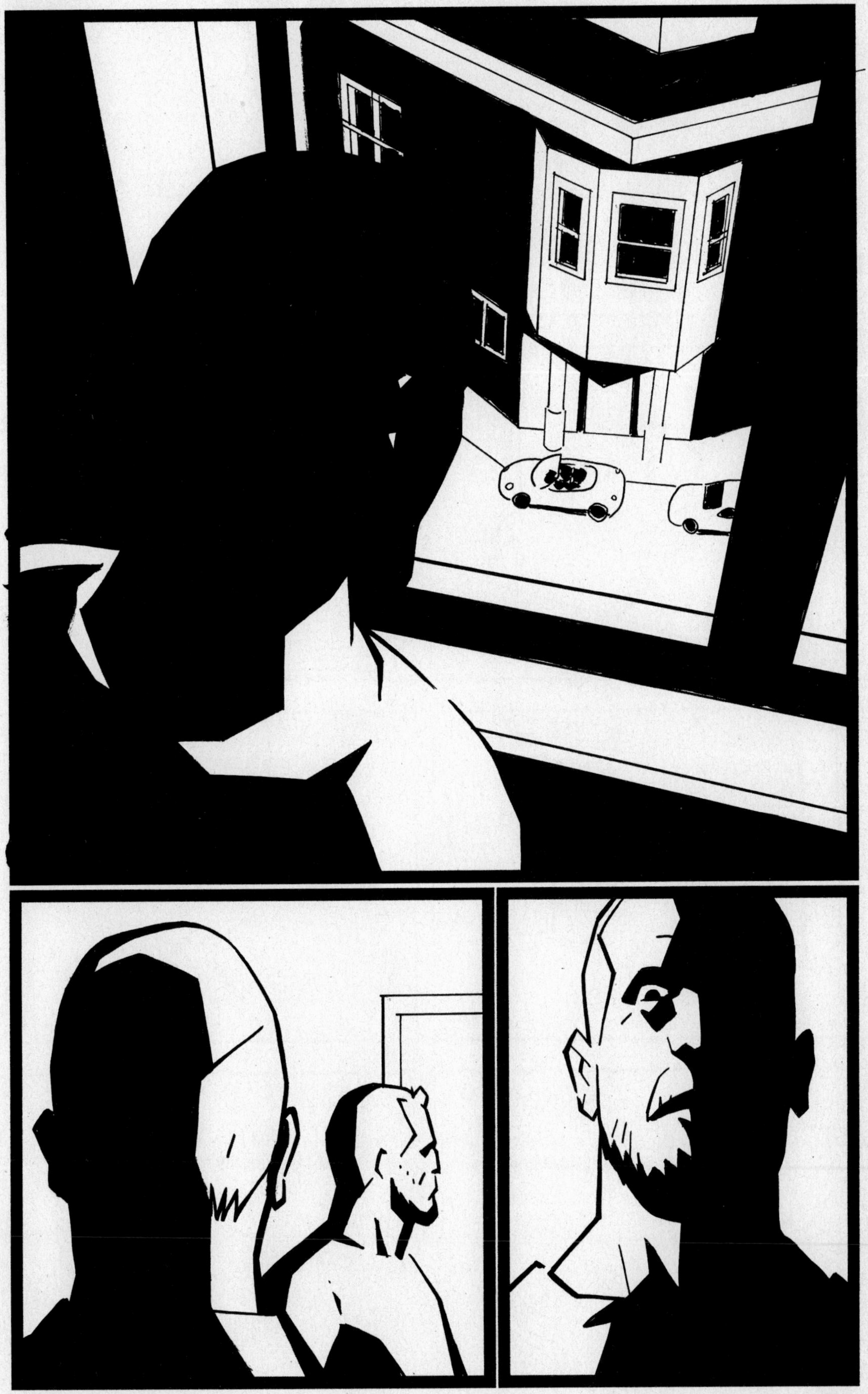

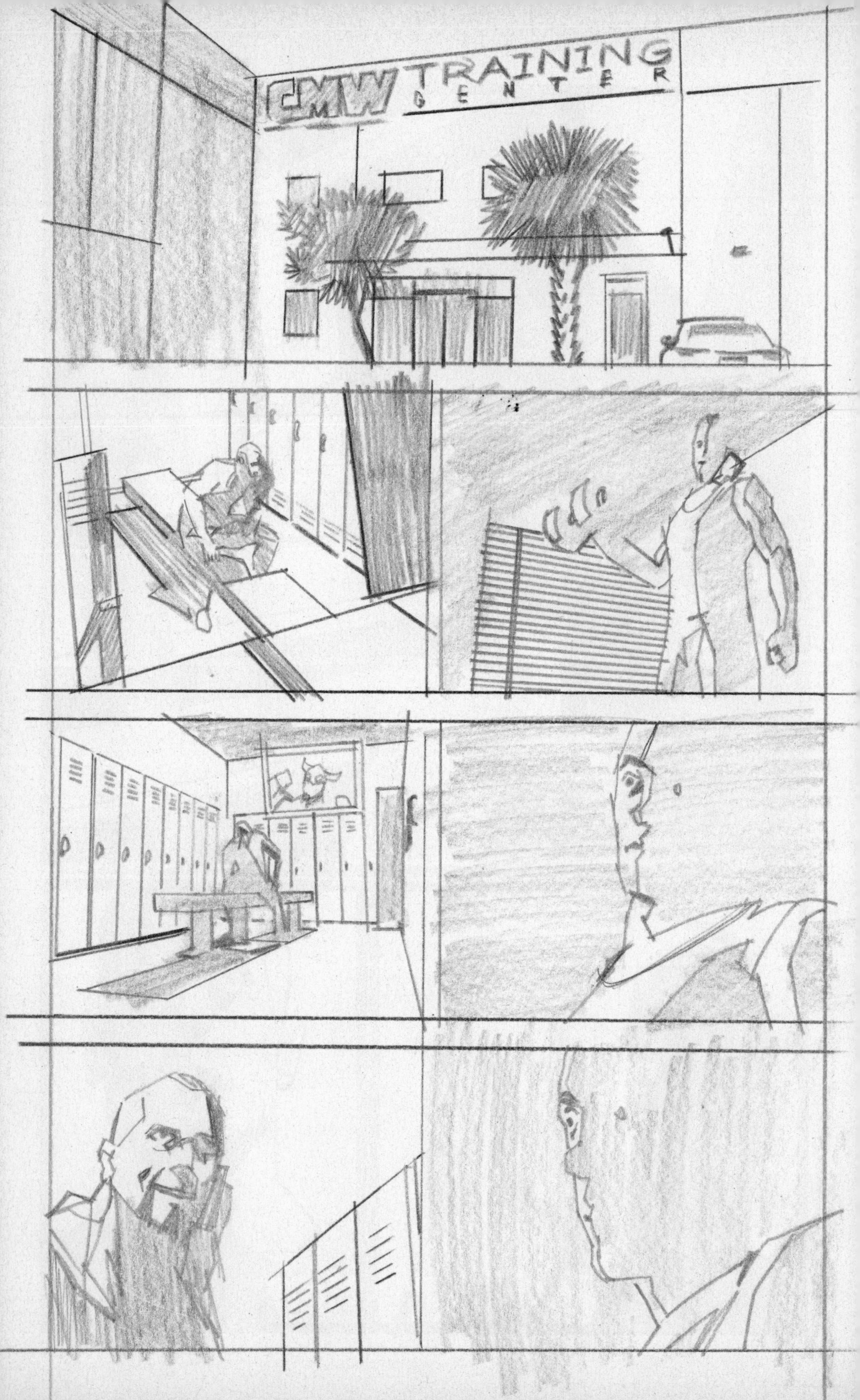
CMW TRAINING CENTER

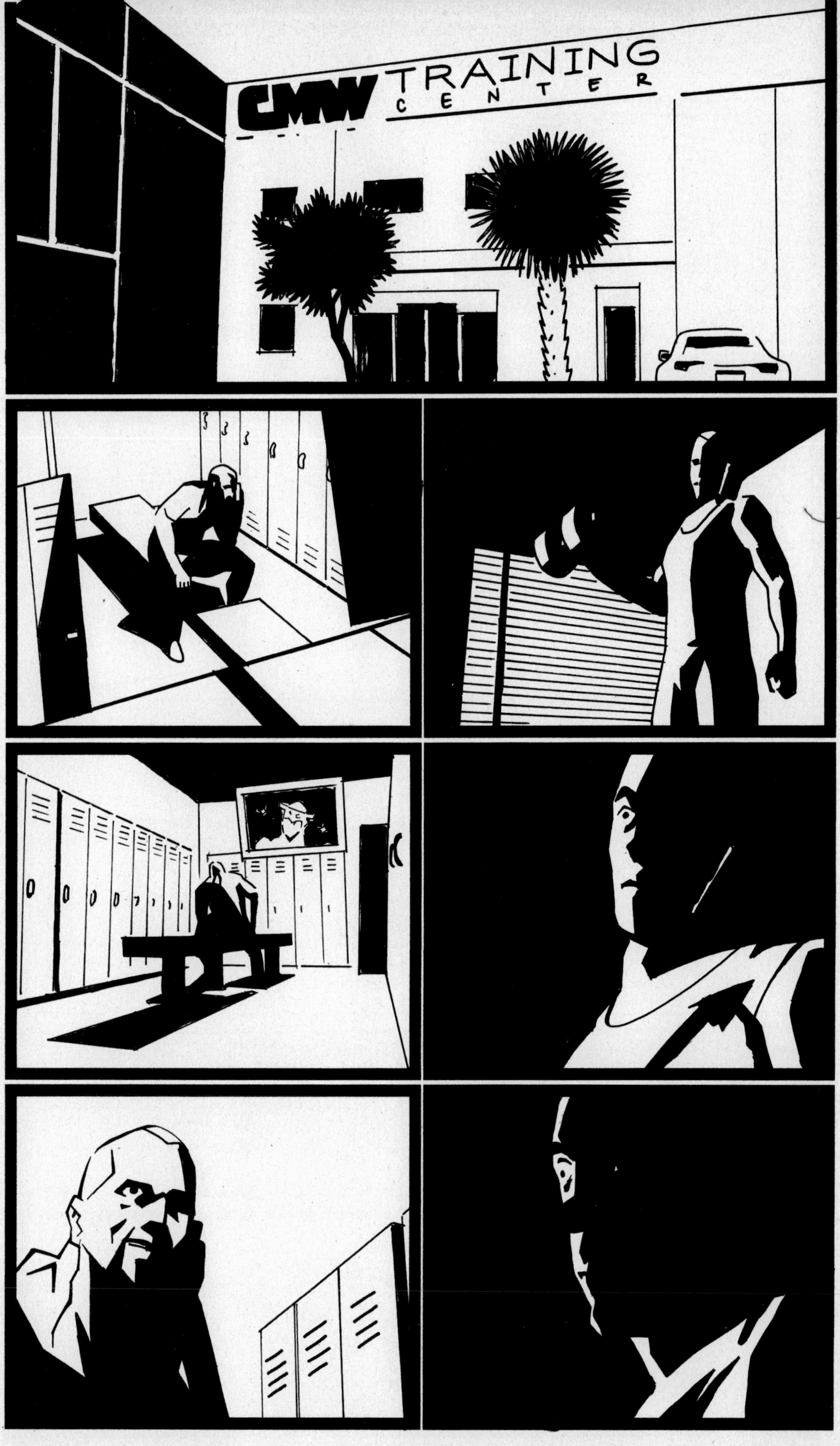
CMW TRAINING CENTER

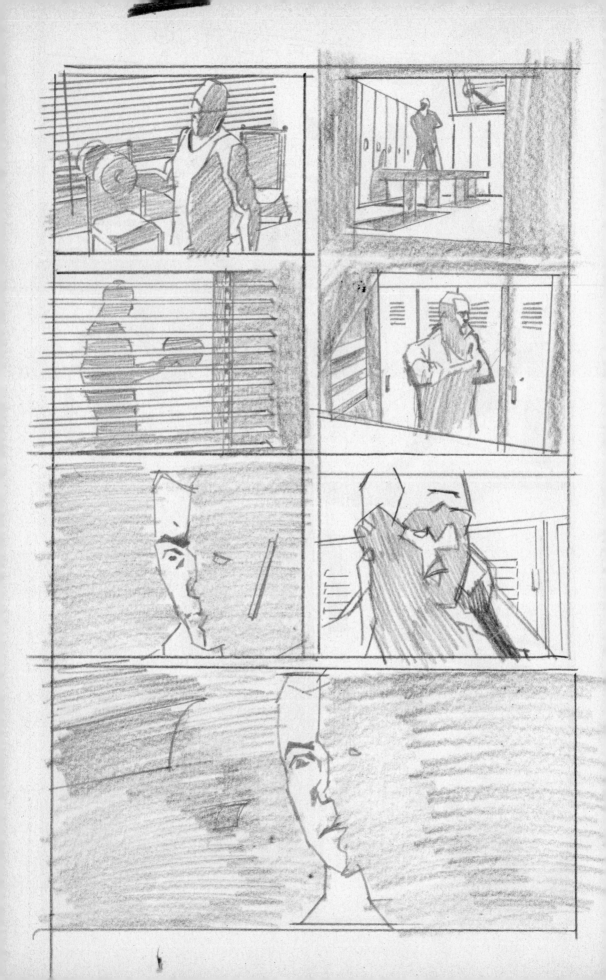

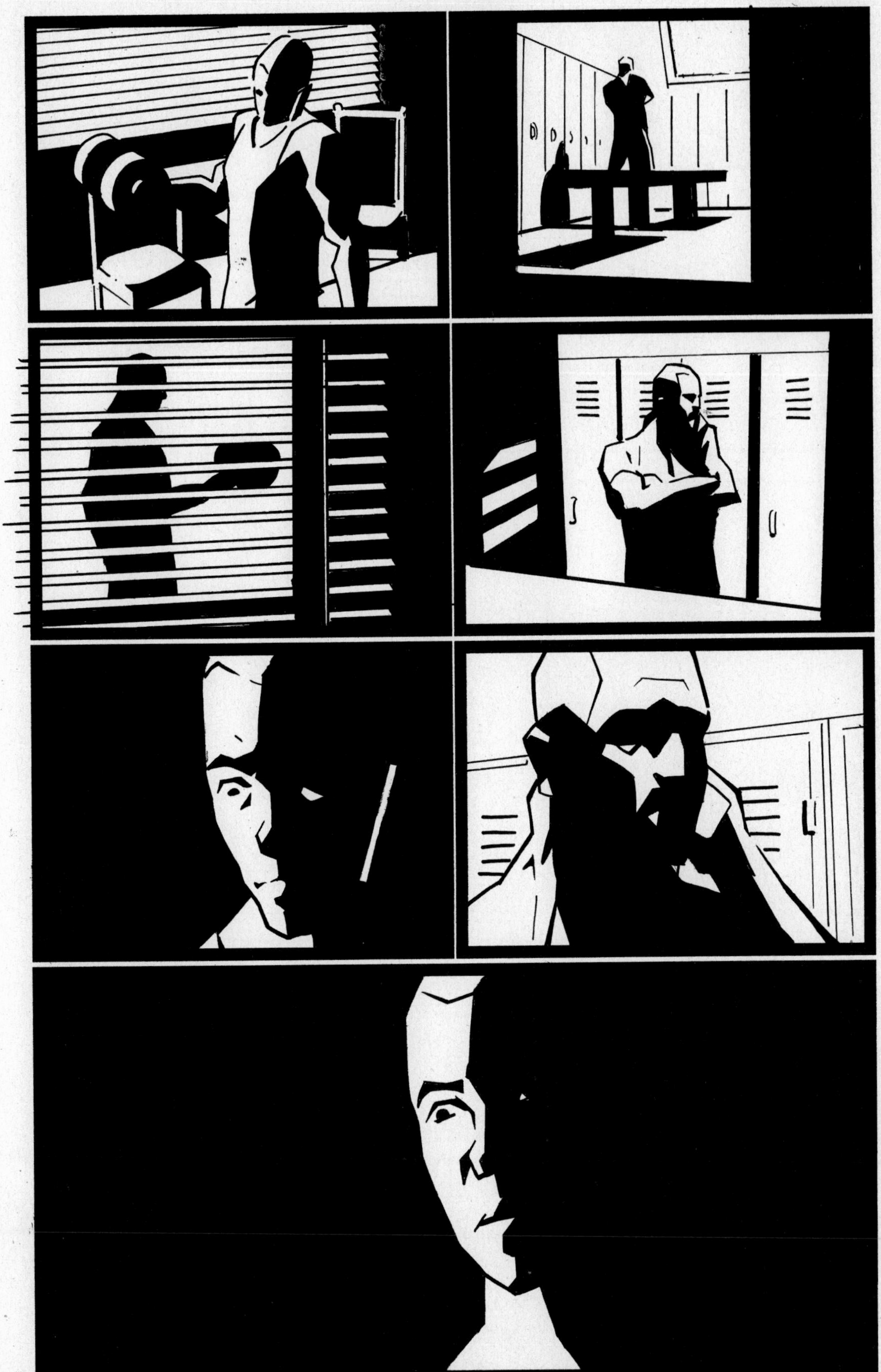

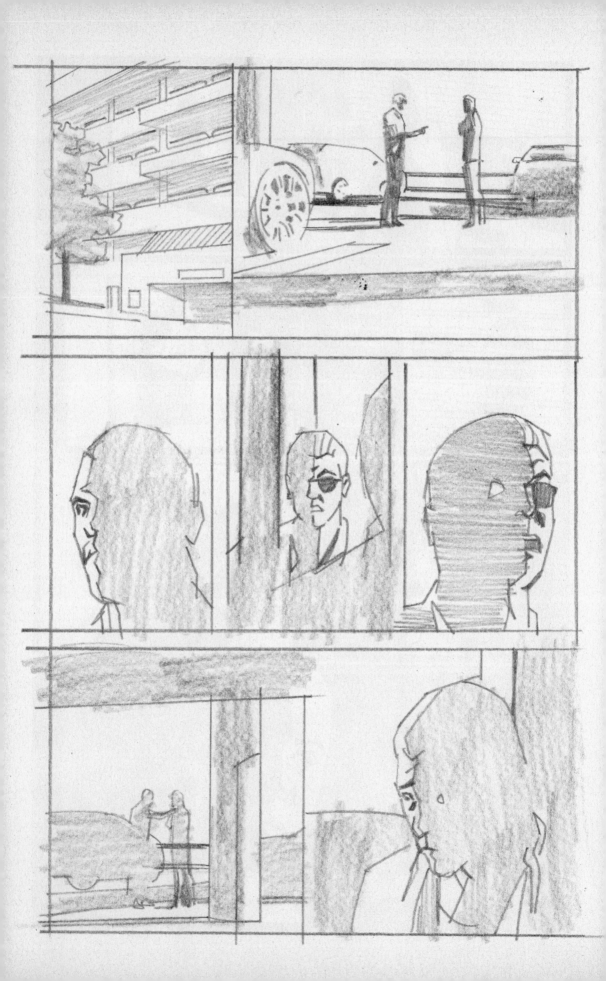

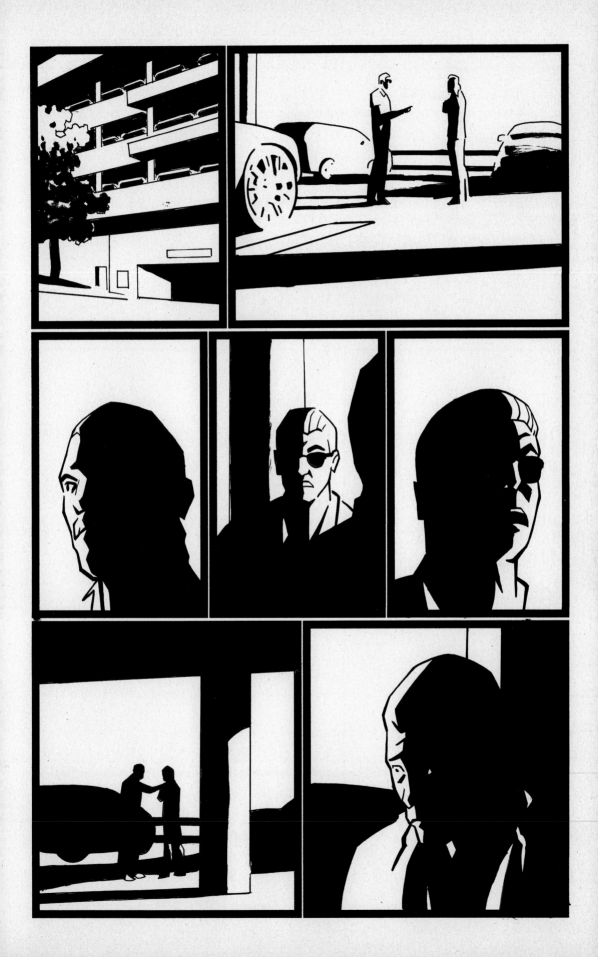

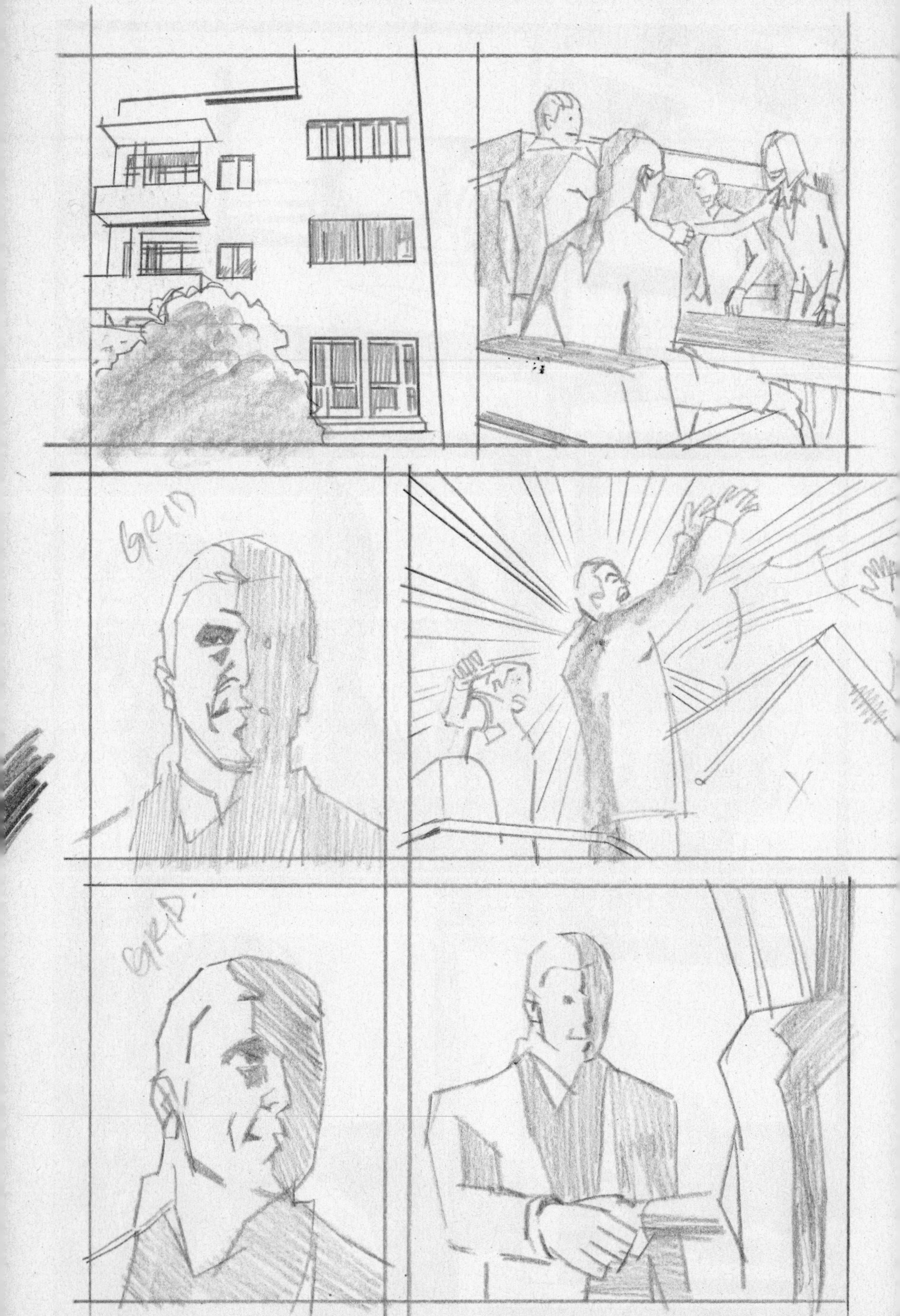
GRIP
GRIP

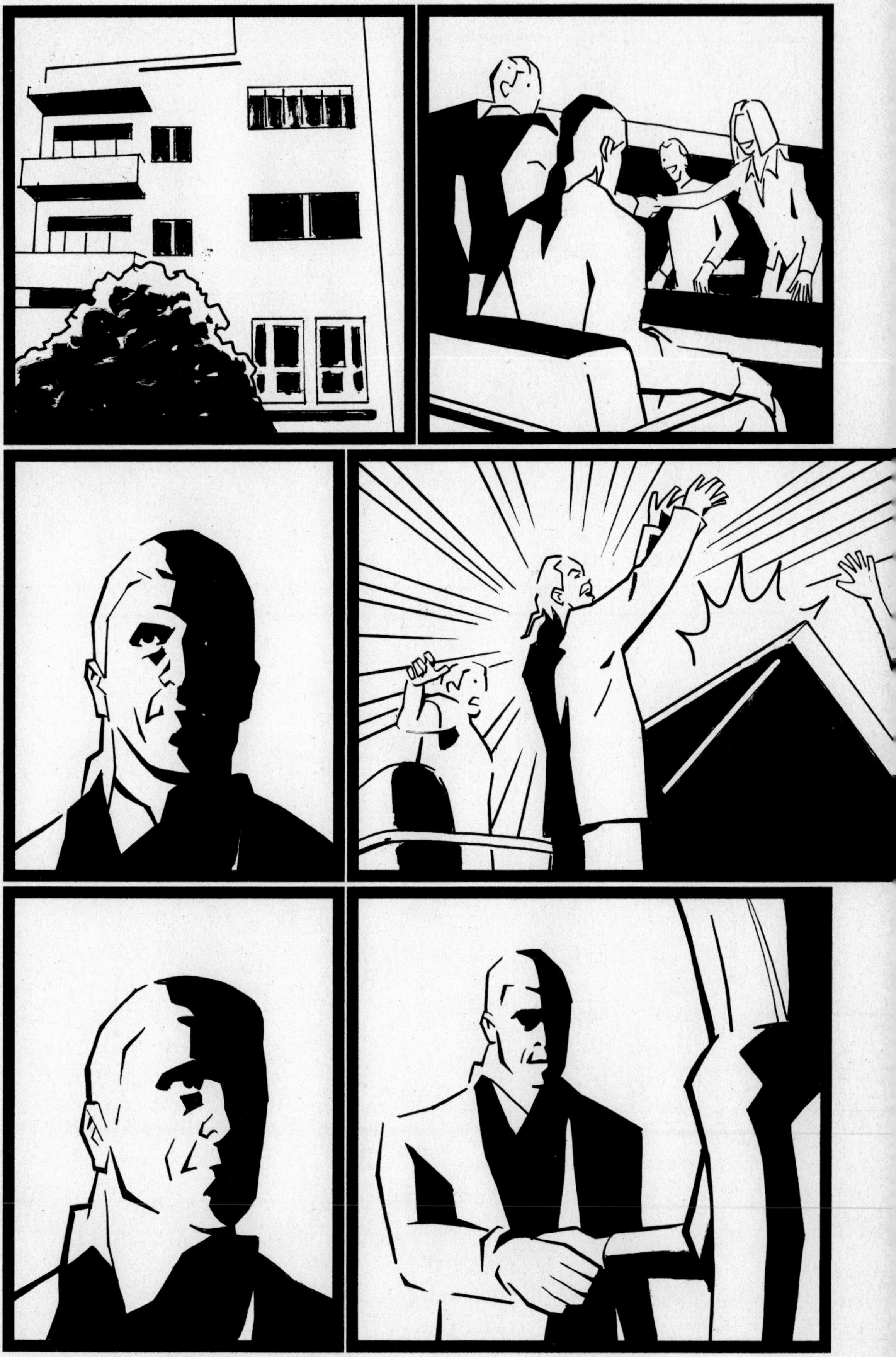

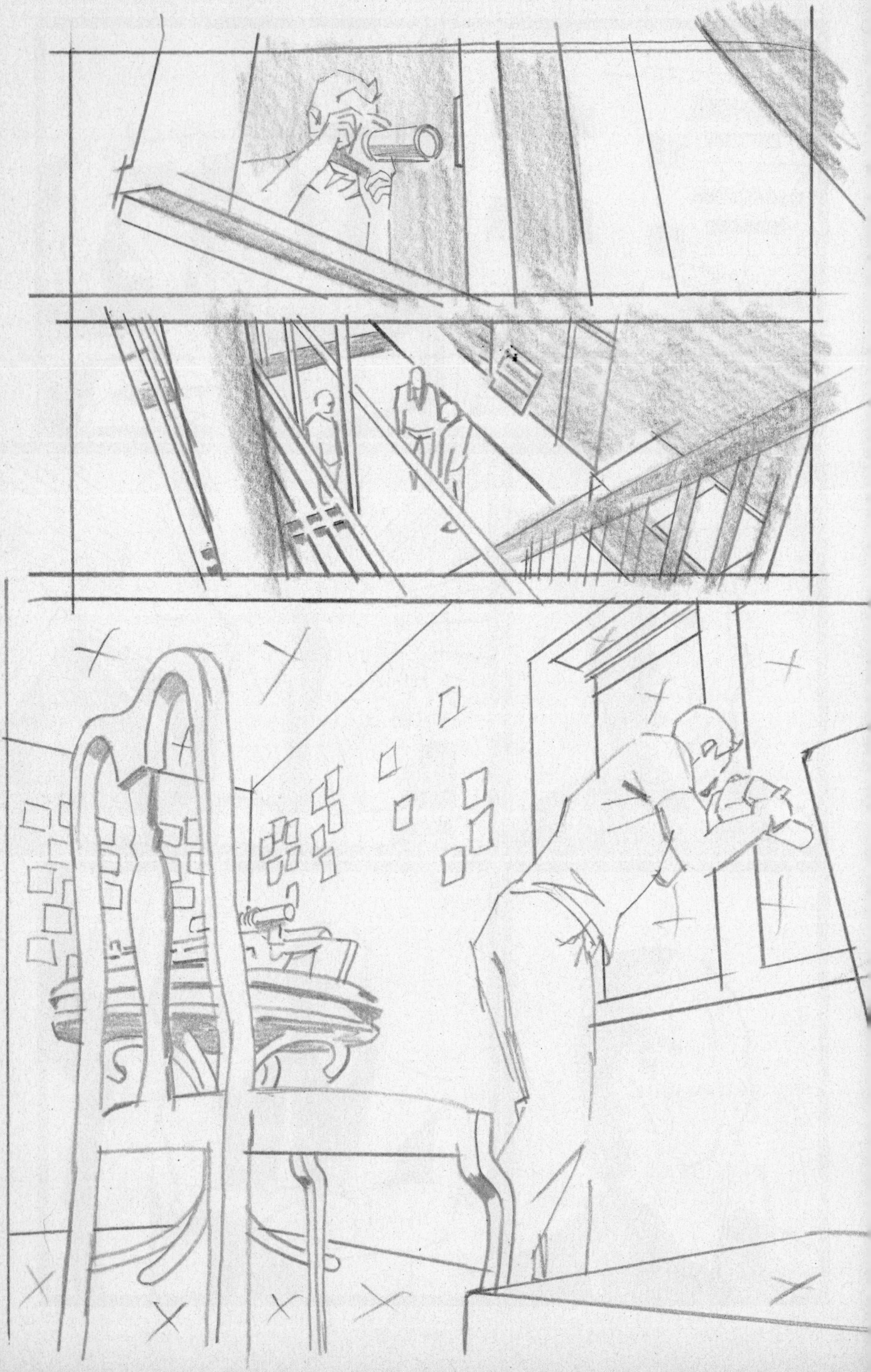

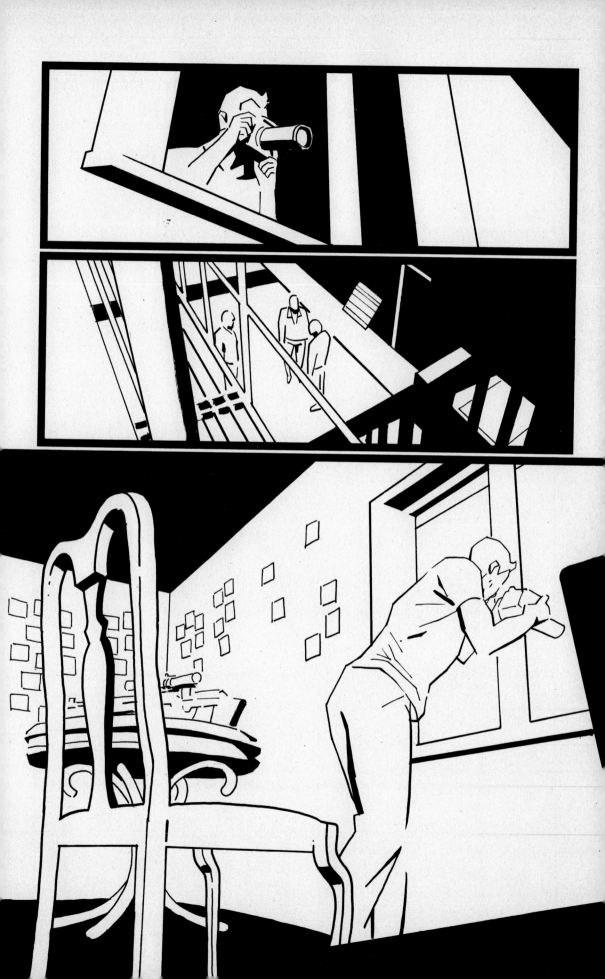

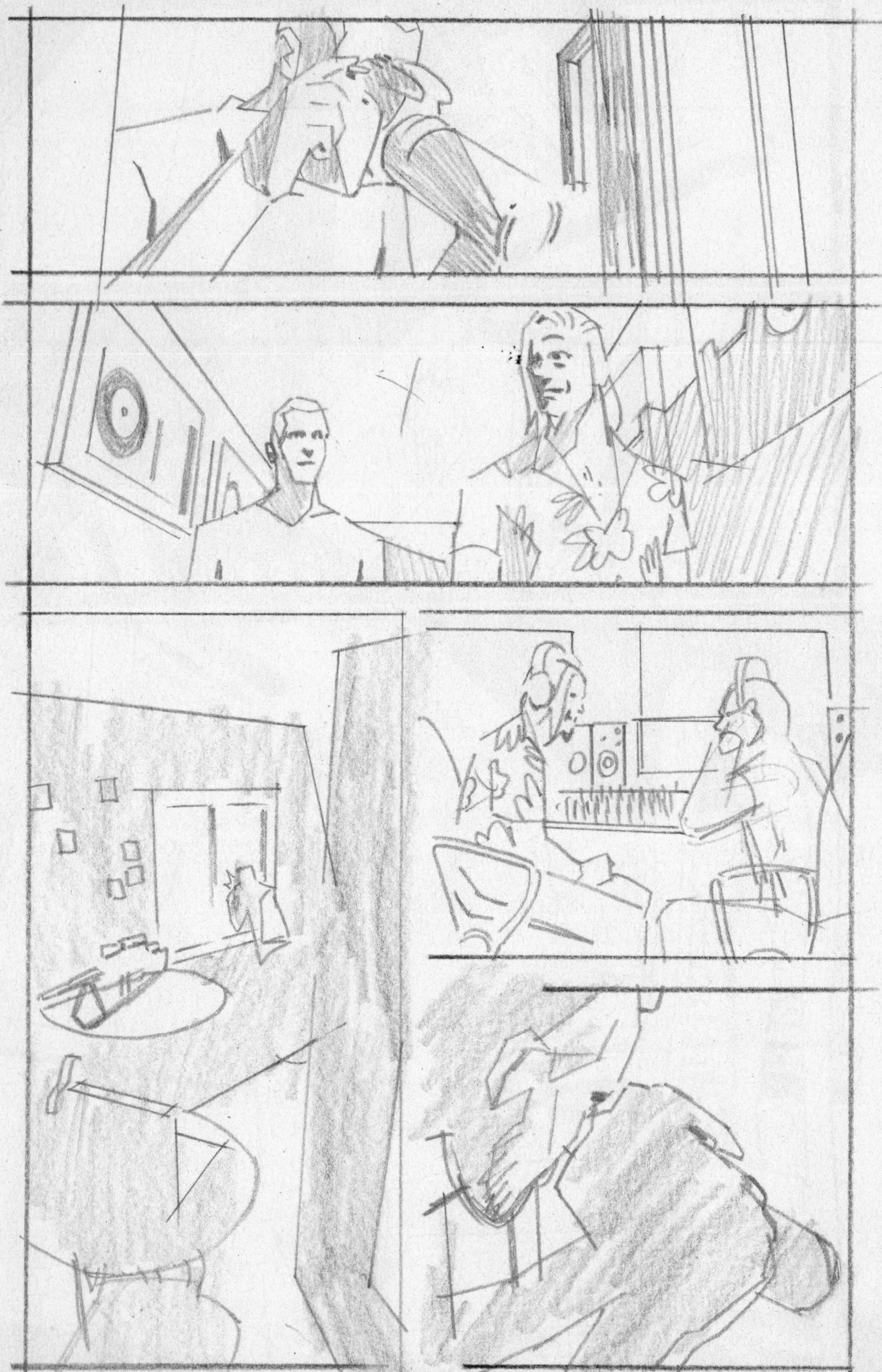

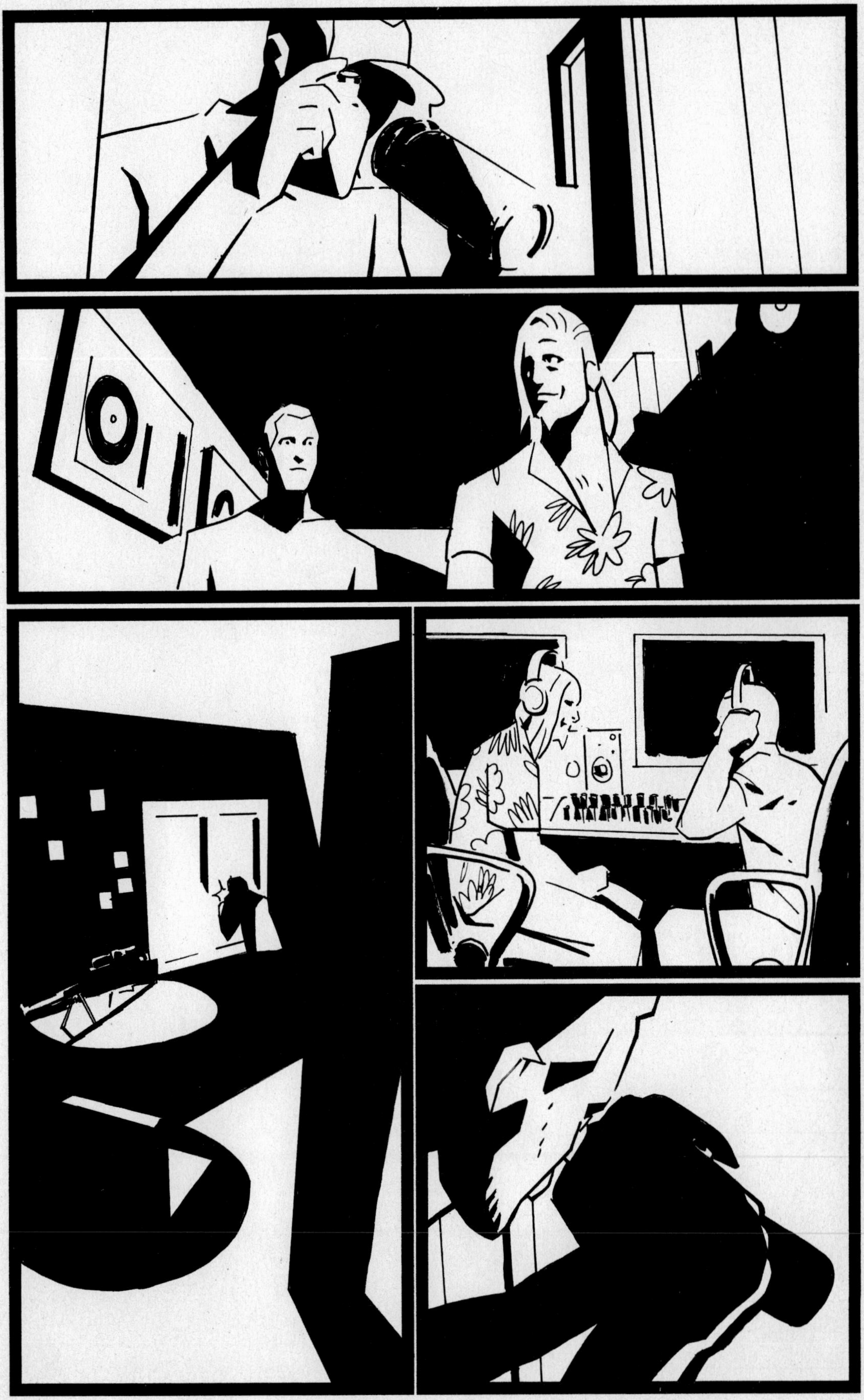

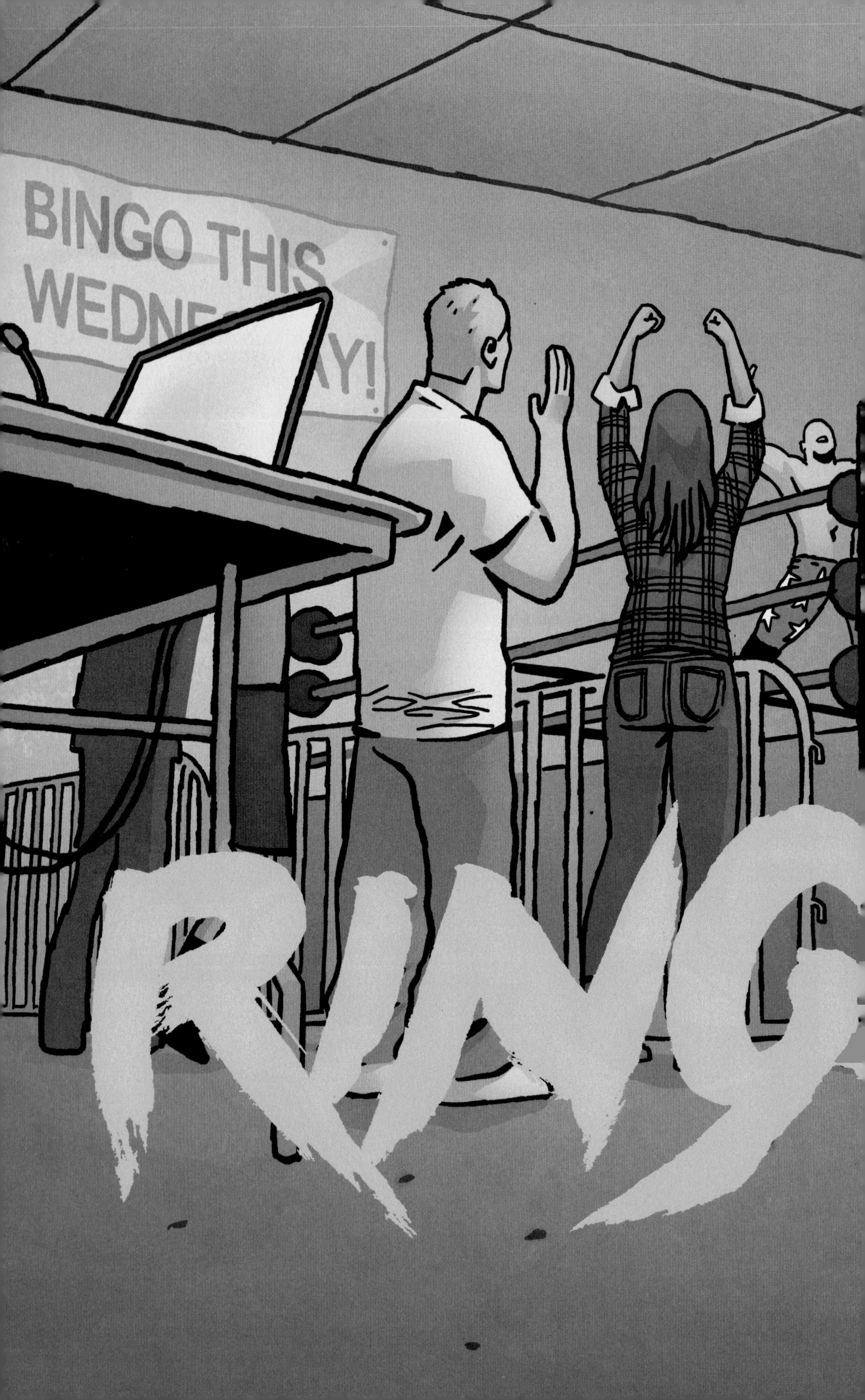
BINGO THIS WEDNE
Y!
RING

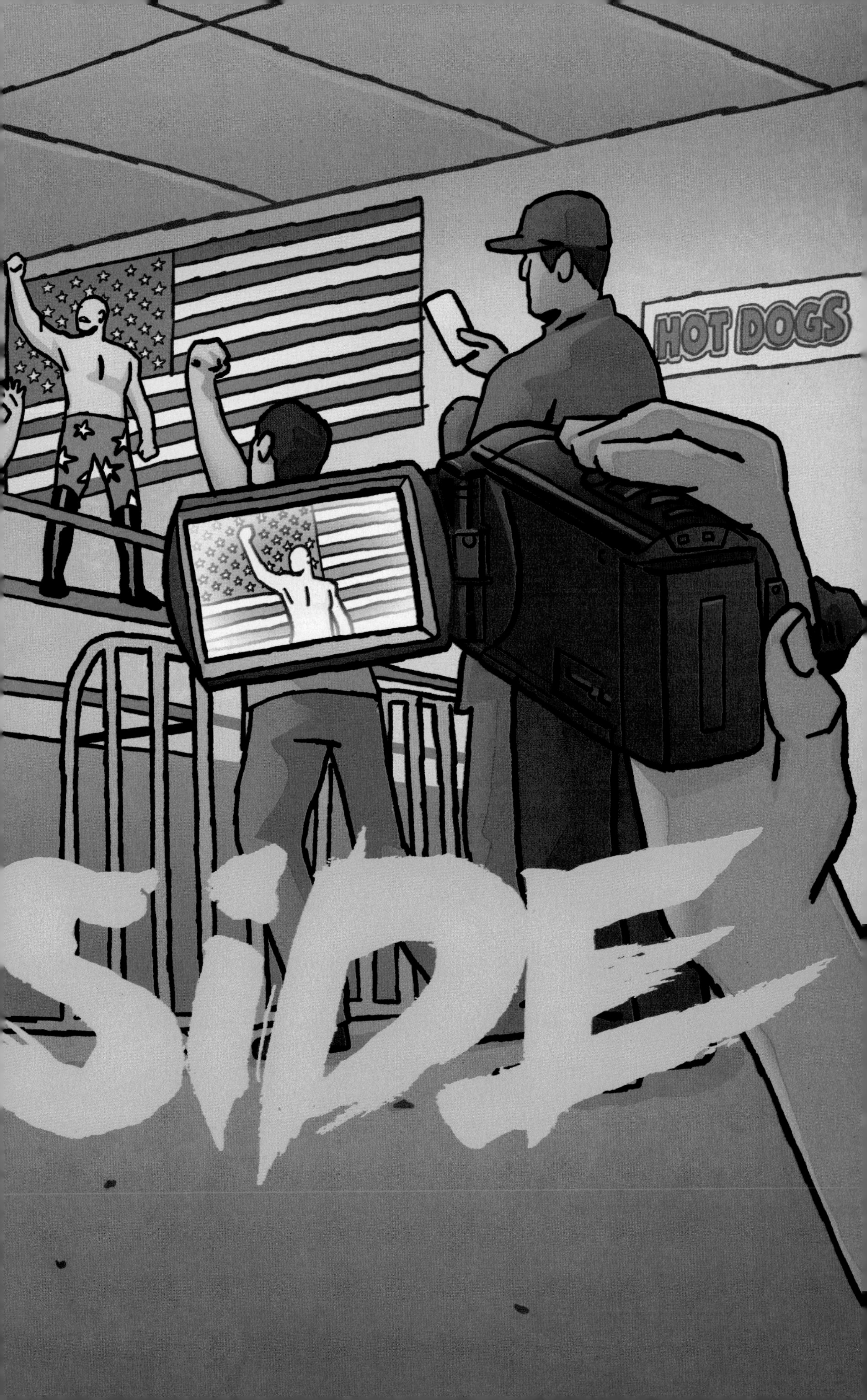
HOT DOGS
SIDE

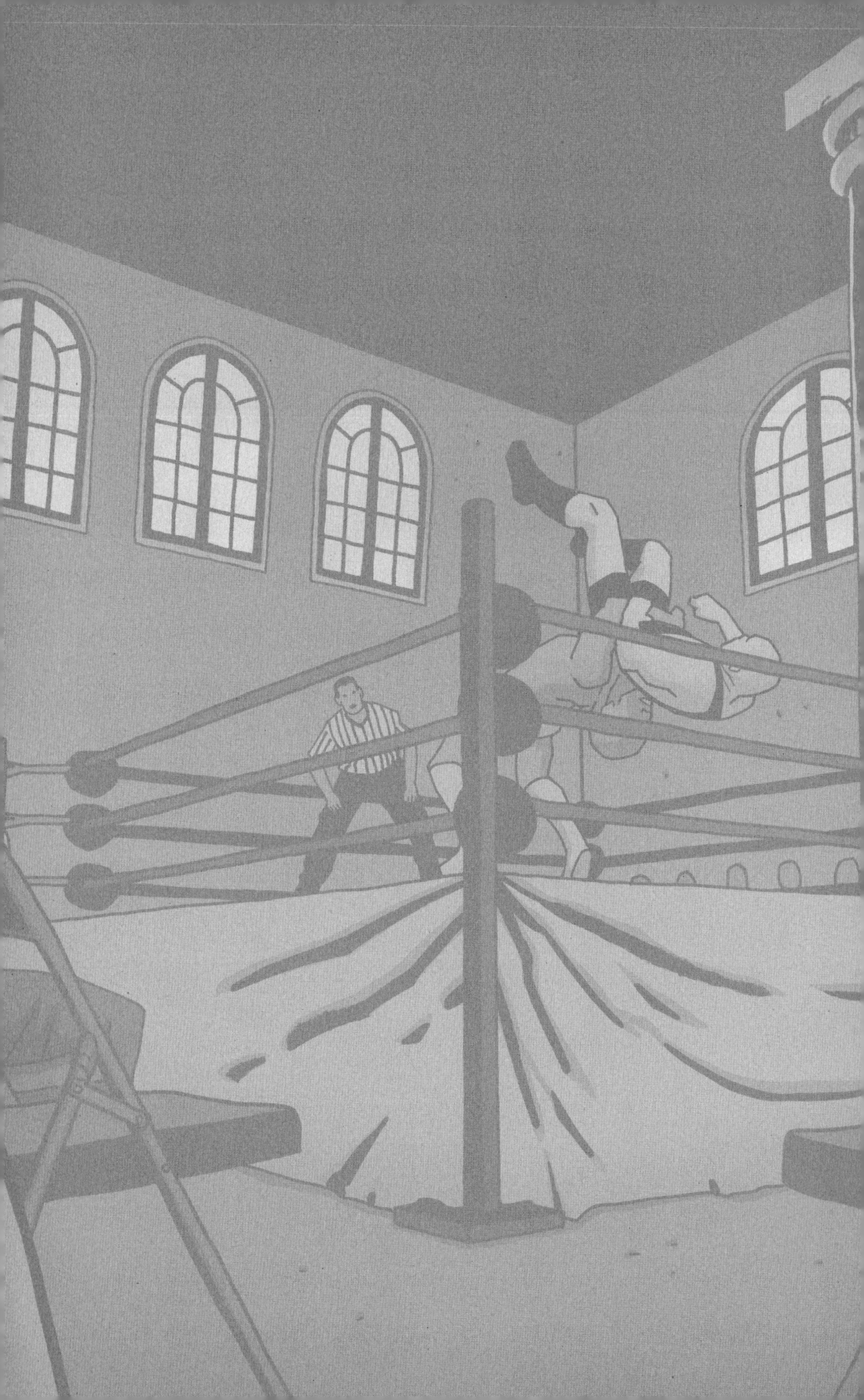

JOE KEATINGE is the writer of Image, Skybound, Marvel and DC Comics titles including SHUTTER, RINGSIDE, GLORY, TECH JACKET, MARVEL KNIGHTS: HULK and ADVENTURES OF SUPERMAN. He is also the executive editor of the Eisner and Harvey award-winning Image Comics anthology POPGUN and the Courtney Taylor-Taylor penned ONE MODEL NATION.

NICK BARBER is from Auckland, New Zealand which means he has a funny accent and a penchant for second breakfast. Nick likes to tell stories and entertain people which he is now lucky enough to do for a living. RINGSIDE is Nick's first professional comic and hopefully the first of many.

SIMON GOUGH is a thirty-five-year-old man with a four-year-old's job, colouring in! Born in Birmingham, in the middle of the United Kingdom, Simon is now living down south in the sunny seaside hamlet of Brighton. Always eager to paint from a young age, and even more eager to read comics, it seemed only natural he would eventually, after many years of exploratory art education, intertwine those two loves into one (hopefully) booming career!

ARIANA MAHER is a Brazilian-American born in New Jersey who spent her formative years in Japan and Singapore. You wouldn't think any one person could talk about comic book lettering for hours... but then you meet her. By day she is an ordinary citizen but by night she transforms into a weird recluse obsessed with balloon tails and text placement. Her last reported sighting was the Seattle area. If spotted, approach with caution and/or more comics for her to letter.

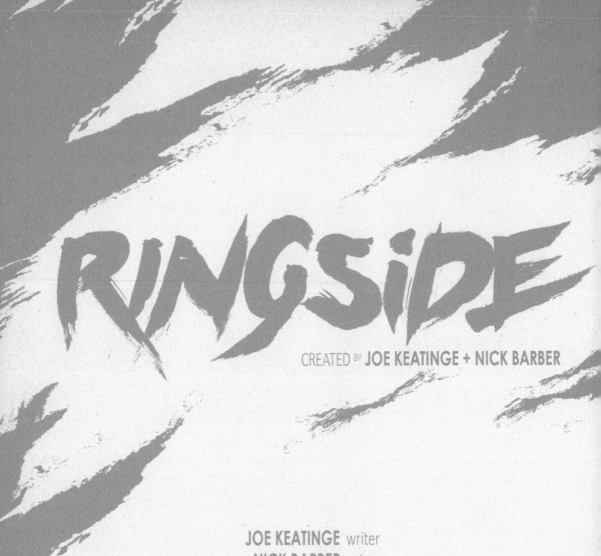

CREATED BY JOE KEATINGE + NICK BARBER

JOE KEATINGE writer
NICK BARBER artist
SIMON GOUGH colorist
ARIANA MAHER letterer

design by ADDISON DUKE
production & layout SHANNA MATUSZAK
logo designed by BRANDON GRAHAM
special thanks to DARREN SHAN
cover art by IBRAHIM MOUSTAFA

IMAGE COMICS, INC. • Robert Kirkman: Chief Operating Officer • Erik Larsen: Chief Financial Officer • Todd McFarlane: President • Marc Silvestri: Chief Executive Officer • Jim Valentino: Vice President • Eric Stephenson: Publisher / Chief Creative Officer • Corey Hart: Director of Sales • Jeff Boison: Director of Publishing Planning & Book Trade Sales • Chris Ross: Director of Digital Sales • Jeff Stang: Director of Specialty Sales • Kat Salazar: Director of PR & Marketing • Drew Gill: Art Director • Heather Doornink: Production Director • Nicole Lapalme: Controller • IMAGECOMICS.COM